WINKLER

WINKLER

Giles Coren

JONATHAN CAPE
LONDON

For my parents

Published by Jonathan Cape 2005

2 4 6 8 10 9 7 5 3 1

Copyright © Giles Coren 2005

Giles Coren has asserted his right under the Copyright, Designs
and Patents Act 1988 to be identified as the author of this work

First published in Great Britain in 2005 by
Jonathan Cape
Random House, 20 Vauxhall Bridge Road,
London SW1V 2SA

The Random House Group Limited Reg. No. 954009
www.randomhouse.co.uk

A CIP catalogue record for this book is available from the British Library

ISBN 0-224-07499-7

Papers used by Random House are natural,
recyclable products made from wood grown in sustainable forests;
the manufacturing processes conform to the environmental
regulations of the country of origin

Printed and bound in Great Britain by Clays Ltd, St Ives plc

Contents

Has this fellow no feeling of his business that a sings at grave-making?

Hamlet V, i

As a general rule the Jews are inclined to magnify their persecutions.

Reginald 'Rex' Leeper
Assistant Under-Secretary
The Foreign Office
April, 1940

FIRST PART

I

The Fathers' Match

Winkler is an Englishman – and his story begins with a cricket match, whether you like it or not. More than likely you have never played the game. Chances are you know nothing of its history or its personalities, do not even begin to understand its laws, don't give it a moment's thought from one summer to the next. If you feel anything at all, it is probably a sort of ignorant contempt. But the story begins with a cricket match, and it could not have been any other way.

Because at the moment when his story begins, Winkler, the hero of all that is to come, is rattling wordlessly to work, chug-chugging all sleepy on the Underground, and thinking about a cricket match. A cricket match, worse still, that was played in the grounds of a small boarding school in the English countryside very nearly twenty years ago.

He will soon stop thinking about it, though, if that's any help. He will return to thinking about his fear of trains, his walk to work, his work itself (which he hates, and which he hates himself for doing), his home (which is rented and smells) and his friends (who are barely friends) and about his girlfriend (who makes him feel anxious and strangely sick) and about his grandfather, who is no substitute for a father, but is better than nothing.

Realising that he has forgotten his keys, Winkler will find himself trapped in the home of the old Jew who lives under the stairs and we will be forced to sit silent, like Winkler, while the old Jew talks on and on and on about the War, the terrible things he saw in Warsaw and in the forests of western and central Poland, and the terrible things he did. (There will be burnings and beheadings and throat-cuttings, rape and infanticide and gas.)

We will see Winkler profoundly affected by the story he hears – an old story, full of old horrors, from a continent that no longer exists, come to haunt Winkler in the modern world – and we will see his friends and his work colleagues, his girlfriend and his grandfather fail to understand the pain of his empathy. And we will witness a terrible assault on a blind girl in a piss-smelling subway underpass, and we will see what happens when Winkler tries to help her. And we will see him push a fat woman under a train.

We will see Winkler out of his mind on pills and powder, being sodomized against his will (as far as we can tell), wanted for murder and hunted by the police. We will see him dance and sing. And we will see him in prison.

We will see an armed robbery go horribly wrong (blood and rhinestones everywhere), we will see an immigrant die shivering above an English pub, Winkler weeping on his grandfather's bed and, in the final pages, following a coffin to the grave.

And then it will end. And you will be glad that at least there was the cricket match.

It is only here, this game of cricket, because on the morning when the story starts Winkler was thinking, as he had been thinking for some time, that he really ought to go and see his grandfather. This gentle guilt of inattentiveness to his almost-family came upon him occasionally, often when he was nodding on the Underground, casting around in his mind for something to distract him. But it usually passed. And when he was in the middle of it he always ended up thinking about the Fathers' Match.

The Fathers' Match was the gala event in mid-July, at the end of the prep-school cricket season, which brought the curtain down on the academic year. A match between the junior school First XI and their fathers, most of them alumni of the school themselves, in a battle for the Corinthian Cup which began at two, stopped for tea at half-past four and then ran on until the shadows crawled out to reclaim the square. In the evening, prickly with heat and grass seed, the winners and losers returned to the pavilion for supper, the boys delighted to be finished with junior school forever, the fathers grief-stricken at the passing of another tide-mark in their adulthood, and everyone, even the mothers, overjoyed to be English.

Everybody came to the match. All the boys and their brothers and sisters up for the day, the teachers and long colourful trains of parents, crocodiling down the path from the school hall after the speeches, crossing the main road into the sports field through the big green gates that were named after a former captain of everything from the 1890s who had gone on to be captain of England too, and who was named after a bank. Or vice versa.

Winkler had feared the Fathers' Match for as long as he had played cricket. And he only played cricket by mistake. He did it without questioning, as he did everything then, despite the fact that nobody came to watch him do it and no one seemed to derive any satisfaction from his being so good at it.

The fear began when he made the first team two years early, at the age of ten, and it was only by pretending to be ill on the day of the match in each of the first two seasons that he had managed to defer the moment until now.

Two ruined years, spent worrying about the day when, despite his efforts to fit in, he would finally be found out in public, and the world would end. Two years poisoned with regret for the day when he had joined in the playground tennis-ball-and-painted-stumps-on-the-annex-wall-at-lunch-time game, been spotted by the geography teacher who also took cricket, PE, and occasional portions of smooth, hairless arse, and been moved from swimming (which he didn't like anyway because of the nakedness) to cricket.

Winkler at ten, eleven and twelve thought of little but how a moment's harmless fun at nine had set in motion the long slide to the Fathers' Match. If he had only walked on past, not picked up the ball in his left hand and thrown it in such a way that it changed direction when it hit the ground, causing Rupert Pennant-Cecil, captain of the under-11s, to swing at it and miss by a mile (making the whole playground laugh), how different his childhood might have been.

If only the arse-fancying cricket master had not grabbed him from behind to ask what class he was in. If he had only walked on past to his appointment with Joshua Bingham in the vault under the dining hall where they planned to play Wombles, how very different a childhood he might have had, in which there would have been room to make friends and meet girls and do all the things you can do when you're not worrying, in every waking moment you have, about the Fathers' Match.

But things were as they were, and no different, and so the Fathers' Match came for Winkler only a fortnight before his thirteenth birthday, at a time when he might have been fearing another, greater public trauma only days away, had things been different, had his parents been around,

had he been at another sort of school, in another part of England. If his
grandfather had ever woken from his endless armchair snooze.

Winkler saw himself, that last summer term, in his cricket whites,
standing in the long grass on the boundary of cricket pitches all over
England, very short, and just becoming short-sighted, without knowing
it, so that the edges of things were always fuzzy.

Standing at fine leg, in the shade, singing quietly to himself to pass the
long over of some foppish fast-bowler (whose father had also played
cricket, and grandfather, and whose home had books about it on its many
shelves of books), did he feel at home?

And when he looked down at his feet in the hard-toed white little
boots, whitened again with a squidgy-ended brush-stick thing for the game,
did they look the same to Winkler as the fast-bowler's looked to him?

The cricket ground was close to a churchyard much like, Winkler imagined, the sort of places the rest of the team would be buried in. Did the
walls and iron gate, with old headstones and willow trees visible through
dips and cracks, look the same to them as they did to Winkler, who would
be buried in a half-unfinished row in a non-denominational municipal
cemetery beside a suburban dual carriageway?

What was he entitled to? What could he have? There was a mighty
rusted iron roller. There was a spire (or possibly a steeple). There were
fields with crops and a small town in the distance, in the sunken belly of
the small hills. There were brown photographs in the pavilion of boys his
age or not much more, with moustaches, wearing caps like his, and bowler-
hatted groundsmen in the back row with no initials before their names.
Could he have them too?

Could he have the games played here a hundred years before – when
his own ancestors were God knows where – the games that went on as
the wicket fell into shade and the clock, which still worked then, chimed
quietly for eight, and the roadless valley shone in the late evening of an
unimaginable pre-War English paradise?

Winkler saw himself standing there, on so many afternoons, as the first
change bowler marked out his run, wanting desperately for him to fail
and be laughed at and so make room for Winkler's own relative success,
or, better still, to succeed, to do so well that Winkler might not be called
on at all and be saved the potential horror of failure. Did he think like
that because none of it was his? Or did the others think it too? And what
about their great-grandfathers on the pavilion wall?

Winkler had his own imagined ancestry, not photographed, containing
bearded, thickset Poles with side-locks, in a wet shtetl, nodding over some

Talmudic riddle, or out in fields breaking bad earth with wooden tools
to plant potatoes. But it didn't make his belly clench with longing. And
he had no idea at all what games they played.

And yet he had only to think of round-arm bowling or Ranjitsinji, or
the giants of Hambledon with their curved sticks, or old-style spiky
batting gloves, to feel a rush of incapacitating nostalgia and heartbreak.

Hedley Verity did not come back from the War. Chest wounds sustained
in a Sicilian cornfield, leading his men under heavy fire, killed the greatest
English bowler of his or any other generation.

Almost none of Winkler's recent ancestors came back from the War.
They didn't even go to it. They were just gassed in their dozens. Or shot
in forests.

Why, of the two, was it the fate of the quickish left-arm finger-spinner
that made Winkler want to cry? What was cricket to him? He was the
only one in his family who could even have told you who Don Bradman
was.

Winkler's grandfather, who didn't know that his grandson, like Verity,
preferred to push the ball through a bit but tossed it up on crumbling
pitches and got a degree of turn that made him, at times, unplayable, told
him to tell them his father was dead.

'Sir, I'm sorry, sir, only I shan't be able to provide a father for the
Fathers' Match as I haven't got one. And what's more, he's Jewish.'

The plan was not appealing. The school had never been given any
reason to believe that Winkler's father wasn't alive – some sort of Trust
paid the school fees (or was it a scholarship? Winkler dimly remembered
sitting exams and answering questions about levels of gratitude) – and it
was too late now to tell them, with only days left of his final term.

And, anyway, Winkler's father was alive. Winkler just didn't know where
he was. His grandfather wouldn't tell him, 'Because if you find him it will
only make you sad.' And he had a point. Having no parents was marginally better than having Jewish parents. But it didn't help with what to do
about the cricket match.

'Well. We'll just have to find you a father, then,' said the old man,
enlivened by the prospect of a task to perform. It was years since he had
done anything.

He sat forward in his chair and Winkler saw his long yellow feet draw
back out of his leather slippers. His grey-green chest showed for a moment
until he hugged up his dressing gown to cover it again. He folded his

newspaper on his knee and said, 'Now, bring me a nice cup of tea so I can think.'

In the kitchen, while the kettle boiled, Winkler sat by the blue table that folded up from the wall and bounced a rubber ball to himself off the floor and the door of the oven six feet away, flipping it out of the back of his hand to make it break from left to right. This was not his natural bowling action, but in the Fathers' Match the men would like a boy who could throw in a bit of wrist spin. This was 1982 and there wasn't much of it about at the time. A novelty delivery that took those boys' fathers back to the heroes of their youth would be useful if things became tricky.

'Stop with the banging will you, sonny. You want me to help you or not?'

Winkler sat in silence, listening to the metal tock of the kitchen clock, until the sound was gradually drowned by the wheezing of the kettle.

'Maurice might do it,' his grandfather called from the living room. 'He was quite a one for quoits, I remember.'

Thin Maurice Mogelbaum. An old poker friend of his grandfather's. He had livid blue-white skin and the network of facial veins was so visible through that thin carapace that he seemed to have walked through cobwebs, or tried to have frightening tattoos removed. His nostrils were long and arching so that you could see the cartilage between them way up inside his nose. His eyebrows met in the middle. He wore grey shoes and a zip-fronted leatherette blouson, perhaps stitched from worn out barber's shop furniture.

Winkler went in with his grandfather's china cup of apple tea, made from yellow crystals and naturally caffeine-free.

'Maurice, then, eh? How about that?'

Winkler said nothing.

'Ashamed because he's such a Jew?'

'No.'

'Where am I going to find you a big yok who doesn't work Thursdays to come and play stickball with a lot of spoilt kiddies?'

The old man sipped his tea with a loud noise through a tiny hole in hard-pursed white lips and said, 'Hot, hot.'

'You think Sammy Patel plays cricket? They do, these Indians, or not?'

'Yes, he probably does, Grandpa. But he doesn't look much like my dad.'

'At least he's not Jewish. Anyway, how do you know what your papa looks like? The photo is fifteen years old.'

He is short in the picture, like Winkler. Standing by a car with his wife and three children, Winkler's unmet brothers and sister. Before he ran off with the *shikse*. Before he left the *shikse* and went back to his wife and three of his children. Before the *shikse* disappeared.

'What about English Dave, whose father ran the fish shop after me? He'd be about the right age. But, now, I think he lost an arm or a leg in an accident. Both, even. Not so good for all your running and jumping, I suppose.'

He laughed. Winkler went to his room down the hall and looked at his Geoff Boycott annual. He stared for a long time at a full-page picture of Boycott in a blue cap, with his sleeves rolled up neatly to just below the elbow, driving a rising ball towards extra-cover, not really forward or back – unusually for him – just relying on timing and a perfect eye.

'There was a good crowd at Perth to see me get up on my toes to play this shot,' ran the caption. Winkler was always struck by the confidence of Boycott's picture captions. He didn't like Boycott. But it was a cricket book, and his grandpa gave it to him, so it was a big deal.

In the end the old man made Ginger Bill promise to do it in return for the use of his car for a week and a waiver on an old debt regarding some second-hand bridge tables.

Ginger Bill was a distant cousin by marriage (like everyone Winkler knew back then) who showed up at weddings and bar mitzvahs and got very drunk and shouted and danced on tables so that yellow-eyed old men with flapping, gynaecological ears stared at each other and said 'farpotchket' a lot, and occasionally 'gevalt!' But he was generally popular with the children because he behaved so much like a goy that it helped them to pretend these occasions were fun and normal in 1970s Britain, and not merely the strange atavistic howlings of a moribund race grumbling itself finally to death.

What Winkler knew about him was ludicrous: he had once been 'a wrestler of some repute' and his father was a circus strongman with Billy Smart, 'Like such a Geoff Capes or a Schwarzenegger,' (pronouncing the Austrian name correctly, with a labial-dental 'w'). The strongman's grandfather was the same contortionist who used to perform at the novelist George Eliot's private parties. It was always 'the novelist George Eliot'.

The Ginger Bills were originally of Ukrainian stock but had been in England for so long that the family, it was reasoned, must know a bit about cricket, among all the other things they knew about, which included dogs and gardening and wine and ladders and Cornwall and Latin and guns – mysterious things which baffled their in-laws. But they were not successful in business and none of them, it was said, had ever lifted a finger.

Ginger Bill was a gentle man, named after his bright red beard more than the strawberry pink of the hair that thinned on his head, and he was bottom-heavy, with trousers that hung low under his belly. He had a huge conspiratorial grin but looked a little mean without it, and Popeye forearms. The conviction, held among those certain Jews who seek silent blood-allies among movie idols and rock stars, that Ernest Borgnine is at least partially Jewish can be attributed entirely to the startling resemblance he bore to Ginger Bill.

Winkler remembered now the rumour that Bill had been one of the Krays' bodyguards, back in the early days, recruited when they saw him killing horses with his bare hands at a long-gone stud farm up in Elstree that was run by his uncle, Black Les. He was said to have killed a number of men, too. Not out of malice but to pay the hospital fees of his only daughter, whose mother had died giving birth and who was stricken with Lupus, a blood disorder that threatened to turn her into a wolf. 'And a kosher wolf,' Winkler's grandfather used to say, 'is an abomination.'

Bill had spent time in prison, fingered – said the old man – for his part in an arson attack on a Quaker school, a crime of which he was innocent. 'But it was time that Ginger went down for something anyway.' Inside, he did well trafficking in drugs which he had smuggled into him in piles of freshly laundered prayer-shawls (a service he inaugurated for Jewish inmates who would not trust the prison laundry with their fragile tallises) and by 1982, the year of the Fathers' Match, he was living the life of a respectable man of leisure in the Northern suburbs.

And so while mothers and fathers sat on compass-rutted benches in the dining hall and clenched each other's hands as their sons' successes were publicly enumerated – and tried to laugh at jokes in Latin – Winkler was sitting on the school's perimeter wall, warming his face in the sun and occasionally squinting down the road for his Grandpa's chocolate-coloured Rover containing Ginger Bill.

At last, around ten past one, while the rest were having lunch – standing about in the memorial garden with plates of sandwiches and potato salad and plastic cups of wine – the old D-reg behemoth howled past.

Winkler leapt off the ragged wall, feeling the newly freed rock-dents in his buttocks, and ran into the road, where he waved both his arms after the Rover with a drowner's desperation, and watched as a single brake-light flickered, heard the gearbox crunch, and saw Bill's flaming

beard, full of sunlight, as he turned to grasp the back of the passenger-
seat headrest and steer himself back down the road.

'Cheer up, Wink,' he said, leaning across to peer at Winkler through
the open near-side window. 'This bucket wouldn't start, so your old man
had to call the AA and pretend to be Uncle Sid, who's a member, but
they wanted to see identification, which is unusual. I think they recognised him. And there was traffic like you wouldn't believe . . . You didn't
think I wasn't coming?'

Winkler shrugged. Bill had on thin brown cords, suede shoes, a white
shirt and a thing made of tweed that might have been a hacking jacket
if either of them had known what one was.

'My English disguise,' he said, with the grin. 'You think the hat is too
much?' He was arranging an olive coloured felt fedora on his big freckled
head. 'Okay, we'll lose the hat.' And he flung it onto the back seat.

Winkler got into the car and directed Ginger Bill to the car park
behind the pavilion, where some of the First XI were already in their
whites, throwing a ball around and testing each other in the slip cradle.

'Have you ever played cricket before, Bill?' Winkler asked as they stood
by the car, looking out at the wicket where the groundsman was going
over it one last time with the heavy roller, while his mute son (nick-
named 'Spasmo') raked up a dozen errant leaves that had been sifted from
the beech trees on the northern boundary by a lazy breeze.

'Once, a long time ago, I went on a company outing with your father,'
he said. 'It was a big house in the country and after lunch there was a
run-around in the grounds. Some of the lads played a game. Your dad and
I stood together at a distance. A couple of times the ball rolled out to us.
One time I threw it back, the other time your old man. I think his throw
was better.'

Winkler wasn't used to hearing his father mentioned outside the flat,
and it quietened him.

'But don't worry,' Bill laughed, clapping him on the back with a spade-
like hand. 'I've come prepared.'

From the boot of the Rover he pulled an immaculate blue canvas
Slazenger cricket bag. Unbuckling it on the bonnet, he went through its
contents loudly in a mock-heroic impersonation of the upper-class accent
of Old England:

'One pair boots. One pair white flannels. One shirt. One pair Bob
Willis fast-bowler's socks. One abdominal protector,' (he grinned the grin
again) 'and athletic support. One pair batting gloves. One pair pads. And
the pièce de résistance: one bat.' Turning the bag over, he unzipped the

bat pocket and slowly drew from inside it a brand new, undeniably well made and perfectly finished baseball bat.

The warmth on Winkler's back cooled for an instant as a cloud passed in front of the sun. The birds in the trees momentarily ceased their optimistic twitter. A church bell in the distance gonged the half-hour which concluded the presentations and would send three hundred people marching towards the cricket pitch. The breeze died and the dry summer air was still.

'What sort of dumb old Yiddler do you think I am?' said Bill, sliding round to the boot again, tossing the baseball bat inside and drawing from beneath a tartan blanket that was faded with ancient sunlight a long-handled Gray Nicholls four-scoop cricket bat, perfectly seasoned, with two stripes of yellowed batting tape around the middle.

'You think I drove all this way on a work day just to embarrass you? Relax, Winky. I haven't played your silly game, but I watch the television. I borrowed this lot from Ronnie Mendelson – you remember Slick Ronnie? – he hupped it from an unlocked Volvo in a church car park a couple of years ago, thought it was a suitcase, and never got round to throwing it out. The rounders bat was my little joke. Come on, show me where I change.'

The train shuddered in a station. Winkler opened his eyes and felt sweaty. It wasn't his stop. Was he dreaming of the Fathers' Match or just thinking about it? It felt real enough for a dream. He could smell the weak coffee in the urn for the fathers and teachers, and the ham on the breath of the mothers from the swift memorial garden sandwich gobble, the woody must of the Victorian pavilion, the leather of the kitbags, the cut grass browning on the outfield and smelling of sweet new rot when turned with a boot; the roses, mostly dead, behind the stretch of picket fence at the school end, still reeking of evenings and jam . . . was this, Winkler wondered, alright? All really how it was? He couldn't be pink-tinting things now, could he? Not developing a sick, unthinking fondness for those awful, awful years?

The train shuddered again, lurched, grunted, sighed and then ground itself forward and up into its rattling canter, and hit the dark tunnel as Winkler shut his eyes again.

At ten to two, Rupert Pennant-Cecil, captain of the boys, and his father, Sir Leicester Pennant-Cecil, captain of the fathers, walked out in their blazers to toss. Rupert, thirteen years old, looked eight feet tall. He called heads ('gentlemen always call heads') and Sir Leicester's coin, which happened to be one of the older five pees in circulation – an ex-shilling, in fact, from 1947 – fell with the trim profile of George VI pointing at the sky. Young Pennant-Cecil, fancying the oldies to flag in the field the later it got, invited his father to have a bat and walked back hurriedly towards the pavilion, signalling with two fingers pushed away from his body in a downward arc that the First XI was to take the field. Sir Leicester, superfluously, presented a firm push of the back of his left hand to his men, indicating that the openers were to pad up. The match began on the stroke of two.

Winkler did not enjoy the first two hours at all. Assuming that Ginger Bill would be batting low in the order, he could not bring himself to bowl well. If the fathers could only rattle up a big total with the first few batsmen there was a chance Bill wouldn't have to bat at all.

At twenty-five past four, three overs before tea, the last ball of Winkler's spell (he was to be removed after a shockingly ineffective performance) landed in the rough outside leg stump, turned sharply and removed the off bail of the Fathers' number seven, who glared at Winkler and stalked off.

Winkler looked across to where the fathers were sitting. There was a brief flurry of activity. And then Ginger Bill, immaculate in his stolen clothes, rose from among them.

Swinging his bat the way a carefree pedestrian, delighted that the rain has stopped, marks his progress along a pavement with swipes of his umbrella, Bill strode out to the wicket.

'Winkler's dad looks pretty shit,' Winkler heard the wicketkeeper whisper to first slip. But he didn't really. It was just the missing button on his shirt which allowed some ginger belly hairs to sneak out, and a barely perceptible suggestion in his walking gait that he had never inten-tionally broken into a run, that undermined his otherwise convincing impersonation of the greats of the Golden Age.

Standing square-on to the bowler (not unlike Grace in some of those dubious oil paintings of his early years) and wielding his bat like an axe (or like the hammer, Winkler briefly imagined, with which he had once been accustomed to breaking rocks) he heaved his first ball into the road. The umpire raised his hands to signal six, and Bill looked around, spotted Winkler at square leg, and waved.

He played the same shot to his second ball and missed. Turning round and seeing that the ball had hit his wicket, he searched for Winkler again and mouthed: 'What now?'

Winkler twitched his head urgently towards the pavilion. Ginger Bill stared back at him, bewildered as a cow.

'You're out, Mr Winkler,' said the umpire, just as Winkler was arriving at a sprint to whisper: 'You have to go back now, Uncle Bill,' into his ear.

'Already?' asked Ginger Bill. 'But I've only just –' And then he saw the panic in his nephew's eyes, the terrible fear that something was about to go wrong, and he turned and apologised loudly to everyone and cupped his ear to pretend he was deaf. And then he trudged off slowly, shaking his head, because that was what all the others had done.

The innings ended at the tea interval and as Winkler sat with the team in the pavilion dining room he was glad to see Ginger Bill apparently cracking jokes with the other fathers and not, as yet, being rumbled. The boys, of course, never 'fraternised with the oppo', even when they were the very men – in every case apart from Winkler's – whom they had to thank, or blame, for the fact that they were there at all.

'Winkler, you'll be number eleven, as usual,' Pennant-Cecil said through a mouthful of French Fancy with pink icing, a fleck of which arced out from between his teeth and lodged between the tear-duct and sclerotic coat of Winkler's left eye. 'I'm trying to precipitate some of the old family duels, but it doesn't look as if your pater is going to be doing much bowling.'

Winkler looked over again at the fathers and saw Ginger Bill swigging heftily from a hip flask which, offered to other members of his team, was being politely declined. He was staggering, but only slightly.

Set 143 to win, the First XI hove to their task grimly and passed the hundred mark for the loss of only four wickets. Truly enough, Bill was not offered the chance to bowl, but one or two of the fielders, as the sun slipped slowly behind the chapel, were taking the odd nip from Bill's flask, which he refilled occasionally with smart dashes to the car in the middle of overs, when it looked to him as if nothing much was likely to happen for a while.

At 110 for 5, the boys' number seven, who opened the bowling for Worcestershire Colts and whose family owned most of the West Country, clipped one smartly to square leg off the military medium of Mr Poulton, who was later to be disgraced in a sex scandal that nearly brought down the Governor of Bermuda. Ginger Bill was in place for the catch. As it shot towards him he raised both his hands in front of his face like a schoolgirl playing volleyball on the beach. The ball hit the palm of his right hand, went to ground, and rolled towards midwicket, to a groan from the fathers and a milky sneer from Pennant-Cecil at the non-striker's end.

At 139 for 8, a cover drive from Edwin Marchmont, of the Port and Sherry Marchmonts, was flying to the boundary (and would have brought the scores level) when it struck Ginger Bill, who had wandered in from mid-off to get a closer look at one of the younger mothers bending to chastise a child, full on the forehead.

A gasp went round the ground. Bill bent down, picked up the ball, and tossed it back to the bowler, whose next ball uprooted Marchmont's middle stump.

And so Winkler, the last man, walked out to join Pennant-Cecil, descendant of the Cecils who bestowed greatness on the Tudors and Stuarts, with the score on 139 for 9.

Winkler's first ball, bowled by a man wearing the cap his grandfather had worn in the Eton-Harrow match of 1902, flicked the edge of his size four Gunn and Moore Magnum and shot through the legs of Ginger Bill, who was just then emptying the last drops from his flask at slip, where his captain had recently positioned him to keep him out of harm's way.

The ball dribbled down the slope towards the boundary, where, in the now-gloomying distance, it was cut off by a despairing bellyflop from a man grown fat at the long dining tables of the Middle Temple, and they ran three.

Pennant-Cecil, now on strike, squinted meanly as the bowler jogged in. The wicket-keeper, whose relatively static role disguised the hereditary limp first recorded when an ancestor had his horse killed under him at Agincourt and was forced to fight on on foot, squatted low and narrowed his eyes.

Ginger Bill, at slip, tucked his empty flask behind his back into the waistband of his stolen trousers. The spectators peered out into the blue-grey field, the ash grown long on their slim cigars.

The ball left the bowler's hand and swooped towards the bat, which swung elegantly, lazily, aristocratically and caught it with a chunky flick of its outside edge as it straightened in the direction of the main boarding houses.

Pennant-Cecil turned his head and saw the ball, brown as the trees now with a hard day's play, bend in the air with the spin it took off the willow, away from the line of second slip, where it had seemed to be heading, towards first slip, where Ginger Bill stood with his hands on his knees.

Pennant-Cecil's upper lip began to curl towards another sneer as Bill put his hands together, one on top of the other, fingers pointing towards the batsman, opened them, crocodile-fashion, and lunged towards the arriving ball.

And in it flew. The jaws closed. The ball remained inside. Ginger Bill looked down and found it nestling in his upturned palm.

The fathers streamed towards him and engulfed the ginger-bearded Jew. They raised him on their shoulders in his stolen shoes as the orange sun showed momentarily in the arch of the chapel before it disappeared behind the plane trees beyond – plane trees that were planted when Nelson was in short trousers – and they carried Ginger Bill towards the cheering crowd, dancing and singing his name as they went. And it was all his. And it was all Winkler's.

Rupert Pennant-Cecil dropped his head as he walked, and Winkler walked with him, behind the rejoicing fathers. And Winkler heard the captain of the fathers say to Ginger Bill:

'The beers are on you for that one, Bill.'

And he heard Bill reply: 'Beer? What do I want with beer? Does nobody around here drink whisky?'

And then Pennant-Cecil, because he had to say something as they walked, with the dark field behind them and the glow of the pavilion and the cheering hundreds ahead of them, said the only thing he could think of to say.

'Your father,' he said, 'snaps at his catches.'

And Winkler said: 'He's my uncle. My Uncle Bill. And he hasn't played in a long time.'

The train nosed into Albert Street station, site of Winkler's first change, clunked – passengers looked up, tutted, glanced around, found themselves in a train compartment, looked down again – and sat groaning for a while, half in and half out of the tunnel.

'My uncle. My Uncle Bill. And he hasn't played in a long time.'

Was it really like that? It sounded, on reflection, heroic. And thus unlikely. Was time beginning finally to play those healing tricks about which he had heard so much?

After the match, term ended and Bill drove Winkler back to his grand-father's place, with his trunk and his tuckbox and his three sacks of dirty laundry. Winkler ran up the stairs of the mansion block when the lift was too slow coming, skidding on the paisley carpet, bouncing off the wood-chip yellow walls with wide portholes of frosted shatterproof glass, pulling himself round corners with his fingers in the wire of the lift-shaft cage, arrived at the flat door and pounded on it.

Impatient with the silently passing seconds he shouted, 'Grandpa, Grandpa, they won, they won. Bill did it all. Grandpa, Grandpa.'

After another minute or so, as the doors of the lift opened behind him and Ginger Bill emerged with some of the luggage, the door opened a crack and stopped on the chain.

'Grandpa, I'm home. They won. Bill did it all. He was the hero.'

'The first time, I heard. It's a respectable building. Not a zoo.'

The flat door closed, the chain rattled, and it opened again, wider.

'The ball hit him on the head and he didn't even . . .'

'Shhh, for the Lord's sake. You'll wake the building.'

'But it's only nine o'clock.'

'Respectable people are asleep now. It's only a game of stickball, boy, dear oh lore. There's no need to shout.'

'I'm not shouting.'

'Don't answer back.'

'But Grandpa,' Winkler whispered. 'It was only one run to win and it was Pennant-Cecil, the one I told you about, who . . .'

Unimpressed by the kingmaker's descendant, Winkler's grandfather interrupted: 'You ate already? Eh? I hope you ate.'

'Um . . .' Winkler looked round at Ginger Bill.

'We picked up something on the way home,' said Bill.

'You didn't feed him from a beefburger place?'

'No.'

The old man took Winkler by the shoulders. 'You ate beefburgers again, sonny?'

Winkler said nothing.

'Bill, why must it be always this McDonald's?'

Ginger Bill pushed past the old man into the flat, wheezing under the weight of the tuckbox and the three bags of laundry and muttering to him, as he passed: 'For Christ's sake, Woyzeck. It's not always. It's the second time in his life he ate a Big Mac. It's not going to kill him. We were celebrating. We did it. Nobody rumbled us. It was just a Big Mac to celebrate the end of school. What do you think they feed him in that fucking prison, anyway? Cucumber salad and gefilte fish? You haven't seen the kid in weeks, you might at least give him a hug.'

'There's no need to get hysterical, William.'

'Hysterical? Jesus Christ, Woyzeck . . .'

★　★　★

The train lurched. And then crawled on down the platform to the end. The doors hissed and parted. Winkler dismounted and shuffled through the crowd to his connection, and his memories of an ancient day were jostled from him as he went, as if by pickpockets.

2

Winkler's Fear of Trains

Winkler stood waiting for his next train and thought, 'If I do get pushed under the hurtling wheels, I hope it's in the morning. Because what a terrible waste to be killed on the way *back* from work.'

Then the red train burst out of the dark arse of the creamy-tiled wall with a great scream, listing, round the bend of the platform, slowed, grunted, stopped, sighed, relaxed.

Winkler never failed to shudder as the train roared in, and he shuddered as usual this morning. But he was in the process of curing himself of the problem.

Today he was standing nearer the edge, even measuring both feet in the space between the yellow 'stand clear' line and the white-painted cliff edge. He was trying to feel reassured by the newly laid grippy surface that seemed to make slipping less likely and gave you something to push against with your soles if you needed to lean back into the crowd to stop from being squeezed out onto the rails.

And he was trying to reduce the number of times he looked behind him to see who was waiting to nudge him quietly onto the track. He was trying not to transfer his weight onto the invisible fulcrum behind the small of his back, where he reckoned he could pivot on his low-ish centre of gravity and recoil in an emergency, and also, in the case of a sudden fit, be more likely to topple backwards than forwards.

But in the end he always leapt back to flatten himself against the dirty wall, near to a phone or a chocolate machine, a bench or a fire extinguisher bracket, so that he was as far from the train's blunt blade as possible and had something to cling onto should a maniac choose that moment to strike.

He blushed, almost, at the thought that he had already tested most of these platform installations (which he thought of as 'bases'), surreptitiously, for strength. On every station on the network. There was a chocolate machine at North Central which he had even reported on the emergency hotline because it yielded too willingly to a firm lean. But it had not yet been seen to.

Not that he had any real confidence in these strategies. They were a joke, he hoped, told to himself to amuse the part of his mind which thought that the fear was funny. Also to relax the part of his mind that was genuinely panicked by the part of his mind that truly believed he was about to die.

It was for this reason, this lack of confidence in his survival strategy, that Winkler always stood at the very end of the platform, by the opening where the train would arrive. That way there was no question of pain.

At the other end of the platform, anywhere past the middle probably, the train would have slowed down enough that immediate death was uncertain. He might be slammed down into the well between the tracks, mashing dozens of major bones and suffering terrible brain damage that would leave him drooling and slurring and pissing himself in public, or maybe lose a leg, or be chewed up down one side. All of which had happened to Cornelius Prane, from school. Winkler shuddered again, just thinking of him.

Cornelius Prane had lost an eye and an arm and the use of a leg jumping to escape his teenage friendlessness, virginity, wonky chin, mathematical genius, and not-actually-carved-in-stone-certainty of university entrance success – and fucked it. And he was now a fully grown friendless virgin who had not, after all, gone to university, and was fully fucked in more ways than he would have dared to dream of back in the days when he thought the lack of a fuck and a place at Cambridge was the worst life could throw at a man.

The smash also unwonked his chin, which might have been considered a small Pyrrhic benefit, had not the impact that unwonked it simultaneously wonked the part of his head that knew what a reflection in a mirror was. For to every wonking there is an equal and opposite unwonking, as any alumnus of the school physics club, apart from Cornelius Prane, knows well enough.

And so. At the gaping entry-point the train was still bombing down at (pretty much) full pelt. If the baddies went for him here, or if his self-slaughter-curious demons got the better of him, a swift end was guaranteed. The hammer of God would not flinch.

But the hammer wouldn't get him this time. He was in luck. There was space on the barrier.

The Barrier. Best spot on the platform. Base Camp. Ground Zero. Campo Numero Uno. Mummy and Daddy's house. The barrier comprised four iron verticals rooted three feet deep in the platform's concrete bed and three rows of well-bolted cross-sections – a rock-solid grid, ten feet wide and five feet high, positioned at the main entrance to prevent late home-leavers, rushing for the train, from bounding off the bottom of the escalator, leaping the last stairs into the onrushing headwind and then, when the headwind dropped off suddenly at the emergence point onto the platform, hurtling onwards with their residual momentum into the path of a train.

The Barrier was usually full. Even at the quiet times when Winkler chose to travel there were generally a couple of station staff idling there as if with a fag and a mug of coffee, but without them, of course, and a couple of others like him, palely loitering. Enough to make any attempt to squeeze onto the rail pathetically conspicuous.

But this morning he had it to himself. Here he could lean for hours and watch the trains – which could not touch him – hurtle by. He often did. No, not often. But he did.

Looking up the platform as the wrong train pulled out he contemplated the other safe points, the other (how embarrassing) bases. These included:

1. *The Chocolate Machine.* Winkler had given this model a safety rating of 7/10. It was of the very newest type: a large colourful plastic unit mounted, crucially, on two wide stanchions. They were good and sturdy. He had kicked them plenty of times in different footwear and was satisfied that they were not hollow or, if hollow, then thick enough as made no odds one way or the other. He imagined them still standing in a grim post-Armageddon future in which the station had been ransacked and the chocolate machine pillaged and then stolen for fuel: two vast and trunkless legs of plastic in the nuclear desert. In an emergency, if he could not get a grip for any reason on the unit itself, and found himself on the floor, being sucked by some unknown force into the path of a train, he was confident that he could save himself by locking arms around these legs.

2. *The Payphone.* Solidly mounted and with a shatterproof Perspex canopy. Only 6/10 but better than the newest models which a̶r̶e̶

themselves attached by two struts to the chocolate machine – this
was at least a separate safety option, with its own structural
integrity. The apparatus was smooth and square with little to get a
purchase on, but in the absence of other options he could
unhook the handset as if about to make a call and, apparently
absent-mindedly, wrap the steel cord thrice around his upper arm.
It ought to work. And if he did go under the train, goddamit, the
phone was coming with him.

3. *The Mystery Doors.* 5/10. Three wooden doors on some sort of
    cupboard marked with flashes of lightning and signs saying 'Danger
    – High Voltage'. Each had a ten-inch horizontal grasp-handle of
    strong-ish plastic. He tried the doors often but they were always
    locked, tending to yield a little, perhaps as much as three
    millimetres, due, presumably, to a not quite snug fit between bolt
    and socket. The handles themselves felt sturdy enough and would
    do to give confidence in a crowd situation if they were to hand,
    but Winkler would not have wanted to stake his life on them.

4. *The Two Light Switches.* 3/10. Just along from the mystery doors
    were two grey boxes that looked like outdoor light switches but
    were not flickable. They were evident in most pre-war stations,
    usually marked with Dynotape strips reading 'when illuminated
    invert light is on'. Winkler had no idea what that meant or what
    the boxes were for, but the cables that ran into each one were
    housed in good strong steel tubes soundly bracketed to the wall.
    He had once grasped them, one in each hand, face to the wall,
    when a group of young black men in gym kit had appeared on
    the platform one evening, moving in his direction and making
    percussion-box noises at the very moment that a train was arriving.
    There had been no emergency but he felt that the tubes would
    delay any attack long enough for the train to become stationary.
    Nothing happened except that the black men as they passed with
    their rolling gaits all turned to look at him clinging to the wall,
    and looked at each other and tutted.

5. *The Fire Hydrant Box.* 3/10. The box was big, steel-topped and
    steel-framed with glass doors. Ideal to prevent lateral movement
    along the platform but not much use for preventing a slide onto
    the track. There was an edge, though, where the top overhung the
    doors, which could buy him a few seconds, depending on his
    finger-strength.

6. *The Help Unit.* Newly innovated. A big round shield-like object

with 'Help!' written on it. A button next to a grid of forty-two
pores in the metal claimed to open an intercom where you could
report an emergency. But frantically banging the button and
screaming 'Help! Help! A train's coming!' would do Winkler no
good at all. There was also a button here for the general tannoy, or
so it claimed, though Winkler doubted it was that easy to
commandeer the means of communication. Again, taking control of
the microphone and announcing, 'Anyone coming within six feet
of Mr Winkler during the approach of a train will be vaporised,'
did not strike him as constructive. The real disappointment was
how shabbily the structure was mounted on the wall, it wobbled
and clanged in every direction as if waiting to be pulled under a
train by a desperate commuter fooled into believing it could
provide succour. 0/10.

A rattle in the tunnel announced the imminent arrival of another train.
From the safety of the barrier, Winkler wondered: what about people?
Could a fellow human provide the protection of a 'base'? Why not? When
did you ever hear of two people falling under a train? There was no reason
why he should not position himself behind a nice big fatty as the train
came in (you'd need a real porker to be safe) and push against him or
her if he felt he was about to be pushed himself. It might be an ideal
way to work himself down off the plateau of anxiety represented by the
'bases'. All he had to do was select a convenient lard-arse, get over the
revulsion he felt at the sight of fat people (a physical reaction almost as
debilitating as his train problem – he told himself over and over that physical enormity was not necessarily an indicator of moral lassitude but it
just didn't help), and then park himself behind one.
    An enormous Jew in a black pinstriped three-piece suit with a moist
bubble of face beneath a round hat waddled onto the platform and rolled
past him, holding a thin, shabby briefcase and loudly crunching a bright
green apple.
    The train's blazing eyes (so dragon-like) flashed into view in the tunnel.
Winkler, taking his life in his hands, sprang from the barrier, marched ten
paces up the platform to where the large Hebrew stood, flayed core in
one chubby fist, shabby case clutched greedily in the other, and watched
the train hurtle in, watching also a roll of neck-fat, filthily grimed in the
crease, and a dangle of curly black hair in front of the ear, which was also
not very clean in the cartilaginous space behind. In fact, inspected closely,
it sustained a population of foetid blackheads. Do people have blackheads

there? Winkler felt behind his own ear and in the act of reaching back he touched something with his elbow.

Was there someone close behind? Why? Not today. Not today when he had finally decided to try. Only seconds before he had been leaning on the hefty rail of The Barrier and now, when it seemed that the moment had finally come, there was nothing between him and a gruesome death, ground beneath greasy black decelerating wheels, but this enormous Old Testament sebum farm.

Winkler put his hand up to touch the back of the man's coat and prepare himself for resistance. Turning, he saw that what his elbow had brushed was a tiny schoolgirl in a green uniform, about eight years old and no more than four foot two, who was now smoothing her hair and looking up at him to say, 'Oi, watch out four-eyes.' He laughed with relief, but now the Jew leaned back himself as the train rushed by, and Winkler felt his hand pressing on the Jew's back. And he felt the Jew feel it. The Jew flinched and turned. He saw Winkler's hand still there, braced on air.

What was in his eye — fear? Anger? Puzzlement? Was it panic? Resignation? Was it what would have been in Winkler's eye at the moment when he realised that he was finally being pushed under a train?

'Sorry mate,' Winkler said. 'That little girl bumped me and I sort of . . .'

But already the Jew had heaved himself onto the train, a door having opened exactly at the spot where they stood. Winkler stepped backwards, walked down the train, passing the gap between carriages as the doors made their just-about-to-close noise, and hopped in.

'I sort of what?' he thought, and looked at his hand, and practised pushing it against air, backwards and forwards, for nearly a minute. Or half a minute. And thought about turning this thing round. Thought about becoming the aggressor and letting someone else worry about being the victim.

'I sort of what?'

At Central Station, where he changed for the monorail, Winkler walked down the platform faintly brushing people as he passed. He allowed the back of his hand to brush backs and buttocks. As the crowd jostled to position itself for an approaching train he saw an arse in a tight Burberry-patterned skirt on bare legs, a sticky-out but small, teenage, female arse, and thought — as a Perspex people podule winked in the tunnel — of bestowing a firm push on it. He felt his cock thinking about it too, perking up in his pants, and withdrew, horrified. This had nothing to do with sex. But there was no doubt that with the general brushing and leaning and the distraction of the arse, he had experienced a far more painless train arrival than he was used to.

Why? The bodily contact, maybe? The sense of physical contiguity with humanity at large?

He sat down opposite a man in a singlet who was eating something with the remains of a Ginsters packet still wrapped around its bottom half.

No. Of course not. This fear of trains was not merely an expression of his existential loneliness, of the cosmic detachment he felt from his fellow man. It could not be overturned simply by the corporeal confirmation that he was not alone on the planet. His fear was not part of some ongoing delusional psychosis. It was real. He was scared of trains. They can kill you. They are really very dangerous. It is quite extraordinary that a society as supposedly 'civilised' as our own can allow tubes of metal weighing hundreds of tons and travelling at speeds of up to sixty miles an hour simply to blast through an underground passage lined with jostling people who at any moment might . . .

Blam!

3

The Puddle

The monorail capsule rocketing along with Winkler inside burst out suddenly into the sunlight.

In sympathy with the jittery confidence of the late 1980s Docklands Development Project, the people who landed the contract to build this monorail (landed it like a slippery trout) decided to make the trains out of glass, or some durable transparent polythene (Winkler knew little of plastics), so that when it finally exploded out from under the city through the big hole that led to the sea, or the estuary or wherever the boats used to come from when they came, it didn't just fill with light, it exploded:

Blam!

People winced, gasped, sighed, tutted, shielded their eyes with hands and papers, or closed them. It always took Winkler by surprise, like everyone. Like everyone, at some point during his forty-five minutes under ground he forgot that it was light outside. Just like when he would emerge from the cinema on a weekday afternoon when he was little, hand in hand with some new foreign woman standing in for a mother, still thinking he was in the enchanted forest or the, no, always the enchanted forest (Snow White, Bambi, Sleeping Beauty . . .) and be smacked in the face with a stick of dazzling suburb.

He usually felt like shouting, 'Bomb!' as if someone had detonated a light grenade in the carriage and everyone should throw themselves on the floor and cover their eyes (should you do both at the same time, Winkler asked himself, or would that mean that you hurt your chin?).

But people did not throw themselves on the floor (for Winkler did not cry 'Bomb!'). After the gasping and wincing and flinching there was a ripple of pocket-and-handbag-rifling and then everyone was wearing sunglasses and staring straight ahead at the seven skyscrapers of the 'Exo-City' development down at the old docks, tall and pointy, screaming in the sun like the Emerald City. Except not green.

Winkler squeezed his eyes tight shut against the light, and then tighter still against the red and green fireworks. And the rolling greenhouse climbed up the overhead rail that caterpillars over the houses and gardens (although there aren't any gardens) and snaked, wheezing, up to the first station on the line, which was the stop for work.

Out on the platform the day, which looked hot from inside the air-conditioned carriage, turned out to be as good as its word. Up ahead, the Emerald City steamed in the sun. And there, when Winkler turned around, was the old city, which has always been there, if a little smaller and dirtier than it is now. The very city which had just spat Winkler out (quite rightly) onto this hot tarmac sideboard – hot enough that the tarmac felt as if it might just be a little bit squishier underfoot than on cooler days.

Winkler descended to the road by the bright metal steps at the end of the platform, and at the bottom of the steps he saw the puddle.

Even when the days were hot and the city was dry and the pavements and the concrete and the mud-packed parks were dust-puffed and grey like embers, there was a puddle at the bottom of the steps outside Cannery Road station.

During the rainiest times of the year it was much bigger, of course. But then it was only part of the general wetness. In the spring it was at its most impressive, holding its inch of depth defiantly at the end, some-times, of rainless fortnights. And remaining perfectly puddle-sized in terms of breadth and length, even when you had not seen standing water anywhere else for a week.

In high summer it shrank almost away, but never quite, and that was when it was at its most disquieting, to Winkler.

He never expected it, coming in under the city from the cool station, through the black tunnel, fast on the Japanese-manufactured track, which made a loud shack-a-tanging noise on the long bend where the round floor sections at the carriage-joins turned sharply, unsteadying old people (of whom there were few) and making the flight (they called it a 'flight') feel faster.

He never expected it, climbing a slight gradient, still in the dark and with occasional flickering of the white overhead lights from the stress of it, staring hard at the newspaper, like everyone else and like always, half in tune with the train for the sake of something to be half in tune with and then out into the sunlight (Blam!) and the world so bright and dry.

How could the puddle still be there? It was a hundred degrees in the sun. It hadn't rained in months. There had been nothing like it for dryness since the Bible. How could it be that the only place, the one tiny spot in the whole country where it was still raining was the exact place where Winkler began his working day?

Yesterday, finally, Winkler had said to himself, 'It will be gone by tomorrow.'

It had been getting smaller and smaller for weeks. He had not seen a drop of water fall from the bridge – up there above the puddle, netted against pigeons – since early June. The puddle, which back in March was eight inches deep at the centre and three or four feet in diameter (so that he had to jump out from the bottom step to keep his feet dry) had dwindled to little more than a saucerful at the converging point of four dirty yellow paving stones, the warted kind that pass secret information to blind people. It had not looked as if it had more than an hour of life left in it.

But there it was, and Winkler was certain that it was – if anything – bigger than yesterday. Although that couldn't be.

Across the road there was the broken chip shop sign: ''ky chicken 'n' lin' fish'. A shitty name for a shitty shop selling fuck knows what grey inedibles to grease-needy morons who don't know any better, which was not made any better or worse by having been shattered by a brick on the left hand side so that the two light strips behind the red plastic were exposed, making it unclear which qualities the establishment's portions of chicken and fish were supposed to possess.

Was the chicken chunky? Was it funky? Was it flaky? Was it sticky? Slicky? Was it finger-licky? No, 'finger-licky' was too long. And it was harder still to tell what they were trying to say about the fish. Perhaps that it was sizzlin'. But is that good? Would these people be happier, perhaps, if their fish were dazzlin'? Were the proprietors so honest as to confess that it was merely middlin'?

'Manky Chicken 'n' Piddlin Fish', Winkler mouthed, sadly, as usual, and thought of how this place might have been when they first opened it up four, five, six years ago – their first attempt at business in this country, just off the boat, plane, train, Eurostar under-carriage tool compartment, whatever, hoping it was the start of something huge, some vast empire of McPatels that would make them rich and fat and happy and beloved. But all they had managed was this bright, scary vomit-shop under a bridge, with a broken sign and a view of a puddle.

Was it a skinhead brick that did for the dream? Some drunken cunt who came out of the pub just opposite and down a bit, and picked up a bit of kerb smashed off by a too-big-for-the-street delivery truck and thought, 'I'll brick a fucking Paki with this' but couldn't see any Pakis (closing time around the Dog and Fuckpig being no time for Pakis to be out) so bricked a shop that was probably run by Pakis instead?

Or was it some rival Pakis, pissed off that fat man Patel's business dreams were bringing hungry, pissed skinheads into the area?

Or was it an Indian who didn't like Pakis either and was protesting about the beheading of a coachload of nuns in Kashmir by throwing a brick through a sign above a chip shop owned, he had heard, by Pakis? But if it was an Indian protesting about something, wouldn't he have just lain down in the road outside?

Winkler was distracted by the *boof boof boof boof* of an overburdened car stereo. Looking up from where he had been imagining that the Chip Shop Gandhi might position himself, he saw a dented hatchback with its windscreen and front passenger window blacked out. But the driver's window was down, and through it he saw the music-lover: a narrow, green-brown teenager with his head shaved at ear-top height and an oiled beetle-shell of black hair sitting on it, the fringe higher on one side than the other, the kid topless and skinny as a lizard with a thin gold chain round his smooth naked neck and Arabic letters on his hard little bare breast. His lips pursed. His head moving jerkily. The driver of the car looked at Winkler. Winkler's heart raced. The car passed Winkler and the driver put his head out of the window and stared backwards at Winkler, not looking in the direction he was moving, looking into Winkler's eyes.

Winkler wondered if the little fucker ever smiled. Did he smile at his mother? Or at jokes? He'd seen them telling jokes. He'd overheard them on the corner. One of them says something meant to be funny, clearly meant to be funny, but they all just nod and purse their lips and maybe touch each other's knuckles together, a couple of them, and then they all look left and right with their little snake-eyes, suspicious that someone might be listening to their witty repartee.

This one he was looking at now lost interest in him, pulled in his head and accelerated with a roar of rusty exhaust towards the brown four-storey housing estate that sprawled ahead of him, to Winkler's right, full of, what? Pakistanis? Or was it Bengalis? Or Bangladeshis? Or were Bangladeshis the same as Bengalis? Not that it matters, thought Winkler, stepping towards the kerb. No, it does matter. It matters a lot. He'd find out one day soon.

The slim length of street he was about to cross was the same slim length of street on which, in the 1930s, the Jews rose up and fought the evil fascists. And the whole city rose with them. Glorious days. No Hitler for us. Did our fascists have a point, though? Come on. I'm not saying (Winkler wasn't saying anything, just thinking), I'm not saying anyone wants to gas anybody but wasn't it all a bit like . . . and then now with the . . . and wouldn't it all have been . . . no, no, of course no.

A wave of pointless love for all mankind came over Winkler when he stared into the depths of what he might think if he were left to think it.

Next to him, suddenly, was a little old man.

It's a little old man, smiled Winkler to himself. With a little beard under his chin, scampering from ear to ear. And a funny little hat. And he's wearing a dress – Winkler smiled some more – he's wearing a little beige dress with flappy trousers underneath, and open shoes. I can see his little brown toes. I shall say hello to him.

'Morning,' said Winkler.

The man looked at Winkler. 'Good morning,' he said, and walked off towards the brown housing estate, hauling behind him a little tartan shopping trolley.

There you go, thought Winkler. Everything's fine. He's got a little tartan trolley.

Winkler walked past the Post Office, where people were queuing. What for? Stamps? Road tax discs? Dole money? Did they still do dole money at the Post Office? Wasn't it all done on the internet?

After the Post Office, the greengrocer. Not a white face to be seen in there. Not ever. Winkler used to go in occasionally to see what would happen, pick up a funny-looking vegetable and stand there with it at the counter, anticipating suspicion, waiting to not understand whatever the Asian man behind the till said to him and to mumble 'Sorry' and run out of the shop and all the way to work.

But the man only ever said, 'Yes, mate? Pand fifty. Anyfink else?' And so that was no fun. The shop smelt of cumin, fenugreek, soft old fruit, armpits and boxes. It brought flashing back with frightening efficiency shops he had been in in Cairo, Nairobi, Goa, Zanzibar, Hammamet, always ducking very briefly off the package-tour crocodile to slip through a beaded doorway. Then, those shops had made him feel adventurous, self-reliant, competent, happy and free. This shop, despite the authenticity of its smell (which was helped very much by the heat), made him feel none of those things. Should it?

Not necessarily, no.

Should the shop even be here with its warm reek of foreign holidays?

Of course. Of course it should.

Outside the shop today a short fat man stood, talking on a mobile phone in a language he may, for all Winkler knew, have been making up as he went along. He was fat, but not overhanging. Not fat like a . . . It was George Orwell, in *Burmese Days*, who wrote the thing about Orientals growing fat not like Europeans, but swelling roundly, like fruit ripening. Should he have written that? Really, should he?

Of course he should. It was 1936 or '37. That was fine.

After the shop, the last thing before the boundary of the main road was the pub, green outside with frosted glass and three silhouettes of Victorian drinkers: two men and a woman, all laughing, all wearing hats, all madly overdressed for going to the pub, even then. The front door was open because of the heat.

Only white men in there, obviously. First pints of the morning.

No white men out on the street apart from Winkler.

And no brown men in the pub. Some of the white men (you could see the corner of the bar and two tables beneath a wall-mounted television from the street) were bare-chested. They had nylon football shirts rolled up and hung over the edge of their jeans, wedged in by the hip, next to the mobile phone holster and the tattoo of something not at all poetic or sensitive syringed into dumb fat.

Over from the pub was what decent people call a corner shop. For years Winkler called them Paki shops. 'It's a term of affection,' he said, when friends upbraided him. 'If I thought it was offensive I wouldn't say it.' Now he calls them corner shops.

This one never has much in it: a fridge full of Sunny Delight and hundreds of packets of crisps. Packets of crisps that the scrawny teenager with the bum-fluff moustache doesn't even bother taking out of the delivery boxes. Just leaves them on the floor for old white women whose husbands may well have fought to keep us free and English-speaking (or just for the fun of killing) to bend over and rummage in for their cheese and onion.

Though why the fat old goats want to eat that crap is beyond Winkler.

Now, after the corner shop, is a gap in the buildings where the road slips off towards the grey housing estate (full of bright washing on lines) which Winkler always cuts through to get to work, the one with the smells that make him want to eat curry at eleven o'clock in the morning. On the corner, a giant poster pasted up by the government (the Home Secretary in the dead of night with a brush and ladder) warns against the evils of cigarette smuggling and tells you what will be done to you if you are caught. And you will be caught. The poster changes every few months but the message is always the same:

DON'T SMUGGLE FAGS!

Nobody cares if these people die coughing and screaming and weeping for their faraway mothers. They waste no money here on posters about cancer, heart-disease or birth defects. Just as long as they pay £4.90 a pack for the pleasure and don't get them for two quid a pop round the back of the market.

The black poster made Winkler's eyes water, it looked so hot. The full sun blazed on it, and hot warps bubbled under its black skin. He looked away to cool his eyes, looking at the pub, the fish shop and the bridge's pale-blue iron side, the chromy metal of cleanish wheel hubs, bicycles and the struts of push chairs flashing in the whiteness. The edges of every-thing surreally crisp and sharp. The sky very blue in the gaps between buildings. The walls cartoon clean. Every brick spotless in the brightness. The floor dirty with stubs and wrappers and tickets and leaves and poly-thene, ash, oil, shit, hair, splintered wood and plastic, rotted food, papers, piss, the puddle . . . as if the director of this ghetto-in-the-morning scene were going hard for urban realism on a set created by a gay set designer who likes everything to look nice.

The extras scuttle in the shadows to keep cool. More lizards. Or spiders even. Little and black and unimaginable.

Then there's some other shit-dirty pointless shop with fuck all in it that stays open all night and then . . . wait, what's this?

It's a sturdy little thing dressed all in black. But, all. Head to foot. With a little black cowl and a little black mask. It could be Batman for all Winkler knows. Apart from being barely able to walk, it's so fat. Let alone fly. Mind you, Batman couldn't fly either. Nor did he show his toes. Oh no, you want to know about modesty, you look at Batman. Batman is a Muslim woman who knows her place. Not like this one, whoring her fat little toes to all and sundry. Look, look, Winkler can see her toes.

'Ooh, stone me to death for adultery, I saw her nasty little toes.'

Or, wait, to be fair, nice little toes. This reminded Winkler that he had more than one option when it came to thinking about this woman. It was no good just seeing things and then thinking the first thing that came into his head. There was a multitude of available thought options. For example, there was:

Thought Option One (and these in no particular order): What is England
    coming to? Where are the old ladies pedalling home from the
    jumble sale on high-handled bicycles with a basket on the front
    full of Cox's orange pippins for a blackberry and apple pie which

will be left to cool by the never-locked back doors of their little thatched cottages? And where are the children in grey shorts who will pause in their whipping along of wooden hoops when they get the smell of the juice bubbling up through the crust through holes made with a pewter fork? Where is all that? Where did it go? It was good. It was better than this.

Thought Option Two: It's not her fault. The bigoted patriarchal system of her own community forces her into this humiliating disguise but she leads her own intellectual life inside the hateful wrappings, a life as valid as mine. And anyway:

Thought Option Two (b): What is so individual about the shell-suit, block-heeled sling-backs and greasy perm of the universal fag-smoking white trash fat bitch on which our nation depends for its longevity? And anyway:

Thought Option Two (c): The men who make her dress like this and who believe that Western women who show off their mottled pink flesh and wear make-up and stunt bras to imitate women made of plastic they see on the television are whores, don't they have a point?

Thought Option Three: I've read interviews with women like this in the papers, where they insist that it is their own choice. I've read about women who, having grown-up in liberal or Westernised Muslim families, subsequently, as adults, decided to adopt the veil, purdah, hijab, chador, burka, jellabir, shalwah kameez, whatever it's called. (Am I good, knowing these words, or bad, not knowing what each one means?)

Thought Option Four: If they're going to come and live here and bring up their families and sow bloodlines, then shouldn't they make the cultural compromises that integration demands? (By which Winkler meant: eat, dress, talk, think, wipe your arse like us, respect the same values, and if you disrespect them then disrespect them like us, and then how you pray, and whom to, and when, and how often, and whether you do at all, is up to you. And you will, of course, stop praying in time, because the freedom to not pray always results in people not praying.) But this demand for integration led to:

Thought Option Four (b): Yes, but look what happened to Europe's Jews in the 1930s. The integrators who thought they could become Germans, Poles, Czechs and survive that way because that was what the German, Poles, Czechs wanted them to do, laughed at the Zionists, the separatists, off to Palestine (buying, forging, stealing certificates) like a swarm of nomadic Old Testament half-wits. And it was the half-wits, of course, who lived. As half-wits so often do.

The integrated ones got slaughtered. For there is nothing so scary
to the racist as not knowing his enemy.

Thought Option Five: These people, whoever they are, have every right
to preserve their traditions, culture, whatever, in any way they
choose, as long as it does not infringe the civil liberties of others
(by 'others' in this context we mean 'us', rather than, say, 'their
women'), which of course raises the point that it is the very liber-
ality and tolerance of the host culture that enshrines their right to
practise their own bigotry, if they choose to. And this leads you
back, in a way, to Thought Option One, unless you press on
quickly – with the grim smoke-stackery of the workplace looming
now, only a main road-cross and backstreet shimmy away – to:

Thought Option Six: Isn't it all our fault, all this, for creating arbitrary
nation states in the dismantling of our Empire, and for being unable
to resist the greedy imperial urge for the last three hundred years?

Winkler emerged onto the shore of the dirty dual carriageway, which he
half-crossed.

Pausing on the little concrete island, Winkler, through the dust and the
petrol fumes, got the greasy refried saturated fat smell of McDonald's. The
smell of death on a grand scale. Big ugly death on a hook, dripping onto
hot griddles and slithering towards his palate up the grubby street. The smell
that had most of the city in its brown grip now. Not just grimy high streets
swathed in dripping from the huge outlets that cluster wherever people incapable of reflection feel hunger, but also the nicer areas, where a 'restaurant'
positioned a mile or two upwind from where local resident associations
resisted planning permission, belched out that smell of a broken crow decom-
posing in a chimney, deliberately to choke the area in its vile headlock.

Stranded on the island with monstrous lorries rushing past on either
side, Winkler was trapped. The smell curled round him and he looked for
traffic gaps to flee its greasy ambush.

He leant on a half-crumpled plastic bollard, yellow, white and blue,
and felt the black soot on the plastic, grainy in his damp palm. He glanced
up at the meaty yellow and red of the drive-thru, and stood there, sweaty-
haired, swaying on the sooty road sign, not vomiting.

When he finally beached on the other side and slid down the alley off
the main road onto the office's cobbled backstreet, Winkler was nearly
killed by a speeding Saab. In so far as a Saab roared past and if Winkler
had stepped in front of it, for any reason, he would not have stood a
chance.

'Wanker!' he shouted up the street after the car as it roared away, bouncing over a speed bump and squeaking on the hot cobbles.

The Saab garage next to the office sold and mended hundreds and hundreds of the big, Swedish cars that once were porpoise-shaped and harmless and now were big angry tanks capable of terrifying speeds, which damn near flattened Winkler every day.

Outside the garage, at the great plastic curtain over the entrance to the loading bay, dozens of bull-necked men with close-cropped hair, or none at all, were employed to stand around in blue overalls ('blue-collar worker' always *sounded* so respectable) with their hands behind their backs and cheap cigarettes pinched meanly between fat, calloused thumbs and fore-fingers, dragging on them occasionally in a cupped hand (wind or no wind) and flexing their necks as they replaced the fag-pinching hand behind the blue-overalled back as if their heads didn't fit properly, and snaking eyes left and right (like the lizards who guarded the puddle) to observe . . . what? Winkler? Surely not.

While Winkler's hatred for these men was immense, he presented no immediate danger, so far as they could see.

'Are they car testers or something?' he would ask himself, more quietly, as he passed the plastic curtain and another stubble-headed man climbed into a plastic-sheeted driving seat, reversed at speed, spun the wheel, yanked on the handbrake to put himself in position on the runway, released it, and launched himself up the cobbled lane like a rocket, throwing up leaves and dust and hamburger wrappers and lettuce strands and torn-cornered barbecue sauce sachets and fag butts and crisp wrappers in a cyclone as it passed. In winter great tsunamis of filthy grey rainwater, too.

'Testing what? Testing that it's loud enough?' he shouted, inaudibly, at the top of his voice. 'Testing that every fucking vehicle can survive hitting a speed-bump in a narrow street at a hundred miles an hour?'

And he always strode to the loading bay to demand an audience with the manager, and then saw them, three or four of them, standing there. Like cattle in trousers. Heads like tortoises, though. Hairless and slow. Smoking fags. Full of menace. And he always let it go.

'Calm down, calm down,' he thought, digging in his pockets for his security pass. 'It's nearly over.'

Winkler found his pass, took it out, and looked at the two-year-old photograph. For he had arrived at the entrance to his office and would soon be challenged by the square-headed, red-faced, thickly bespectacled and Brylcreemed security man to prove that he was, indeed, Winkler.

And, by God, he was.

4

The Office

Winkler took the stairs one at a time, slowly. It was only two flights, there was no need to risk the lift. Halfway up the first flight, he stopped.

'I walked the stairs like this on the first morning of school terms,' he thought, bored, sad, sorry to be thinking about it again but unable not to. 'I took off my outdoor shoes, black slip-ons with elastic webbing, and put them in the box marked "Winkler" – I know this, why am I bothering? – and put on my spongy-soled brown sandals (which were perfect in length and width because my foot had been measured in the holidays on a measuring board shaped like a monster's claw with a sliding rule that pressed up against my big toe and made me feel the texture of my sock) and walked up the stairs one at a time, and stopped halfway up each flight. And then walked on up the rest of the flight putting both feet on each step, halving my speed and touching the banister each time with my left hand after my right because the feel of the polished wood felt uneven in only one palm, and always thinking to myself the same thing:

'Okay, this is it, this time, it really is. I'm not going to talk at all. And then they won't be able to say that I talk too much. And they'll see I've changed. And they'll wonder why. But I won't say a thing. And then they'll see I'm strong and that I can be quiet when I want. That's what I'll do.'

That's what little Winkler thought on the school stairs smelling of floor polish, with the low sunlight howling in through the big window at the turn in the stairs so that he couldn't see much when he looked up (or was that just his memory being lazy?) walking with an exaggerated stamp so his sandals wouldn't slide and squeak on the lino. He promised himself silence.

At the top of the first flight Winkler turned left, through the grubby white double doors with shatterproof portholes, and walked down the ramp that would come in useful if the office ever decided to hire a disabled person, or a dalek. Winkler always used the ramp instead of the three steps: it made a nice, cheap, hollow sound when he walked on it.

'Winkler!' said the shiny-faced one with the beard on the media desk, the one whose name, after three years, Winkler still never remembered. 'Jesus H. Rinkydink. I don't believe my eyes. What brings you in at this hour? Couldn't sleep?'

Winkler looked around for a clock. There were hundreds. The office was nothing but clocks. It was five past twelve.

'Big lunch today, is it?' said Roger Skelton. Roger Skelton was the drooling gimp to whom Winkler owed his job. So he couldn't tell him to fuck off.

'This is about when I always get in . . .' Winkler began.

Skelton and the bearded shiner and a couple of others who had been sitting there in their ties since nine o'clock exchanged glances – as if they had the wit, soul or originality to impart meaning in a look. As if there were any music inside.

'Well it is,' Winkler insisted. 'It's not especially early. I don't . . .' And here he could go two ways: he could play along, making a self-deprecating gag about his habitual lateness, or protest that it was an aberration. Either of these would be considered acceptable responses to the familiar goad. Winkler played the game of office banter reluctantly, but it had to be played.

What he really wanted to do was to remind them that he, Winkler, came and went as he pleased because he, unlike them, was not paid to occupy desk space and perform tasks in an endlessly repeated pattern hour after hour, day after day, week after week. He was paid to perform under pressure and to be unique. He was paid to be Winkler. He wanted to remind them that he was special, different and better than them.

He said, 'I don't usually come in much before this.'

'You're telling us!' said the thin one who wore very narrow ties that reached down to his fly and smoked roll-ups in the loo. Barry, was he called? Winkler had fed him a line, because he knew that was what they wanted, the desk. By conceding this defeat, so much more was gained in the long run.

It upset Winkler only because of the 'us'. What sort of a man was this who turned even a cliché like 'you're telling me' into a group utterance empty of individual consciousness? The grunt of a primate cursed with language. It tipped him just far enough over that he said:

'I don't have to come in at all, Roy. You know that. I'm self-employed.'

They all thought, and some even mouthed, 'Woooo!' But they didn't say anything. And his name must really have been Roy, which was a stroke of luck.

'Big night was it?' Ronnie said, looking up from the gossip page of the paper, which he had been looking at since his first greeting.

They measured life in terms of lunches, nights, weekends, jobs, fuck-ups, and all of them broken down by size. And 'big' only ever meant 'before, during or after which, a lot of alcohol was drunk' – their spiritual poverty corrupted even the very concept of quantity.

'Not particularly. You know I don't really drink anymore,' said Winkler, who drank a lot but always said this, because then they would say he was gay. And that made them happy. Particularly if he protested.

'And before you say it, no I'm not . . .' But on this occasion the desk had decided, a few seconds earlier than usual, to fall silent, and suddenly appear to be going about its business. They all looked at the bits of paper in front of them as if to say, 'Listen, pal, you may not have work to do but we have.'

If he said anything now then one of them, most likely the bald one who always wore a pink shirt that was losing its colour at the armpits and said 'myself' instead of 'me' and talked to you with his fingers locked behind his head, would have said, 'Shh, Winkler, not now. We're up to our ears here.'

Bristling with irritation, Winkler walked on past the media desk towards his own, tucked in a corner, pausing briefly at the big, square, semi-subsidized drinks machine to pick up a plastic cup of boiling brown, dusty and undrinkable coffee. And he remembered how on those first mornings of term an opportunity would always present itself when he had no option but to break his silence. Often it came immediately. For example, Adam Rosen asked a question. Miss Maxwell answered it. Adam Rosen said, 'Oh, well, ask a silly question.' Winkler said, because he knew how to finish the phrase, 'Get a silly answer.' And he was yanked from the kneeling group of six-year-olds, yanked painfully by his arm and pulled, faster than he could keep up so that he was half-trotting and half being dragged, like a man with his coat caught in a train door as the train pulled away, to the door, and thrown out into the corridor by the coat pegs and shoe lockers to explain himself to the headmistress when she came past. Explain what? He buried his face in his parka, where it hung on the wall, feeling the fake fur trim on his wet face – wet from the pain, not from crying – and looked at his name, written on the wall in marker by his peg, with the 'k' back to front. And that was the silence done for, for that term.

Winkler's own sorry little grey plastic work station was empty apart from yesterday's evening paper, folded, with a ring-bound typist's pad on it, and on top of that a colour guide to boarding houses and hostels on the Isle of Wight. These were only there because when he left the night before, Winkler had noticed that his desk was entirely empty and looked as if it had been wiped clean, which made it look as if it belonged to a mad person. So he had made a few small adjustments, using items he found in a nearby cupboard.

Winkler saw that his desk looked neutral but not obsessively so, and was pleased. Winkler was not a man to express himself through his desk. Everyone else, it seemed, was. Every other desk in the building, all two hundred (six hundred? A thousand? Who knows?), contrived to deliver a message about the desk owner. But as well as the intended meaning, they also carried (which each desk owner did not know) a secondary meaning, easily decipherable to a man of Winkler's sensitivity.

Everything on a desk spoke to Winkler, sometimes even sang. He glanced, as he walked, at fat Marjorie's desk and saw the polka-dotting of Post-It notes. 'I want you to think my mind works so fast and unconventionally,' it warbled, 'that I have to scribble little monuments to my thoughts as I go or they'll be lost forever. But the truth is my short-term memory is shot to pieces because I'm getting old.'

And Winkler listened to the cries from other desks:

A framed photograph of a baby muttered sadly, 'This is my only achievement, my life is over.'

A computer monitor plastered with cut out newspaper headlines coincidentally featuring the desk-owner's own surname in funny/relevant contexts beamed, 'I cut these out myself, but I wish someone else had. It would mean they had seen something in the paper and thought of me.'

A desk buried beneath an avalanche of papers and capsized polystyrene coffee cups announced, 'You think I am a bit of a dilettante? A bit of a card? Too busy to tidy up? Ha, what you don't know is that at home I have cupboards full of my own shit in jamjars, fully labelled and dated.'

A Gary Larson Far Side calendar with a hilarious talking animal-based cartoon for each day, clenched its fists and wept, 'God help me, I live alone and own a cat.'

A spider plant in a brown plastic pot on a delft plate said, 'My husband left me but I got to keep the crockery, now the office is my home.'

A packet of Marlboro reds and a box of Swan Vestas drawled: 'Even though this is a no smoking office you should know that I smoke in my spare time because I'm a bit like Marlon Brando.'

A Twinings herbal teabag selection simpered, 'I am serene, I ride a bicycle, my flat is impeccably tidy. My ex-husband is a bastard.'

Sherwood Glaub said, 'Ho, Winkler! Got a job interview?' Sherwood Glaub was not a desk, he was the squat, open-pored bean-counter who sat at the desk next to Winkler's.

'Yeah, Sherwood, sure I have,' said Winkler.

Winkler had ironed his shirt that morning, standing in the corner of the bedroom, cramped in the little gulley made by the chest-high bookcase and the bed with a broken leg propped up by a fat, brown Cassell's German Dictionary, a Yellow Pages and two unread Isaac Asimov compendiums, cramped there with his tide-marked yellow-grey ironing board right up against his hip, banging his elbow on the yellow wall, because that was the only other plug in the room apart from the one with the television and clock in it and he wanted to watch telly while he ironed but couldn't be arsed to reset the clock when he'd finished. And even then, tucked in that little hole, with the room occasionally shaking from overloaded lorries rumbling down the dual carriageway, and the creases not keen to yield to the piddle of steam that the iron with its lint-filled pores wheezed out, he had thought, 'If I wear an ironed shirt then Sherwood Glaub will ask me if I've got a job interview. Maybe Ciara in the messengers' office will ask me who died. And one of the Barrys or Rogers is bound to ask me what time I'm due in court.'

And so he thought to himself, 'No, I haven't got a job interview you sad, fat little fairy with your mauve shirt and your purple horizontal striped, metallic-finish tie. I don't have a job interview because I already earn three times what you do for the same fucking job because I'm so fucking good at it, and they know it. And you should know that, sitting next to me. I've never had a job interview in my life, twat, because people come to *me* and beg *me* to work for them and, you little oily poofter, if I did have a job interview I wouldn't specially iron myself a shirt for it because I, unlike you and every other sorry-arsed useless motherfucker in this place, have more to sell myself on than my neat appearance, discretion, conformity and ability to exactly fill the space left by the last bloke without anyone being any the wiser that a change has been made. Now fuck off, you little toad and let me get on with the business of being me, Winkler, who doesn't give a fuck.'

But all he said was, 'No, the truth is I just woke up with an odd feeling of wanting to do a bit of ironing.'

'Ooh, you're turning into a proper little poofter,' said Glaub.

Winkler said, 'When that happens you'll be the first to know,' and was suddenly aware that he hadn't yet had his morning crap. He wanted to grab something to read, though, and moved his weight from one foot to the other, clenching his arse cheeks as he pulled a stack of newspapers apart looking for something suitable.

'Got anything shite-worthy?' he said to Glaub, pushing his hand up against his rectum to try and slow things down. 'I'm growling for a pone, but I've gotta have something to read.'

'Here, take *Honcho*,' said Glaub, tossing him a magazine with an over-muscled homosexual swimwear model on the front. Glaub was everyone's favourite office queer. He made jokes about being gay so that everyone else could feel comfortable doing so, too. But what – thought Winkler – about his dignity?

As he flicked rapidly through the pictures of enormous, half-tumescent cocks, thick-veined and oily, the turd emergency subsided somewhat, and he wondered if he could postpone it, until he was able to walk round to the loos without the embarrassing 'tortoise-head waddle' which he was so quick to point out in other men on their way to the bogs with a paper in one hand.

And while he weighed his next move in the balance, mousy Millfield Spawn (formerly McSpawn) with his wide arse stitched into grey poly-ester trousers worn shiny with restraining it, rounded the corner with a fat faggot of bundled paper under his arm.

'Wink, how are you?' he said cheerfully, emphasising the 'are' and singing the vowel very long, Winkler noticed, in the way Scottish people have developed over centuries, as a way of injecting brief tonal excite-ment into a grim life of oats, thistles and punitive taxation. A tone super-fluous now in most offices, filled, as they were, with the little Scots fuckers, so that some days you thought you'd never hear a properly rounded 'o' again.

'Hey, Millfield, we're honoured,' said Winkler.

Spawn had been promoted the week before. Once, Winkler and he had been more or less contemporaries, but Winkler took a couple of years off to sort himself out after a crisis and when he came back Spawn was ten years older than him and out of sight up the promotion ladder, casting the shadow of his monstrous arse onto the slower climbers below. But now there was nowhere for him to go. The firm was run by four simpering directors who were too dependable as corporate flunkies to be removed, and too talentless to be poached by anyone else. So they just kept giving Millfield more to do, and every six months they changed his job title to make it sound more important.

As it happened, they were friends. Six months ago, remembering this, Spawn had told Winkler 'it's too long since we did an evening together'. They made a plan, and then Spawn cancelled an hour before because something had come up with The Owners. Vague dates had been made half-a-dozen times since then, and each had been broken by Spawn for some very important reasons, an unexpected radio appearance, problems at the Amsterdam office that necessitated a flight, a speech to write, a bout of flu brought on by working so many late nights.

When Winkler, eventually, became convinced that Spawn was doing it deliberately to reinforce the status gap that now existed between them he began, quite naturally, to hate him. Then he decided that Spawn was, in fact, the unfortunate one, the beaten, emasculated, bought one, the voice-activated mantelpiece puppet operated by clicks of The Owners' fingers. And he began to pity him. Which was why he said, so magnanimously, 'Hey, Millfield, we're honoured.'

'Och, don't be silly, Wink. I'm expected to show my face down here occasionally. That's all they need me for, really: to keep an eye on you.'

'And to carry things to the recycling bin.'

'Oh, this?' Spawn drew the rolled-over wodge from under his arm and watched it spring open in his hands, easily 350 pages, smallish type, not even double-spaced. 'It's nothing.'

'So I see,' Winkler said, as it thudded onto his desk and made a drop of coffee leap up from the middle of his polystyrene cup and land on the title page, inking a little brown crown on the fat paper.

'Really, you've seen most of it before.'

Winkler lifted the corners of the first few pages.

'Oh, God, Mill, do I have to?'

'Come on. It won't take more than a couple of hours once you get down to it.'

'By when, then?'

'Close of play today?'

'What? Fuck, Millfield. I've got a lunch.'

'So go to your lunch. Tomorrow morning is okay, as long as you promise.'

'Can't Sherwood do it?'

'No.'

'Why not?' Winkler knew, but wanted at least to hear it said.

'You know why not. You're the only one who can do it quickly enough. And you can do it with that lightness of touch, which nobody else can, and you won't get bogged down, because, well, you don't give a fuck.

Look how different it is for you here. You get away with murder most of the time. So occasionally when they need someone who . . .'

'Doesn't give a fuck.'

'We must do that supper some time,' said Spawn, leaving.

'Right. Next week maybe.'

'Next week I'm in Dusseldorf. I'll email you.'

Glaub overheard this and Winkler could have sworn he smirked. Winkler seemed unable to convince anyone else, Sherwood Glaub in particular, that he pitied rather than envied Spawn. And he tried again now. And when Glaub goaded him – 'Of course, Wink, you wouldn't want to be compromised by the big house, the money, the car, the respect,' – Winkler became furious and shouted, 'What respect?', and explained how it was gracious of him, in fact, to pity rather than hate Spawn for his gutless-ness, and how everybody, everybody in this place trod the fine line, oh, the fine, fine line between Winkler's hate and Winkler's pity.

'And which do I get?' Glaub asked.

'Both!' was the obvious answer. But Winkler was not the most tactful man in the office for nothing. He laughed and said, 'You're just a big fairy. You don't count.' And then, because he was disgusted with Sherwood Glaub, disgusted with Millfield Spawn, and disgusted with himself, he went out for a drink.

Three pints of thin, sour Guinness in a dark pub under a bridge put Winkler briefly in a more optimistic mood. The sun at least brought girls out. Walking back to the office, he kept trying to watch bouncing breasts in sleeveless white blouses, as well as arses and even occasional legs that weren't so bad, go by. The legs were rarely any good, though, because the girls were all secretaries at best, and while working-class girls often have nice fat tits they never have decent legs: too long in the thigh bone and too short in the calf. The great thing was that they all wore sunglasses which rendered their facial shortcomings at least ambiguous. Fat tits, bleached hair and shades – you couldn't ask for more.

Winkler walked behind one of them all the way back to the office, coming back from her low-fat sandwich and bottled water lunch. He enjoyed for at least a hundred yards the waistband of her G-string, which arced above the rim of her low-slung skirt into the flesh gap below the cropped blouse, and he fingered the mild beginnings of a hard-on through his trouser pocket. Other girls passed him and he looked at them, too. With three pints of beer in him he half-felt like fucking them all.

Arriving at the office he stepped in front of the one he had been following to hold the door open with an outstretched arm and she said 'Thank you'. He considered pushing his pelvis out a little as she walked past him so that her G-strung hip would brush his cock. But he decided, in that tiny portion of a second, against it.

It was now four o'clock and most of the serious work of the office day was being done. Winkler went for a little walkabout, as he almost always did when he was pissed.

There was a girl called Mandy who he quite liked. She was coffee-maker, memo-taker, letter-writer and tight-sweater-wearing available arse-glance to Roger Skelton, and the one with the beard, the one with the rollies, and the one who said 'myself' all the time (or were they all the same person?). He walked over to where she sat, pacing deliberately, bumping into only one desk. His arrival at the desk was enough for two or three of the ruminants to look up from the over-farmed information pasture on which they were pointlessly grazing, and sniff the air. They all fancied a bit of Mandy, and Winkler's occasional drunken passes at her were not popular with the herd.

This was because, Winkler believed, he was a genuine threat to their casual, impotent lechery. Mandy could see that he was different from these cattle, these gnus. He perched himself on the edge of her desk and said, 'Alright, Mandy?'

She looked up at him, began a smile, and then put her hand to her face, covering her nose and mouth, and said with a grimace:

'Yuk, have you been drinking?'

'No.'

'What is it, beer?'

'I had a couple of pints of Guinness.'

Mandy, who was tall and rangy and rosy-cheeked, rode point-to-point, lived with her mother, enjoyed skiing, swimming, hill-walking, hockey (which she had played for Kent) and tennis, flapped her hand in front of her nose and said, 'Well, it's gross.'

Winkler stood up and walked away without saying anything. He didn't look at the gnus, who had fallen to their grazing again, heads down. He didn't have to see their little gnu-smirks to know what they looked like, and to be angry because they were wrong to smirk. Mandy had not done this because she found him disgusting. She had done it because she knew that his confidence, his supreme sense of his own individuality, was undentable.

He returned to his desk, picked up his wallet and keys and rummaged in his top drawer for anything else he might need, and then looked at Sherwood Glaub. Looking at Glaub made him think, again, of the turd he had been meaning to have.

'I'm off mate,' he said. 'I just can't be bothered today.'

'What about that?' asked Glaub, gesturing at Millfield Spawn's paper-stack.

'That?' said Winkler, pointing at it. 'Fuck that.'

He picked up the pile in both hands, held it high above the bin and, after a short melodramatic pause during which he opened his mouth wide and stared madly at Glaub, he let it fall with a thud into the black liner bag, unhooking the bag from the edges of the bin as it fell, so that the whole thing disappeared, as if swallowed by a giant steel python.

'Fuck it completely.'

'Bye, then,' said Glaub.

'Yeah, Sher. Bye.'

And Winkler strode for home, stopping only to disburden himself of the infuriating faecal ingot that could not wait another second, hitting the porcelain hard with it, almost with an audible clang, and not bothering to flush.

5

The Smell

The smell of the house came skipping to meet Winkler every evening like a dog, yapping and wagging its tail.

It was the smell of boiled head. Recently boiled, the scummed water just cooling off the simmer with a great fuss of meaty steam. Specifically, the head of a man, Winkler thought. Some others said it was the head of a woman. And Winkler was certain the head was old.

The smell was worst at the first floor landing, where it was sticky in the carpet and in the velvet of the six little lampshades on the wall lamps, and in the tassels of the table lamp that stood over the phone. And the lace table cover the telephone stood on was yellow with the smell, too.

The telephone, which was cream-coloured and cracked and heavier than it needed to be, with two rows of buttons above the dial as if it had spent the busier part of its life functioning as a small switchboard, was for the three bedrooms on that floor. Each room contained someone who came and went not when Winkler went and came, but at other times, and even then not stopping to nod. Well, barely. The fourth door must have been the bathroom, from the way the grey lino where the door was often ajar was always puddled.

The fifth door was the kitchen, and was the home, or at least the source, of the smell. 'Its *fons et origo*,' Will called it. Will was a cunt, if you asked Winkler.

The fifth door was almost always damp with condensation, beaded with sweat from the wet heat of a head being boiled inside.

From there, the smell descended the stairs, slowly, dragging its feet, greasily steadying itself on the banister, stalking through the gritty brush of the carpet. It curled around the foot of the tall clock at the foot of the stairs. And as the clock tocked quietly it curled on, over the cool red floor tiles, rubbing its back on the skirting board, depositing a pearl of moisture, or two, clinging to the carpet-runner which was red and blue, machine-made in the Turkish style, now threadbare and full of odour.

The smell made a camp in the grey net curtain that hung on the front door, not bothering to penetrate to the cold stained-glass, which was orange and red and green and had '32' on it, in lead italics.

And the smell crawled the yellow paper on the walls like a spider, leaving cobwebs. It passed Madame Moranges' door (perhaps crawling in underneath, nudging through the plastic bristles of the draft-excluder), heading down the corridor that ran between the wall and where the stairs came down, and climbed, clinging to the painted-over-with-emulsion chevronned paper of the creamy ceiling, looking down on pictures, three of hunting scenes, one a photograph of a man in uniform, all in brass frames, none glass-covered, and at four empty coat pegs and a banded hatstand, down to the little sub-landing at the turn to the basement stairs.

There, there were three doors. One, with two glass panels, led to the dark basement stairs. Behind each of the other two lived an old person who had been in the house for years. Fifty years, supposedly, if you want to believe that. The room that faced you as you walked down the corridor contained a man. Immediately left as you left his flat (though nobody ever did) was the other door, behind which lived a woman. Neither of them seemed to notice the smell.

Down further still was the cellar, containing mice, wood, meters and fuseboxes, furniture, tricycles, pipes, boxes, broken things long concealed by the darkness.

And the smell went up from the first floor landing, too. Up the five steps to a landing with a loo and a door. And that door, too, because it was cold in the daytime on the other side, was often wet with head sweat. And down under the door the smell went, though it was double-locked, Chubb-locked and Yale-locked, latched and chained, and climbed the grey stairs to the attic where Winkler lived with his friends.

And so that was the smell. They could smell it from the moment they walked in the door. They could smell it before that. Meriel said she could smell it squeezing out through the keyhole as she approached it with her stubby little brass key. Will swore he could smell it from the pavement. Putting his hand on the mossy gate to push it open (dry, dusty moss in summer, wet moss like cold mucus in winter), looking up at the house (its late Victorian red brick, its ivy, its fourteen dirty windows, the small, cracked paving squares through the wild front garden to the blue door with the orange, red and green stained-glass and the number 32, he swore he could smell it then.

But Winkler knew that it did not stop at the gate at all. Even emerging from the subway, he could smell it. Out of the station, under the racing dual carriageway, and up the steps towards home, then, then he smelt it. Boiled head – or maybe not boiled head, but the boiling and boiling and boiling, long after the flesh had collapsed into ghee and the bones turned as white and as brittle as chalk, of unfamiliar flesh, sweet like our own is supposed to be – skittering down the hill to meet him from the train, and bringing with it the carpet and the lace and the netting, the clock and the hunting scenes, the people on the first floor who came and went, and the old ones who didn't, the wet lino and the red tiles, the broken stones and the moss and the lamps and tassels and the cold, sweaty doors, the stained-glass and the briny, bristly carpet, all stewed up with the gamy smell of something from the farthest undreamt-of end of the food chain, now whistling in a pot.

'I swear some fucker's cooking his wife,' Mary shouted, walking in some hours after Winkler (and after Meriel and Will), letting the door on its heavy iron elbow slam shut behind her, dropping her satchel on the hard brown carpet, and dropping, with a crunch, a bag of shopping (eggs maybe, sausage-rolls, packets of noodles, dented tins of tomatoes and tuna and peas on special offer, cola in a fat plastic torpedo, and the tops of big, stringy leeks sprouting from the top), and standing in the middle of the low-ceilinged room under the roof (the ceiling full of sharp angles, with two windows pressing out through the slope and a skylight on top and a bent floor, so that if you were lying down on its sandy surface, head tilted, one eye at ground-level, it seemed to have a horizon where the walls had sunk and the floor warped to sink with them) and wedging her small pink fists into her wide white hips.

'I swear, I fockn' sweeer. He's killed her and he's chopped her into tiny little pieces.'

Mary lived in Winkler's room. In Winkler's bed. In Winkler. She was squat, tough and noisy. She was from Belfast and had a face like a broad bean. She believed, like the rest of them, that human flesh was being boiled. But Mary talked about it the most, pronouncing 'cooking' as 'kyoo-cn' and 'bitch' as 'batch'.

'He's chopped her up into tiny pieces and he keeps her in that fockn' greet freezer in the kutchen. He's kyoo-kn the batch into fockn' soup so's the bastard police'll never feynd her.'

'Your accent makes it sound like some sort of super-violent Ulster cookery show,' Will said, misjudging Mary as he always misjudged her. 'You know, sort of like Tarantino meets Gary Rhodes meets, meets, I don't know, Henry Kelly . . .'

'Henry Kelly is from Cork you fockn' arseho . . . Jaysus Christ, Wink, I've had a long day, will you tell him to shut up?'

'Steady on, Mare . . .'

'And tell him to stop saying "Steady on", and I'm not called "Mare". I'm called Meery. Meer-fockn'-ree.'

'Mary,' said Winkler. 'Stop it.'

'No, fair do's, Wink. She is always telling me not to call her "Mare". Fair dos, fair do's.'

'Aaaaargh. Tell him if he says "fair do's" again, if he says it one more fockn' time, I'm going to fockn', fockn' . . . arghhh, I'm going to have a bath.'

On her way out she poked Will in the stomach, meaning something only half-conciliatory that he didn't understand. Then she went and had a Boots aromatherapy bath with scented candles and the radio on, for *The Archers*. Winkler liked hearing her humming along to the theme tune from behind the bathroom door (beaded with the sweat of aloe vera or pacific lemonweed or Papuan edelweiss). But then something in it, in the radio programme, always made her angry so that she would come down with a stolen hotel towel turbaned on her head and the cleavage line in her wobbly chest-flesh slanting at a bizarre diagonal because she had knotted the other towel so aggressively under her arm, and shout: 'Those fockn' Archers, they get right up my arse. You'd think nobody ever lived on a fockn' farm before . . .'

When she went for the bath she left the groceries on the floor, right where she'd dropped them. Even the things that needed to go in the fridge, and the frozen things. Mary was not a great taker of care. Will and Winkler looked at each other again. Will raised his eyebrows and pursed his lips. Winkler closed his teeth and clenched his lips to express a lipless, long-chinned admission that this was how things were.

'I was only trying to be amusing, you know, with the TV show thing,' said Will.

'Yeah, I know,' said Winkler.

'I suppose it was about as amusing . . .' Will began.

'AS A BOMB IN A PLAYGROUND!' Mary shouted from upstairs, where she was stripping for her bath.

Will smiled, sadly.

'Or were you going to say something else for a change?' Mary sang.

Meriel, who hated these exchanges, said: 'I'll just put this shopping away, then. Shame to let it spoil.'

'Maybe we'll go and have a quick drink across the road, then,' said Winkler, who usually offered to buy people drinks after they had caught the sharp edge of his girlfriend's tongue.

'Mm,' said Will, who was usually the person. 'A swift halferoo.'

'Oh yes,' said Meriel. 'Why don't you two go and do that? And perhaps Mary and I will knock up some supper for about nine-ish if you come back then.'

Winkler and Will only stared silently at Meriel.

'Well, okay,' she said. 'I'll make us all something. And we'll have a nice chat. We haven't all sat down together in ages. It'll be like the old days.'

'Great,' said Winkler. 'We'll bring back a couple of bottles.'

Rather than take the subway pass under the main road, which was one of the few places in the world that smelt worse on a warm summer evening than at any other time, Winkler and his flatmate chose to cross the roaring dual carriageway over ground. The traffic was all on their side, the tail-end of the north-bound rush hour out of town, and when a gap came they bolted for the central reservation across three lanes – two horns screamed, a lorry flashed – and hit the railings hard: bang, bang.

Will went over in a standing vault, one hand on the grubby rail, feet together like an acrobat in the horse-dismount. Winkler walked down twenty yards and squatted through a gap in the railings where someone had hit them, and probably died. Then they both jogged across the empty into-town lanes, Will with a too-upright gait, forearm across his middle, holding his jacket closed (protecting important imaginary documents from falling in the road), shoulders back, neck high, nose up – the run of a rugby player rather than a footballer. Red socks and black loafers giving no grip, so a sliding step, straight-legged, new blue jeans affording not much movement to the thick thigh. White work shirt rolled up to the elbow to signify mufti. An Etonian in late youth, not too bright, but more harmless than many.

He held the door of the saloon bar open for Winkler, whose own running style was more crouched, a probing bow-legged scuttle, head down, shoulders in, nudge nudge, quickstep, nudge. Ready for anything.

'Sorry, Will,' said Winkler, when he had ordered drinks and was leaning at the bar with this strange, tall man he had met at university and to whom he had said nothing at all on the way.

'S'okay. Really. No problemo.'

Winkler laughed.

'What?' said Will.

'Oh, nothing,' said Winkler. He was thinking how much a phrase like 'No problemo' would have upset Mary. She'd have mock-retched and almost certainly said, 'Actually it's a very fucking big problemo.' Fortunately, Will was someone to whom you could say 'Oh nothing,' and leave it at that. There were not many of those. And then to poor old Will he said,

'You know, Mary thinks she's the great democrat among us, but she hasn't seen anything much, and doesn't know anything really at all.'

'No,' said Will.

'You know when I first met her she'd never seen a black person before?'

'I was there,' said Will.

'That is, she made a big deal about how she had not seen one until recently.'

'I know,' said Will.

'She talked all the time about how she hadn't seen one until she came to England.'

'And I fockn' *steered* at them all day,' said Will, recalling the ancient conversation and attempting Mary's accent as well as he could. 'I used to go *roynd* and *roynd* the ondergroynd *steering* at them. I'd barely even seen any on the television apart from Maykle Jackson and Eddie Morphy. Nobody real, yi noah. For months ay just walked aroynd steering at black people's hands. Jaysus Fockn' Christ Almoighty, Ay was almost eighteen fockn' years old. Ay mean, at home Farder used to call them . . .'

Winkler was pleased. For Will, it was probably enough to take the piss out of Mary's accent for a bit. And her Irishness. She hadn't seen black people. She hadn't seen Etonians. She was naïve, she didn't mean any harm.

'She'd never seen a Jew either,' said Winkler, suddenly, surprising himself, and interrupting Will's vaudeville impersonation of an Irish racist before too many people noticed it.

'She genuinely thought they were something out of the Bible that didn't exist any more. Like Medes and Sumerians and Ammonites. But then we were shagging one afternoon a few weeks after we met and . . .'

'I thought you weren't Jewish,' said Will.

'Ah. No. Well, I'm not. Well, only a bit,' said Winkler, caught out. 'On the Spanish side, probably. You know, bit of gypsy, bit of Romanian Catholic, maybe even a bit of Greek . . .'

Will's eyes looked suddenly sleep-filled. This was always the best tactic, to waffle the subject away with confusion and diffidence, as long as it didn't come across as evasiveness, and then go straight into soupy detail with a 'long story' weariness in your voice, as long as the weariness didn't sound contrived – they can smell that. There was never any need to be transparent about it, to confront a twelfth generation Gloucestershire Etonian with the image of a bearded *mohel* in black robes tearing away at your eight-day-old foreskin with a dull flint in the living room of your grandfather's suburban mansion flat. And, anyway, the anecdote he had been on the verge of accidentally beginning was best kept private.

It was the one about the blowjob, early on, when Mary had spat his cock out, grabbed it very hard in her right hand, stared at its startled red end and screeched,

'Are you Jewish?'

And Winkler, not used to making conversation at such times, had said: 'Er . . .'

'You're circumcised aren't you?' she had said, pulling it this way and that, pushing it right down low to get a look at the top of it so that Winkler's eyes watered. 'I've never seen that before. That's fockn' weird. It looks like a fockn' fish.'

'Hey, Wink. You alright?' said Will, panicked by Winkler's wordless reverie. 'I told you, it's fine. It's fine. Mary and me get along fine. House on fire stylee. We love having a go at each other. I know she loves me really. Come on, let's have a couple of spins on the triv machine and I'll get us a couple of sly halves, eh, a couple of cheeky ones, and then we'll head on back to the ol' homestead, and see what Meriel's brewing up.'

6

The Old Jew who Lived Under the Stairs

Later, after screwing Mary under the grim white strip light of their attic bedroom, Winkler rolled off her onto his back and threw his arm over his eyes to keep out the glare.

He felt the running sweat on his head, running down into his eyes and onto his neck and into the hot pillow, and heard his breathing, which was like it had been whenever he tried running in the park. If he closed his mouth to make it quieter the air came out wheezing in a shrill groan through his nose and sounded like death.

'Am I dying now, on top of everything?' he thought. He rolled over onto his side, aware of the wide, blotched canvas his back would make in the squealing brightness, the light peering in through layers of yellow skin to the spots and mottles and moles of the future, on their way out from the inside.

Winkler was embarrassed by his exhaustion and by the noise of it. Any minute now she might say, 'Well, Jaysus Chroist – I don't know what you've got to be so fockn' exhausted aboyt . . .'

He pulled the wetted pillow out from under his neck and used it to prop his sweaty chest so that he could lean into it without having to think about staying on his side, and reached out with his right arm so that his finger pads bridged on the cool wall. With his head flat on the lumpy mattress his breathing felt quieter. But he could hear his heart more loudly, thumping against the flax.

'That was nice,' Mary said.

Winkler rolled back onto his back. He dragged his arm away from his eyes and let it fall on her, the back of his hand on the top of her back, the boniest part of the top of her spine hard under his knuckles. Her

back was cold. The thin curtain fluttered just a little, night air brushing
past and evaporating the wetness and cooling her.

Mary wouldn't care that it was just the back of his hand. Ethel Frinn
(or Errol Flynn, as Will often observed she was nearly called) had left him
when, too often, it was only her holding hands, and his was limp in hers
because he was thinking about something else.

'It's nice with the breeze,' said Winkler.

'Aye,' Mary said.

The ceiling light fizzed and went out with a pop.

'Mulligan is such a fockn' cont,' said Mary. Mulligan was their landlord. They had told him that the electricity kept shorting out and he had
told them it was nothing and all they had to do was go and flick the fuse
switch in the basement, and so they kept on having to do it and they
kept on telling him.

'Aye, well, I wanted a glass of water anyways,' said Mary, moving her
cold back away from Winkler's hand, his hand dropping on the bed.

'No,' said Winkler. 'It's alright.'

He felt at the end of the bed among the day's clothes, and the clothes
of the day before, and found a pair of pants and wiped himself with them
and then threw them towards the corner of the room where the dirty
and half-clean clothes were. He pulled on a pair of grey towelling shorts
and that day's shirt, ironed in this very room not twelve hours before and
smelling of sour armpit and fried fat and smoke, and said:

'Just water?'

'Aye.'

Winkler pulled the thin, hollow bedroom door quietly behind him, not quite
clicking it shut. Feeling the painted banister in his hand and the glossed wood-
chip wall against his forearm, he descended the six steps to the first landing.
He felt the carpet under his toes and tried to be soft-kneed to minimise the
floor-squeak. In the living room, the big window behind the television stared
south over the city, which twinkled in the distance but showed also big round
blobs of dark which were the tops of trees in the street below, blotting the
lights. Winkler felt the big acorn at the banister turn.

Air nuzzled in through the window of the small kitchen, smelling of
the warm street and picking up the sweetness of empty tomato tins perched
in the jaw of the swingbin. The white and brown tile-rolled floor was
striped with moonlight, this being higher than the orange lamps in the
street below, and the shadows of the tops of trees waltzed backwards and
forwards across it.

Before he turned his hand on the fat shiny acorn Winkler noticed the cigarettes-and-shoes smell of the living room shuffling lazily out to meet the high whiff of tomatoes.

The room where Mary lay, asleep again almost certainly, on her side, with a trickle of his sperm running out of her more than averagely hairy crack and down the circumference of her thigh, hugging the line of the buttock, clinging to the crease, would smell, when Winkler returned, of the high, lamby smell they made together. At least the window was open. If he took his time the room might air a little.

The nine stairs down to the little landing outside Will and Meriel's room creaked pathetically. Pathetically, because they were not ancient or interesting stairs being descended by someone with an urgent need for silence, but only oldish stairs covered in coarse carpet with exposed tack-boards on the wall side, and Winkler didn't really care if he was quiet or not.

Meriel and Will were asleep. No, not necessarily asleep. There was no light under their door because there was no light anywhere, thanks to that idle Irish cunt, Mulligan. Although Will and Meriel probably were asleep, as it happened, because they always slept well. Meriel thought she was a light sleeper, but only to convince herself of her own pale delicacy. She and Will slept instantly, deeply and silently, against each other on sofas in front of the television, in the backs of cars, on planes, in bed. Not like Winkler and Mary, who smoked and argued in front of the television, took it in turns to drive and shout, panicked on planes, fucked and fretted in bed, and nodded off stiffly at odd times of the day, waking suddenly, filmed with sweat.

Winkler paused by the sash window exit to the roof, which was at 90 degrees to where Will and Meriel lay on their backs with their hands clasped on their sternums, or spooning, and looked at the twinkly city again, seeing it differently from this different angle.

He pushed his forehead to the glass, withdrew it from the coolness, saw the steamy print of his head, and rested it back on the greased pane. How many souls fell, at this moment, under his gaze?

'Two, three million . . .' he said aloud, but only in a whisper. Nevertheless, as he said it he stood back again from the glass and looked around him for signs that he had been heard. But it was very dark in the flat and he had got used to looking at lights. He went back to them.

How many of these two or three million whom he could encompass at a glance were alright? Eight, ten, twelve? How many? Who? No one at work: not Glaub, Spawn, the Gnus. Mary? Maybe. Will and Meriel?

Will, possibly. Alright but not useful in any way. Winkler looked at the door of their room.

'As cunning as a cat in a cheese suit,' Will always said, and looked around for a reaction. 'She puts the chest into Chesterfield,' he said frequently of his mousy, titless girlfriend whom he insisted had the best breasts he had ever seen. Winkler could do without him. The world, too, if it had to.

As for Meriel, she was merely kind. Amnesty would miss her standing order, and Oxfam and Friends of the Earth, Terence Higgins, the local homeless shelter and the WWF ('Huh, Merry, I didn't know you were into wrestling,' Will had said twenty times since they moved in – every time, in fact, that a World Wildlife Fund letter appeared on the doormat); she made rhubarb crumble more often than most girls her age but when it came to it, if she were hit by a bus, he wouldn't really . . .

'Hey! Helloooo-oo!' Mary shouted from the bedroom. 'Get away from that bloody window and sort the leccy out. Come on, it's late.'

Winkler looked up the stairs into the darkness. 'Sorry, sorry, yeah,' he whispered, too quietly for Mary to hear. 'I'm going'. And down the grey stairs he went, softly, to the door at the foot of the staircase with its Chubb lock which you had to turn while you pulled the handle from the bottom step, because there was no room for the door to swing open if you stood in the little well, and eased it open.

'Winkler enters the realm of the anthropophagi,' muttered Winkler, pushing his nose out past the edge of the half-opened door, out into the damp air of the landing.

The smell was not so bad, to be fair, at this time of night. It was there. But it was asleep.

Winkler put his hand round the door and felt the back of it, lightly oiled but not dripping. He stepped out onto the carpet: again, not wet, just strangely grassy. He padded across the black grass away from the downward stairs, perversely, to stroke the kitchen door in the pitch, pitch dark (for there were no windows), and found it still wet. A cold sweat. The door moved gently in at his touch, showing suddenly some of the kitchen wall, the enamel draining-board, the sink, a corner of the floor, all flickering orange-red because a street light was dying outside the window. Behind the door was the freezer, containing mysteries. Or maybe just peas and chickens.

Winkler backed away from the door, readjusting to the dark after the streetlight. No light under any of the doors, of course: it was late. They were asleep, and unaware of the electrical problem. He trod on a mantrap and gasped 'Fuck!'

Raising his naked foot he plucked a sharp thing from it that clung to his soft sole as he raised it. He rolled it around in his fingers. Just plastic. He wasn't cut. 'A lady's hairclip,' he said, squeezing the object and finding it to be hinged. He should have worn shoes. The carpet is not so lovely underfoot anyway, never mind hairclips.

Winkler took the frail banister in his left hand and felt it wobble as he aimed to walk the middle of the stairs down to the hall, staying away, barefoot as he was, from the edges, where the tacks lay exposed and sticking up.

Landing in the hallway on the red and blue ragged runner Winkler, full of purpose, pivoted on the last large acorn, turned his back on the stained-glass front door, which was coloured briefly by a swish of passing headlight, and walked down past the door to Madame Moranges' flat, full of dragons, past the hunting scenes, pacing the cold red floor tiles and leaving brief but invisible footprints of condensation, stretched kidneys sprayed with toe-dots, nearly bumping the downstairs phone on its lacy table (which would have made a single protesting ping), towards the three-stair drop to the two old people's doors.

Just then Winkler crunched something soft and crackly into the carpet, just where his foot was still tender from the hairclip. He froze. It was possible he had killed something. Though not anything important. But it might also have been a chocolate praline coated with crushed nuts, a hard-boiled woodcock's egg or a bit of cracker stuck with a cheese blob to the floor.

Again he lifted his foot, arching his sole to contemplate its newest prey. But it was black dark in the deep corner of the corridor and he could see nothing. He wouldn't touch it, not knowing what it was. He stood on one leg, paralysed.

'What you need,' said a long pointy nose, sliding out from behind the door nearest the cellar entrance, lit by a moonbeam and dangling (like a lantern) a long drop of mucus, 'is a candle.'

'No, I'm fine, honestly. Thanks. I just trod on a beetle or something. There's plenty of moonlight.'

The man looked up through the window that was half-lighting Winkler and contemplated the moonless sky. 'Ah, but down there you won't find moonlight,' he said. 'Down there is very dark. It's where you're going, no? To the cellar.'

'Yes, lights gone again. Yours okay are they?'

The old man laughed.

'Yes, yes, mine, they're fine. Come in, come in, I have plenty candles, just to find one with the correct, you know, such a holder, is the work of moments.'

'Really, it's very . . .'

But the man had retreated into his home and Winkler, off guard at this first meeting with what Will called 'Hobbit One', wanted to be polite. And, anyway, a candle might make things easier. Then again, who on earth has candles just lying around?

Winkler, who had plucked the thing from his foot now and had balanced it on the gently curving surface of the fluted dado rail, failing twice, but making it perch at the third attempt, edged towards the door.

A glow came from behind it, and Winkler said: 'I see you're lit up okay.' When he got no reply he pulled the door open a little more and stepped round it into the room.

He saw immediately that the light was provided by candles: two on the mantelpiece above a bar-heater set in a tiled fireplace (the tiles featured bucolic scenes, threshing, harvesting, milking, but Winkler could not see that in the dimness). One on a table. One, Winkler thought, behind a bamboo screen. But he couldn't be sure.

The smell, here, was a mild one of fish. In the flickering light the place seemed tidy, but outside the aureoles of light that bloomed from the candles the roomscape disappeared into brown semi-visibility.

A hatstand had on it several hats – brown and green fedoras, a tweedy deerstalker type of cap, a yellowed borsalino and what appeared to be a homburg. There were also coats on hangers, too many for the stand, jostling with each other for room to hang free, all failing, crowded round the central pole like a rugby scrum.

In an alcove next to the fireplace was a bookcase with six shelves, containing plenty of books, and some spaces left for photographs in silver frames. Advancing deeper into the room to look more closely at the pictures, Winkler creaked a floorboard loudly and froze.

'Come in, come in, Mr Vinkler,' said the old man from a doorless cubicle off the main room in which Winkler could see only a sink. 'I'm just here finding a suitable holder for you.'

How odd that he knows my name, Winkler thought. But then, of course, the old man would have seen his name on letters. The post was always neatly sorted when Winkler came down in the morning. Maybe it was the old man who sorted it. Winkler had assumed it was Madame Moranges, or maybe Meriel. Still, there were four or five other men in the house, and he had not hesitated in identifying him as 'Winkler'.

And he had pronounced it 'Vinkler'. Very few people did that. There was a Latin teacher who Vinklered him throughout his schooldays, no matter how often Winkler corrected him, and made him sit in the dustbin whenever he complained. Winkler could feel the sharp metal edge of the bin in his lower back and upper thighs even now, standing at the book-case, squinting at the photographs. The Latin teacher, Mr Cookson, used to push down on his head, forcing him deeper into the bin, saying, 'Fully wedged are we now, Vinkler? Good. Now shut up, Vinkler, and stop showing off.'

One of the photographs was of a newly married couple, presumably the old man and his bride, looking like everyone did in the 1930s or 1940s or whenever it was. Knowing that it must be the old man, he recognised the pointy nose that had dribbled in the moonlight. Black eyes and shiny black hair parted in the middle. But hard to know how black everything really was, his suit, his shoes, the car, because the contrast was so stark in those old pictures. Her dress, for example, could hardly have been that white, or her skin, or the flowers. Her eyes were shut, apparently not just momentarily, but because of the sun. They wouldn't have even bothered to print that one now. But photographs were rarer then and more special, which made it seem as if life also was more rare and special, and made more feasible the assertion that these people had, minutes before, been gathered together in the sight of God.

Another picture showed a black Labrador, sitting, head and shoulders only, like Caesar. Another showed a group of seven or eight men standing smoking on what might have been a small airfield. One of the men, who was cupping his hand to protect a flame from a match held out by another, was looking at the camera. This must have been the old man, too, because the rest were all in shadow or had their backs to the camera. Unless he was one of the ones with their back turned, and this was all he had from that time. Winkler compared the face with the newly-wed. But everyone looked the same back then, and everyone over eighty looks the same, so there was no way of knowing.

There were some piles of old-looking magazines and yellow news-papers on the bottom shelf of the bookcase, and piles of newspapers on the floor, too. There was a bed which was made, but ruffled, and would be

folded back into a sofa in the morning, which looked a heavy job for a
frail old man.

There was a table under a plastic cloth with a dark floral design on it,
three unmatching chairs, a radio, no television, empty vases, dried flowers
in a coffee tin on the bookcase, a burgundy wastepaper basket, a pile of
toilet rolls in the corner. And the room was very, very cold.

The old man emerged from the cubicle − which might have been a
bathroom, a loo, a kitchen, perhaps all three − carrying a small delftware
candle holder which contained an inch and a half, at most, of red candle,
a tiny flame just catching under the gaze of the old man, who cupped it
from the draft of the open door as he shuffled across the room.

'So,' he said, 'here we have a candle.'

As the old man looked up from the candle and into Winkler's eyes,
his face was lit from below by the reddish flame. And Winkler recognised
him.

In October of the year before last, Winkler had ducked into the sad, dirty
Payless mini-market on the high street up the hill for tea or deodorant
or cigarettes and, annoyed as ever at being filtered up and down two aisles
of food to get to the till, he had almost tutted as he was called upon to
avoid, in a hurry, a crooked old man, whom he could now identify as *this*
crooked old man, hobbling with a stick very slowly along the rows of
cakes and biscuits.

'Wondering if you've got enough change to buy the Mr Kipling French
Fancies instead of the povvo brand jam tarts past the sell-by date, are you,
old man?' Winkler had thought, slowing down to be revolted by the liver
spots on the parts of the man's head that were not covered by a damp
deerstalker.

But he had become immediately sad, entertaining the thought.
Immediately full of self-loathing.

The man's spine was arched over like a question mark and biased to
the left, and he was getting very close to the shelves and then leaning
against them on his knuckle with the stick in his palm, and with the
other hand lifting varieties of cake and biscuit to his face − Penguins,
bakewell tarts, Jammy Dodgers, mince pies − and pulling them close to
his eyes, above the line of his spectacles.

Winkler felt suddenly sick with pity for the man's life outside the cakes.
This pity-sickness was real and creased his stomach as efficiently as ever
love-sickness had (the last time, funny to think now, had been with Mary,

when she called him back the first time and he heard her voice on the telephone asking if he was in).

It was like this because all he knew about the man was this cake-selecting deliberateness and so all he could make of his life had to be built on it, and, because he was old and bent, it all had to be sad and lonely. And this had to be the highlight. Here he was witnessing the man's attempt to find happiness in his last days with plastic-wrapped processed sweet matter. He felt like crying, and only didn't cry because if he cried about shit like this, then where would it end?

The old man dropped a box of Cadbury's Boasters onto the blue and white dirtily-tiled floor, onto a brown spot where two tiles had cracked away at the corners to reveal the gritty concrete beneath. He was unable to pick them up, but looked down at the box and flapped an arm like a drowner's desperate paddle. Then he straightened up, marginally, and twisted slowly round to see if anyone had noticed (Winkler had moved out of the man's restricted line of vision in the moment after he had rejected the first impulse to reach and pick up the box). The old man took another box from the shelf, this time of French Fancies, not daring to stop and look at the price, and hustled off up the aisle to turn the corner and get back down to the till, a journey which must have felt like an age, thought Winkler, on those cracked old feet.

When he got to the counter, the middle-aged Indian woman took the box from him and said, 'Good afternoon, Mr Wallenstein,' quite loudly so that he could hear, and also loud enough that other people in the shop turned around to get a look at this Mr Wallenstein. Yes, Wallenstein, that was this fellow's name.

She swiped the box across an infra-red scanner and the LCD read out announced that these biscuits were going nowhere without the exchange of £1.79. Mr Wallenstein could read the display perfectly well, but the woman said loudly, 'That's one pound and seventy-nine pence, Mr Wallenstein.'

As he rummaged in his little clip purse a queue built up behind him. His hands shook as he plucked each coin from the dark inside of the little bag, held each one in front of his squinting face, turning it to catch the light, and laid it on the ice-cream fridge next to the counter. His mouth was open all the time, with his tongue forward, resting on the bottom lip so that he looked not only blind but stupid.

Winkler was with him in spirit, guiding each coin onto the fridge, counting it for him in his head, desperately wanting him to get this right and hold on to the flimsy dignity Winkler assumed he must believe he still had, to have bothered putting clothes on to go shopping.

Oh God, he had come out in the cold and the rain for a cake for his tea. Oh Christ, he fancied something sweet. Something sticky. Like when he was a boy. Life is not just pissing yourself and waiting for death, sometimes it's cakes and tea.

The people in the queue remained patient, indulging the old man's decrepitude, faintly aware that they would end up like that one day and would want to be treated well. They started exchanging glances with the Indian woman, and one of them who was only buying instant coffee handed her the money and didn't wait for the penny change. The old man, thought Winkler, is thinking that he doesn't mind if they all pay for their things while he struggles, but to indicate this would take more energy than he can spare. Thinking about this, Winkler thought, the old man had lost count, and perhaps also forgotten how much it was he was supposed to pay.

'How much was it again?' said the old man. There was a sigh behind him which he couldn't hear.

Gradually they all paid and slid past him, between his crooked, trembling body and the end of a row of shelves. Finally, his gnarled little paw, wobbling at the wrist like the nodding dog he put in the back window of the Austin 1100 when he was still allowed to drive, put the money in the woman's hand.

She recoiled slightly at the touch of the cold claw, it seemed to Winkler. And the old man took the blue plastic bag with his small box of iced sponge cakes and hooked it into the claw that was resting on the walking stick. When a very fat woman opened the door of the shop and waved him through, he went off drooling at the thought of the cake he was soon going to be scoffing with a nice cup of tea. Maybe even having two cakes, just this once.

'You're sure you won't have a drink, perhaps a cup of tea?' Wallenstein asked, now, as if he had asked once already.

'No, I'm fine, really. I've got to go and do that fuse, my girlfriend will be' (Winkler wondered if it was wrong to introduce into this lonely old person's death chamber the idea of extra-marital cohabitation) 'wondering where I am' (wrong to conjure the image in this cold place of Mary's still flushed and sticky body sprawled naked on the mattress upstairs). 'Thanks so much for the candle though. I'll drop it in on my way back up. There'll be light by then, with a bit of luck. Lucky you're so well prepared for these emergencies.'

'For me there is no emergency.'

'I mean the electricity.'

'I know what you mean, Mr Vinkler. I don't use it.'

'You don't use . . .'

'Electricity. Candles is always how I light my home. See.'

And he flicked the main light switch noisily on and off to show how it didn't work. Though, of course, it would not have worked then anyway.

'I won't use it in this house. He doesn't pay for it, Mulligan, you know.'

'Yes, I know.'

'Oh, you know?' said Wallenstein, pausing on his way to the bar heater where he seemed about to stoop and to flick one of the two black plastic paddle switches at the side of the metal grill to demonstrate, again, the absence of current, but losing interest, turning, and looking silently at Winkler, from under his hump, like when he dropped the cakes.

'Yes, or, well, I *assumed* he didn't pay for it when he said our rent would include all the bills apart from the phone. You wouldn't do that if you were a landlord, unless you were sure of profiting by it.'

'Profiting, yes. He's an Irisher, you know.'

'Yes, I know. And when I first went down to the cellar I saw all that business with the wires, where he's bypassed the meters. It looks fucking dodgy. Sorry. I mean, you know. It looks dangerous.' Winkler regretted the 'fucking'. He was too free with his fucking and cunting in front of old people. But dodgy just doesn't work on its own, without a 'fucking', that's the problem.

'Dangerous,' said Wallenstein. 'And also wrong. To steal is to steal. I told him I would have nothing to do with it. When Mulligan first came, this would be 1993, or '94, he told me I wouldn't be getting electricity bills anymore, he'd put it on my rent as flat fee and pay the electricity board himself for the house as a unit. He said this was to make the bills cheaper because by splitting up the bills with different meters they could make more money from us.

'So I went down to the cellar. And there I saw what he had done. So I said to him it wasn't right and I would have none of it. "Oh," he said, this Mulligan, "Oh, so you're not worried about money? Where have you hidden your millions then, Grandpa?" This he said with that rough, rough accent of his, and he tried to look past me into the flat. "Under the floorboards, is it, with you? Or in the mattress maybe?" An uncouth man. A dolt. And always wearing such a tracksuit and running shoes, which I don't understand. Never do you see him run. Never. Like such a bear he lollops along.

'I said to him I wanted my electricity back on the meter, but he said that wasn't possible. I told him it was possible – it is, you know, I could even have done it myself, just the wire you put back through the meter – but he started shouting so I said I wouldn't discuss it any further and that I would telephone to the electricity board. He said that if I did that he would kill me, he would kill me right there in the house and feed my flesh to his dogs – such nasty little dogs they are, not trained at all – feed me, he said, "Piece by fucking piece." And he meant it, too.'

'So, what, he cut off your electricity altogether?'

'No, this I did myself, not to use his stolen goods. I went down to the electricity shop to tell them what he was doing and they sent me away because I am a crazy old man. "Yes, yes, Mr Wallenstein, thank you for coming, we will investigate." But inside they are thinking only to themselves, "Who is the crazy?"'

'So I went next to the police to tell them what is happening with the Irisher. But they want nothing to do with me also. So I went home. I went to the cellar with a pliers and I cut it off myself. And so then eight years I am cold and reading always by candle.'

'Um, hold on. So you told them about Mulligan even though you believed him when he said he would kill you?'

'So, what should I care if he kills me? If the Irisher thinks he has something to gain by murdering me, so he murders me. And that you worry about after. Such a death I don't fear. I am an old man. He comes to me with such a hammer or a brick – I don't know what he imagines – and bang! He strikes me here,' the old man slapped the side of his forehead with a hard palm, 'and so I am dead immediately. This I am not afraid of.'

'And anyway he wouldn't have killed you, would he?' said Winkler. 'So I don't see . . .'

'Wouldn't have killed me, you think?' Wallenstein said in a raised voice. 'Why not to kill me? You think because a man is a dolt that he will not suddenly kill a man for reasons of his own? You think because Mulligan has not murdered before, ha, or so you imagine, that he will not start now? You think a murderer is such a one kind of person, and a not-murderer is something else? You know to tell me who will kill who? From what do you know how to judge this? Ach, such a threatener is always harmless you think, and maybe it's so. But if you have made these threats yourself, and then with your own hands you have killed them, then you know to believe a man is best, when he says he will kill you. And then it is easier not to be afraid of it. It is not such a big thing to be killed. You should kill somebody yourself one day. Then you see what I mean. It is not so much to be afraid of. There you are and then, pop, there is the end of it. It is not so much of a thing.'

So, what, the old man wanted Winkler to know that he had been a soldier? He just wanted to get round to this, in his old man way, because this was how he could make himself interesting to young people. And then they might want to talk to him.

'I don't know about "should", Mr Wallenstein,' said Winkler with a laugh. 'For a start I'm not a soldier, and also there's no war, where it would be appropriate for me to try out your theory.'

'I was not a soldier, Mr Vinkler. I have never been a soldier and I was not in a war. It was not a war that I was in.'

'So who did you kill, then? Or are you just kidding me?'

'Not kidding, young man. I am not joking with you. This was in another country and this was terrible times. Another age, Mr Vinkler. Everybody from there is dead now, if they survived or if they did not survive. So it doesn't matter now did they survive or did they perish. You see, Mr Vinkler, for what I did I am sorry. But also I am glad. Because after the killing, then for fifty years everything was easy.'

So, obviously. Wallenstein. He hadn't really sounded anything other than English until now. Winkler had only noticed, in his late-night dopiness, a bit of funny-sounding old man grammar. But, of course, this was not an Englishman. Wallenstein was an old European. From the East. He spoke not with the accent of a Croatian tennis player, though, or a German pop singer, or some black-eyed waiter at Café Rouge. It was something much older, with the bang bang bang of shots in a forest about it.

'It was in the camps, then?'

'It was in the camps, yes. And it was out of the camps. It was every-where killing. So. Your candle is guttering and it will go out soon. You don't want to hear me on about killing people in another world.'

Winkler did and did not want to hear. He wanted it over with, for the most part, because it was clear now that he was going to have to hear it at some point. This old man had some fantasy of the War he wanted to tell Winkler about. Or whoever happened to be around, presumably. All old people want to witter on about shit from when they were young and Winkler was probably lucky this stuff wasn't just about wooden toys and milk carts pulled by donkeys. But he had a fuse switch to flick, a clammy Irish girlfriend asleep upstairs, no shoes and a need to piss. You have a lonely old man living under your home in a dark cell. You wonder about him for two or three years and then you bump into him at two in the morning during a power cut and he wants to tell you how he killed people.

'You want perhaps a tea or a coffee?'

'I would, really, Mr Wallenstein, but Mary will be wondering – well, she must be asleep if she hasn't come looking – and I said I'd get her a glass of water.' Winkler thought of how he would run the tap for a while, leaning against the basin with his right hand and feeling the stream with his left forefinger until it cooled, then give the glass a real sloosh and swirl to get any possible dust out, and allow for further cooling of the water then a second sloosh in case he missed anything. Then two more slooshes because he always did four. He had always done four. He did not know what might happen if he did not.

'If you said, then it's best. Here. Take this. It's enough to get you down to the fuse box.' He handed Winkler the stub of flame.

'I would like to hear about all of that, though. Maybe if you're around tomorrow?'

'Ach, it's not such a big story you never heard before. But as for around. Around I always am.'

'Well then, tomorrow maybe.'

'As you like. Mind the stairs, the mildew is slippery at night even in such a drought like this.'

He showed Winkler into the hall and shut the door behind him.

The cellar steps were indeed slithery and cool, and felt, to Winkler's naked toes, mossy. At the foot of the stairs was a lot of broken furniture. Things scuttled. There was a light switch on the wall. Winkler flicked it, of course, and then tutted at his stupidity. And then he tried it a couple more times.

A doorless frame on his right led to a cell full of broken wood that was not even recognisable as furniture. Firewood, possibly. There was also a whole chest of drawers, with broken wood and pots and cables and bent shoes and dusty magazines on top of it. Winkler opened the top drawer and found it full of the sort of stuff top drawers are full of. Or were until quite recently: identity cards with black and white photos, paper clips, brown boxes of staples, pots of ink, pens, embossed business cards, three-minute rounds of cine-film in yellow envelopes with hand-written addresses, corks, pencils, springs, string, coins with holes in the middle, dirty white rubbers rubbed round at the corners, pencil sharpeners, the smell of shavings, fat rubber bands, bull clips, a round of ring-reinforcements, loose boiled sweets and crumbling Fisherman's Friends, small hardbound books with floral print covers, diaries with gold trimmed page-edges, papery bus maps . . .

Feeling his way over the sharp, cool rubble with his soft soles, Winkler stumbled as a half-brick rocked under his foot, threw out a hand to steady himself and with the other spilled hot wax onto his thigh. 'Fuck!' he whispered, moving the steadying hand to brush his thigh, overbalancing and spilling more wax and snuffing the candle and throwing out the balancing hand again and finding nothing so going over into a bent-double position and finally feeling rubble on his outstretched fingers and so stilling himself and pushing himself upright again.

In the dark he stood on the cold pile of brick, domestic dust-mud and scuttling things, which scuttled louder with the light gone. Moving his foot to let a different part of his fleshy sole take the jagged brick he wobbled again and steadied himself on what he knew was the fusebox. Something fluttered past his ear. A bat. Of course not a bat. A moth. Probably a small moth. Or a leaf.

Feeling along the row of switches, all down, all on, he bumped one that was not. This would be the one. He rested two fingers on top of it, applied pressure, felt its resistance, knew it would take a firm push and thinking – even as the pads of his two fingers took the pressure and yielded to narrow the gap between bone and switch – how the bare strip light would blaze on upstairs in the bedroom and wake Mary, and piss her off. But the act of switching was under way, and the act of switching is a short one . . .

7

Grandpa

Blam!

The rattling box filled again with the bright hopelessness of another weekday morning and Winkler stirred once more after the dark half-hour of tunnelling. It was hot, still and bright and dry and airless. Everything was in place.

Puddle: Check.

Paki-basher's bricksmash evidence in the shitty chip shop sign: Check.

Little fat lady on her way to a fancy dress party disguised as a bowling ball: Check.

Morning lads, no, actually, we don't want to say that — it could easily unperch them from that railing, all of them, like a flock of little sparrows, to swarm and muster and then, skinny as they are, to pulp us into lassi with their hard little brown fists, leaving back-to-front sovereign ring insigniae in the froth.

No, we won't be smuggling any fags today.

Yes, yes, curry smell and traffic roar: Check.

Stationary Saab boys out the back, snake-eyed, sucking the hot yellow juice from their smuggled fags, pinched brown at the filter.

ID card swipe, swipe, swipe, come on fucking register us, fucking swipe, swipe, swipe. Fucker never works. From behind, Mandy's long arm reached round and swiped her own lovely photo through the barcode reader and the door swung open.

Winkler followed her through.

'Excuse me,' the security man at the desk rose to his feet for the first time, no doubt, in hours, probably since the beginning of the morning shift. 'Excuse me, hey. Can I see your . . . hey, you!'

Winkler ignored him, walked on and up the stairs, just ahead of Mandy. Into the valley of the gnus.

'Morning, Winkler. Heavy night?'

Winkler hadn't ironed his shirt. His night was no business of theirs. He couldn't be bothered with this bollocks. He had an old Jewish killer in the cellar of his flesh-smelly spook house up north. He had depths in his life of which these fucking cattle knew nothing. And besides, right behind him, coming through the door and appearing to arrive simultaneously with him this bright, blue, twinkly morning, was:

'Mandy!' This involuntary ejaculation from the one with the beard contained astonishment, jealousy, awe.

She touched Winkler's shoulder, gently, en route to her desk. Only politely in passing, but it mightn't look like that to the gnus. And so he didn't answer their question about his night. His night, after all, had not been much to talk about.

Winkler's phone was ringing. He accelerated towards his desk to catch it before it gave up and grabbed the handset from the wrong side of the desk, which was a little too far for the tangled cord so that the flat phone unit leapt, flipped, and landed upside down.

'Yup,' he said into the mouthpiece.

There was a silence on the line. The leaping phone must have cut itself off.

'Yes, yes, hello,' Winkler tried again, just in case, finger poised for a futile rattle of the clicker.

'Hello? Could I speak with Mr Winkler, please?'

'Yeah, speaking, who's this?'

'"Who," he asks. What do you think? It's your old dad.'

Winkler's father was dead, as we know. Or at least missing.

'Oh, hi, Grandpa.'

'Is "Yup" how you answer the phone these days in your big city offices?'

'Sorry. It's early. I just got in.'

'Early? It's gone eleven.'

Glaub slid across towards Winkler on his rolling posture-paedic chair, still attached to his own phone, the main unit of which he had, infuriatingly, secured to the desktop with bolts, and slapped a Post-It note on Winkler's keyboard.

'Spawn's looking for you,' it said, and then slid off the keyboard because there was not enough flatness for its feeble stickiness to get a grip.

Winkler mouthed 'What for?' at Glaub, and got a shrug in return, while at the other end of the phone his grandfather was saying:

'. . . best hours of the day. Of course, as you know, I don't sleep so well so I was up anyway. Time goes slower in the morning. You can get so much done. By eleven o'clock you can have everything in order and then . . .'

'I know, Grandpa,' said Winkler, opening post. 'But nothing happens here until afternoon anyway. I've told you that. And anyway I can't think before ten o'clock.'

'Think? He can't think. Dear oh lore. With all that education and . . . anyway, I didn't phone just to criticise, whatever you imagine.'

'No,' said Winkler, scrumpling paper: press releases, invitations, conference agendas, and throwing them over his shoulder towards the corner where the bin would have been had Sherwood Glaub not moved it next to his desk to make his own post-sorting more efficient.

'How are you? You don't mind me phoning just to ask? You could phone sometimes, you know. It wouldn't kill you.'

'I phoned you last week.'

'To talk about money. I mean just to say hello. Just for a chat.'

'We chatted. We talked about your bridge game with the Rosens and the Greenspan girl. You said she responded to your three no trumps bid with something that she shouldn't have because Maurice Rosen had already passed and you didn't know why you bothered to play with such amateurs when you could be playing on the television if you put your mind to it, and how you once beat Omar Sharif in a newspaper competition . . .'

'Yes, but . . .'

'. . . and you said that with all the smoking of the Greenspan girl it was a wonder you had been able to get any sleep at all, and with the cooking of Barbra Rosen you had had trouble with the toilet, because the potatoes, you thought, were underdone, not like his first wife who cooked such beautiful fish and could have opened a restaurant if she'd wanted. You said Maurice made a thing of driving you home and so you called a minicab in the end just to show him, and he had protested but you wouldn't hear of it. And then when the cab came he paid it to go away, such profligacy you couldn't bear to see, and it was — I believe I have this right — some *schvartze* who couldn't believe his luck — and so then he gave you a lift home, but he also gave the Greenspan girl a lift and she smoked in the back and it gave you hiccups. You see, we chat.'

'But you could call sometimes just to say that you love me.'

'To say . . . ? Okay, Grandpa. I'll try.'

'So then. What's new?'

'Oh, nothing much.'

'What's wrong?'

'Nothing's wrong. There's just not a lot going on with me at the moment.'

'But there's something.'

'There isn't, really.'

'So why are you being so short with me?'

'I'm not being short. Nothing has happened since I last spoke to you that I can think of to tell you about, that's all. I've come to the office every day. And I've sat here doing nothing surrounded by morons and then I've gone home to my fat *shikse* every night.'

'Don't say such a word! *Shikse*. You don't know what it means.'

'But *shikse* is what you . . .'

'I just telephone for a nice chat and you start swearing and getting hysterical.'

'I'm not hysterical, Grandpa.'

'Calm down, son. I'm sorry I caught you at a bad moment.'

Winkler, unusually, did not feel at all at this moment like smashing the telephone unit to splinters with the handset and tearing his hand up a bit along the way – which he sometimes did during these sorts of conversations because he knew the sight of his own blood running down his forearm would shock him into calming down. This type of conversation was pretty much a routine for him, and usually ended with his own blood dripping onto something clean.

'Honestly, Grandpa, it's not a bad moment. I'm really, really well. Everything is better than can be expected, by comparison with most other people. I've just got to work. I've opened my post. I'm going to get some not very nice coffee from . . .'

'And is Sherwood Glaub there?'

'Yes of course he's here. You think anyone else would offer him a job?'

Glaub looked round without understanding. Winkler's grandfather said, 'Why do you only open your mouth to say something unpleasant?'

Glaub's mouth was full of crisps. A red packet of Golden Wonder lay split open on the desk in front of him next to a can of Diet Coke from which he slugged occasionally to help mulch the dry flakes and ease them down. There was a fleck of potato slice on the left ridge of his long grey filtrum, and a Coke splash on his shiny tie.

'Oh, come on, I was joking.' A flicker of comprehension lit Glaub's face momentarily and he returned to his paper, fingering another salty handful into his mouth as he turned.

'I knew his grandmother in Walsall, you know, before the War.'

'In Warsaw?'

'Walsall. Up from Birmingham.'

'Oh, right. Yes, I knew that.'

'A very good-looking woman. And her father had an Alvis. An eight-seater. But she married Glaub. You should give him my regards.'

'I know. You've said that before.'

'But you didn't.'

'I did.'

'How do I know that?'

'Because I did.'

'He would have sent his regards back.'

'Yes, well, he didn't. He's a bit funny.'

'A poofter, you said. Well, now give him my regards. Now, while I'm here on the line.'

'Grandpa. I've got work to do.'

'Nothing happens till afternoon, you said.'

'Okay, okay.'

Winkler said, 'Hey, Sherwood,' and then squashed his thumb over the four little holes of the mouthpiece, 'get us a coffee.'

'Eh? Yeah, right.'

'No, go on. Get us a fucking coffee just this once. I've got some loony on the phone, it's going to take for ever.'

'What do I get in return?' Glaub said, twinklingly.

'You get the pleasure of getting me a coffee. And a glass of water, ta.'

'Oh, alright. But you go and see Spawn or he'll be furious.'

'Fuck Spawn.'

When Sherwood Glaub had gone Winkler unthumbed the phone and said to the empty wall, 'Yes, I'll be sure to tell him, Sherwood.' And then into the mouthpiece, 'He sends his regards, Grandpa, and says he wishes he'd had a chance to meet you before he emigrated to Australia. But he's going next week and he wants you to write to him when he gets there.'

'Really? Oh. Well, what's the address?'

'What's the address, Sher?' he said to the wall, then covered the mouthpiece with his palm and held it at arm's length while he muttered, 'I donnle knowdle rurble staynle at theboyffle parentnurdle skittapool a marbing eedle.'

Then, into the phone again, 'Grandpa? You still there? He says he doesn't know the address yet because he's staying with his boyfriend's parents when he arrives. They're going to go flat hunting immediately and he'll write when they've settled down.'

'The boyfriend's parents have him in the house? Ye Gods. And sleeping?'

'I guess so.'

'In the same room?'

'I imagine.'

'In the same bed? In the father's very house?'

'God, Grandpa, I don't know.'

'Still, at least he wants to write to me. That's more than a lot of grand-children.'

'I'm not going to write to you. I'm only ten minutes away.'

'So, why don't you visit?'

'I came round the other day.'

'It was in April.'

'Was it? Shit. I thought it was the other day. Still. You don't visit me either.'

'Very funny.'

'What's funny? You could have your stair-lift extended out of the front door and all the way down into the Underground. It wouldn't take much, just half a mile of extra stair-lift track and then you could dock into the larger gauge on the main line. With a heated seat you could even come in winter.'

'I'm glad my disability amuses you.'

'It doesn't. I've got work to do.'

'I only called for a chat. I thought you weren't busy in the mornings.'

'Well, today I'm busy.'

'Oh. Sorry then, son. I couldn't know. I won't bother you at work anymore.'

'No, Grandpa, it's okay. I've just had a funny week. Maybe it's the weather. I'll come round and see you. What are you doing tonight?'

'Oh, rats. Tonight I'm going dancing.'

Winkler laughed.

'Okay, I'll come after work. I'll come about eight.'

'Eight is quite late.'

'Seven, then.'

'I'll have Irene stay after she cleans and knock up some supper.'

'No, I won't need supper.'

'You're sure? Just an omelette?'

'No, I'll eat later with Mary.'

'It's not good to eat so late. I'll have Irene make an omelette. You eat mushrooms, don't you?'

'No, Grandpa. I don't need to eat.'

'Just a cake then. We'll have a cup of tea. And Irene will get a cake. A nice sponge cake.'

Oh, Christ. A sponge cake. From the cakes and biscuits aisle.

'Okay, great. We'll have cake. I'll see you later.'

'It's a date then?'

'Yes.'

'I love you.'

'Yup. Bye.'

Winkler put the phone down.

'Jesus fucking Christ,' he said.

'What?' Glaub was arriving with Winkler's coffee.

'My granddad. He's a fucking nightmare.'

'You've got a grandfather? At your age? You should be glad. Mine are all dead. Most people our age don't have grandparents at all.'

'Yes,' said Winkler. 'But some have parents.'

'Oh yeah. Sorry.'

'Not an issue. And anyway it's not grandparents. It's just one mad old Jewish grandfather.'

'I saw Spawny again. I said you were in.'

'Oh, you cunt.'

'Well, I wasn't going to lie. He'll be after the Werther report.'

'The what? Oh, fuck, that stuff I binned. Well, there's not a lot I can do now.'

Maybe he would be fired now. That would be interesting. Winkler glimpsed briefly a world where he was in complete control. Not shackled to the office, not excusing himself to the gnus for being different from (come on, better than) them, not forcibly moulding his natural romantic recklessness into something resembling a work ethic so that at least he had some sort of tangible scale by which to measure his success or failure as a human.

Deprived of a spiritually decrepit arena in which to take moral centre stage and of a population of midgets by comparison with whom he could not help but appear a giant, he would be forced to grasp life by the throat and shake it into something commensurate with his capacity to dream. It was only a shame that he had to depend on his employers making the terrible mistake of firing him to catalyse his assault on Olympus. The bourgeois dilemma that set short-term comfort against eternal reward, the stifling smother of option paralysis, made it impossible for him to take the first step on the road to self-definition. But if someone pushed him, if someone pulled the chocks and gave him a nudge, then, once he was rolling . . .

'Oh Winkler . . .' sang Sherwood Glaub. 'Ohhh Weeenn – kurrr – lurrr . . . Look what I've got. Look what Uncle Sherwood rescued from the dustbiiiiin . . .'

The big file of paper – even bigger than Winkler remembered and now stained from its spell in the bin – dangled between Glaub's thumb and forefinger.

The cunt. Winkler's new self-image was destroyed at a stroke. Moments before he had been a great man preparing to deal with the aftermath of a gigantic nihilistic gesture, either to survive it – in professional terms – and emerge more powerful for the wilful display of egomania, or to die by it, to lay down his immediate worldly comfort for a greater good, a bigger fortune, a richer hope. A boy on the brink of manhood. But now, with the moist paper mass swinging in the pansy's little pumice-buffed paw, he was reduced to the position of a payroll flunky who hadn't done what he was told.

Winkler groaned. He would rather die, really, rather leap in front of that fucking train and have done with it than grovel for an extension and apply himself to the work now. He couldn't, simply couldn't, flick through page after page of drivel, trying to make sense of it, and then set his mind to the creation of something the company was meant to believe was the best he could do. On the far side of the room Winkler saw the vast arse of Millfield Spawn, trousers hoiked into the long pink crack by the leather-strapped red braces for which he was famous, as he bent over Mandy to . . . to . . . who knows what?

'Quick, Wink,' said Glaub, thrusting the manky bundle into his arms. 'Run up to the smoking room this way,' Glaub threw open the door to the fire stairs with a great flowery flourish. 'Read through it quickly and then go up to the transport department and find a spare terminal while they're out having lunch and just bang it out. I'll say you had to go to the doctor. And by three o'clock it'll all be over.'

He pushed Winkler with his little hands out into the cool, white paint-smelling well of the fire stairs, with its outsized breeze-block brickwork, flaky metal tubes of banister and shiny green lino floors smelling of polish (why polish a floor that is merely for escaping death? Who would go back to be consumed by the fiery maw of hell because the lino was a bit grubby?) and pulled the door shut.

Winkler was left standing alone in the well, clutching the mystery paper-bundle, aware of the sudden silence and of the smell of cigarette smoke wafting up from where some bull-necked delivery man was snarfing a cheeky fag before heading back to the loading bay.

'It'll be all over before that,' he said.

The next hour was spent, horribly, in the smoking room on the third floor. Brown carpet squares, school common-room furniture with fag burns in the upholstery, deep wormy melt-holes through the foam and long black scoops in the varnished blond wood from canoes of forgotten fags balanced on arm-rims when furtive smokers were hailed from the fumes by fragrant, unsmoky bosses, risen to that position of easy dominance by assiduous use of the collections of seven minutes scattered through each day of their working life that they had not spent in here, smoking.

Winkler lit a cigarette. Allowed the smoke to begin easing its way out of his mouth, then gobbled it back with his lips and tongue and gulped it down. Exhaled it now, less thick, broken down into more thinly linked molecules of tobacco soul. And felt instantly miserable.

He began leafing through the pile of papers, killing cigarettes in the speckled carpet every ten minutes. If it were only in the bin and he at home, in the bath, contemplating a wank, cooking some lunch, renting a video, walking in the park, waiting for Mary, taking her out for supper, seeing a film . . . No, fuck. Grandpa. He had to go and see him now. And he'd have to tell Mary, who'd be pissed off. Unless he went early to Grandpa and she never knew.

The door of the smoking room opened to admit Red Lev, truly Leo Sneel, the office's trade union representative. A conspiracy-theorist, a grammatological pedant, a philosophical somnambulist with sour-cigarette breath who, if you were fool enough to catch his glance, would lock you with his grey eyes, reel in a crooked finger and herd you into a corner, glancing round furtively, to tell you something only he knew, which only you could understand.

'Hey, Winkler, hey, hey,' he would mutter. 'Get this, no, no, get this.' And he'd produce a column from a month-old local paper, the page folded down and down to just the width of that column, and there'd be a ringed paragraph that might say, 'Enid Smimming, 48, an enthusiastic amateur entomologist and secretary of the Northside Allotments Association, was admitted to the Royal Hospital accident and emergency unit yesterday with suspected Portuguese nettle rash. Locum Dr Raj Khalil said, "The welts are unlike any I've seen, but have responded well to a smear of

Savlon".' And Sneel would look left and right and then narrow his eyes and say quietly, 'So it begins.'

And Winkler would say, 'What begins, Lev?' And Sneel would say, 'Shhhh,' and put a finger to his lips and smile and chuckle noiselessly and touch his teeth with his tongue and say, 'You know people, Winkler. Talk to the papers – it's no good coming from me. They know me.' And then he'd shake your hand with his middle finger bent in to touch his palm and he'd stroke the top of your thumb with his thumb, and then slouch away with his hands in his pockets, almost whistling with inconspicuousness.

And they said that was why he had kept his job so long. 'If we sack him the union chapel appoints a new representative,' said Millfield Spawn. 'And better a nutcase who can't do shit than an unknown quantity who might actually try and change something.'

Even as Sneel drew breath to say, 'Ah, Winkler, I've been meaning to . . .' Winkler was up and out of the smoking room and saying, 'Shit, Leo, I've left my car on a zigzag, I just remembered.' It was all he could think of, even though he had no car.

Winkler, with his paper-bundle under his arm, bolted for the marketing department which was emptying for lunch with dizzying efficiency. Men with earstuds and shaving rashes made bottle-of-beer-drinking motions to each other as they rose and logged off their computers, as one, with the coming of 12:59 and 59 seconds. And as one, or even less than one, they poured out of the office in their short-sleeved shirts and ties, and the girls all with smeary fake-tan legs, to stand outside a converted bank consuming not quite cold enough Czechoslovakian beers served by Australians with neck sizes in the low twenties.

Winkler sat down in a recently vacated chair. He could feel not just that it was warm, but that the buttocks of the warm individual recently departed were large.

He logged on. Username: Winkler (of course). Password: 'fatcunt'. Recently changed from 'fuckingcunt' after a security scare required everyone in the office to change their passwords (though the rumour was that the scare was bogus – created by the head of systems as a smoke-screen for the fact that the computer systems people never had anything to do). Before selecting 'fatcunt' as his password Winkler had tried to make it 'fuckingwanker' but had been denied because someone else in the building was already using it. Who? There were only a few hundred people in the building. Who was it who enjoyed typing the words 'fucking' and 'wanker' so much, first thing in the morning, that he had programmed his computer to remain dumb until he did so?

Some fucking psycho he would do his best to avoid.

The machine, on learning that 'f-a-t-c-u-n-t' had been tapped into its outstretched palm, plinked and fizzed for a minute or two and, when it was ready for him, Winkler created a Word file, typed 'cunt' at the top of the page and attempted to save it under the file name 'cunt'. But just as the screen was denying him that pleasure, he remembered that he already had a file called 'cunt' in his document folder, containing a letter to Mulligan, so he called it 'cunt2'.

'Do you want to replace the original "cunt2"?' the computer asked.

Winkler said that he did not, for he did not know what the original 'cunt2' contained. He opened his documents folder to see how many numbered 'cunt' files he had made. He was surprised. They went up to 'cunt14'. But there was no 'cunt7' or 'cunt12'. He created a 'cunt7' file and wrote 'fnark!' in it, and then closed it. Then he created a 'cunt12' and wrote 'qekvnvjiqer' in it, and closed it. Then he closed the folder menu and reopened it and observed the nice column of numbered 'cunt' files, and was glad that he had sorted that out at least.

He got up and went to the window. Across the cobbled street down which the stubble-headed Saab pilots strove for take-off velocity were more bits and pieces of the office. Long sheds of sooty brick, headless chunks of lorry drooping in vast lonely parking lots, a wooden tar-roofed shed with a creased old woman in it selling filter coffee and hard Danish pastries tasting faintly of pork, ramps and lifts, forklifts, men in hard hats, black men dragging wooden trolleys full of lukewarm food under metal lids, tottering women with pink legs carrying papers, something like a helter-skelter tower down which things on coasters slid which cannot have been good, a forty foot sloping window of glass which leaned against a block of grey concrete to provide a dazzling façade of modernity to foreign visitors – who drove in round the small oval of artificial grass and shimmied through sliding doors – all of it encircled by ten foot walls of brick, yellow and black and also sooted with ancient carbon, the detritus of Victorian industrial enthusiasms unscrubbed in the hundred years since the end of that particular daydream. And looming above it all was the giant chimney of unknown purpose which could be seen for miles around.

Well, perhaps not miles. But from a long way. Taxi drivers' directions to lost pedestrians usually began, 'You see that massive chimney . . .'

Winkler saw this morning, for the first time, how the chimney resembled what he imagined the chimneys of the Auschwitz ovens had looked like. Visible from across the plains of Poland, belching satisfied fumes of roasted Jew into the clouds, to rain down on Europe for years afterwards. Not this one, of course, which was smokeless. You can't go around incinerating Jews nowadays. You can't even smoke.

But, wait, where did the gassing come in? Did they burn them or gas them? Did they gas them and then burn them? Wasn't that a waste of gas? And time? And manpower? Why not just chuck them into the ovens alive?

'Who knows?' he said aloud and returned to the desk. It occurred to him that Wallenstein would know the answer.

He created a file entitled 'work21', to indicate the day's date. He wrote his name on the first page. Then he wrote a prefatory sentence and got up to go to the loo. When he got back he read what he had written:

'Nobody is pretending that Werther 2001 has turned out the way we all expected.'

Winkler stared at the ceiling. Finally he returned his gaze to the computer screen and wrote, 'But then who the fuck are we to know anything? And why should we give a fuck what happens to a project intended to provide gratification only for three or four greedy motherfuckers whom I would like to see eaten by hogs from the arse inwards?'

He chuckled to himself. Then he opened all the 'cunt' files and read what was in them. An unsent letter to Mandy gave him a hard-on and he contemplated a wank. But that was sick. So he closed the file. When he had read everything contained in the 'cunt' files – bits of poem he had forgotten writing, long emails from tiresome people dumped for further perusal, unsent letters to newspapers, proposals for projects that were supposed to allow him to get out of this fucking place and do something with his life but had not got past the first page – he sat back and looked at the ceiling some more.

Someone tapped him on the shoulder. Had he slept?

'Oh, sorry,' said Winkler. 'Hot-desking today, I'm afraid.'

Gaaaahh. He had said 'hot-desking'. Winkler never said things like 'hot-desking'.

'No worries,' said a plump man with a feeble goatee floating on the formless surface of his face who wore a white short-sleeved shirt out of which emerged chubby, hairless arms, one of which sported a big steel wristwatch.

Winkler closed his fourteen 'cunt' files with a single click to the master X in the top right corner of his screen and watched them all tinkle back to where they came from (where was that?). He logged off.

It was three o'clock.

He picked up his bundle of papers and went back to his desk.

'Done?' said Sherwood Glaub.

'Yup,' said Winkler.

'There now, isn't that better? Now the rest of the day's your own.'

'Lucky me,' said Winkler.

The rest of the day was, in fact, his to avoid Millfield Spawn, and to visit his grandfather and to book somewhere for supper with Mary and to have supper with Mary and to speak to Mulligan about the electricity and tell him this shit with old Wallenstein was not acceptable, and maybe even to mention the smell if he got on a roll, and to go down to the cellar and see just what was in those drawers and . . .

Eh? Was he planning to do that? Look in the drawers? Yes. Not a bad plan. That might be interesting. Possibly.

Winkler had too much to do, suddenly, for one man. He put the paper-bundle into the bottom drawer of a desk that nobody ever used and said to Sherwood Glaub,

'I'll just go up and tell Millfield that it's done. No, actually, what I'll do is I'll just leave it in the "General Projects" file and let him find it there. Then he can assume that I filed it first thing this morning and that he just didn't look for it properly.'

Sherwood Glaub smiled and shook his head, indicating what a hopeless maverick he considered Winkler to be. How, Winkler wondered, could a man who put his dick up other men's arses be such a square?

'I'm going to go and have a look at Mandy,' he said and then headed off towards the gnus, turned left before he reached them, skipped down the stairs to the turnstile, zipped through the big glass front door and strode out into the hot afternoon.

As he stared at the rushing highway, dazed with disgust, squinting fat fists of cheek into the outside corners of his eyebrows to keep out the dust and the diesel and the rapid murderous flashes of sunglint in the windscreens speeding towards the Exo-City, Winkler could not help seeing how it used to look, years ago, when it was only fields, stitched together with dark hems of hedgerow.

Above the hedgerows, small birds swooped and sang and climbed and Winkler could see, if he looked hard enough, clouds of insects there for them to feed on. And there were hundreds of coloured flowers in the hedges, too. The people working in the fields wore soft brown three-cornered hats, red-brown breeches and stockings and frock coats, not formal, the sort of coat you might have worn when frock coats were what one wore, and you happened to be in a field.

There was a scarecrow (also in a frock-coat) and there were thick-trunked trees with swollen bowls of leaf throwing long shadows. The men who worked, worked silently with blades on the end of long sticks. There were haystacks and in the distance the smoke of what might have been a charcoal burner's pile. A trickle of stream in the foreground containing otters. A copse, wood or even the edge of a forest where the roll of the fields ended. A squat church tower visible through trees. Away in the dip of a valley were the spires and domes of a small city with no urgent ambitions to grow, perfectly contained, nestled in the green and brown, puffing thin plumes of blue smoke. And, though they were too far away to be seen, there were strings of pigs and sheep being walked by herders through the gates of the city to be sold.

Implicit in the scene was the knowledge that America was there, though mapped only on its eastern side, the feeling that people, very soon, in another year or two, would start playing cricket, that there was plenty of water and the land was not overstretched, the fear that the world beyond England contained roaring animals that might eat you, that a well-sealed bellows squeezed into the guts of a furnace gave you an awesome feeling of power, that the flour in your bread was milled by a stream . . .

And the sight of how it used to be caused Winkler terrible, terrible pain. He could not understand how men could have chosen, *chosen*, to deprive themselves of this. And he could not bear the anger of knowing that he couldn't go there. He couldn't bear the weight of awareness of things so fundamental, important and beautiful and so perfectly inaccessible.

And from this rage and sadness and longing, which came on so quickly whenever Winkler saw fields, there was no escape but death. Not suicide, though, because to take that route out would reduce his rage and sadness and longing to the level of a general bourgeois malaise, diminish him to the status of some grunt who had lost his job or couldn't pay his mortgage or whose wife had left him or who hadn't bought a lottery ticket the week his numbers came up. And Winkler did not want his rage and sadness and longing – the gloom of his special aesthetic – to be made to look anything like that.

And so he longed for Armageddon: a righteous external justice to sweep it all away. A vast tidal wave, asteroid hit or concatenation of volcanoes would do it. Or the slow environmental revenge of global warming, species mutation, tidal change and famine – self-inflicted and well deserved. Why weep for the rainforests, really? The world is an old man: the organs fail, the man stoops and the man wheezes and the man dies. To be here at the end is almost a privilege.

On the train Winkler stared dully at the metro map, traced with his eyes the long grey line on the colour-coded tangle of places to go, and eyed wearily the words 'Eswich Central' where his grandfather lived, eight stations – twenty-four minutes – past his home stop.

Returning from the day, wiping off on the map the traces of his having travelled the other way a few hours earlier, Winkler would this afternoon slide through his own station and open a new route, north, to the old man who was all that was left of his family. All that was left of Winkler apart from Winkler. No other trace on earth. Christ. And what had his grandfather ever done for him that he hadn't been compelled to do by the demands of decency and familial responsibility? What was to be gained by visiting the old fucker? Nothing at all.

So he didn't.

8

What Wallenstein
Did in the War

The air was hot when Winkler emerged from the station. Crap still swirled in wide cyclones in front of the underpass entrance but he didn't mind the walk under the road too much today. At least he was going home. Climbing the hill to the house he even stopped to look at a hedge that somebody had clipped nice and straight since the day before, and to look at a nicely mown front garden and through the big bay windows of a house with a high-ceilinged double drawing room where there was a table with a big vase of flowers.

Entering his own house, which was nice and cool, though smelly, he remembered his plan to go down and have a good look in the drawers. He turned round and pushed the front door shut quietly, turning the lock-knob back and then releasing it slowly, to keep it from clicking. He didn't want Wallenstein coming out, loaded with stories.

Upstairs, he changed into shorts and a t-shirt and made the closest thing he could to a gin and tonic, which was vodka and the last of some flat lemonade Meriel had made for a picnic nobody went on. He took it onto the roof and drank it looking at the city, which appeared to steam in the heat. The sky was very big and very blue, with seven planes visible but no vapour trails. He was always surprised by how quiet everything was, relatively speaking. The drink wasn't all that bad. More of a Tom Collins. Except with vodka.

He could see – navigating by the Emerald City – more or less where the office ought to be. And he smiled at the thought of Glaub and Spawn and the gnus in there, wondering where he was. He closed his eyes and faced the sun, allowing his eyelids to get hot. He walked to the edge of the roof and sat down. Using his hand to lower himself, his palm had been embedded with dozens of gravel crystals, which he brushed off on his shorts. He dangled his legs down over the wild garden of man-high spiky weeds and monstrous dandelions. The sharp gutter on the back of his knees made it uncomfortable so he dragged himself further back on to the roof and lay down. It was gritty. It was too hard for his head to get comfortable. But he put a hand behind his head and rested on its palm. Like that, he fell asleep.

He woke up sweaty. A few minutes later or a couple of hours. The movement of the sun across the sky was not enough to give Winkler any idea. And he never wore a watch because it made him feel rushed.

He got up to go inside and make himself another drink. But then he remembered the drawers. Leaving his empty glass in the kitchen sink he flipped on his moccasins, congratulating himself for remembering the rugged terrain of the basement, and went downstairs.

Pulling the flat door shut he squeezed it firmly but quietly so that the ball rolled out, caught on the edge of the socket inside the lintel and then dropped in no louder than a wishbone snapping. As it clicked, Winkler thought how it would have been even quieter to hold it with the key and release it slowly once closed – why had he not done that? Because he wasn't holding the key. Where was the key? He patted two front pockets and the back one. Patted them again. Shook the shorts for a locatory jingle. No. They were on the draining board, where he had put them down to pick up a glass to drink from.

Trapped. The opposite of trapped. Locked on the outside. But also trapped in the house, because if he went out and shut the front door he had no way of getting back in. And he had not picked up his wallet, obviously, to go down to the cellar. So there was no question of time killed in the pub, a café, or bookshop or going to see his grandfather after all, should his troubled situation bring about a change of heart.

Trapped until Will or Meriel or Mary came home. Which would be about seven – but how far off that was was anyone's guess. And anyone with a watch would guess better than Winkler.

Down through the house, at any rate, he went, for want of anything better to do. But, preoccupied with his entrapment, he forgot that he was trying to be quiet and instead of tiptoeing mouse-like down into the well containing the door to the cellar he stepped like a medium-sized man killing time by going for a poke amongst other people's stuff in a cellar.

'Electricity gone again, has it?' said Wallenstein, who must have been standing by the door since Winkler left the night before, to have responded so swiftly to a single floor creak. Turning round, Winkler was certain he saw the other door – the old woman's – close as Wallenstein spoke, which must have meant that it had been opened even quicker than his and then closed again with troglodytic panic.

'No, ah. Oh, hello again. How are you? I think I, um, left something down there.'

'The cellar storage is for long-term residents only. It's already so full of rubbish. What are you keeping down there? Cases, is it? Firewood? Items for selling is not allowed under any circumstances.'

'No, no, nothing. I dropped something last night, I think, maybe. I just wanted to check.'

'What did you drop?'

'Oh, just my . . . my keys. I can't find my keys. That's all. I seem to be locked out and I just wondered if I'd left my keys down there.'

'Locked out since last night?'

'No. Just now I . . .' (wait, he couldn't have got home, let himself in and then locked himself out if the keys had been in the cellar since last night) '. . . I got back from work and found I didn't have them' (not that this was any better, because how then did he get into the house?).

'Like that you dress for work?'

Winkler looked down at his stained shorts, t-shirt and moccasins.

'It was a dress-down day for charity.'

'A what?'

'You come in in casual clothes and give ten quid to the office charity.'

'Casual it certainly is. Well, I hope it's a good cause, to look like that.'

'Oh, yes, it's an excellent cause.'

'So maybe at work you left your keys with all the excitement of this dressing up day.'

'Dressing down day. No, I don't think so. I think I left them last night.'

'I think you didn't have keys.'

How would he know, the old fucker?

'I'll just go and check anyway.'

Winkler descended into the bowels of the house. He made some noises, as if looking for the keys. He was about to open and shut some of the drawers, but then how would his keys have got into a drawer? He went to the back room where the fusebox was and scanned the floor. 'What's wrong with me?' he thought. 'I'm actually looking for the keys. And yet I know that the keys are on the draining board upstairs.'

'Any luck?' said Wallenstein, very close by.

Winkler's heart leapt, and he gasped. Wallenstein stood behind him.

'Christ almighty!' said Winkler. (How did he get down here so fast, so quietly?) 'You scared me.'

'What's to be scared?'

'I don't know. I didn't think you were there.'

'Well here I was. Did you find your keys?'

'No. Not yet.'

'So.'

'I'll just look a bit more,' said Winkler, refusing to be dictated to by the scary old cripple. He kicked aside a broken brick. Beneath it was movement.

'Oh, shit, fuck. Rough. Rough,' Winkler said. A small dead bird – a starling or a blue tit thought Winkler at first glance, though he knew nothing of birds – seethed with maggots. Winkler retreated.

'A sparrow,' said Wallenstein, leaning forward to look. 'Such a shame. There are not now so many in the city. You'd never have thought years ago it would one day be an extinction.'

'Yeah, well. That'll do me. No keys here.'

They reascended to the light.

'So now, maybe, you'll have that cup of tea?'

'No, can't, sorry, Mr Wallenstein, I've got some things I've got to get done this afternoon.'

'Without going into your home? Without your clothes?'

Tricky. Tricky. The thing with the keys was good cover to begin with, but it was always going to come home to roost. Unlike the sparrow in the cellar. You meet an old man in the night, you strike up a sort of chat. You promise to come by again, planning to avoid him for a month or two and then move out without saying goodbye, and then, like a fool, you return to the scene of the encounter not eighteen hours later. And then, dear God, you let slip that you are locked out. And you expect sympathy?

'No, I forgot I was locked out.'

'So then it seems best I invite you for a tea.'

As Wallenstein opened the door to his flat Winkler hung his head, and like the condemned man who, now out of all hope, follows his executioner quietly to the block, he walked inside, the old man leading the way.

The curtain was drawn on the only window. But it was a thin curtain and glowed with enough light that Wallenstein had only two candles burning. 'You don't take milk I hope?' he said, disappearing into his little cubicle to make tea and emerging surprisingly quickly holding two small teacups by their saucers. 'With no refrigerator, you understand, in the summer months . . . Sugar there is plenty.'

He offered Winkler a jam jar full of sugar, with a red and white checked pattern on the lid. Winkler shook his head and looked around for a chair. Not wanting to sink irredeemably into something too soft, he sat on the edge of a hard chair close to the small table on which Wallenstein had just placed the sugar.

Wallenstein pulled a similar chair up close to a bulky, joyless armchair and rested his cup and saucer on it while he settled back noisily into the cushioned depths, which, making room for him, emitted a puff of dust.

'Forgive me for asking, Mr Vinkler, but you are Jewish?'

Winkler replied: 'Um, yes.' Which felt as much of a lie as when he replied 'no' to the same question when asked by English people. It was a question to which he could not give a truthful answer.

'You go to shul?'

'Um, not really. Well, no.'

'You read Hebrew?'

'No, I'm afraid I . . . I remember bits of the Manishtana because it was written down phonetically for me once one time when Grandpa didn't want me to embarrass him in front of the Mogelbaums. And I guess someone will do the same with the kiddush for me when my grandfather dies.'

'Kadesh.'

'Yeah, kadesh. I never had a barmitzvah, though. I don't know the difference between a Tora and a Talmud or a Ganesh or a . . .'

'Gemara, you mean? Or Midrash?'

'Um, both. All of it. Not a clue. I was brought up by my grandfather, who . . .'

'A Jew?'

'Yes, a Jew. And he . . .'

'A Jew from where?'

'I don't know where from. England. Poland, maybe, originally. Russia, Lithuania, somewhere like that.'

'Does he speak Polish?'

'I don't know. I doubt it.'

'You don't know?'

'Not really. He speaks bits of Yiddish I think to some of his friends. But he speaks English properly. Not like . . .'

'Not like me?'

'Well, without an accent. You know what I mean.'

'He was born here, then?'

'That I don't know. I think so. I couldn't swear to it.'

'There is family?'

'Yes. I guess. I don't know how much. Some cousins. I saw them a few times when I was little, but then I went away to school, you know, and, hang on . . . I think I heard Mary come in,' (heard that heavy slam of the door and that loud, mannish scraping of her shoes on the doormat, as if a farmer scraping the mud of vast fields from rubber boots). 'I ought to go and say hello. I only came in to . . .'

'The person what just came in is Mr Mather.'

'Really?'

'Really. Edgar Mather, author. Such a scribbler of romantic rubbishes what you boil in a pot. You never saw him? Often he goes out at this time with walking boots on and comes back later and scrapes on the mat like a mad thing.'

'Oh. I just thought . . .'

'Your grandfather. He never talked to you about the Shoah?'

'The what?'

'The Shoah. You never heard of the Shoah? The Nazi Holocaust?'

'The Holocaust? Of course I have. I'm not with you. Why would he talk about it? He wasn't involved.'

'Not involved?'

'No. I asked him a couple of times if anyone was in the concentration camps – because of people at school going on about it – and he said not. He said we weren't refugees. And we asked nobody for any help, and . . .'

'But about the camps you were never told?'

'Of course. At school. All the time. Except I didn't pay much attention because I just wished the teacher would shut up about it. Every time he said the word "Jew" the classroom went funny. And they all made hook-nose gestures with their fingers at me while the teacher was reading. It was a mistake, doing Modern History for "O" level. I wanted to do Medieval but there was a test and I failed so I got put on the Modern course, which was basically the War.'

'In the Middle Ages there was plenty of Jew-killing also.'

'Yeah, maybe. But it doesn't get on the syllabus anymore. With the Holocaust it was all that detail that everyone thought was so funny. The piles of spectacles, and the hair, and the lampshades. They used to pile up my shoes on the bed and . . .'

'Your shoes?'

'Yes. You know, they're always going on about the piles of shoes. At boarding school you have to have indoor shoes, outdoor shoes, gym shoes, football boots, slippers . . . so there's enough to make a reasonable pile. At least, enough of a pile so that if it's in your mind from photos or a video or something about Auschwitz, then you know when you see it what it's meant to look like.'

'And when this happens you did what?'

'I suppose I . . . well, there was nobody in the dorm when I got back and found the pile. I think I . . . God, I haven't thought about this in fifteen years. I suppose I took all the shoes and put them back where they came from.'

'That is one thing you can do.'

'Yes. But it isn't what I'd do now.'

'Now you would do what?'

'I'd fucking . . . sorry. If it happened now I'd definitely . . . I don't know. I wouldn't just put the shoes away and let it go.'

'And so what you would do?'

'I'd go after whoever it was with a baseball bat.'

'You think? Where would you get such a bat?'

'Okay, a cricket bat.'

'Who would you go after?'

'Whoever did it.'

'And who was that?'

'I was never sure. It must have been boys in my boarding house, to have been able to slip into the dormitory.'

'And in your house was how many?'

'Seventy, maybe eighty. But some were my friends.'

'And your friends you don't think it could have been?'

'Of course not.'

'So there are maybe fifty, sixty who might do such a thing, and which do you hit with this bat?'

'A couple of the most likely. I wouldn't care really if they did do it. Just to show I wouldn't be pushed around by some fucking Nazi kids.'

'And so then you hit the wrong boys and then what? What do you think they think about you after? And their friends? And the teachers who they go and tell? You attack some innocent boys with such a weapon and the parents complain, and then what?'

'I tell them everything that happened. And I'm sorry if it's the wrong kids but I'm all messed up by the persecution and then they make an effort to stamp it out.'

'You tell them what?'

'About the pile of shoes.'

'And you explain what you think it means?'

'Of course.'

'And if they say, "But it's just a pile of shoes"?'

'Then they're Jew-hating psychos as well.'

'But, of course, you are twelve years old, so you do not tell them this.'

'I suppose not.'

'They exchange glances with each other, the parents, the teachers . . .'

'They're thinking I'm a neurotic Jew fabricating all this to get attention.'

'And now the other children, how do they behave? They all think you're a squeal and so now no more you have friends even. Now what? You hit them all with your cricket bat?'

'No. No. But, look, at least I didn't just sit there and take it. At least I know that I made a fight of it.'

'But you didn't.'

'No. I didn't.'

The old man got up to make himself more tea. He looked into Winkler's cup and saw that it was still full. He disappeared into the cubicle, leaving Winkler silent in the glow of the candle at his elbow. From the cubicle he called out, 'So the shoes you know about?'

'Yeah. And the gold teeth and the scratch marks on the inside of the doors. And about the giving them towels so that they would believe that they were really going for a shower. All the clichés.'

The old man's head appeared at the door. 'Towels?' he said.

'Apparently,' said Winkler.

'From where came the towels?'

'I don't know.'

'Towels, I don't think.' And the head retracted again.

'Right, well. That's what someone told me. And there were the lamp-shades made of skin and the socks made of hair – though why a German soldier wants a Jewish hair sock, I don't know.'

Wallenstein came back into the room and sat down.

'And the soap,' Winkler continued.

'*Reine Judische Fett*,' said Wallenstein.

'Eh?'

'RJF. It was stamped on the bars of soap. "Pure Jewish Fat." With such soap I washed my own hands. And such soap I . . .'

'Was it really greasy?'

'No, it was just like soap. Like a Lux or Imperial Leather, a white bar. Creamy.'

'But it was made from fat.'

'Soap always is made from fat. I didn't know it was such a soap, of course. It was in the hostel in Danzig when I was living as a Pole near the end of the War. When I was back from the forests. I washed, like so, my hands in a bucket with the soap, RJF. And the woman who ran the hostel, a big Polish woman with red hands and a purple face, she said to me when she was ladelling me out a *bigos* from a pot – she said bigos, but it seemed to me the seventh boiling of a squirrel or a rat or even . . .'

'And she said?'

'She said, "I see your hands are clean." And I said, "Yes, I hope so." And made a joke, because I knew it was a thing with them how the Jews were dirty and carried disease. And I wanted to join with her in the big Polish story about clean hands. Which is strange because in fact the Polish people are not clean at all, they . . .'

'And so then she said?'

'She said "It is good soap, no?" And I replied that it was fine. I had not noticed it was anything special different from soap before the War. During the War, of course, we did not have soap to wash. And the woman, she grinned and said proudly, and very slowly, "*Reine. Judische. Fett.*" Pronouncing it badly like that because probably she knew no other German words. And when she said it I remembered upstairs the print of "RJF" on the bar. Still now I can feel the imprint of the letters on my fingers.' The old man rubbed his fingers on his thumbs and in his palms.

'So. To tell how I came to this place of the soap, really it is to begin five years before this time, also in Poland.'

Wallenstein drank a mouthful of his tea. And then rested the cup on the saucer in his lap. Winkler thought it must be about four o'clock.

'I was only sixteen when the bombing started. And straight like that I was an orphan. We didn't live in the middle of town where was the main Jewish area, but still in the suburbs was plenty of bombing. This was the beginning of Hitler's blitzkrieg, the "lightning war" – which of course you know.'

'Yup. Like in London during the . . .'

'Yes, like in London, but also not like in London. England was already a year at war and knew what would come. Bomb shelters there was, and

plenty underground stations where you could run, and it was expected
to come the bombing from what already you knew. But in Warschau it
was only talk. All the summer it was talk, talk, talk about when the
Germans would come. In September they came into Poland and only for
two, three weeks did we know. But how they would come, this we could
not know. What was in Spain, in Guernica, of course we knew, but what
was this to us? The sky every day was blue, and it was such a hot, hot
summer, not like in London, but . . .'

The underground stations, thought Winkler. Shit. They ran to the underground stations. Of course they did. What a place to run to – dark and
damp and full of rats and piss and tramps. Perhaps to be trapped down
there for ever, maybe in a gas attack, with the adverts and the jostling
and the smell of ashtrays. And not even any trains coming through that
you could jump in front of. And, anyway, why did they need an underground train in those days? There can't have been much traffic. You'd just
get a bus, or drive . . .

'. . . And when finally I could open my eyes, there I saw Yitka's arm
reaching from the rubble. I was myself trapped, and I had such a pain in
my head, terrible like you cannot imagine, and when I freed my hand to
touch my face I knew it was bad for me. Like such a smashed melon it
felt, only warm. But all I could think was to help Yitka from the rubble.
I made myself free from where I was trapped, but it was not easy to move,
my leg was hurt also – and I reached to Yitka's hand. I knew it was Yitka
because she was twelve and her nails always she polished with Mother's
nail polish even though my father would not allow it . . .'

'Were there trams?'

'What's that?'

'There were no underground stations to hide in, so obviously you
didn't have a tube system in Warsaw. I'm just trying to get a picture. Did
you have trams?'

'I don't understand.'

Winkler was wondering whether, if he had been going to work every
day in Warsaw in 1939 he would have been okay because there was no
tube.

'To get to work, were there trams?'

'Yes, trams. And also buses and cars. Not so many cars like today,
everyone rushing, rushing, but why . . .'

But then maybe Winkler would have had the same trouble with the
trams. A tram could kill you, presumably, just like a tube train – Winkler
shuddered. And he saw the old man see him shudder. And then he

remembered that the old man had been talking about bombing, which Winkler did not understand because he thought all this was meant to be about the Holocaust. But still, he didn't want to offend him, and said:

'Sorry, Mr Wallenstein. I didn't mean to interrupt. I was just trying to get a picture, you know, of what it was like. Anyway, yes, there were trams, good. I've got a picture now. Sorry, you were talking about your brother.'

'My sister.'

'Of course, yes, with the nail varnish. So, what, she was alright, was she?'

'No. She . . . No. She was not alright.'

Fuck, thought Winkler. She was dead, and he looked like he wasn't interested.

'Her hand, Mr Vinkler, when I took it to hold, to let her know I was there, and maybe to pull her free, was cold. As I took it, it moved, and so I pulled gently, not thinking, and it came away, it came through the rubble, some of the rubble shifted, and her hand came out nearly to the elbow and then it came free.'

'Christ almighty.'

'I was sick and sick and sick. Later I saw much worse, but by then I was accustomed and not sentimental. This with my sister was on a sunny day in the end of summer. There was talk. There was in the newspapers speculation, there was August, and then there was in the sky, such a blue sky, hundreds and hundreds of aeroplanes, and then there was this with the hand of Yitka. And I didn't know suddenly where I was, and I was sick and sick and sick.'

'And your parents were killed too?'

'Yes, they also were killed. My mother in the kitchen and my father in the doorway of the house, where he was looking up at the sky and with his pipe in his mouth, not smoking, he hardly ever smoked it, but just holding it there. He called to me, "Yitzak. Take your sisters and your mother and –" I don't know, some instruction, and then, pof!, like that it was all gone.'

'God. How terrible.'

'Terrible, yes. But also it is perhaps why I came out from the War. For one boy to hide is hard, but for a family. It is not even to hope. I couldn't know this then, of course, but for me, it made me free. Not to have the responsibility for my family, no person to betray, none to disapprove if later what I did to survive was immoral. I was free to die, and so also to live.

'And anyway, my parents would have lived only till the first Aktsia, the first purging of the ghetto, or not so long even, to die from typhus, or starvation, or from a shooting or a beating. They never knew all what happened to Warschau. Even about the ghetto they never knew. They died as Poles, not as Jews. And after, when the Germans came, and the ghetto, never was I sorry for the bombs. Even I was glad. It was best for them that it was like that. Never was I sorry. Not until after . . .'

Free to die, thought Winkler. And so also free to live. The absence of parents had never felt particularly liberating to him. He was still unprepared to die. Was he, then, unable to live?

'. . . when the Germans entered the city, there was such order like the world had never seen, not since the Romans. They came marching in ranks, and ranks also of motorbikes, and men on horses and tanks. We younger boys even ran down to watch them enter the city. The Polish soldiers were not like these. They were drunken brutes, unshaven, who would shoot you dead for a joke, or to show off to girls, but here there came thousands of Germans all the same, the same height and the same faces, clean and smart and their boots making such a noise, crack, crack, crack on the stones.

'In the beginning it was not so bad. There was everywhere soldiers and they kicked sometimes at Jews, the religious ones what they could easy identify. They knocked off their hats and laughed at them running in the wind to pick them up. I even also felt sometimes like laughing because they looked funny. But then I was ashamed.

'In the beginning it was only like that. It was not so different from with the Poles. It was better, some said, than the Poles. In the beginning we thought it was just they wanted that we stopped being Jews, because they cut off the beards and the locks in the street. But always the Polish hoodlums did that for a party at Easter. The hair grows back, and so.

'I was living then with the family of my schoolfriend, Abba Korczak. A religious family, not like mine. And for them it was worse than what would have happened with mine. The Germans did not know always what was a Jew and what was a Pole. Only later, when the Poles were helping them, denouncing all who they knew were Jews, did it turn bad.

'For an example, right at the beginning they stopped the kosher butchers, which upset only the religious, but for us boys to be told to eat such a *treif* like pork sausages it was something to laugh about. But it was not often that there was meat for us, so it was not often to laugh. And later, in the last days, to go somewhere and they had a bucket of horse blood to eat, you thought it was a holiday.

'But there was not immediately a ghetto. First was the Jewish stars, and the curfews and the rations, which for everyone was bad but for the Jews was much worse, hardly human – though at that time we could still get on the black market enough to eat – and then the Jews had to register their shops – this was before they were all turned over to the *Treuhander* – and then it was not allowed to go by rail and then not to sit down in the parks, and then not to go into the parks at all.'

'Not go in the parks?'

Winkler thought of the parks of his youth: Regency gardens still maintained with sharp-edged lawns and delicate English flowers, boating lakes, timber-framed pavilions, great oak and elm trees surrounding you with green and the smell of grass and earth and blossoms and then in winter their bald, spindly clutches keeping out nothing and the shape of the city reaching in. But in summer there were the bandstands and deckchairs and ice-creams and kites and tiny bicycles with stabilizers, pushed in a pram by his grandfather. The old man singing, 'Will you still need me, will you still feed me, when I'm sixty-four?' And the joke was that he was sixty-three.

And later there were occasional glimpses of a park life that never quite happened for Winkler. One or two games of rounders – enough to persuade himself, in certain moods, that his life had been full of that. Some Frisbee throwing, the odd kite, some lying in the long grass (not much) before the last cut of summer, some duck feeding, some conkers collected, some football played, some games watched en route to somewhere else, using the park to cut through the ugly city. Intermittent joggers quietly crunching the gravel with each step.

And once Winkler had his cock grabbed from his trousers on the little bridge across to the island in the middle of the lake by a Spanish au pair whom he could only take for walks because the orthodox Jewish family for whom she worked wouldn't let her out at night for more than an hour. She had taken it at dusk and leant on it like a banister, giggling at the hardness and Winkler's wincing, and then shuffled it and shuffled it, dribbling into her palm to keep it sliding, until Winkler had exploded through the railings of the bridge into the water, where a pair of ducks paddled briskly up to the floating wax, sniffed at it, and let it lie.

'. . . Then they came with the prohibition that Jews should not practise the law, and then not to borrow from libraries, and some streets we could not go to, and then not to go in Piludski Square, which at the same time was renamed Adolf Hitler Platz which . . .'

And here the old man actually laughed.

'. . . Which was enough to know anyway it was no place for a Jew.

Then I think after the trains it was the trams and then, this I remember exactly because it was October 31st which would have been my father's fifty-fourth birthday, they made a law: no Jew can buy a first day cover. You know what it is, a first day cover?'

'Um, yes. Stamps, isn't it?'

'Exactly. Stamps. The first day of new stamps what they stamp with the date for philatelists. This they banned on October 31st, 1940. Already Jews had less rations than Poles, earlier curfews than Poles, could not as doctors treat Aryan patients, we could not go in cafés or restaurants, we must do forced labour, everyone between fourteen and sixty, and then, after all this, they decide, the Nazis, no more stamp collecting.

'What do they think a Jew is? To a man who already is forbidden meat for nine months and still is alive, to him you say, "No more stamp collecting" and then what? He gives up now and shoots himself?'

And the old man laughed again and put a two-finger-and-thumb pistol to his temple and mouthed, 'Pffff!'

'But of course there was for Jews no guns. And this with the stamps they did on my poor father's birthday. And he always was a collector of stamps. So what I did, I went to Gdankysc Street and there I went in such a stamp shop and I bought an envelope of stamps. A first day cover. The shopkeeper didn't bat an eye. Always I looked like a Pole, even a Volksdeutscher, with my blond hair and blue eyes. I was careful not to gesture too much or talk more than I needed, and to speak Polish like a Polack, slow and dumb, not like at home. And for three zlotys I bought them. And I took them home to my house, where it was before the bombs, and I sat there and looked at my stamps. And I said, "Look Papa, what I bought." And then I cried. And there I sat and cried, and sat and cried, until it was night. And –'

The old man stopped. He didn't cry. Which Winkler was glad about. He didn't think he could handle that. He wanted Wallenstein to get a grip. Maybe the story was coming to an end now and he could go upstairs and see if anyone was home.

'And then back to Abba Korczak's house I went with my stamps,' the old man went on. 'And always I kept them. All through the war. And then after the stamps, only two weeks later, it came the ghetto.'

'What do you mean "came"?'

'Overnight with bulldozers and bricks they put up a wall. It's not true: overnight. But not much more. And where there was not yet a wall was barbed wire or planks, guarded until the wall was done, and it was quick quick, thirty-six hours maximum. Around a few streets, a small area, and into there eventually it would come all the Jews of Warschau, half a million, and from the rest of Poland, and eventually also from further even away, Germany, Belgium and so on. It was in accommodation not more than two or perhaps three metres square for each person.

'It was the forced labour Jews what built this wall. Weeks at a time, when it came their turn, they disappeared for labour, skilled men and not skilled, good and bad, weak and strong, Abba's father who was a cellist in the orchestra, for example, and ruined his fingers the first week, and usually they came back — beaten and thin, but they came back — and this is why when they came later for "labourers for the east" it seemed at first not so unbelievable.

'And we went to see the wall, and it seemed at first like a miracle, how quick it came. Sometimes in the work gang you saw one you knew. An uncle or shopkeeper and you thought maybe to shout hello, but there was always plenty Poles saying hello, and not just hello, but other things what I don't choose to repeat. And one time I was watching from a broken house with Abba and some others, and little Viktor, my cousin, saw Grosstein, the maths teacher, in the line and he shouted, "Look, look, it's Grosstein the gay!" Always we thought our teachers were homosexual, but especially Grosstein. He looked up and also some of the other men looked, and Viktor picked up a rock, a piece of house rubble, and threw it at him from where we were. But it was not a good throw. Viktor was small. It fell a long way before Grosstein and bounced and hit the boot of a soldier — it was not a soldier but an SS officer, from such an Einsatzgruppe, what we didn't understand yet at this time — just beneath his knee it hit him. He turned around and immediately came a shot that hit the wall behind us, where was an old wardrobe, and it broke a mirror that was already broken but was hanging anyway.

'Someone shouted, "Run!" and some more shouts came. And we ran, down the stairs into the alley, there were maybe eight or nine of us and we knew our way better than the Germans. But with the bombing every-thing looked so different and the houses they blew up looking for spies made all the maps in your head sometimes wrong. We made it away, all but little Viktor. How he ended we heard later from one who was in the work group.'

But if you kept your head down, thought Winkler, in the dark after-noon, in the room smelling of fish, then you were probably alright. And if you did what you were told and just kept working and didn't do anything bad you'd be okay. The only thing was, how do you build a wall? Winkler had no idea. Would the Germans have explained that or just expected him to get on with it? Do they have foundations? What if he had said he didn't know how to build a wall? Would that have been okay? As long as he was trying his best and not being insolent? He spoke a little bit of German so they might have favoured him a bit. And at the end of it at least he would have known how to build a wall.

'. . . And this place I found myself when I stopped running was full of boys, my age and a little older. And it was held safe, they said, because the Germans thought under the collapsed masonry was nothing. And they had there food and even a gun. The leader was Ringelblum and he told me all what was happening in Lodz and Krakow and Vilna, how it was in the streets everywhere corpses and starvation and tuberculosis, and hangings every day and shootings and worst of all there was selections, when they gathered together all who was in the ghetto and chose which from them was good for labour and which was to be immediate killed. And this all was coming to Warschau and we would be ready for that, to survive until the Allies came, or to fight back, but not like dogs to be rounded up and killed.

'After a few weeks all this came true in Warschau. The wall was three metres high all round, not a chink, except where there was gutters and gaps for water and sewage and here sometimes the smallest children could fit through to buy food from the Aryan side. For every three or four, maybe, only one returned. Whether on the other side they escaped to live as Aryans, which happened with many thousands others, or more likely they were found and shot, we never knew.

'Certainly in the morning among the bodies what was taken out from the houses and left in the road to be taken away like so much rubbish bags were more than once a child half in and half out, trapped under the wall, where his booty had been snatched, and the head smashed from one stamp of a great boot.

'The bodies soon was a daily thing. Every morning forced labour Jews came to take them away with carts – these were appointed by the *Judenrat*, the Jewish council set up by the Germans to make us go quieter to death, even there was Jewish police, who thought that to maybe keep their heads down, cooperate, speak a little German, would save them for a while but in the end they all went the same way with everyone else – and on the carts was sometimes a friend or maybe your doctor, sometimes shot or beaten, but as the months went by, and in winter, from just cold or hunger or disease.

'Soon then it became very crowded because all the Jews what the Germans evicted from their homes in all Poland came to here. And soon others, Ukrainians, Russians, Austrians, what didn't even speak Polish but only Yiddish. And in houses for six people was maybe fifty. And no food, and the bodies came more and more, so that it was everywhere you were stepping over them in the street, usually new ones, died since the morning clear-up. It was so many people you could see that many, many must die all the time just so that there is room for the others to live, and during the hours when it wasn't a curfew, it was a jam something terrible of people, all a hustle and a bustle, where you were choked by the force of bodies.

'And then suddenly would come a Gestapo on the pavement and Jews must clear the way, so everyone leaps in the street and truly there is no room at all and for me, small, young, it seemed so dark, especially in the winter. In truth we were not supposed to walk on the pavement ever, this was for Germans and Poles only, and so when it came a German, and especially SS, then just like that, the pavement was clear and the road was full.

'But sometimes they fired in the crowd bullets and then it was panic, panic, panic, screaming and running, always I was quick and small and felt safe in the crowd — always Jews felt safe in the crowd and that is the shame. But even in the crowd little thieves were working, once I had an apple in my hand for which I had worked two days, and I was thinking about how to eat it when I got home, because to eat in the street was not advisable, when sudden a little hand grabbed it and I reached to grab but missed and it turned round such a face, tiny, like a mouse, and if I had caught him then probably I would have killed . . .

'But so. These SS would shoot in the crowd and there was running, running and when the people were gone then you would see the bodies, seven or eight, and two or three dying what was finished off with a *genickschuss* — a bullet in the bottom of the skull — and if young mothers was in the bodies then sometimes was babies screaming which they finished off not even with a wasted bullet, but with a stick or a brick or sometimes I saw just a hand. With a big man's hand holding a baby by the neck and squeezing — a baby no more than a year, two years — it snaps so easy with a little pop. And so quick the baby stops his noise that you hear the pop sometimes.'

Wallenstein was holding out his fist and making squeezing gestures by way of dramatising long forgotten murders. But Winkler, ever since the old man said 'underground', was thinking of nothing but tube stations and barely noticed. When he became aware of Wallenstein again, the old man was talking about less crowded times.

★   ★   ★

'When it began the emptying of people to Sobibor and Treblinka, to the gas, it became occasionally less crowded. After a selection there was then room to breathe a little. But soon came more from we didn't know where. "I had no idea there was so many Jews," said Abba, when the new ones came with their boxes and their fancy coats. "If we knew before there was so many maybe it would have been the other way round. We would have put the Germans in a ghetto." This was a big joke in the ghetto at one time.

'And soon with the new people it was the same: dark and busy and crowded like in Hell you imagine. So dark and such a smell, and everywhere hands held out – children and cripples and respectable people resorted to beggars, collapsed on their knees with their palms up in the air brushing you, tugging you always as you go, their eyes hollow and weeping, weeping, so that it made you angry to get on your way.'

People flowers, thought Winkler. White, five-fingered flowers buffeted by the storm of souls.

'So you fought back?' said Winkler, hoping to force the old man to his conclusion. 'Is that who you killed?'

'Mm?' said Wallenstein. 'No. Yes, later in the April rising it was Germans killed, but for me it was first outside the ghetto that I began to kill, in the forests. This was very soon after I escaped.'

'You escaped from the ghetto?'

'If not then how am I here?'

'I don't know, I . . .'

'This was not a community with a future, Mr Vinkler. It was in the Spring, we had heard no news of the Allies for a long time. It was only optimists what held out for an end to come from outside.'

Winkler moved in his chair, stretched his legs and moved his head exaggeratedly from side to side and it made a crack loud enough to be heard by the old man, who looked up.

'But I bore you, Mr Vinkler, with my story. There is perhaps not action enough. It is only to tell you how it was before and then there is no big surprises because here after all I am. Perhaps a slice of cake you will have?'

'Okay.'

'Not to please me, I hope?'

'No, of course not. I'd love some cake.'

Wallenstein went into the cubicle and ran a tap, rattled a metal lid, struck a match, and returned with a tray containing four French Fancies. Winkler took a pink one and bit. The small cake crumbled like plaster in his jaw.

'They are, perhaps, a little dry,' said Wallenstein. 'But there is nothing of danger, sugar is the best natural preservative by far. I eat such things not so often, but I keep them for guests. You should use your tea, a little to moisten.'

Winkler peered into his cup. There was a hard water scum floating on the top, twinkling in the candle-flicker, like a plastic bag on a pond. A candle guttered and blinked out, leaving a corner dark.

'So, now, I was sitting one afternoon with Issy Dalman, from Solec,' said the old man, lowering himself into his chair again. '"Thin Issy", we called him – although what was funny, everybody was at this time thin and Issy even was one of the fatter ones – and horse-blood we were pouring from a big bucket into pots, flower-pots I think, to sell. I mentioned this before, no, the blood? With a little sawdust it was a meal, like such a blood-sausage, and with maybe a green potato or some turnip greens was a feast. Although perhaps it was not horse blood because on this day, my last in the cellar, we killed a cat. Cats and dogs by 1941 was not to be seen. Every one of them was eaten quite early. And because of this came rats. And rats was not eaten, but this cat had appeared at the little window of . . .'

Why cats and not rats? Rats are much closer to our natural diet – not so far from rabbits. Cats seem so sour and dogs so high and tangy and shit-tasting. Solve the dog-shit problem, though. Winkler shuddered.

'. . . when sudden Issy's brother, who we have not seen for six or eight weeks, rushed into the house and said for Issy to come quick, he had a truck, a German army truck even, and if he came quick they could hide in it and get away. "They'll kill us first," Issy said. "No they won't, they're driving," said the brother of Issy.

'It seems that since his escape a few weeks back the brother of Issy – what we thought was dead – was working in Zamosc, a nearby town, in a factory making switches for the army. He was no electrician but the boys' father, old Dalman himself, had before the War an electrical shop – he was taken early away – and they knew a little from fuses and circuit boards because as children they played often in the shop while the father worked, making believe. The factory owner was one of these Schindler types, not such a big-shot hero but filling his factory with Jews, and to get the most money from the army he needed more electricians. There were not so many now who were not in the army or sent away or already working. But in the ghetto was plenty electricians, he thought, and so he came with five or six of his Jews to find them.

'Quick as a flash I said, "I'm coming with." But the brother said I was not an electrician. Neither was Issy, I told him. "I can't take two," said this brother. I had to think quick. I said if they do not take me with them then I scream and denounce them and expose all in the truck – because it is all now coming to a finish with the ghetto, the selections had started again and the Germans were going from house to house. It was, we knew, only a matter of time until the liquidation about what we knew from Lodz and Krakow and about the resettlements in the east there is now no more any illusions. So now it is here a chance of salvation what my instincts tell me is the very last for me. The brother looks at Issy and Issy says to him that I will definitely do this, even though he knows perfectly well I will never do such a thing.

'So we ran to where was this truck and the brother says, "Quick, hide in here," and he lifts a tarpaulin and under it is eight or ten men. Jews. With terrified faces and blinking eyes from the light. "What's this?" he says. But it is with everyone the same, every Jew sent to find electrical parts comes back with at least one more Jew – a brother, a cousin – and here they hid them under the tarpaulin. It was no time to argue. Issy's brother was not wearing a star and for this you could be shot right there in the street. A patrol would come at any minute. "What are these Jews doing climbing into a German truck?" they will think, and then it is all up with everyone.

'So in we climbed to the tarpaulin. A few minutes later there are footsteps and the sheet is lifted. There it is Dosseker, the Schindler type, and he asks what is this? And they tell him it is relatives. And he swears likes this: "*Scheisse, scheisse, scheisse.*" Not at them but at the ground. And his hair he pulls with one hand and in his eyes he seems angry and also scared. And again he says: "*Scheisse!*" And then he says, in a whisper that is like a shout, "Okay, okay, you keep your heads down and you shut up, so help me, not a word, not a breath. One of you sneezes and we all die. Myself included, maybe."

'But this is not such a terrible threat because after all if we do not sneeze but get out of the truck and go back to our lives then we die also. And the prospect that he perhaps will die himself, such a big-scale businessman, is not anything to us.

'And so down again comes the canvas and we drove only a hundred or two hundred metres to where was an exit gate. And we stopped. And there is conversation in German, and laughter. And then we drove on. I think the German drivers never suspected what was there in the back of the truck.

'An hour or so later, maybe more, we stopped again and Dosseker came and opened the canvas and said to get out. "You are a long way from the ghetto," he said. "Thirty kilometres minimum. To the west is villages. To the east is forest and the river. Partisan gangs is there. You can try your luck with either . . ."

'So we came out from the truck, me and Issy. And his brother begged for him to stay but it was not possible. He had no papers and Dosseker could not get him back into the factory. So then the truck went. Issy's brother looking back at us all the way. And then the brake lights came on and it stopped suddenly. And a few seconds later the brother of Issy jumped out. And he and Dosseker stood speaking at a distance from the truck. The brother with his head down and Dosseker shaking his head. And then he put his arm on the shoulder of the brother of Issy. And then he got back in the truck and it drove onwards and Issy's brother came to us walking. He preferred to be with his brother.'

Wallenstein paused. He was out of breath. Moved, finally, Winkler thought. Wallenstein stood up and walked to the bookshelf. He brought down a picture of two men. 'Here is Issy and here the brother,' he said. 'This was taken in the forest, would you believe. Near the end of the war. By a German girl who joined us later.

'Here is Issy,' he said, indicating a moon-faced boy who looked, to Winkler, to be in his early teens, with a high forehead and tight black hair and skin blue-white like milk. 'And here this is the brother of Issy, who was called Janusz' – bigger, meaner, hairier – 'he did not come out from the War.'

'And so this was the choice, to throw ourselves on the mercy of villagers, Polish peasants for whom the penalty for hiding us was death, or to hide in the forests, maybe to join a band of resisting ruffians – again Poles who hate us anyway and blame us for the War and will surely shoot us as quickly as any German. Or to hope that we encounter the ZOB, the Jewish Combat Organisation which we hear is out there, but we do not know where.

'So we sit for a long time here where we have been left, not on the track but maybe a hundred metres into the woods. And nobody says anything for a while. And we lie on our backs and above is trees leaning over and touching their branches and leaves, and sun that makes us squint and lay our arms over our eyes. Then suddenly Issy says, "Hey!" and we all sit up, and he says, "At least there are trees."

'And nobody says anything, and then we all laugh. Because in the

ghetto was no trees. Not a green thing, except it was a rotten corpse. No
bushes or grasses – all this was eaten – or even weeds. And no trees, which
all were chopped down by the Germans for barricades and fences or by
Jews for firewood. And here it was trees and trees and trees. Like in the
time before there was people and towns and ghettoes. And so here must
also be water and animals and we could maybe live . . .'

Like in the Golden Age, thought Winkler. Before the dual carriageway
that sliced his mornings, before the Underground, the chimney, the Saabs
and the smokers, muslims and monsters, seeking asylum, and finding
one, and the Emerald City. The simple world. World of his dream-visions,
where he cannot go, and the only place he believes he can live. Impactless
living, nature thick with resources, hogs and chickens turning fattily on
spits, rivers of harmless water to wash in, noiseless machinery, millstones
and wood, horses, the road open, the routes limited, the options
unparalysing, the world tiny but dimly perceived, the universe incon-
ceivable, the fear great, hope abounding, man small and little expected of
him, little imagined. Men acting on faith and belief, intuition and sense,
nothing proven, nothing tested, nothing known, all possible.

'. . . it was with this group in which I now found myself only little
sabotage actions, occasional killing. It was a mixed band and among them
was Jews. Not many. And not in the hierarchy of the band, only cooking
or mending or digging. But alive. And from them we heard stories of
what it was in the rest of Europe. The killing. Where it was not ghettoes
but just random in the street. From Kovno in Lithuania was a girl who
saw with her own eyes one man kill sixty Jews in a morning with a
crowbar on the forecourt in a petrol station, and the crowd all counting,
"One, two, three," and singing afterwards the Lithuanian national anthem.
A local prisoner it was, set free from prison by the SS to get things going,
and after this, and one or two like it, was no more encouragement needed,
and the German left them to it, and like this the Lithuanian people,
Christians, killed their Jews, all of them, three or four hundred thousand
with no help from the Germans needed.

'It was there among them a boy from Austria who told how he
escaped a convoy from his town, where was a massacre even before the
War in '37 or '38. He recounted their names every day, to remember,
and all the time he was under his breath muttering, "Massinger, seventy-
three, hanged from school gates; Dreizler, twenty-four, suffocated with
pillow, standing up, by wrestling champion; Theodora Mizener, seven-
teen, strung up by her feet and quartered and her baby daughter drowned
in a horse trough by the greengrocer, Haider, with his strong arm from

carrying cabbages; Frisch, fourteen —" And so on like this. And always he muttered, muttered. All from his town in the mountains was killed, Mochsholden or something like this, and he thought to remember each one out loud was something useful. But it depressed me terrible to hear and sometimes I shouted to him to stop, when he was sitting there rocking – you know what is davening? No, well it's no matter – and saying names as he stirred perhaps a soup of fox meat, and he would stop when I shouted, and look, and then start saying with a different recital, "Mochsholden, population 4,304, a picturesque market town in the Austrian Alps, principal industry, dairy, also some tourism. Hill-walking and skiing. Excellent rail links to Vienna, Berlin, Geneva. The church and townhall dating back to the 14th century is in the late Gothic style and boasts . . ."'

Winkler thought of the blue Alps, bearing witness, the pointy-spired churches and the schools with their gates and kitchens and gymnasiums, the rivers and trees and woodland, the firs and spruces and the birds and bears, the fishermen and the milkmaids, blacksmiths and violinists, woodsmen and hunters, big and pink and healthy. Forest people, mountain people, dairymen and women and old people with half-true fairytales of monsters and midgets, demons and dark-dwelling elves, simple lads in shorts with axes, woollen checked shirts and hats with feathers in, Alpine horns and melted cheese, strong-cured sausage and schnapps for winter expeditioning, cold weather hunting and chopping, and if they thought the Jews, squat Jews, serious, furrow-browed, black-eyed, unlaughing Jews were a threat to all that, a lapse of taste, quiet accumulators in the back-ground of all the wealth such a world can generate, sneering and mocking, reading and writing and counting and planning, dreaming of different things, symbolising with their strange way of walking and talking and dressing a different future, a challenge to ancient tradition and unfoetid outdoor existence, well then, wouldn't they want to protect it, kill them, beat them down, string them up and throw them off the mountain? Was their Austrian dream not a beautiful one? Was their way not the way it was meant to be, from the beginning, in the *Urwald*, in the very birth-moment of the mountains? Did not the end, here, in this instance, in some way, aesthetically at least, justify the means?

'. . . I felt I must do something to show I was more than a Jew to cook and to dig, and with winter so close it was no time to fool around. The town, what was really a big village of eight maximum nine hundred people, had food stores enough for plenty but to raid was foolish since we had nowhere to run where they would not find us and kill us, every last one. They said that a Jew was a stupid thing to send as an infiltrator, but also they did not want to risk a Polish life. I explained to them how I had always been told in Warschau that I had "good looks", which meant then not handsome but like an Aryan. And at this it was laughing because I stood there telling to this one-metre-ninety Polish with a yellow beard and thin lips and water-blue eyes how I looked good. "Not so good as you maybe," I said, smiling at him, and again there was laughter. "But you we cannot risk." And so I went like that to pass myself off as a peasant who was willing to work for food, and to find ways of helping also my band in the forest.

'This obviously was a dangerous thing. It was previously in the town forty per cent Jews but very quick after the War began they were killed. Not by the Germans but by their neighbours, what rounded them all into the synagogue and set light to it. But still I thought it was nothing to lose so special if I am killed, and I insisted.

'"Okay, you go," says the yellow-beard, "but if they suspect then you better hope they kill you, because if they torture and you tell them about us, it will be so much the worse when I catch up to you, and maybe for your Jew friends here also . . ." and he snarled at me such a snarl like a wolf. And I said I will die before I talk, and so he nodded, and if I am a Polack then maybe he hugs me, but he shakes me only the hand, which is still something, and . . .'

Were Winkler's looks 'good'? Certainly, he was in no danger of being taken for a Swede or a Pole or a German, but in places like Greece, Spain, Italy, France, even Turkey, the locals seemed to assume he was one of them. He sometimes had people asking 'Are you Jewish?' but it usually transpired that it was his name that had 'given him away'. People would say, 'I didn't notice it at first, but now you say "Winkler" I can see it.'

But these people, so keen to show that they were fooled by nobody, were only identifying Winkler's relatively un-British looks, rather than any cartoon *Yiddishkeit* he gave off. He was not especially short and his walk was fine and straight. His nose was relatively small and very straight. His ears were sleek and well-fitted. He did not gesticulate too much when he spoke and he rarely suffered from sinus trouble. This was all thanks to mongrelisation of the blood: he was a robust cross-breed rather than a frail thoroughbred. But then, of course, there was his cock.

'. . . the daughter of this family was maybe fifteen, a year younger than I, and her name was Adriana.'

'What about your penis?'

'I am sorry, Mr Vinkler?'

'Your penis. You were obviously circumcised. Supposing they saw that?'

Wallenstein looked puzzled. 'I have said only that there was a daughter. It was not to produce suddenly my penis in the first meeting. I was sixteen, which in this time was a man in many ways that is not expected now of such a boy, but it was not all sex, sex, sex. This was not my thought when I —'

'I'm sorry Mr Wallenstein,' said Winkler. 'I didn't mean to suggest that at all.'

Winkler had not, in fact, heard anything of what Wallenstein said about the girl or her family, busy as he was contemplating his looks.

'I shouldn't have interrupted. I meant only, what if they suspected you and pulled your pants down? I mean, when I was at school, I pretended not to be a Jew and had to keep mine away from view. I never had a bath or a shower at school in eleven years.'

'Interesting,' said Wallenstein. 'What is so terrible for you if they should see it? In my situation it would have been different. Not an embarrassment because suddenly my friends discover I am a liar, but a death sentence immediate. But I did not have to worry such a thing.'

'Why not?' Winkler asked. And Wallenstein laughed. Laughed so that he coughed as if he were drowning in treacle. And he rasped three times, the last sounding dry and deadly. And then he neither spat nor swallowed, but grinned a grin that from inside, no doubt, felt playful, nostalgic, wistful, but from outside looked toothless, reptilian, evil.

'I did not have to worry because . . .' and he leaned back and opened his dressing gown and began to reach into his pyjamas.

'No, no, no. Christ. Don't do that. What?' Winkler stood up and backed away behind his chair. 'I don't want to see anything. Forget I asked. It was just something in my head I should have kept to myself.'

'Ach, it's not such a horror. My *schwanz* only is damaged. *Nisht kaput.* Sit down, sit down. I was joking only. It is not here to expose myself to a stranger after all what I've been through to gain back a little dignity.'

Winkler sat.

'It was a bad *mohel*. You know what is a *mohel*? Mine was Nadolnik, a lazy man, a drunk. My father was poor and maybe they argued. Not it was deliberate but he was perhaps angry, perhaps drunk, this I heard from my uncles and great-uncles all who were at the *bris*, all what did not come out from the War, and so he cut wrong, so that my schwanz was irreparable damaged and became infected. Afterwards it grew wrong and the urethra was blocked so that I had to have operations and operations and when finally it healed, it was neither circumcised nor uncircumcised but only twisted and blunt and then when hard so like a strange and terrible thing . . .'

'So it wouldn't matter if they looked because it just looked like an illness?' said Winkler to stem the onrush of detail.

'*Ja, exact.* But also of course it was for me terrible embarrassing growing up. Not so easy for me to hide like with you. It was a poor house in a poor place and always in summer playing naked by the river, not with such swim trunks and changing cubicles. And also when it came girls and to kissing I was afraid that soon I will have to show. And so never I got close enough with a girl to let this be a possible event. And this of course made me unhappy. Though after only a year, or two years, it came the war, and then a pretty *schwanz* to put to a girl was the least of my worries.'

Funny that Winkler kept his hidden, and fled contact for fear of its being something hideous, even though it was, as it turns out, quite well done by whoever it was. And there was old Wallenstein back then only wishing he could have one like Winkler's to wave around. How much better for owners of a Jewish prick to grow up in a Jewish community, with Jewish girls expecting from their first few pricks exactly what you've got in your trousers.

'. . . just sometimes hands we held when nobody looked. But most I didn't want to raise any suspicions with the villagers or the father. Jews always was thought lascivious, you understand, rapers of girls and thinking always of sex, sex, sex, and all was going so well, they had no thought of me being a Jew, only a fellow peasant like them. And so I could this way bring news to the band of the outside world, what is happening in the War, and also local troop movements and most important food and also maps. I worked in the field of this man and slept in his barn and his daughter gradually I liked more and more – five months I was there through the winter at the end of 1942 – and one day in March when there was a smell of Spring I remember how well she squeezed me and said, "Later you come to the clearing," (it was a clearing in the woods what we always kept for a meeting place) "and I show you how much I love you." I thought this finally was it and maybe I can get over my shame and make love with her, although if only it would be a night meeting with no moon so that her first view of it would be less shocking . . .'

Winkler was stunned. 'And I show you how much I love you.' He remembered Lydia, a tall blonde athletic girl he met on a school trip, when he spent some weeks in a grammar school in Bavaria. She was gorgeous. And for no reason that anyone knew she chose Winkler. Because anyone English was a good thing for a German girl. Any Englishman better than a German boy. And then after school one day she kissed Winkler as they rode next to each other on bicycles to the big open air swimming pool. The Freibad. And Winkler loved her, and swore to return to her and never leave. He saw her to her garden gate on the way home and kissed her for a long time as they stood straddling their bicycles and she whispered in his ear, 'Come tomorrow to my house after supper. My parents are going out. Then I show you how much I love you . . .'

He cycled home thinking, 'This is it, this is it,' spoke the words over and over out loud in the wind as he rode. And all the next day he feared the evening. And when the time came he didn't go, because he couldn't bear for her to see his circumcised cock. And she was hurt. And they argued. And gradually over the next week they made it up, but were never alone in a house again. And she didn't offer to show how much she loved Winkler. And then it was time to go. And for a couple of weeks Winkler planned a return to his first love, which is what he suddenly realised she was. But he did not go.

She wrote him letters on coloured paper, covered with love-struck doodles and he kept meaning to reply, and then the summer ended and he went back to school, ignored the letters, left them unopened on the house post-board to be grabbed and torn and laughed at by others. Until finally a letter came that was not on coloured paper, to tell him that he had betrayed her and destroyed her ability to love, forever.

'. . . And so what was I to do? He was a *szmolcownicy*, a blackmailer. If I tell him where is the camp in the woods he will at best blackmail me to bring to him money or weapons, and at worst simply inform to the Gestapo. How he found out I do not know, but sudden he was very angry because he has been tricked. If there is one thing a Polack does not like it is to be tricked by a Jew. In his eyes was furious anger and they cast about, I thought, for something heavy to hit me to teach me a lesson.

'The future now was terrible. One minute I live in his barn and love his daughter and have food and warmth and also for my friends provide basic needs and now in the barn he is murderous mad and though he says it is a blackmail he wants I think maybe it is to kill me.'

Winkler sat up in his chair, the intrusive daydream of first love burst, and he was angry with himself for drifting yet again.

'I saw his eyes stop and I looked and there it was a spade, a big field shovel, and before he could move I went for it, grabbed and swung. It missed, but as he ducked he tripped on a hay-bale and fell. Like a flash I swung and hit him his head so hard the noise was like I hit a wall. He was silent on the floor. The noise I thought would alert his wife or sons, and I listened, listened, and then he stirred. And so I hit him again, on the floor, and I hit and hit and hit with the spade and was aware then of something and turned to the door where was Adriana, looking.

'When I did not come in the clearing she had given up and was just now back from the woods. At first I thought she was about to faint. And I looked down at the mess of her father at my feet and saw only now that his head was off from his shoulders mostly and he was very much more than only dead. And I looked back to her to say something. How he was going to kill me and my friends in the forests, dozens of young boys and girls all would have died and how I was sorry. And then she opened her mouth and made such a noise like air from your neck when you go to vomit and I knew it was a scream that she was trying to make. And she gulped then air, and was opening her mouth then once more to scream and what can I do but save myself and my friends? Not with a thought of this even, not a thought of anything I swung with the spade, but she was further than the length of the spade handle, and so I let go with my right hand and swung it in an arc with my left hand, what was my strong hand anyway, and it travelled in my hand at full length and was just long enough to have a contact, with the side of the blade, the edge −'

The old man paused. But only because Winkler's face was clenched like a fist, wincing with horror, his hands clawing at his thighs.

'Ach, it is now sixty years, Mr Vinkler,' said Wallenstein, dismissively. 'The spade crossed her face and opened her head up like such a boiled egg. There was no scream. The top of her head went up as the blade came through, like a glove puppet, and the force of the swing turned me right around, hundred eighty degrees. When I turned back then was the head settled back together for a moment, and then was blood, blood, blood. She fell. And so.'

Winkler made a noise. A sort of whimper.

'Ja, but it is the truth, Mr Vinkler. It is what happened. You want I should not speak of these things?'

'No, no. Of course I want you to,' said Winkler, who must have looked pale to the old man, and green. Even in the poor light of the clammy flat. 'It was just a surprise, you know. I was thinking of your girl and . . .'

'Adriana.'

'Yes, Adriana. And obviously to me she looked like a girl I once loved.'

'This is not likely.'

'No, I mean in my mind. If you say "girl" and "love" then I don't make up a whole new face, I use one that I already know. I was thinking of a girl I loved, and then I was just trying the face of a different girl I loved when . . .'

'All while I talk you think of your girlfriends?'

'No, no. I'm not thinking of something else. It's just, you know, in my head, in my mental cinema screen I have to . . .'

'In your head is a cinema?'

'No. Yes, sort of. Surely when you read a story or −'

'This I have never heard.'

'Well, anyway. It was horrible what you described and I −'

'For me also.'

'Yes, obviously. But −'

'Me, I have no need for a cinema.'

'I'm sorry, Mr Wallenstein. It is a moving story and I was momentarily transported somewhere rather unpleasant. Maybe I just need a bit of air.'

Winkler stood up and went to the window. Drawing the curtain back he saw that it gave onto a small yard and then the back of the piano factory in the next street, and would not have provided much light even if the curtains were fully drawn. He grasped at the two cold metal hooks at the base of the frame and lifted gently. They didn't move. He pulled harder and felt a small pain from the effort in the small of his back.

'Painted in,' said Wallenstein. 'For the purpose of security.'

Winkler banged at the window frame with the heel of his palm and heaved again.

'It is not so much air outside today anyway. A glass of water perhaps?'

Winkler looked up into the jagged portion of sky visible above the piano factory. It was, as it was every day, very blue indeed. And very dry. A jumbo jet, passing very high (obviously), left no vapour trail. The puddle might even finally be gone.

'Unlikely,' muttered Winkler.

'Excuse me, Mr Vinkler?'

'Water. Yes. That would be lovely. Thank you.'

Wallenstein handed him cold water in a white enamel mug, tasting of metal.

'So then what?' said Winkler, trying to sound breezy.

'Then it was no choice but to flee,' said Wallenstein, settling himself again in his chair. 'To get back to the band and to warn them. When the bodies is discovered then will the villagers immediately raise the alarm. They will search everywhere till they find us and kill us all. But it was already too late. When I came out from the barn and walked quiet into town, not to raise suspicions, I saw that only it was women and children in the streets.

'What the father knew about the band of Jewish partisans in the woods, all of them knew. Most of the men had gone out already to hunt down the band, and the father only had suspected me. And had stayed behind for blackmail, to see what I had. He knew well that the band was to be attacked, so there was no plan in his mind but to kill me.

'When I got close to the hideout I saw already it was too late. A crowd of perhaps a hundred fifty local men, many familiar to me, including teachers from the school and a doctor where I got drugs two or three times for my friends, was gathered with also many Gestapo. From branches was hanging ten or fifteen: Ovadia, Mirjam, Szlomo, the Pecynowicz twins what was only eleven years old, Judes, Gitele, Judke and then others still. Two or three villagers were already pulling from them their shoes while they kicked, and later they will be stripped and their teeth even pulled, there in the forest, for gold.

'From the middle of the crowd was rising now smoke and it was here eight more of the band naked, tied round a tree and they were burning from the bottom where was piled straw and stick-bundles and logs, all taken from our firewood what we collected every day. The clothes were some metres away where they had been stripped, and at the tree was three or four dead perhaps, or unconscious, and the rest screaming, screaming, including one was Janusz, the brother of Issy, what I forced to take me from the ghetto.

'I had with me the hunting rifle of the father what I took from the barn when I left, and immediate I went to the crowd and barged through to the front. Still they do not know about what happens to the father and the girl and think nothing but I am a Pole like them.'

Surely, thought Winkler, he wasn't going to claim that he started shooting people? How could he still be here if he shot people? He wasn't going to claim he rescued them or something? This was getting silly.

'. . . because it was all what I could do to stop them their pain. A Gestapo came forward and said, "What is this? We have not gone to all this trouble building a fire to just shoot them. Desist this!"

'But already I had been shouting "Jew bastards!" as I executed my friends. And now I shouted, weeping real tears of course, that it was Jews such as this what stole from my friend the farmer his food for his children and my beloved Adriana. And my gun I raised again and I pointed at the brother of Issy his head who looked me straight in the eye and, I thought, nodded, but perhaps just bowed his head and like that, blam!, I put the bullet through his skull.

'Then cold on my temple I felt the point of a Luger, and the Gestapo said, "Cease, Polack, from this, or you go over a tree on a rope also." And at this I stopped to shoot, but now four of my comrades I have saved from burning to death at least. And the villagers all thought it was funny but some was angry saying that it spoiled their fun. And the children too, which their fathers held above the crowd to see the burning, were crying because of the noise of the shooting, and now when I left they started again to smile and clap.'

They'd still be alive now, Winkler thought. Not just the laughing children but some of the men. Now would be the perfect time for Winkler to go back there, just a tourist, to the village, and kill them. What a surprise they would get. What a joy, to walk the streets of their little town with a machine gun, putting fat sprays of fire into the bellies of old fucker after old fucker. And how sweet, after all that time. Better than hot blood. Better for sixty years to think you'd got away with it and then one day, on a cold morning, a tourist in a brightly-coloured anorak pulls from his rucksack something black and shining and blam! Blam! Blametty Blam Blam Blam!

Only, how? Winkler had no idea how to fire a gun. Or where to get one from. And would he go alone? They'd kill him first, and not just for old time's sake. What alternatives? He could push one or two under cars and trains. A few, even. Mosey round town pushing them quietly under vehicles until there were none left. Yes. Good plan. And why not start here? Tomorrow. A big fat German. Well, clearly a German. How would he find a Pole? So a German or an Austrian, Norwegian or Dutch. Much difference? Hardly. So just someone big and fat. Good. Tomorrow, then.

'. . . For a while I sat in the woods after all the crowd was gone, with the naked bodies what had been hanged, such hair on their bodies the women had that I was ashamed, such big bushy black triangles on the white skin. And I thought that soon they will find Adriana and her father and come for me. But where else do I go? Here was fifteen or twenty from the group dead and the rest fled to I didn't know where, but only to more death. And then forward out from the trees came Issy. And he was worse than what I was. Trembling and weeping and crying out. All what had happened he saw. And I was glad he had seen because if not I will have to bear it always on my own.

'And so what to do now, we wondered. To stay was not an option because the hideout was known and even if not to look for us they would anyway come to dig the bodies in graves. Issy said that from the shouting and all what he heard with the lynching, the Polacks thought it was a ZOB camp what had been sabotaging trains in the winter – so probably there was ZOB somewhere near in operation. To find them was our only option.

'"And when we find them what then do we do?" Issy asked me. And I told him, "Now in one day I have killed five human beings what I love and one what I hate. This is a mathematics that now I will not rest until I have changed . . ."'

And so Wallenstein talked on, into the afternoon. And Winkler listened, drifting in and out of concentration. Sometimes transported to the forests and towns of occupied Poland, and, not liking it there, drifting out again into his own life, his work, his journey, his girlfriend, his grandfather, the puddle . . .

And Wallenstein talked about his introduction to the ZOB and of being too late to join in the April uprising and his despair at that. As a newcomer to the unit, which operated in the forest of Wyskow and raided Warsaw sporadically, he was given no responsibility initially but soon made an impression with another action that shocked Winkler upright.

'. . . The SS what we have kept now captured for three weeks with barely food, is two of them dead and the other four emaciated like corpses. Weak they were and shrunken down and their eyes all bulging from hunger and their skin from dehydration grey and terrible. "Ha! You look now like poor Jews yourself, scum-eaters," cried out one of us, and sudden I had a thought. I kneeled down by one and drew from my belt my knife and he screamed like a woman, thinking it was now his death. But only I cut from him all his hair with eight, nine choppings and then called for one of the girls to bring me a razor and I then shaved his head of all his yellow hair so that now, truly, he looks like a Jew such as you see liberated in pictures from the camps. With the fat and muscle gone, and the body broken and tired and no hair it is astonishing what similarity it is between people. And we all laughed at this German and cried Jew! Jew! Jew! And then I said to them that now I have something to do what I must do myself alone and not in front of nobody. And I dragged away this shaven one behind the shed where is our stores. The others shouted to me not to kill him because we need living Germans perhaps to bargain for our lives later but I said this was not what I plan, although it is a possible outcome and if so I am sorry. And they see I am mad crazy to do this and they keep then shtum.

'What they hear then from behind the shed is a terrible bump, which is what noise it made when I hit him his head with my rifle butt to make unconscious. And then, maybe twenty seconds later, is a terrible screaming and two or three come running to me but I am already standing and coming out from behind the store and I toss to them a small red item what one of them catches. And the one who catches he cries aloud to God and throws it down on the floor.'

'His ear?' said Winkler.

'What for I cut him his ear? It was his foreskin what I threw. I circumcised the German is what.'

Winkler groaned and clutched at his groin.

'What face did you put on this German in your cinema, then?' said the old man, laughing.

'Boris Becker,' replied Winkler, smitten to honesty by the grimness of the image, and the sense that this old man was not an old man worth lying to.

'So. But small and bony from starvation?'

'Yes.'

'And shaved at the head all clumsy and bloody?'

'Yes.'

'And now what happens to him in your cinema?'

'I don't know. He gets an infection and dies?'

'Hmm. In this case, no. Antiseptic a little we wasted, and bandages, and after ten days, maximum a fortnight, it was pretty good healed.'

'What was the point of that?'

'All I had figured out as soon as it was said to the Nazi, "You look like a Jew." And what I planned, the rest accepted, although some was not happy. It was to march him naked to a village and set him loose to be killed by the people as a Jew.'

'But he could have told them that he wasn't one.'

'Na, obviously I cut him out his tongue before. This way he seems just a Jew who runs away mid-torture and finds himself here.'

'But if the villagers make enquiries –'

'Make enquiries is not what happens with Poles and Jews. It is just bang bang dead and put in a hole.'

'So they did kill him, the Poles?'

'As it turned out this first time was even better than that. The Nazi had no idea what we planned. We took him to near a village and untied his hands and he thought we would shoot him, so he ran. He ran straight towards the village, which was better than we hoped, and it was clear that he had no idea what is going on. But outside the village is two or three labourers who stop him and look at him all over and he shouts, shouts and makes tongueless noises and points to where we are hiding in the trees, and they look towards us but obviously they think he is mad.

'And then a Gestapo appears, and another, and this is not what we thought and we prepare to run and I take one last look, and the farmers is pointing at the man and the Nazi is waving his arms and making noise and then sudden up comes the arm of one Gestapo and blam! Down goes our Nazi, shot dead on the spot. The two Gestapo turned and went back in the village, and the farmers stood looking at the body, and straight away we fled.'

Winkler listened as the old man disburdened himself of his memories with greater and greater relish. For a while he focused on this gruesome circumcision procedure:

'. . . The blow to the head this further time was perhaps too light, it was a big man, and he came round right at the wrong time and slip, I opened him up like such a banana peeled by a hungry child – zzzzipp! – and it was such blood I was head-to-toe covered and he immediate fainted the big Nazi and I ran because it was terrible and a girl, Lala, came running to see and near vomited, but then shot him his forehead straight away . . .'

And the more grim the memory the greater seemed Wallenstein's relish in description. He told Winkler how he became better and better at this 'procedure' and was laughingly called the '*Mohel* of Wyszkow' by his comrades. And how he 'improved a little the mathematics' of his killing career.

It occurred to Winkler to ask, 'Didn't the local people start to get suspicious about these deliveries of tongueless Jews?'

'*Na*, it is not all the same time in the same place, this is now a year, year and a half what I am talking, and over a wide area. Perhaps some was not shot, but most. And what survived were never probably so happy like Larry from there afterwards.' And he laughed a little laugh.

'My comrades after a while told me it was enough with the *Mohel* of Wyszkow, that it was a trail that would lead the Germans to us. And that it was not what we were needed for, and it was no help to win the War and no time yet for revenge. And here I became angry and shouted to them, "Ja, so when will come the time to revenge? Mm? When it is over the War and we are all sitting nice back in our homes with our feet up and a nice bowl of soup and hearing on the radio how it is now a Jewish state in Poland what is shooting in forests all the Germans and all the Poles, women and children, millions, millions, millions? When will come this? What war? What win? What is victory? If even the Allies come and defeat these Nazis then you think we simple go home? To what? Is your home there still? Is yours? Is yours?" like this I pointed at each man there standing −'

And he pointed now at Winkler, and at imaginary men and women next to him.

'"And your parents?" I shouted to them, "Your families, are they there to welcome you? Are they living? And yours? And yours? So. What is then victory? Where we will go? People like us what have lived as animals here in the forest killing and killing and eating such *treif* like in the Torah was not even imagined to forbid," some at this moment laughed a little at my joke but then quick stopped, "And even if we find somewhere a home then how will we revenge? And on who? They will put maybe some Nazis on trial, maybe Hitler, maybe Himmler, Blobel, Ohlendorf, Nebe, Hoss, maybe they hang them − this is if the Nazis do not win the War − but the rest, the rank and file? The Poles? The bastard women and children and old ones who laugh to their men as they beat us? It is not in peace-time to kill everyone. They will say how the peace last time was too unfair and made this war − ha! − and to not be barbaric so like the enemy, but to turn like this their Christian cheek. And some to prison perhaps. But no, this is not revenge. And what do they do now for us, that we should help them in this war? The Polish government in London, what does it do? What did it do for the uprisings? What in January? What in April? Where is the food drops? The railways that go east with thousands baking there in the trucks or freezing, to the gas, what do they do for this? Do they bomb the lines? The stations? Where are they? They are maybe drinking a whisky in London and thinking one day maybe we land in France if the weather is nice and we go nice and easy through the summer and liberate a little Italy, and maybe after winter we go see what is happening in the East where is only Jews and Slavs what nobody cares about.

'"No, we will die here, me and you and you and you. And we live as long we can to kill as many we can, and I do it in this way because this is my promise. Like Abram made with God his covenant in blood, so now I make mine. I make for each Nazi a blood-bond for himself, to present to God on his day of reckoning. And we see then if God honours or if He does not."

'And after was silence. And they look to me and they look to Grabowski, the leader, and he makes no sign to them. And it is for a moment unclear who is leader and who is not leader. And for days it is like this. And there is a little what seems fear in the eyes of the others, and nobody confronts me. And then it comes the thing what I only regret of all this, the thing what makes me leader.'

Winkler did not have to ask the old man to go on.

'The boy Tadek, a fourteen-year-old from Riga who is with us six months, is sent to a village from where we camp only five, six kilometres. His job is only to bring bread or potatoes, what he can get, and if by chance some news of the front then so much the better. He has good Aryan looks and countryside Polish fluent like you would never hear from even me – so good we call him Chlop instead of Tadek. "Chlop" is in Polish the word for "peasant". But by nightfall he is not returned. There is some what thinks to make a search party, perhaps the boy is captured, and these have the ear of Grabowski. This makes me angry. He is just a boy, a fourteen-year-nothing what is not to be sentimental, if he is captured he is captured – though of course I am myself no more than nineteen at this time. We do not risk men for him. This is not why we are here. He has no skill, he has not taken even a weapon. None is impossible to do without, and most of all him. What we do if he is not back when is coming dawn is we fly immediate from that place because he will surely talk, and then it is up with us all, and complete.

'This is harsh words, but Grabowski knows it is right words, and he nods, and the others go back muttering. And some hours later comes back the boy, Tadek. And he is even singing. What is to sing? And out comes everybody and gather to him to find what happened. And he is not talking sense and he is staggering and in the dark they think he is beaten terrible or something like this, but I know instant what it is. "He has been drinking, the little bastard," I say, and with the back of my hand I cut him down onto his knees. The others cry out, and a girl runs to him to hold him his head. And he looks up scared. And he weeps now and says, "I did not say to them anything, one or two what I was talking with in the square says to come and drink a little schnapps. There is there an inn and I drank with them only one or two."

'This of course was not true, even though only he was fourteen, still it takes more liquor than one or two to bring a man to this kind of drunk. "Did they enquire you where you came from?" I asked him. And he said that he did not think so. "Do not think so?" I shout to him, "Here is fifty comrades hiding, what every man in that village will hang gladly with their own hands from these trees, waiting for you to come back and you go to drink with such a group of Polacks and do not remember even what you said? Did they see you leave?" I asked him. "I don't think so, it was dark," says Tadek. "Were you followed? My God they might be out there now in the trees, you dumb little bastard!" And then the woman holding him, Yitka she was called, like also my sister what died in Warschau, she said to me to stop, that they had not come, the villagers, and that he was only a boy.

'Only a boy she thought. "He must be punished," I told her. She says we decide this in the morning. And I tell to her in the morning maybe we are all dead, we punish him now and then we strike camp and we retreat some distance to hiding and we see if they come a couple days. And I told her to let him go, and she did not, and I pulled him away with my hand by his forearm like so —'

Wallenstein with his spotted yellow arm, weak and limp, made a frail snatching gesture in the feebly lit room.

'And I looked to Grabowski and he looked me in my eye with his eyes, what hanged down like such a bloodhound, and then turned away. So then the boy I dragged away to the trees and he looked back at the girl what had held him and she cried to me, "He is just a boy." And then it was dark around us, and I did what it needed to be done and I returned to the men and women. And they stared at me. And I stared back. And I said, "So." And Grabowski said what was maybe he thought a joke, "I thought for a moment you would shoot him." And to him I looked and to the others, and I said, "If we want to live to tomorrow we will not shoot our weapons in the dark on a quiet night." And to the floor where they sat I threw my knife. The knife of the *Mohel* of Wyszkow. And in the moonlight it was covered all over the blade with blood. And then some of them they gasped. And Grabowski stood up and went to his bed. And the girl wept, "You killed him? You killed him?" and to her I said "What you think, woman? Circumcised he already was."'

'You killed him,' said Winkler.

'Cut him his throat. He felt nothing, nothing. The joke only I was sorry about at the time.'

'The joke?'

'About he already was circumcised. It was not to joke of such a thing. Now, of course, for years I worry is it right what I did, is it right, is it wrong? Who's to say? He was now a liability. He can be sent no more on missions. Never trusted. It was not a holiday. There was not room for baggage.'

'Yes, but, Christ,' said Winkler. 'I mean, shit, you killed him?'

'And then from now people will not put in danger the rest of the band. This will no more happen. It is just a life. It is not such a thing. He had not already done so much with his years that it was a tragedy to end them. And what world was there for him after? Probably only to die like the rest of us in the forest. Or to come home to no home. Really, to me it was no life any more important than another, my own including, so long we kill plenty Germans.

'And so now it is understood I am leader. Grabowski said he was going to make a contact with the Armia Ludowa, the Polish underground. It was also a Polish underground called Armia Krajowa but this one was not so happy to make partnership with Jews. And he said "I leave in charge the *Mohel*," what was a joke but did not make anyone laugh or giggle.

'Truthfully, Grabowski was not going to the underground. All what I had said he saw was true. There was no future for us but killing and he saw also that I would use these men to kill what I could of Nazis and his time was no longer this. It was coming the end of the War, Grabowski thought, and he left the band to me and went maybe to find the front, to go perhaps to Palestine, maybe to kill himself somewhere alone, as many did. Whatever it was I never saw him after that. Which of course meant nothing. For it was almost nobody I saw again from what I knew before the War and during.

'And he was right in both: the War nearly was over, and it was now only killing. The Nazis were narrowed and narrowed with the Allies on one side and the Soviets on the other. The band grew smaller, some were killed, others left because they did not agree with the killing what I thought was necessary. For example, a German girl, fifteen or sixteen, what Issy saw at a well, collecting water near to the Stutthof deathcamp, what was maybe the daughter of a high-ranking German or maybe a cook only or housecleaner, what suspected nothing of who we were, he began speaking with her and another from us went to them, a Russian Jew what was recent arrived with us and he grabbed her and I was away a little distance, but when I got there were nearly at blows, perhaps I think, the Russian thought to rape her. They began shouting at each other, Issy and the Russian, and I told them to be quiet. And then again they shouted, and straight like that I took the girl and broke her neck. And this stopped them from shouting. And they looked at her body and I told them Germans is not to love and we are not to rape, but to save if possible Jews and kill if possible everyone else. And from this action I lost maybe half from what was left in the band. Not the Russian, who was without a heart. And not Issy. Never I lost Issy until the end.

'And days after this I saw at Mauthausen a death-camp for the first time. It was liberated only days and here and all around the bodies, bodies, bodies and the smell, and what I saw it is not necessary to tell, surely, Mr Vinkler? All this you know?'

Winkler nodded.

'Here went now the last of my men – not to count Issy, the Russian and one girl – to the Russians what had liberated the camp. For them they wanted only that the War was over. But for me it was not to trust the Russians with Jews from the forest what had no papers and wore only rags, any more than the Germans.

'And so we bent our way back towards the advance of the Allies, where to perhaps be picked up by Americans or British was our best hope. And we came in this way to another camp, smaller, what I didn't know even the name. Here was a group of partisans I had not heard of. They had taken control of the camp and had as prisoners what seemed maybe a hundred Hitler Youth aged not above, I think, fifteen.

'The leader of them explained me that everywhere the Germans were destroying the camps to have no evidence of what they did, but here they had not had time and fled west as soon as they heard what happened at Mauthausen, not to be caught by the Reds, what was killing German prisoners by thousands. These Hitler Youth, what was under the control of the SS, who now were gone, had been found wandering in the forest and rounded up without a fight and brought here. The leader now was anxious to be away from the Russians himself. It was a new world coming and a Polish man can choose to live under Stalin or not under Stalin. And so I said them to go and I would look after the Germans till came the Russians.

'Issy and the girl what was left, Mala, they knew what I will do. The Russian begins to ask me in Yiddish why I agree to this, that Stalin has ordered partisans killed like Nazis, and this is not our job to guard children. Why I agree to this he asks when they can perfectly good look after themselves? And in the middle while he is talking he stops. And he turns to look at the other two and his face is white.

'"No, comrade," he says. "Not this."

'"I am your leader," I told him. "I do not ask for consultation."

'"They're boys," he said to me, the Russian. "It's over now."

'"So. If it is worth to save the lives of these Nazis that you risk your own life," I told him, "then perhaps you do something."

'And he stood for a short time, and looked to the others, and then he set off walking towards the west. And Mala and Issy turned also away and walked.

'And to my friend from all those years I said,

'"Ha, Issy, even you?" So like a Brutus he was betraying me.

'And he said to me, "*Ja*, Yitzhak. It is now enough. I ask you once, come. Leave here the boys."

'But I turned away from his eyes to look the other way and when the next minute I looked back he is walking with the others away to the forest.'

'And so you killed them?' said Winkler.

'With gas,' said the old man.

'How?'

'Ach, it is not difficult. You think such monkeys would have killed so easy millions if it was a thing difficult to perform? It was potassium cyanide. Pellets. What is the same in any language. Plenty there was in the gun lockers. When they ran, the Nazis, they took only guns, bombs, grenades. But gas pellets, what need is this for men fleeing? There you empty from the canister plenty and then some more and this turns straight to gas and soon after everyone is dead.'

'And you did that to a hundred children?'

'Nazis. Eighty-seven of them. What killed all my family, my home, my country, my past and my future.'

'Yes, but —'

'I am not now interested to talk about the morality, Mr Vinkler. At that time, yes, it was I alone who made this decision, and I alone who killed them. And it is I who has survived, alone, to tell you.

'It was I who roused them from where they were sitting in the yard, on stumps and rocks, cowering from the rain by the low walls. Roused them with my gun, waving it towards the chamber — there was only one at this place — and shouting orders. No, not shouting, because this would have panicked them. Speaking just adequate loud to be heard over the rain. And not orders. Only instructions.

'"On your feet, you lot. Now."

'And up they got without a murmur.

'"Form a line. No, two lines. Hands on your heads. No. No. Four lines, then. Four lines of twenty. And the rest on the end of the last line."

'And so they did. Well drilled, they were. And also well defeated. I was lucky. I had them at a good time, when they were already broken. But still, eighty-seven of them, and just me with my old rifle. I was very weak by then. I didn't show it, perhaps. They could have rushed me. I would have hit one, maybe two, maximum. If they had done this then they would still be alive. Not even so old. Some would have died — cancer, suicide, traffic – some suicides is certain. But probably most of them still alive. Some still working, even. Writing books maybe, in barbers' shops cutting hair, making food. Or, like me, sitting in a chair and telling how it was.

'The oldest were sixteen, maybe. And the youngest perhaps thirteen. Perhaps twelve. But not children.

'I think really they did not know what would happen. The War was over. The Russians were almost through Poland, headed for Berlin. And the camps were being liberated one by one as the Allies came from the west. Everyone was talking about the gas. The ovens. Huge, terrible numbers. But the War was over. This was clear to everyone. And so my comrades thought it was not necessary to kill these last few. More blood, they thought, it was not necessary. Now all we can do is run. But run where? To the forests, Italy, South America, where?

'I would not run. Such a business started, the fulfilling of an ideal for which you have lived four, five years, is a thing to be finished. And so I let them run, my comrades, and stayed myself with the eighty-seven that remained to die. These were only young men, but this is what it was always about, from the beginning. The men and the women and the children, every one of them. And if the War really was over, there was still my duty.

'"Right. Into the bunker. From the front, to the left, the next row following on to the tail of the first, nice and slow. March."

'There was no marching. They stared at me. One said, "But Herr Kommandant. The War is over. The War –"

'"Don't tell me the War is over," I said to him. "You little bastard abortion. You hear the shooting? You hear that? You hear the bombs?" I pointed and they looked. And in the rain you could hear just the noise of the front, booming. "That's the War, over there. Nothing is over." And I walked straight up to the talker and pushed him with my bayonet, not hard, just so he doubled up. How I wanted to shoot him there. But, again, a general panic would be disaster. To see one drop dead at my gun right then, with the gas chamber right ahead of them, might have been enough, for these young ones, to make them see that all was lost anyway and so maybe, this time, they would come for me. It was all about trust, you see, at this point. So I laughed.

'I said, "What do you think, you stupid boys?" (To treat them like this, like an angry teacher, was to make them automatically obey.) "That I'm going to kill you? What do you think I am? I'm just going to lock you in there so that I can get away, and rejoin my friends and get a nice distance away so you don't catch me up and do me a mischief. Don't

pretend you won't. Now, come on, just get in the bunker. Smoke a cigarette. And the Russians will be along to round you up in a day or two.
Or the Americans if you're lucky."

'One of them, a big one, took a step towards me. I raised my rifle and
sighted him down the barrel. But the rain was so hard I could not do
this properly to shoot him. In fact the rain was so hard I think they maybe
couldn't hear what I was saying.

'It is possible that the rain helped them decide. We were all soaked
through. They hadn't eaten in days. They knew the front was moving at
ten or twenty miles a day towards us, and that they needed only to stay
alive another day or two to be saved – and inside the bunker it was at
least dry. Slowly, they shuffled in.

'The last was a very small boy. Not even one metre fifty. Very sad
looking. Weeping. Or maybe it was just the rain. "You're not going to kill
us?" he said.

'"I told you, no." I said. And I pushed him in with the butt of my rifle
to his hip, and he squealed and grabbed at it as I threw the door shut
and dragged the bolt across. I dragged the other two bolts across and they
made a terrible scream of metal above the rain.

'And then I went back to the gun lockers and picked up a canister of
the pellets and climbed the ladder – which was greasy with the wet –
onto the roof of the bunker. Standing there, I was a little higher than the
nearest fir trees and to the east I could see the sky bright with orange
from the burning, perhaps of a small village. Or possibly of the conflict
of armies. The land between was very still and dark. Only the banging
of the little raindrops on the flat roof of the gas chamber and this rumble
of the guns.

'I opened what seemed an entry place for the poison crystals and
poured them till it was empty, the canister. Only after it was empty did
I see other ducts for putting crystals, probably to better disperse the gas
around the chamber. But now it was too late. And I did not feel like
going for more.

'So I sat down on an ammunition box, what was left there thoughtfully
by the last executioner who came to pour in pellets. And I listened to the
rain, what was very loud on the roof and all around me, and to the wind.'

And in the room it was also silent. Winkler thought he heard floorboards
creak above. The flesh-boiler, perhaps, back on the job. He yawned, nervously. And wished that he hadn't.

'Then after is not much to say. Quick soon I fled from there, and a couple days later came across a patrol of the Palestinian Brigade, what I could hardly believe. Jews in British uniforms with the six point star on, which they chose to wear from pride, not was forced from shame. They spoke only English and Hebrew which was a strange language to hear in that place. But one or two from them understood Yiddish and so by and by it came that I was in Palestine.

'Very quick I was wanted to fight in the Independence war – partisans what came together there who had fought in Europe were immediate recruited. But I did not want to kill now more people. Not British. British had not killed Jews. The only ones. The only ones, what had not killed Jews. And by one way and another it became possible for me to come to here, to live, in a place where Jews are not taken early from home in the morning to a place where the trees have been cleared . . .

'And so. This is now fifty-four years. The fancy cakes I see you do not touch. More tea, perhaps, you need?'

Winkler said, 'No thank you. I'm fine. In fact, if you don't mind I really must get some air and I think someone must be home upstairs by now. I should change my clothes, too. It's pretty much evening.'

Winkler, in his t-shirt and shorts and in his moccasins, rose to his feet.

'No, no don't get up, Mr Wallenstein. I can see myself out. Thank you for your story. It was . . . it was a great story.' And he took the old man's hand to shake it in his. It was yellow and cold and Winkler looked at it cradled in his own large-looking, warm, pink hand.

'Perhaps too grisly for such a summer afternoon?' said Wallenstein, looking up from his chair. 'And for a long time I think I talked. I am tired now. It is only when I start to think from that time then is there nothing missing, not a detail. Look, Mr Vinkler, I have here the stamps.'

Wallenstein reached into the pocket of his dressing-gown and drew out a small see-through envelope of stiff plastic containing four small yellow envelopes, each addressed and with a small, differently-coloured stamp on it. He handed them to Winkler who took them and, tilting them towards what light there was from the curtained window, saw a man's head and the strong outline of the franking stamp, validating the new issue. He handed them back.

'Take,' said Wallenstein. 'I want you to have.'

'No, I . . .' Winkler said.

'Take,' said Wallenstein, pushing them deeper into Winkler's hand and folding his fingers around them. 'Maybe you come again to give me back if I cannot bear to be without them. What I told you is only what comes first to mind. There is more what I can tell. But all from that time. After that is not much to say. I was a small child in Warschau with my parents and with Yitke and my brothers. And then it came the War, and then it ended the War, and so here I am in my chair.'

'Another time, maybe, the rest,' said Winkler, turning the door handle. The corridor outside was dark like the room but at the end, behind the curtain, bright light was outside the front door. Like outside the cinema when some foreign woman standing in for a mother . . .

'*Ja*,' said the old man quietly, as Winkler pulled the door quietly shut behind him, 'I was a small child in Warschau with my parents, and Yitke, and my brothers, I forget what is now their names, and it was such a sky, blue like you never saw . . .'

MIDDLE PART

9

What Winkler's Flatmates Thought About It

As Winkler left the flat, a shape appeared at the front door, shadowed on the screen of the dirty net curtain. A key jabbed at the lower lock, rattled impatiently and heaved the bolt over. A slimmer key made a higher pitched din in the Yale chink. The door of the Wallenstein flat clicked shut behind him. He heard Mary say, 'Ah, fock it.' The front door opened and in she came.

She stopped in the doorway, surprised to see Winkler standing in the part of the hall corridor that led only to the old people's hovels and the basement.

'Do you not go to work at all any more?' she said. 'Look I've broken my fockn neel on that fockn lock. It's so fockn stiff. I could have broken my fockn finger.'

She was wearing her black and white horizontally striped tights with the big round clumpy shoes that had Minnie Mouse on the buckles, a shortish skirt that was bunched up between her thighs from climbing the hill on a sticky afternoon and a white singlet which made her light brown underarm hair – which was moist – visible to Winkler.

'And have you seen this oyt here?'

'What?'

'This. Oyt here. The fockn evidence. Look in the drearn.'

Mary led Winkler to the big street drain at the edge of the pavement directly outside the house. He shielded his eyes from the sunlight, too bright after hours in the dark room. There was a tangle of what looked to Winkler like hair – he would have said about a handful, the right unit of measurement for hair that was no longer attached to a head – clinging to the bars

of the grating and dangling down into the shallow darkness above the oily
water, whose surface supported motionless sticks and crisp packets.

'So?'

'Human hee-yur. It proves it. It's from whatever poor bitch that bastard's
kyookn opsteers.'

'You think?'

'Christ, isn't it obvious? He shaved it off because he can't eat it.'

'But why would he get rid of it in the drain outside his house? If he's
really killing women for food he must know it's against the law. He
wouldn't just throw it in the gutter outside his own front door.'

'He's a fockn psychopath, Wink. For Christ's seeks, he's not a rational
person.' And she stormed back into the house.

Did she really believe it? That there was a psychopath living in the
house who was keeping butchered portions of his murdered victims in the
freezer? Mind you, he half believed it once, too, while all the time . . .

Winkler, remembering that he didn't have his keys, ran into the house
before the front door swung shut and caught Mary on the stairs.

'Forgot my keys.'

'So where have you been just now?'

'In Wallenstein's flat.'

'Who?'

'The old man downstairs.'

'What for?'

'Talking.'

'Aboyt what?'

'About him, mostly. What he did in the War. He was in the Warsaw ghetto.
I had no idea. He saw some terrible, terrible shit. His parents were in . . .'

'Aye, aye, all very interesting I'm sure. I've seen some terrible terrible
shit, too. Did you get anything for supper?'

'No, I –'

'You mean you focked off out of work in the middle of the day while
the rest of us were fockn slaving away at oor desks and you came back
and sat about in your pants with some old twat all day, and you didn't
even buy any fockn food?'

'Well, I'll go out now and –'

'And what? It's twenty past six. The shops are all shut now.'

'I thought maybe we'd go out for supper.'

'Oh, don't bother. I'm going oyt anyways with Sheena and Keet.'

The front door opened. Feet skipped noisily up the stairs to where
Winkler and Mary were standing on the first landing inside the flat.

'What ho!' said Will.

'Jaysus!' said Mary, and barged past him on her way up to their room.

'Day?' said Will.

'Yeah, fine,' said Winkler. And after a pause during which he wondered whether it was still such a good idea, them all living together, and whether maybe it was a good time to say goodbye to Mary, too, and, in fact, probably to can his stupid job and go and live a long way away for a while, and hook up maybe with the sort of girl that was split open by Wallenstein, a nice, foreign girl, he said, 'You?'

'Bloody hell,' said Will, who was waiting for the opening. 'Bloody hell. There's been a massacre at a school in Wales – loads of children killed. Sayonara to the sprogs of the valleys. It was about three o'clock. And it was all hands on deck at the office as you can imagine.'

Will worked on the diary of a national newspaper. One of five Old Etonians who sat at a round desk in tweed jackets, writing about jolly goings-on at product launch parties and hoping one day to become editors, which they all would.

'Even us diarists were nearly involved,' he went on, 'because the Ed considered dropping the diary out of respect – twenty-two daisy-pushers at the last count – but then we pointed out that you have to give the readers a bit of a chortle even unto the darkest hour and all that and he agreed but there were loads of really grismal photos of these kids all mashed up, the killer took off some of their faces with a hunting knife before they shot him and anyway the designers did this graphic of where each child was killed in the school of course most of it was speculative because we don't have many details yet but it'll be the best layout in the first editions we reckon and so Tufty, he's the news ed, he phoned down for a case of poo for after the edition had gone to celebrate doing the best splash in years it says,' [and here Winkler's friend put up his stretched palm and wiped a banner headline in the air as he spoke] '"Slaughter of the Innocents", and under it is a photograph of some bodybags – in fact they're corpses from Rwanda as they haven't released the actual real Welsh bodybag pics yet but nobody'll notice because the bags are zipped shut and it's in a municipal building of some sort it was really funny because Jane P, she's the pics ed, she said that they never even got in the paper when they were just a row of bags full of little dead coons but now we're pretending it's white babies inside they're front fucking page and then anyway the grog was delivered and we tucked right in and the Ed made a speech standing on a desk about how this was real journalism and stories like this were why we had gone into it in the first place and then he

announced that they were extending the print run, moving back the deadline on the last edition and going for two million copies and we all
cheered and anyway then I was allowed to come home because the diary
was done so even though it was all pretty exciting and some of the other
chaps decided to hang around I thought I'd take advantage of the tragic
sitch and miss the worst of the traffic.'

Winkler wondered what to say.

'That's all a bit sick, isn't it?' he said, although he was rarely bothered
by lapses in taste, and was not much moved by this one, across town, in
the offices of a newspaper he never read.

'Well, you can't bring them back by being sad, so you might as well
just get on with it,' said Will. 'And it's our job to focus on the tragedy
and stop it happening again.'

'By doing what?'

'Well. By writing about it and getting across the human tragedy and
saying how awful it is.'

'In case people thought that, in general, killing a roomful of children
and cutting off their faces was a good thing?'

Will stared at him.

'Hark at you. Since when did you get all lefty?'

'Oh, Will, for Christ's sake.'

The sun was streaming in through the window from behind Will's head
so that he was silhouetted and Winkler had to shield his eyes to see what
was going on in the big stupid face of the Old Etonian. Will wasn't saying
anything at all. Which made it difficult for Winkler to know how to go
on.

'I mean. Christ. It's a bit fucking sick. No? This fucker's killed children
and they're all drinking champagne and celebrating about their fucking
diagrams.'

'It's the reality of hard news,' Will said slowly. 'I'm sorry if you find it
difficult to stomach. What civilians sometimes fail to −'

'Civilians!'

'Look, you can sit there crying about it, that's all very well. But somebody has to make the attempt to describe and explain.'

'And drink champagne?'

'Listen, Wink, that's newspapers, okay? Tomorrow's fish and chips,
perhaps, but also the first draft of history. Okay?'

'First draft of my fucking hairy old arse,' said Winkler. 'I've just done
an afternoon with that poor old cunt from downstairs. He had to pull
his dead sister's hand out of the rubble of the family home, shoot his best

friends to save them from burning, gas a load of German kids and cut his girlfriend's head off with a spade.'

'Why?'

'Why? Because he had no choice.'

'Seems a bit extreme.'

'It was the Shoah. Of course it was fucking extreme.'

'The what?'

'The Shoah. Christ, Will, don't you know anything? That's what the Holocaust is called in Hebrew, or maybe Yiddish.'

'Ooh, Wink. Don't be racist.'

'What are you talking about? Yiddish. It's a language.'

'Yes but it comes from Yid, which is insulting. They don't like it. You should call it "Jewish".'

'You idiot. It's the other way round. Yiddish is a language. It's where "Yid" comes from.'

'Well, even so.'

'Christ, Will. Did they have any fucking lessons at that school of yours in between the boat races?'

Will stood up.

'Where are you going?' said Winkler.

'Out.'

'Out? You never go out. Out where?'

'I'm going to meet Ru and some of the gang.'

'Ru. God. He's such a prick. You're going all the way across town to see that cocksucker with his silly hair and his voice like a racecourse announcer choking on a golf ball?'

'He's actually a bloody sweet guy.'

'Oh, fucking spare me.'

'No, shut up, Wink. You don't know what you're talking about. You're always down on everybody and it's just sad, that's all. Ru is a bloody lovely bloke and he knows how to have a laugh without being a bloody knob about it.'

'With his fucking tinted spectacles and his sandals and his fucking million quid house and his fucking DJ-ing. Shit, he doesn't have the first fucking idea.'

'Of what, Wink?'

'Of . . . I don't know. Anything.'

'Well, maybe neither have I.'

'No. That's not what I'm saying. That's not it at all. It's just them. Those fucking arseholes with their dancing and their parties and their drugs and their getting "rarely bugled up" and all screwing each other and going to fucking weddings in the countryside, all that *Four Weddings and a Funeral* shit – except not enough fucking funerals.'

'There's nothing wrong with dancing, if it makes you happy.'

'Oh. Oh. Ohhhh, right then. Nothing wrong with dancing. I thought we agreed on that one.'

'Well, yes, but, I mean if you're really, really pissed and just with mates . . .'

'No, Will. No. No mitigating circumstances. Not booze, not drugs, not friends, not girls, not nothing. Dancing is not acceptable.'

(It may not be possible, in the end, to convey the importance to Winkler of not dancing. Truly, he had never danced a step. Never, in public, even tapped his foot. Winkler's refusal to give up his body to a tin rhythm in a low space under the ground was itself, he felt, a form of aesthetic expression. One in which he saw the uniqueness of his artistic soul most emphatically reflected.

Winkler did not dance, because he had pretended to be ill on the night of Nicky Raymond's twelfth birthday party. Panicked by the possible presence of girls and of a requirement on the night to dance and kiss, neither of which he had ever done, he stayed home. Did not tell his grandfather. Watched *Jim'll Fix It* and *The Dukes of Hazzard* and went to bed.

He felt at the time that he had avoided being made to look like a malcoordinated and friendless fool who had never met a girl in his life – and so that was exactly what he remained.

In the years that followed, Winkler built an impressive list of things that he had never done, and thus would never do. To kissing and dancing he added singing, playing a musical instrument, skateboarding, roller-skating and skiing, speaking a foreign language, riding a bicycle, horse or motorcycle, going to the countryside or anywhere very far away without very good reason, swimming in the sea, showering naked in the presence of other men, or, of course, women, going into a pub he had never been into before on his own and ordering a drink, and other things which, when he thought about it hard enough, were almost numberless.

But dancing was the most important. Sitting in a nightclub, alone at a table, keeping watch over the drinks and the bottles, the phones and the bags and the coats and hats, while the others went voluntarily to twitch involuntarily in response to a noise coming out of boxes mounted on the wall, Winkler felt like the only dissenter at a Nuremberg rally, felt himself perched on the very edge of civilisation, staring into the abyss, hidden by the shadows from dark, unconscious humanity, a fugitive staring over the crest into the valley of the Yahoos, flesh-pit and totem-pole, where naked monsters take human form and surrender to the bloody-fanged fury of the music god.

Never did he feel more alone than when he saw his friends blended into the roiling throng, tossing their hair around their heads, staring at their feet and at the ceiling, legs and arms moving without reason or directional intent. There was no will to communicate – defining privilege of the human – no possibility of distilling and expressing meaning from the stinking animal soup that bubbled there, no hope of enlightenment or understanding. Only the wild orgy of movement before death.)

'Yes, well anyway. I'll see you later.'

There was the heavy skip on the stairs again. The diminishing percussion of Will descending this time. Suddenly, there was a shout from upstairs.

'Will!' called Mary. 'Will you give us a lift into toyn?'

'Yah, if you're going right now.'

'Yeah, sure, great. Two secs.'

Mary put her head round the living room door.

'Don't wait up,' she said to Winkler and blew him a horrible kiss.

Then there was the skippety-clunk of Mary going down the stairs, and the small clatter of the two metal locks being simultaneously dragged on the downstairs door. And the slam of it behind them.

Now Winkler had nothing to do. His social default options – Mary and Will – were simultaneously unavailable. Where did they say they were going? Didn't he and Mary have plans? Wasn't Will his best mate? Winkler needed to talk about this Wallenstein thing. This Holocaust thing. This Jew thing. This Winkler thing. He had been looking forward to talking about it. And yet clearly they weren't interested. More interested in their own turdy little lives. Will off to wherever with his tosser gay boy Eton friends, no doubt they'd end up dancing with each other. Mary troughing snortily in some cheapo pork-hole with those bog-trotting slappers Sheena and Kate – the three of them so richly Irish their DNA profile differed only by one per cent from that of a medium-sized baking potato. Fuck 'em. Winkler didn't need shitbags like that around.

Then again, he wasn't sure his own company would be enough this particular evening.

The television gawped stupidly at him from a corner of the room, under the eaves.

Still, fuck 'em.

Wallenstein cut off their foreskins with his eating knife, cut out their tongues and sent them to be murdered by their bloodthirsty countrymen.

You wouldn't be afraid of Mulligan, would you, if you'd done that?

'I haven't done shit,' said Winkler aloud.

But he'd nearly a pushed a fat man under a train yesterday. A Jew, even. Wrong choice. He'd touched the garments and arses of random women and thought about pushing them under the train. Better. And then just now, downstairs, he thought about going all the way to Germany, Poland, wherever, and pushing them under trains and trams. Stupid. And all just thinking, thinking.

'I haven't actually done anything. Not ever.'

If he really did push someone under a train, though, if he really did, then that would be something, now, wouldn't it?

Imagine. Paf! All over. Some fat old housewife splats and Winkler is made more than mortal. Why fat? Because it leaves at least a sliver of rationality in it. Fat people are gross. Moral lassitude is all it is. A failure to apply the normal moral restraints to action is what makes fat fuckers fat. To that extent they are no different from murderers, rapists, paedophiles, the more widely reviled sociopaths.

Do they explode when the train hits them, or what? Do you see it all or does the locomotive rush them away from you in the moment of dying?

And what about killing a good-looking slim woman? The sun warmed Winkler's lap. One minute she's standing there reading the paper, train hurtles in, she looks up, feels a firm shove on her arse, thinks it's just routine pervery same as always, but it isn't, not this time . . . pointless, though, she'd never know it was him, never know anything. She would have no idea of his power.

Wallenstein shot the young German girl. The fourteen-year-old girl the Russian wanted to rape. She would have been slender, slightly tanned, cornflower eyes, wearing a peasant sort of a smock thing, no doubt. Physically confident beyond her years from all that rustic living, a little bit dirty, fleck of mud on her forehead . . . Winkler slipped his hand into his shorts, cupped his balls, yanked the waistband down with the back of his wrist. The door opened and Meriel walked in.

'Hi-de-hi-iii! I'm ho– oh, ah . . .' she said, and backed out, turned round and scuttled into the kitchen.

Winkler was stunned. 'Fuck,' he said. And immediately he didn't know which was worse: that his delicate, slender, strawberry-blonde flatmate had seen his dick, or that his wank was spoiled. Piling his reproductive organs – tubes and stopcocks, reservoirs and pumps – back into his clothes, he went straight for the kitchen, pausing on the way to fasten the top of his three-quarters hardened penis into the waistband of his pants and then lift the waist of his shorts over that and secure it firmly, so as to avoid any telltale pokey-pants. Best to behave as if nothing – or almost nothing – had happened.

'Hi, Meriel. Didn't hear you come in.' (She shuts the door and climbs so quietly. Creepily.)

'No. Well. Hey-ho. Where are the others?' She wasn't looking at him. She was turned towards the wall and was unpacking a blue plastic bag: carrots, supermarket-brand spring water, double-sided pot-scouring sponges, three for the price of two, and some violet-coloured bath foam.

'Will went west to see Rupert Fuckwit-Bandycock. No idea where Mary went. She was in a strop. Probably gone out drinking.'

'I dare say. Probably back in a minute.'

'Yeah, probably.'

Winkler had a thought. The way his hand had been when she came in – cupping his balls and moving the shorts – it was possible that she hadn't actually seen his dick and it's semi-preparedness for whatever his troubled imagination was about to throw up. He had not been caught mid-wank. There were other interpretations. Difficult ones to breach with a girl like Meriel, but better than the idea that she had caught a man in the act of gratifying himself – an act for which, in Meriel's personal moral universe, men almost certainly went to hell. He couldn't just let it lie.

'Sorry you caught me scratching my balls in there,' he said.

Meriel's head, which had been pointing downwards at the hob, where she had put the groceries, lifted.

'I didn't hear you come in and, you know, it's a bit embarrassing but . . .'

Meriel was motionless.

'. . . but if a chap can't scratch his goolies in his own front room when he thinks there's nobody home, then where can he scratch them, eh?'

Meriel spun round with a big smile on her face, showing her perfect, though large, white teeth. Her cheeks were rosy with suddenly blushing. Her whole face was rosy.

'Oh, Wink,' she said. 'Don't be silly. I thought you were . . . well, anyway, there you go. I'll knock in future.'

The relief, visible in all that frantically pumped faceblood, that she had not interrupted a great hairy beast of a man in the act of replicating the sin of Onan (well, not replicating as such, but, rather, improving upon), was pathetic.

'So George and Julian are off gallivanting,' she said eventually, when the food was unpacked and Winkler was still in the doorway, making it impossible for her to leave the room without passing within inches of his penis. Which, in view of recent events, was unthinkable.

George and Julian were two characters from the *Famous Five*, the adventurous tomboy and the tall, grown-up boy with blond hair. Meriel saw the flatmates as The Famous Four, each of them modelled on the character he or she most closely resembled.

'Yup, they're gone.'

'So what are Anne and Dick going to . . . oh.' Meriel put her hand to her mouth and giggled. A giggle like a baby duck learning to quack.

'Dick, yeah.' Winkler laughed. It wasn't his fault. It was her game. She was Anne, obviously, the square one who wears an Alice band and makes the picnics, and he was Dick, the other boy. No major hilarious similarities. If Dick had been a depressed office flunky stirred to a desire for decisive action by the stories of an old Jewish war hero, now that would be funny.

There wasn't any Timmy the Dog. Winkler would not have a dog in the house. Dogs are for people with bowel problems who achieve vicarious relief by watching some hairy prosthesis shit onto a cold pavement every morning. Occasionally, when they all went for a walk together, which didn't really happen any more, a dog would come bounding up to greet them – some monstrous bear-like retriever trapped by the dumb incomprehension of human identity that comes with having momentarily lost sight of its owner in the pursuit of a stick – and Meriel would cry,

'Oh look, it's Timmy. Timmy! Timmy! Good boy. Hello, yessssss, yesssss. Who's a handsome boy? I'm Anne. Yes, Anne. And this is Julian, Dick and George. Say hello.'

Quite often, the dog would then bark, which excited Meriel more than she could bear, and she'd say, 'Look, Timmy's trying to tell us something.'

And Mary would say, 'Jaysus Christ alive,' and strike out on her own in another direction, looking for alcohol.

Winkler would say, when the dog was safely back with its owner, 'I hope you're going to wash your hands before you make lunch.' And Will would put his arm round Meriel, all flushed with excitement, fresh air and dog-love, and tell her that they would soon have a woof of their own, yes, and keep all the puppies.

There would be no point at all in discussing the Wallenstein-Holocaust thing with this woman.

'I don't know,' said Winkler, still in the kitchen doorway. 'What does Anne usually do with Dick?'

'Well, she's very rarely alone with him.'

'Is she fond of Dick?'

'Oh yes, very.'

'You could say that she loves Dick?'

'Of course. They all do. But Anne loves Dick more than anyone.'

Fuck me, Winkler thought, she is utterly without a clue. And he felt the swelling of his balls again, just from tricking Meriel into talking about his penis.

'Does she like to grab hold of Dick and really yank?'

'What?'

Oops. A double-entendre too far.

'Nothing. Do you want a drink?'

'Ooh, rather. Let's finish that rosé.'

This was good. They went up onto the roof with the bottle and glasses and sat on the wall in the last of the afternoon sun. They drank two glasses each, and then the bottle was empty.

Winkler thought he'd get the other bottle. With two glasses inside him Meriel looked a lot better than usual. She was quite tall, after all, with long legs. She couldn't help having a nice, high arse. A change from Mary's old kit-bag, which remained stubbornly sitting on the bed when she got up to go for a post-coital piss, only finally sliding off the mattress and waddling irritably after its mistress some time after the rest of her had gone. The Cheshire arse.

And Meriel's neck was nice, too – long, and in the windowed sunlight lightly downed with light brown hair. From behind, she'd be quite a thing. He'd get the other bottle. They'd drink it and play a game of chess. He would lose, which was not possible under normal circumstances, and it would excite Meriel. They'd order a takeaway and Winkler would pick up a video. They would sit on the sofa together, the smelly, grey, recti-linear, foam-filled sofa, and drink champagne. They had never spent an evening together before. It was unmapped territory. Maybe there was something there that could be dug up with enough wine. He'd press his thigh against hers. She wouldn't move. Gradually, the occasional half-wriggle would end with a new bit of leg or arm touching. They might accidentally look at each other. Kiss. And then . . . whamola! The step

from kiss to cock-in-her-mouth was a very short one among friends. The
kiss was the barrier. Pass that and intimacy is accepted. No more courtship
is necessary. He was only hours, he felt, from letting go of three days'
worth of frustrated semen down Meriel's swan-like throat.

'I'll get the other bottle,' he said. 'And maybe we'll get a takeaway or
something.'

'Sorry. Can't. I'm going to my parents' tonight. Mummy's cooking fish
pie.'

Mummy?

'I thought you asked what Dick and Anne were going to do?'

'Yes, but that's just the game. You know, George and Julian go adven-
turing and Anne and Dick are left to keep watch on the camp.'

'Yes, but we're not. You're going out.'

'Well, I am. Yes. But we've played camp now.'

'Have we?'

'Mm hm. And I'd better get my skates on. I promised Mummy and
Daddy I'd be there by half-past-seven.'

'Oh, well. Fine. I'll just stay here on my own all night, then.'

'Ah. Sorry.' Anne thought for a moment. Winkler could hear the cogs
grinding. 'I'm sure you could come and have supper with us. Mummy
always makes lashings. Shall I phone and see?'

'No thanks, Meriel,' said Winkler. 'That's sweet of you. I'll be fine.'

Meriel picked up the bottle and the glasses and crossed the tarmac
roof, from which the sun had now gone. As she climbed in through the
window Winkler very briefly saw her knickers and the taut tendon inside
her right thigh.

He stood up on the roof. He curled his toes around the edge of the
tarmac, which was hot and gritty and green with moss. He thought what
a two-faced Irish cunt Mulligan was for saying he would put a railing round
the roof and 'fancy it up all nice, like,' and then doing fuck all except harass
the old man in the basement. He thought of the stamps the old man saved
all through the War. He thought of the little girl's arm. Wallenstein's sister.
The boy he had to kill because he got drunk. His plans for Meriel.

The cracked terrace down below, no more than a clearing in the violent
forest of high, sticky weeds and thistles, looked a long way down. Just like
that he could dive, and . . . blam!

'Bye, then,' said Meriel from the window. She had tied her mousy hair
back with a green twist of towelled elastic. 'Be good.'

'Yup. Right. Have a nice time. Love to your folks.'

Winkler went inside and switched on the television.

What the People on the Tube Thought
About It

Winkler did not sleep well. Mary did not come home. Wallenstein would not leave him alone. Not the spade-wielding Wallenstein of 1944 nor the old and crooked Wallenstein three floors below, shuffling around his flat with blood on his hands. When Winkler slept he dreamt of the Polish girl and the boy called Chlop and the mutilated Nazi captive shot by his comrade and the child shoved into the gas chamber with a rifle butt jab to the hip. When he didn't sleep he rolled and sweated and thought of them again.

And then he thought of his own life. Its close boundaries, its inevitable repetitions, its same old smells, its dull horrors. Wallenstein woke up some mornings in the ghetto happier than others, surely? And people in Auschwitz, too. Once every day is the same, looks the same, plays out the same, then you settle again into the ups and downs. And if some days you wake feeling better than others then that means that even in Auschwitz there was a sort of happiness. Like there sometimes is in Winkler's life.

It's all relative, Winkler thought, lying there, not sleeping, thinking of Wallenstein's heart and how it must have raced when Issy's brother didn't want to let him in the truck. Good days and bad days. Emotions are only how you respond to experience and their extremes are guided only by what you know. Winkler's miseries were suffered as painfully as Wallenstein's. As anyone's who'd suffered in the Holocaust. He was as unhappy as any Jew has ever been.

As soon as there was light, about six, he got up. He wanted to be dressed and up and outside and to leave the horrors of the house, all the horrors of the house, behind. His nightmares couldn't follow him to work.

They couldn't even follow him to the train, there were too many other nightmares there already. No room.

In the street, birds whistled. The sun occupied an unfamiliar place in the sky and its rays broke full on the front door. When Winkler opened it he found himself bathed in light and in fresh, green morning warmth. He sniffed at the pollen.

Down the hill and under the road, Winkler bought his ticket at the ticket office window, not at the machine. He felt like purchasing it from a person.

The small, oddly-shaped man took Winkler's money from the metal trough under the bullet-proof Perspex window and then slid a ticket into the trough down a curved tube (a little grey helter-skelter) and slid his change into the trough down another.

'Thank you!' roared Winkler, more grateful than the ticket vendor had ever heard a man for his morning ticket.

Turning, Winkler realised that the man had been missing an arm. Initially, morning-slow, Winkler had not noticed. He paid, he focused on coins and tickets, and, briefly, the fellow's weak-chinned, bespectacled face. Now, with time on the way to the turnstile to reflect on the ticket office tableau now splashed on his still pretty vacant mind, he saw that there was an arm missing from it.

He turned, glanced, saw a short stump ending in a forked flesh claw, shuddered. And as he shuddered he caught the eye of the stump-owner, glancing up from a transaction.

Did he see Winkler shudder? Or guess why he shuddered? He meant nothing by it. It was just like the thing with dog shit. There were some things that, moments after he had looked at them, sent a shiver through him. Dog shit mostly. Also very sick people. And sometimes heights. This morning, because he felt sick and tired and unslept, the shudder came with a little bile, bubbling up at the back of his throat like in a coffee percolator, but subsiding again and leaving only an acid tang above the toothpaste smell on his breath.

At this early hour there were far more travellers (vampires fleeing the sun to the death-darkness of their office-coffins) than at Winkler's usual time, and they were rather less repulsive. They were slimmer, better dressed, quieter, less ethnically adventurous, far fewer women, purposeful, focused, industrious, clean – this was a mass of common humanity among whom Winkler felt he could come to feel almost at home. More so than the noonday crowd which wobbled with unrestrained obesity, heaving its flaccid flesh into skin of a thousand hues, wheeling its carbuncular young in trolleys; arse, paps and dangling cunts in greyed jogging pants and defeated tops. This marching colony of workers had order, integrity, logic.

At the bottom of the escalator, by the wall, lay three drunks, unconscious, with their dirty faces flush on the filthy floor, clutching polystyrene cups empty of coppers. The human volume was thicker-flowing at the bottom and wound out in space-seeking tentacles to fill all the gaps and crevices. They had to step over the bodies of the tramps, there was no other way.

On the platform itself the mass seethed. It had seemed a calm traffic in the descent. But any gap of more than a minute or two between trains meant a build up of souls with which the narrow shelf by the track could not cope, and the build-up teemed and teetered on the edge.

Then in the tunnel the distant murmur of the train, beginning as a whisper that held the attention of those nearest the entrance.

As the whisper rose to a growl and then a vast, open-throated roar of imminence the crowd shrank back from the edge, to reveal the bright yellow 'Do Not Cross This Line' line. Winkler was thrilled by their obedience.

The doors opened, the train filled, the platform emptied, the train was gone. And Winkler was alone on the empty ledge which curved away round the corner and out of sight. A pavement cleared of pedestrians in an instant. Nothing but the now-revealed bodies of half-a-dozen sleeping vagrants. And station guards in uniforms kicking them gently to see if they were alive.

'THE NEXT TRAIN AT PLATFORM ONE IS THE . . .'

Winkler started. Alone on the suddenly cleared platform, alone except for the heaped bodies and the guards, he missed the instructions that came over the tannoy. All he heard was the officious bark. And looking up he saw the double speakers, pointing away from each other, up and down the platform.

In no time the platform was full again. Winkler pushed himself into the next train, hot and cramped, and down through the tunnel it rocketed with Winkler inside – hungry (alone and angry and sick with self-pity he had not bothered to feed himself last night) and thirsty and uncomfortable, desperate to sit down, held upright by living flesh, fat and bone, desperate to get off, unable to get off.

At Central Station, Winkler, to change lines, had to join successive fast-moving lines of people.

Sometimes so many rushing, rushing, that to stop moving – even this was dangerous.

One line swerved violently right down a corridor where a sign said, 'Escalator out of order. Use stairs to Platform Three southbound.'

Everywhere was notices with orders, posters telling us where to be and what to do and, more often, what not to do.

Winkler noticed how dark it was.

The darkness, oh, the darkness you cannot imagine.

And how bleak, how grey, how strangely lacking in the line-breaking landscape features that make the mere act of looking a pleasure and more than just a rushing and necessary hypnosis.

It was everywhere nothing green. No trees, no bushes, even weeds it was uprooted immediately for soups and teas.

Descending at a military skip the spiral stairs with hundreds of others, Winkler regretted his leather-soled shoes which occasionally slid on the floor and might, hustled by this democratically determined optimum pace, lead him into a slip, trip, stumble and broken neck.

To fall in the line of prisoners was not tolerated. Only bang! Such a kapo if you stay more than a few seconds on the ground shoots you your head and that is it for you. All finished. So.

A child brushed past him with a melting choc ice in its little red hand and chocolate round its mouth. A thin, pale, green-faced man in a shabby suit rootled in his outside jacket pocket and Winkler saw the lips of a packet of crisps gasping for air as he choked it, searching for salt and crumbs. The lips were pink. Prawn cocktail. Winkler thought of the Jew and his apple the day before. Couldn't they wait? Did they have to consume so desperately even as they marched? Was storage such a risk?

Then again, Winkler was starving. He had not had breakfast – he only woke up hungry if he had eaten a lot the night before, but he had eaten, remember, nothing at all. Now, suddenly, the thought of all that tingly salt on his tongue and the mouth-filling potato starch . . . On the plat-form Winkler saw a vending machine. Sugar, even better.

In his pocket he felt with some satisfaction a single coin, which was enough for something sweet. He had never before looked for food on the Underground. He dropped his coin in the slot and tapped out his alphanumeric selection. And he thumped the side of the machine when nothing dropped into the tray for him to eat. The thump of a chim-panzee, furious at an arbitrary change of lab rules that is keeping him from his banana.

He kicked at the machine, stepped back and kicked it high, twice, and again. He swore at it and pummelled its lid. People shrank back from the fight and stared. Winkler looked at them and was revolted.

'It fucking robbed me!' he said to them. 'They always rob people, these things. They've been robbing people for years. And we do nothing. If we all tore them down. If we all acted together they'd have to do something.'

He saw through the crowd the peaked cap of a guard picking his way towards the commotion. He ducked through an arch onto another platform and tried to bustle through this new crowd, but they did not want to let him past.

Searching the walls for an exit, Winkler saw the boy with the choc-ice again. He reached out and grabbed the food from the boy's tiny hand and, in an instant, crammed it in his mouth, tearing the remaining wrappings from it as he pushed it in.

The chocolate was thick and sickly and so full of sugar that he could feel the grains of it jostling in the gooey mouthful.

The boy stopped, stunned, and stared at his empty hand, but his mother was already dragging him away into the crowd as he started to cry, so Winkler didn't hear the screaming begin. And if he could not hear the screaming he would probably survive the guilt.

He wiped his lips on the back of his forearm and was surprised to see a wet brown smear on his white sleeve. Looking at his arm, he noticed also that his armpits had sweated out into his shirt from the heat of the morning.

He broke off from the crocodile of contained panic into the man-jam of the monorail platform. The glass train joined him there, rushing in just as he did, and he wondered if the only thing to do was to charge in a diagonal line towards it as it came, scooping ten, fifteen, maybe even more people into its path and diving after them – one huge gesture of resist-ance to the forces that enslaved him, chained him, and made him angry, dirty and wet. Or just to shuffle towards it as it slowed.

In general, Winkler considered himself a policeman of politeness, ensuring that, at his door at least, the proper decorum was observed, that those waiting to board kept back, allowing free egress to disembarkers, that elderly people, especially women, were helped onto the train, and that able-bodied men under sixty-five did not take a seat as long as anybody outside that category was left standing.

Today, though, damp and smeared and desperate, he pushed up into the fleshpressed wagon through the disembarking dozens. Two or three tutted as he passed and Winkler stood on tiptoe to turn back and shout over surprised heads, 'Yeah, what? Fucking what? Fucking tut at me, you wanker!'

Seeing a vacant seat, he drove hard through the mass and, arriving just ahead of a crooked old man with huge ears and a bald yellow head spattered with liver spots, smartly pressed old brown suit and big, thick, square Reactolite (probably post-cataract) glasses, flopped into it heavily.

He was stared at disapprovingly, but silently. The old man clung shakily to a chrome pole as the train took off.

'What are you muttering about?' Winkler said, randomly, to a woman next to him who immediately looked down at her newspaper.

Winkler stared around the carriage, his eyes slashing wildly from side to side like a torchbeam looking for something in a forest, fixing people with his eyes who would meet his stare bravely, momentarily, and then look away. He looked at the old man, standing. About Wallenstein's age. But not Jewish. Very possibly German. And thought, who knows what this old bastard did in the War?

People continued to stare. At what? Winkler saw himself briefly as he imagined he looked to them, a cornered wolf, slight and bloody-fanged and snarling, eyes red and wide and terrible, panting – and thought of his childhood, when he feared wolves more than anything and would curl the sheets around under his toes so that none of him was poking out, and how he hoped that the big hunter in the bearskin hat (like the bearskin hat on the guard at the palace where Christopher Robin went down with Alice) and the big red coat with a wide black belt and a big brass buckle (like Father Christmas when he came and knocked at the door because the flat didn't have a chimney, and was sent away by Grandpa because Christmas we don't celebrate) would come with his long, long musket, horned at the end like a trumpet, out of the medieval forest, out of the German fairytales, down from the mountain and

Blam!

The train shot out into the light. The city spread wide around them. The black hole of the tunnel was sucked back under the city. The train, full of light, climbed over the roofs and Winkler saw the old man clinging to the rail.

'Sorry,' he said. His voice sounding dry and foreign. 'I didn't see you there.'

He stood up, and the people standing near shrank back. The old man sat. The sky arced huge and blue overhead, down alongside and then under them, tucking itself in, under their toes, and the Emerald City loomed, and the old town smoked quietly in the sun.

The train slowed into the station. Winkler squeezed off with the thin flow of anxious disembarkers trickling like a summer stream between the rocks and boulders of immovable commuters, holding position, straphanging, glancing greedily at the fabric of vacated seats as arses, cleared for lift off, rose to go.

He stood on the platform, stared down the track which shimmered and wobbled in the sun, while the other disembarkers descended to the street, fanned out, slid apart into the weave of streets, until they were absorbed by the city, and soon forgot about Winkler.

And Winkler descended too. And saw the puddle, no more than a patch of sweat on the pavement, perhaps visible only to him. He squatted and stared hard – no, it was there. It was.

It was hot in Warschau at this time like you cannot imagine. There was not water to go round except from ditches and drains and a puddle sometimes in a dark place of moisture you didn't know what. And to drink this was straight away cholera and so it is finished for you just the same. But anyway people drank such a water, not to suffer the thirst.

And why not drink it? Why not get cholera? How bad can it be? You shit and die. That's life.

From his squat Winkler dropped onto one knee and put his hand towards the middle of the moist concrete. He drew it back and looked around him and then dropped the other knee, felt gritty ground on his palms, leaned towards the puddle with his tongue hanging, wondering how bad, how bad . . . and then a car klaxonned loudly and he rose. The driver stroked an imaginary penis in the air with his fist, luxuriously, and asked him what his problem was.

Winkler walked on through the valley of the shadow of death and found himself not at all afraid of the massed hordes of wiry immigrants.

Perched on the corner road-barrier by the zebra, all but charging a toll to cross, were the half-shirted crow-boys with their golden Arabic injunctions to holy war glinting on bare breastplates, and Winkler looked at them and they looked at him and he carried on looking at them and two of them hopped down from the rail and paced like caged things, rolling-shouldered.

'Morning, boys!' said Winkler airily, and thought, 'They might stab me now. For that? No. They're just kids bunking school in the sunshine.'

But they didn't reply to his greeting and so he said, 'Shalom aleichem to you all.' And they looked at each other. And Winkler wondered whether they thought he had said 'Salaam aleikum' and whether, in their ears, that would be better or worse.

And if they stabbed him they stabbed him. They were small. Fuck it, he'd take a couple of them down with him. And if they stabbed him then he wouldn't have to go to work.

But the young immigrants only bristled and glared and made clicking noises with their teeth. And five minutes later Winkler was at his desk.

What the Office
Thought About It

Malcolm Pritchard, a freelance troubleshooter of about Winkler's age who came into the office only very occasionally, was sitting in Winkler's chair and talking to Sherwood Glaub when Winkler rounded his corner.

Pritchard's hands were wide apart, gesturing, and he was firing little salvoes of half-laughter in advance of the next part of the anecdote he was in the middle of telling, during which he had recently paused, the better to enjoy what he was about to say. This was no wild guess on Winkler's part. For Pritchard spoke only in anecdotes. Long, slow, heroic anecdotes that delayed their denouement as selfishly as Scheherezade herself. Though not for the same reasons.

Convinced of his own brilliance as a raconteur and of the fascination his life story held for his fellow man, Pritchard's technique was to digress and digress, introducing numerous sub-anecdotes from the vast volumes of the hulking *roman fleuve* of his life which (he even acknowledged) you might have heard before but would no doubt wish to relate temporally and thematically to this one.

These digressions might relate to men whom he had nearly killed before common sense got the better of him (he regularly forbore, when touched by pity, from slaying giants), women he had pleasured, lands he had travelled, languages he had mastered, towns he had charmed, cities he had tamed, compliments he had garnered, theories he had derived and philosophies rejected, humbug he had scorned, fraudulence he had punished, meekness he had mocked, pomposity he had pricked, dissimulation he had penetrated, barriers crossed, bounty he had conferred, witticisms with which he had reduced whole streets to smoking rubble. The trail of cultural and carnal conquest that shimmered in his wake was almost certainly, like the Great Wall of China, visible from Space. To be alive on this earth, ran the moral of *La Comédie Pritchardienne*, and not to be Malcolm Pritchard, was to be a small and senseless thing, and to have only oneself to blame.

Malcolm Pritchard spoke in slow, muddy, murderous torrents of words that dried up occasionally in the flow, the gaps to be filled with winks and nods and laughs while he gathered his tongue for further action. If you tried to speak into this slow trickle of oral fudge then whatever you said reminded him of something that he too had seen, done, or experienced, that was considerably more authentic, amusing and archetypal (he introduced many of his exploits as 'archetypal', saying 'this was the stuff of pure archetype', as if to emphasise that it was he – in this modern age – who set the experiential paradigms for poor imitators such as Winkler hopelessly to pursue).

Pritchard, whose apparently bottomless reserve of inherited wealth meant that he worked only occasionally for 'beer money', appeared to despise the office regulars (and these included Winkler, of course) for the greed and lack of self-respect that allowed them to be shackled by the bourgeois restraints of formal employment. And they, unaware of the contempt in which he held them, seemed genuinely interested in the continuous oral epic of Pritchard's experience.

Winkler, on the other hand, was physically sickened by every word, wink and ear-waggle of it. When Pritchard spoke at him Winkler treated the passing moments as time that could be spent arranging in his mind things that needed doing over the next few days.

So while Pritchard related again the story of how he had saved two girls from a rapist in Buenos Aires only for them to turn out to be transvestites who took him to a nightclub where he danced on stage and won a prize because he had natural Latin rhythm (despite his blood being a hundred per cent Aryan – unmongreled in 1,000 years) and ended up going home with Kylie Minogue but not actually having sex with her because when she saw his cock she said she was scared of being entered by something that big but went to suck him off only to be told that he wasn't going to be told what to do by some skinny Australian bint and left and went to a brothel, a bit like, funnily enough, the one in Lisbon where he once . . . Winkler would be costing out in his head the bill for the week's groceries, reminding himself to get his bicycle fixed, planning a letter to the bank, running through the logistics of chucking it all in and moving to Cuba, wondering whether, if he now dropped his pants, turned, squatted and shat on one of Pritchard's (handmade) beige suede loafers the fucker would even notice.

And Pritchard was none the wiser because Pritchard appeared to believe that when he opened his mouth time stood still. He assumed that nobody else had anything better to do than listen. Real minutes – during which his audience might otherwise be getting work done, speaking to spouses on the phone, watching television, shopping, sleeping, talking to each other – were not, as far as he was concerned, passing.

And so they remained friends. For without this ability of Winkler's to absent himself mentally from Pritchard's presence he would by now, if he had not actually stabbed him in the eye with a letter-opener (a blow Pritchard would have parried using the yow-kwun blocking manoeuvre favoured by experts in the little known Hunanese martial art of Spling-Chee, taught to him by a trio of large-breasted Tibetan Zen mistresses who worshipped him as a God after he saved their village from a flood), then at least have said something irreparably damaging.

'What ho, Sher!' said Winkler, disguising the terrors of the morning with false jollity and even enjoying the act of interrupting Pritchard enough to feel almost cheery. 'Ho, Malcolm!'

'Heavens, Wink,' said Sherwood Glaub. 'What are you doing in so early? You . . . you look really awful.'

'You think he looks terrible?' laughed Malcolm Pritchard. 'You should have seen me at seven o'clock this morning . . .' and he laughed. And paused. And winked. 'It was a fucking archetypal hangover. But not just any hangover. A grappa hangover. I was in this Genoese restaurant until four in the morning, the owner just wouldn't let me leave, it's probably the best place in England for Olioracao, which is a kind of liqueur that you only see in . . .'

And as Glaub listened Winkler decided that he would begin the Werther Report today, and worked out in his mind how he would do it, and imagined the relief he would feel when it was over and he could forget about it forever. And meanwhile poor Sherwood Glaub heard about the great three-week absinthe hangover of '94, during which Pritchard learnt that the only true cure for a hangover was a blow job delivered by an East African woman who had previously filled your arse with a silk handkerchief moistened in oil, only to whip it out sharply at the moment of orgasm, prior to feeding you a pint of warm saline solution from a traditional Bantu gourd.

Pause. Wink. Stare. Laugh. Lip-purse. Nod. Stare. Laugh.

Only, this morning Pritchard didn't have time to find a black woman

before work so he made his archetypal hangover cure, which nobody
knew about apart from him, which involved blending raw pig's liver in
a Moulinex – pause, pause, eyebrow raise, half-laugh – and then floating
a raw duck egg on top, lots of Tabasco and downing it in one . . .

'Christ, Sherwood. You don't actually believe that he drinks that, do
you?' Winkler thought.

So many times Winkler had challenged Pritchard to prepare and drink
one of his preposterous hangover cures in public. So many excuses. So
many cries of, 'No need. You call this is a hangover? I once had a hangover where . . .' Winkler was certain this was an area where Pritchard's
fraudulence could be exposed. But Pritchard always wriggled out of it.

Most recently he had done it by saying loudly, in front of two girls
whom Winkler had only just met, 'You can't drink the miracle elixir –
you're Jewish!'

And so there followed the usual conversation with the girls:

'I didn't know you were Jewish.'

'You've only known me for an hour and a half.'

'Well, you didn't say anything.'

'Of course not.'

'Now you say it I can see it, though.'

'See what?'

'That you look Jewish.'

That would always make Winkler sigh, involuntarily.

And Pritchard, on that tiny provocation, would begin needling with
the little phrases he reserved for these 'Winkler is a Jew' conversations:
'Don't be so sensitive, Wink', 'stop fussing', 'don't be such an old woman',
'don't overreact', 'don't get so easily wound up' – all of which meant
'Don't be such a Jew.'

And when he was finished Winkler would protest that he was not, in
fact, a Jew, at which point somebody, usually a girl, would say,

'Are you circumcised?'

If you're a Jew it is always okay for people to talk about your dick
within minutes of meeting you.

'Course he is.' Pritchard would say.

'Did it hurt?' the girl would ask.

'They do it when they're babies,' Pritchard would interrupt. 'He doesn't
even remember it. Christ, if they came near me with a fucking knife
trying to take the end off my dick I'd fucking . . .' Pause. Pause. Wink.
Pause. Laughter all round. Almost all round.

And you can bet that if, for any reason, Pritchard had been circumcised, it would have been the best circumcision ever done, performed by the revered Mohel of Vronsk in his very prime as a fleshcutter, who, when he had finished the now famous 'Pritchard Job' – to gasps of admiration from the gathered throng – declared it the perfect cut and retired on the spot. Men who saw it in locker rooms would have recognised it from photographs in the Guggenheim . . .

But he wasn't. So the whole procedure was disgusting. Circumcised men didn't get as much pleasure from blow jobs because of the permanent exposure of the glans. Pritchard once had a blow job from a dancer in Balukistan which . . .

And after all this, Winkler, desperate to expose the Pritchard hangover cure lie, said, 'Yes, well, look, this is all very interesting but I'm not kosher. I eat pork. I'm not the sort of Jew that doesn't. So let's all drink your pig liver miracle, shall we?'

'No I couldn't, Wink. I'd feel like I'd bullied you into it. It would be wrong. It would be disrespectful to your culture.'

Nobody respected other people's cultural peculiarities more than Malcolm Pritchard. Nobody. There was a time when he was standing second in the main competition at the Oatapaka cliff-diving festival when he realised that discretion was the better part of valour and allowed the local favourite, Pedro Hojito Cojones, the Aztec champion and later, of course, his own blood brother, to . . . And the tales of Pritchard's Mexican adventures steam-rollered the pig's liver issue once again.

Now, today, this day of difficulty for Winkler, dreaming of the Ghetto and altogether lost and adrift in his own world, the nine minute anthology of Pritchard's past hangovers over, he looked up at Sherwood Glaub, as if time had not passed and said,

'Do I? I wasn't drinking last night. Couple of glasses of rosé and an early night.'

Pritchard, who was pacing around their part of the office with his thick, hairy calves growing like inverted cactuses down from the twin pots of his Bermuda shorts into assault sandals that showed his gnarled yellow toenails and hairless feet, and wearing on his top half a pale pink monogrammed poplin shirt, ironed to a razor edge, did not think much of rosé.

To avoid hearing again about the vineyard in suburban Tripoli where Pritchard, who was dining with the owner, drank six bottles of the only decent rosé bottled since the War (an archetypal rosé, in fact), Winkler went on quickly to say,

'But I had a bit of a freaky tube journey and . . .'

Malcolm Pritchard did not think much of the tube. He never took it. He took taxis. But he always ended up having to direct them because they never knew the quickest route. And then they overcharged. If they did that he refused to pay. If they gave him any lip then he told them to get out of the cab and say it to his face. Once, in Bangkok . . .

'Yes, well, I got the tube and it was really packed and something very strange happened.'

'What?' said Sherwood Glaub. Pritchard had found nail-clippers and was clipping his fingernails to kill time while they spoke about something in which he had no interest.

'I don't know exactly what happened. But last night I met this old bloke who lives under the stairs —'

'Very Victorian.'

'And it turned out he's a survivor.'

'Oh, we're all survivors, ducky.'

'No, idiot. A Survivor, you know.'

'What did he survive?'

'The Holocaust. They're just called "survivors".'

'By each other, maybe,' said Sherwood Glaub. 'So you met a Holocaust survivor who lives under the stairs and you're feeling depressed about the shoes and the soap?'

'You know about the shoes and the soap?'

'Everyone knows about the shoes and the soap.'

'I suppose. But it's not only that. You know, the poor fucker, he's been living in that manky room on his own since 1947. More than fifty years. His whole family blown away, the lot of them. His home gone. Everyone who was ever there, gone. The whole world gone. Man. I mean fucking nothing and nobody. And he saw all this terrible, terrible shit.'

'With the soap and the shoes and the babies' heads . . .'

'You know about the heads, too?'

'And the showers and the roll-calls and the clearings in the forest and the quicklime and the shovels and the lampshades and the clogs and the spoons and the arses . . .'

'The arses?'

'One of Mengele's tests in the roll-calls. File past the Herr Doktor and if there's no arse, straight to the gas.'

'No arse?'

'No good for work.'

'You would bring it down to arses.'

'It wasn't me, it was Mengele. They killed poofs too, you know.'

'I suppose.'

'Well then.'

'But poofs had a choice. Not like Jews. The option was always there to not be a poof.'

'Another debate altogether . . .'

'Either way. He wasn't in the camps.'

'Mengele, Shmengele,' said Malcolm Pritchard.

'Eh?'

'Mengele Shmengele. Every bloody Holocaust survivor,' and he raised two pairs of twitching rabbit ears to indicate inverted commas before the 'H' and after the 'r', 'claims he met Mengele. Mengele is always there in the bloody story somewhere, miraculously glancing the other way as they file past, thinking that the bloke must be Aryan because he has lighter hair, or recognising him from a favour he did him in Berlin years before. I tell you. It's archetypal. They can't all have met him. How many can he have met? He must have shaken more hands than the Queen. If you ask me . . .'

'He didn't shake their hands.'

'. . . urban myth. Ran to Argentina, my arse. It was Columbia. There's this little bistro in Bogotá where I . . .'

'Anyway, Sher, the fact is I got cornered by this bloke and he just desperately wanted to talk. He's obviously very lonely.'

'Obviously.'

'I think survivors often don't talk about it. Maybe he had finally decided to, before he died. And maybe I was the only one possible. I just felt I really ought to sit there and listen for him.'

'Winkler the Good Samaritan. Who'd have thought?'

'. . . then, when the clay is baked hard, they split it with an axe and eat the flesh of the hedgehog right from the split halves. Most people would probably find it too challenging to their Little England upbringing, but I . . .'

'No, it was interesting though. He was in the ghetto and then fought in the forest afterwards and in the Uprising, and even liberated one of the camps. I forget which one. And then afterwards he, well. It's terrible. And he had to kill loads of people. Dozens. Hundreds.'

'Hundreds?'

'Women and children, too.'

'What a terrible bastard to have living under the stairs.'

'No, no. He had to. Shit. It was another world. They were fenced in for months without any water. Fucking eating cats and dogs and crapping themselves to death from dysentery . . .'

'. . . and by the time they finally brought me to this old man I was pretty fed up. But the moment I saw him I knew he was SS. You can tell these things if you've been around a bit. Probably an *obergruppenführer*. Over eighty-five, but still with that gleam in his eye. Archetypal SS. I was in Berlin last year, as you know, researching for a major motion picture – of course I can't tell you the director's name, it's still in development – and I was given access to a vault under the Reichstag which nobody had . . .'

'Still. It's not news, is it, all that? It's terrible, but we know about it. It's nothing new.'

'Yes, but. I don't know. It just was driven home to me how very fucking terrible it all was. So blatantly the worst thing ever. We can't just go on as if it never happened. The Germans got away with it completely, that's all. And the Catholics. And the French. And the Poles and all the cunty little Baltic republics. And poor old Wallenstein never had shit but some piddly pension. No real reparations. The Krauts should have been bled dry.'

'. . . and I knew that Mossad were still paying big shekels for a Nazi head. Even small fry. I'm not saying it's right. I mean, for fuck's sake, the Jews should get over it. It was sixty bloody years ago. But money is money, so . . .'

'Bleeding the Krauts dry after the First World War was what started the Holocaust in the first place.'

'Oh bollocks. Crap. Fucking rubbish and you know it. It was anti-Semitism, pure and simple. The fucking Krauts, the Russians, the Czechs, the Austrians, French, Romanians, Poles, Ukrainians, the fucking Pope. Fucking everyone. And Britain, too. Don't forget. Silent on it. Not bombing the rail lines to the camps. Not giving a shit. Sniggering. That cunt Edward VIII and the cunting aristocracy and the cunt Churchill. They knew. They knew. And if it happened here they'd be the fucking first in line spooning the fucking fat back on the flaming heap to help it burn.'

'. . . of course, the bodyguards were big and heavily armed, but when they saw how I dealt with the first two, snapping their . . .'

'Jesus Christ, Malcolm!' cried Winkler, turning to Pritchard, who was chuckling at the ease with which he had dispatched the beefy Columbian bouncers. 'What the fuck are you going on about?'

'I was saying about that Nazi war criminal I nearly brought in.'

'Winkler was just saying how he'd spent last night chatting to an old man who was in the ghetto and lost his family and his home,' said Sherwood Glaub. 'You know Winkler. Sensitive old soul. He's a bit upset by it, Malc, you see.'

'Well he should get a grip. I don't see how it's his problem.'

'It's everyone's fucking problem, Malcolm,' said Winkler.

'Oh Christ save us,' muttered Pritchard, low. 'Not another Holocaust bore.'

'Holocaust bore? Holocaust *bore*? Jesus. From you? How dare you be bored by the Holocaust? How dare you? And how, Jesus, how dare you call anybody, anyone or anything on the face of God's earth boring? You? You of all people? You? You? At least these Holocaust bores – whoever you imagine them to be – are boring only in a specific field. Unlike you, whose crippling boringness recognises no boundaries of time, space or subject matter. Or does that make you in some way a better bore? No doubt it does. You are the fucking Hercules of Boring. The Jesus and Mary, the Abraham, Isaac and Jacob of epic tediousness. You talk nothing but shit, shit, shit all fucking day and I can't fucking stand it anymore. I'm going home. Fucking Hell. Sherwood, where are those fucking Werther papers? I'll take them home and do it there. Fuck.'

Pritchard was standing in the middle of their corner of the office with his brow furrowed into a deep vertical crease. His lips were pursed and he picked at something on his chin.

Winkler gestured at Sherwood Glaub with a hurried, beckoning hand, demanding the papers be delivered quickly so that he could make his exit on the impassioned back of his last expletive. Obediently, Glaub dragged the Werther papers from their drawer, knocked them into a block and laid them on his desk with the coffee-crown on top and then slotted them into his own thin black briefcase with its gold clasp and extravagantly scripted 'S.G.' monogram.

While Glaub was making these quiet manoeuvres, Malcolm Pritchard gradually unfurled his forehead and then raised his eyebrows so high that his ears moved discernibly back along the side of his skull. He pulled at the wattle above his Adam's apple, looked at Sherwood Glaub and raised the eyebrows again, scratched his nose with his middle finger, looked at the ceiling with abstract curiosity and then walked slowly away across the office floor and out of sight.

'Bloody hell, Wink,' said Sherwood Glaub finally. 'What brought that on?'

'You heard him. You saw him. It was about fucking time.'

'Time?'

'To fucking take him down. He's a boring cunt.'

'Yes, but –'

'But, fuck. That's eight fucking years that's needed saying.' They both stared at the floor and thought of all the other things that had needed saying for eight years. Winkler shuddered. And thought of what would have happened if he had said them all. He'd be in prison. Or dead.

'I felt a bit sorry for him,' said Glaub. 'He's only trying to be interesting. He wants people to like him. He doesn't have any friends. I've never seen any of these girlfriends he claims to have. He probably makes it all up.'

'Probably?'

'Well, okay. But still. I bet he tells himself every night as he lies in bed that he must be less long-winded and less domineering so that he will be more popular. And then in the end he is so desperate to please that it all goes wrong. He's one of those people who just don't really understand why people like each other. He's never been able to make people like him and he knows that. He really likes you, Wink. And admires you, too. You overdid it a bit. He'll probably go to the loo now and stare at himself in the mirror. He won't cry. He'll feel like crying but he won't be able to. The poor little fellow.'

'Oh Sher, you daft poofter. Don't be silly. You heard him. The man's basically a Nazi.'

'No he's not. He doesn't know what he is. He wants to sound butch and intolerant, that's all. You don't need to tear him apart.'

'Well, I —'

'That was all terribly unmellow. He's just a bit of a twerp and you got all emotional about it.'

'Stop it, Sher. Don't tell me "emotional" — that's the sort of shit he pulls on me. Fucksake. Like everyone's in control of themselves and having a banter and I'm the emotional Jew who ruins everything by not being made of concrete.'

'And that's because you're a Jew?'

'Well, obviously.'

'And nobody else gets that sort of treatment?'

'No.'

'Nobody at all?'

'What are you talking about?'

'Not like, for example, me? Ooh, it's queero bender Glaub the weepy faggot who you mustn't upset because he can't handle it . . .'

'Mm. Well, yes, that's bad, too. But you heard him, "Holocaust bore"! The fucker.'

'Maybe it was a clumsy phrase, but you hear it. I read it in the *Daily*

Mail only the other day where Quentin Letts wrote it about an MP. Malcolm's only parroting a phrase that he thinks goes with his macho image.'

'He doesn't read the *Daily Mail*, remember. He only reads *Figaro* and *La Razon* and sometimes the *Economist*.'

'Wherever he heard it, I'm just saying that it's not a big fascist statement that makes him a Nazi. Some people aren't very interested in the Holocaust. I mean, Wink, until yesterday you weren't exactly –'

'They're not entitled not to be interested.'

'They are. It isn't really all that interesting. Once you've heard one story about it you've heard them all.'

'Bollocks.'

'Woo, I feel so guilty that I survived while millions died. It was a miracle: the *untersheissenstormer* took a liking to me and what with my fluent German and Aryan looks and my skills as a watchmaker . . .'

'I can't believe you're even saying this, Sherwood. What's your point? I mean, I doubt they were planning for future pub anecdotes to entertain you and Pritchard when they were having their fucking babies bayoneted.'

'I dare say not. I'm just saying that similar conditions applied in all the camps, and to all the Nazis and to all the Jews, so it's usually just the same old crap about . . .'

'It's not crap. It's the most gruesome . . .'

'Yes, yes, it's very gory. But that's really all, isn't it? People get a hard-on for the death-porn of it all. Trying to imagine a world that unlikely, is like the impossibility of porn film situations. That's what makes it so exciting. The girl in *Schindler's List*, the one Ralph Fiennes shoots from his balcony and she just falls over. One minute alive, doing her best to keep going, thinking something at the time, maybe about the misery or maybe about home or maybe about Goethe or Milton, and then pop, she keels over. It's got to give you a bit of a hard-on. Like the idea of dropping your pants and pooing when Millfield's talking to you, which you can't deny you think about all the time. Or like if Tommy the work experience boy caught me having a wank in the stationery cupboard, and . . .'

'Shut up, man. That's sick.'

'It's the unlikeliness. The incomprehensibility. The way in which the whole thing just won't fit in your head. Like if you were walking past some woman wheeling her pram on the road outside and a big articulated lorry was passing and you just rushed over and pushed her in front of it.'

What? What was the death-wish fat bitch doing in the imagination of Sherwood Glaub?

'. . . it's all about the excitement of things that are impossible to comprehend like screwing someone you're clearly never going to screw like Prince Andrew or Eminem . . .'

Winkler thought how many times he had felt an erection uncoil itself last night, in the old man's flat. With the half-beheaded Polish girl, the teenage German girl shot in the head, the knife execution of the drunk boy and the tears of the girl who tried to save him.

'Look Sherwood,' said Winkler, but then the phone rang. 'The point is that any opportunity' – ring, ring – 'for people like Malcolm Pritchard to display their' – ring, ring – '-ism without any comment or' – ring, ring – '. . . the end of . . .'

'Aren't you going to answer that?'

Winkler looked at the phone. It rang again. He picked it up and waited for it to say something.

'Hello?' it said.

'Hello, who's this?'

'It's me.'

'Who's "me"? Oh, shit. Grandpa.'

What Winkler's Grandfather
Thought About It

'"Oh shit, Grandpa", yes.'

'God. Sorry. I was supposed to be coming round.'

'Were you?'

'Yes, when we spoke yesterday morning I said . . . oh.'

'Oh, indeed.'

'She cooked, didn't she?'

'Coq au vin with dumplings and red cabbage. Your favourite.'

'But Grandpa, I said I wasn't hungry.'

'You said you were coming round. How do I know what to believe?'

'I'm sorry. I'm sorry. I had a very strange afternoon. I was coming. I was. I was on the train. On my way to see you. I even picked up a sachertorte for you, from Wilkomirsky's, the one with the white chocolate on one side that you like –'

What a strange lie to throw in. What a funny fib to pepper the apology with.

'– And I was holding it in my lap on the train. I was a bit worried that it might melt because it gets so hot down there.'

'If you had looked after that car . . .'

'Yes, but I was on the train.'

'You don't like the train.'

'No, you're right, I don't. But to come and see you I can make an exception. And so I was holding the cake and we pulled into my station, which is on the way to yours, and I got off the train.'

'You got off the train?'

'Yes.'

'Oh.'

'I had to get off the train.'

'You had to.'

'Yes. Because I suddenly remembered I had an icebox at home and I wanted to go and get it to put the cake in.'

'A great big icebox for one little cake?'

'It was quite a big cake.'

'The one with half white topping from Wilkomirsky's? That cake's been the same for forty years. Seven inches in diameter. Two inches deep.'

Winkler decided to have one specially baked that was twice the size and take it round to the old man to show him that he wasn't always right. He even imagined the conversation with the young Polish waitress and wondered if you could get the same chocolatiness with a bigger cake, because it would take longer to bake and then the outside might be dry. And if there was one thing punters at Wilkomirsky's would not accept it was dryness in a cake. Or a chicken. Except Wilkomirsky's didn't do chicken. Strictly cakes only.

'But I was also going to put in some sandwiches. Roast chicken sandwiches, lovely and moist, with mustard pickle, and fruit and a bottle of wine and potato salad and all sorts of things. I thought it would be nice to have a picnic. In that garden you all share. And I bought salami. The pink one from Bloom's that you always have, and a big crusty loaf and pickled cucumbers, new greens, a bunch of radishes and eggs to hard boil and even hummus, the deluxe brand with whole chickpeas.'

Oh stop, stop, this is too much. Said Mole. Winkler remembered Ratty's list – coldtonguecoldhamcoldchickenpottedsomethingblahdiblah – when he packed the picnic to go boating with Mole. And Mole said 'stop, stop' and Winkler, brought up hard by the old man, thought this was rudeness. Rudeness to turn down food. Rudeness to interrupt Ratty when he was speaking. Rudeness to appear unenthusiastic after all the trouble Ratty had gone to, what with the shopping and the carrying and the parking and the queues and then the cooking all day . . .

'But you weren't hungry,' said the old man.

'I wasn't hungry, *then*. But by the time I left work I realised that I was, after all. I had a bit of a stomach ache early in the day –'

(The old lies are the best, so easy, so familiar, they ease the way into mendacity; it was so old, the lie, that he almost said 'tummy' ache)

'– and anyway I was thinking of you, and how it would be nice for you to be outside a bit.'

'I go out enough.'

'In that little grassy bit.'

'It's for the dogs to foul.'

'Well, I'm sorry if you're in a bad mood, Grandpa. But I thought it would be nice.'

'Not so nice that you came.'

That was true.

'Yes, but when I got home – to get the icebox – there was this old man from downstairs. And he, um, he wanted to talk.'

'Talk? What are you talking about, son? You're not making any sense.'

'He wanted to tell me about his life. He had been trying to tell me about it for ages, and I thought I should listen.'

'Suddenly you're interested in old men who want to tell you about their life.'

'No. But I just thought I should.'

Winkler heard the old man laugh. His dry little not-really-genuinely-amused laugh.

'Why are you laughing?'

'I'm not laughing.'

'You are. Why? What's so funny?'

'Oh, son. Don't make such mountains out of molehills. It's just, suddenly this sense of duty.'

'Yes, well. I know I don't come to see you very often, but this –'

'So I'm a duty call now?'

'No, of course not.'

'Because if that's how it is, then –'

'No. It's not. I really meant to come. I was on my way and then –'

'This old man suddenly kidnapped you and chained you to a radiator. This life story of his, it couldn't wait?'

'No. I don't think so. He was in the Holocaust, you see. And –'

'Oh, the Holocaust. We were all in the Holocaust, son.'

'No, but in Poland, he's a survivor of –'

'Really. And this was interesting to you?'

'Yes, well –'

'Suddenly you care so terribly about Hitler and the War and the Jews?'

'It's not sudden it's –'

'You never mentioned it before. You never asked anything about it.'

'I guess not. But you never brought it up, either.'

Winkler's grandfather never brought anything up. Winkler, now, was not sure that the old man had ever started a conversation with him in his life. Except about what was for supper, or to ask him what he was

doing. The old man always asked him what he was watching on television, and if the answer wasn't quick and clear and explanatory – if the
answer, God help him, was 'I don't know' – then it went off with a click
at the loud button on the set. Or he would ask him what he was eating.
If Winkler was caught eating a sandwich of dry sliced bread and low-
cholesterol margerine with a slice of processed cheese and a straggle of
pickled cabbage fished from the old jar with a teaspoon – the best he
could ever hope for from the old man's fridge – then he had to explain
himself. It was not even two hours till supper. Did he not have self-
control? Must he give in always and so easily to his appetites? And if
not that then why was he not doing his homework? Why was he not
out with his friends? Why did he not have any friends? Did he know
that he had a big spot on his neck? Why must he always answer back?
Why did he never read books, why always comics? Did he know how
many books his grandfather read every week at his age? And even his
useless father? Why did he always think he knew best? Did he not
understand the meaning of respect? Did he know how his own father
used to thrash him? His big bristly bandy-legged father with a cane he
brought specially from the old country to thrash him with. Did Winkler
know that that was all he brought, the stick? That and the language.
They didn't even speak the same language, father and son, did Winkler
know that?

    'Brought up what? You wanted to hear about the shoes and the lamp-
shades and the babies' heads and the ones who crawled still alive from
the quicklime and when they looked down at their feet . . .'

    'What is it with everyone and the shoes?'

    'Don't get hysterical.'

    'I'm not hysterical.'

    'So. What's so exciting about your new little friend?'

    'Wallenstein? He –'

    'Wallenstein? That's not a Polish name, you said he was Polish.'

    'I said he was in Poland. Maybe his family came from somewhere else.
But he is definitely Polish, he –'

    'It's the name of Nathaniel West.'

    'Eh?'

    'Nathaniel West. Real name Nathan Wallenstein Weinstein. You never
heard of him? You call yourself a literary type?'

    'No I don't.'

    'And so what did he have to say? He was in the camps, I suppose?'

    'No.'

'And he told you about the drills and the showers and the selections
and the terrible cold and how they would throw your hat over the fence
and then make you get it and then shoot you from a watchtower just for
fun, and how the clogs didn't fit and how guilty he feels, and he almost
wishes that that time when he was nearly selected for the gas he really
had been, but at the last minute Mengele himself . . .'

'Mengele?'

'They always met Mengele, the survivors. If I could show you one old
Yid who felt the icy stare of Mengele's good eye on his buttocks I could
show you a hundred. You know that the buttocks were very important?
If you didn't have −'

'I know about the fucking buttocks, Grandpa.'

'What tone is that to speak in? Do you speak to your Mr Weinstein
like that?'

'Wallenstein. No, I don't. And, no, he didn't talk about all that, or about
Mengele, because, like I said, he wasn't in the camps.'

'No? So what did he survive, the flu?'

'He fought in the forests.'

'The forests, noch?'

'Behind German lines. He was in a Jewish partisan group and they
saved people from the ghetto and liberated a camp.'

'He told you that?'

'Yes.'

'And you believed him?'

'Why not?'

'Why not? Why believe?'

'Well, I don't know. Why make it up, now? What would be the point?'

'Oh Winky, Winky. So grown up the way he speaks to his grandfather
and yet so naïve. When you're a little older. Then you'll learn.'

Winkler's credulousness. An ancient trope. A prehistoric tactic. The
things he didn't learn in that private school of his.

'Learn what? Stop it, Grandpa. Why would he lie? He has nothing to
gain from making it up.'

'Except your time. It's more than I got. You sat, didn't you? You listened.
How much do you think an old man needs? What do you think he counts
a triumph? Maybe it isn't all made up. Embellished, then. How can you
know?'

Winkler was about to speak but paused. Thought that his grandfather's
point was a fair one. Wallenstein had got his attention, his grandfather had
not. What if his grandfather had been there, in the ghetto, in the forests,

in the camp at the end with the bodies? Winkler would be bored with it by now. God, but the old man would have waved it at him over the years, when he failed to eat his fat, or complained about the cold apartment or, anything. But he wouldn't have been there and he wouldn't have done it. He wasn't the type. Just into the queue with the rest of them, and into the gas. Grumbling, saying it was an outrage, posturing power, noisily croaking in a pile by the door, with blood under his nails. If he had been there, though, and survived, he'd be different, presumably. That was the whole point. The whole point.

What was his grandfather doing then? A young man with a brilliantined centre parting pushing fish around city streets in a wheelbarrow. Meeting some Jewish girl as he went about his business, marrying her round about the time when Wallenstein was living on weeds, having a kid towards the end of it, when the last Jews were screaming. A kid who would do it all properly right up to just after his third child and then, one warm spring evening, full of the moist air and grass smells and jangly guitar waftings of the relatively new decade, break the chain, pop, in a moment of madness. And thus, Winkler. The old man's mongrel burden these thirty years.

Ah, but fuck the old man. Be patient. Don't row. You'll feel sick all day. You'll feel sicker still when he's dead. Make up. Say you'll go round.

'I'll come round.'

Say that you'll go round right now. Tell him you'll make it possible by taking your work home. Which you were going to do anyway – look, it's already in Sherwood Glaub's gay little attaché case – but he doesn't know that. Tell him you'll leave work early, to impress on him how important he is, still is, and always has been, to you.

'I'm coming round now. I'll leave work immediately. I'm sorry I didn't come. I'm so sorry. I'll take my work home with me and then I'll come straight round. We'll have our picnic.'

'And even if it's true,' began his grandfather again, 'which I doubt, why do you want to hear about it now? Why do you want to make such a big fuss. Why do you want to show off to everybody? It's not your tragedy. Why must you always be so emotional?'

To control his anger, Winkler told himself the old man was just jealous. He would die soon, and Winkler would be sorry. It was Winkler's fault, this, now. He said he would come and he didn't come. And so Wallenstein had made use of him. And now Winkler was suffering. And it was not the old man's fault.

'They're all the same, the Survivors,' said Grandpa Winkler. 'All they want is pity, pity, pity. Always long-faced. Always complaining. Never grateful. Expecting us to help with everything. Everything. As if it was our fault. And so they played right into the hands of the Jew-haters again. In the War we were all British, we all pulled together. And then came these Czechs and Hungarians and Romanians. We had to absorb them, all of them, like nothing happened. Sticking out like sore thumbs with their accents and their clothes. Like your mother's family. Not your mother. Your father's wife. They came weeping from the Shoah. Always staring into the distance, drawing attention to themselves, and then refusing to talk about it – as if we wanted anyway to hear it all again. Pitiful, it was.

'I don't understand for a minute why you would listen to this old man's drivelling. You have problems of your own enough without all this. You could get married, you could have children of your own, you could buy a home. You should apply yourself to something grown-up for more than a minute before you go worrying about some old fraud in that disgusting dosshouse you live in. You were never remotely interested in being a Jew. Never. And now suddenly you're Primo Levi the second. You should have come round to visit your grandfather who brought you up, instead of listening to all the old lies again. He made it up. He made it up. A hero. A fighter. It's what they all say. If they were such heroes why did they die, eh, son, why did they all die?'

'I don't know, Grandpa. I'm sorry I didn't come. I don't think today's such a good day after all. Maybe next week.'

And he put the phone down.

Sherwood Glaub, who had been looking at Winkler during this conversation and during the long silence before he hung up, looked down again at his keyboard, and punched, stupidly, twice, at a key in the middle of it.

'Sure it's okay with the briefcase?' said Winkler, rising.

'Sure. Course. Everything okay?'

'You heard. My grandfather.'

'You shouldn't –'

'No, I know. But he can be a cunt.'

'Well . . .'

'He always thinks I make a big drama just to get attention. How would he know? He's always been so obsessed with not spoiling me that he has all but ignored me for thirty years. How could he possibly have imagined that I was a person in need of attention? And if he did, then how could he have deprived me of it for so long, knowing how much I craved it?'

'Bit of a cunt, then, as you say.'

'Cunt is right,' said Winkler, smiling. 'Cunt is exactly it.'

There was a second or two of silence in which the two scrutinised each other quite carefully, unsure whether the other thought this conversation was funny or deadly serious.

'He always thinks he knows exactly what is inside my head. He thinks he knows every fucking thing. He thinks I've just woken up to the horrors of the Holocaust and the vague relevance of my being a sort of Jew, basically in order to have something to make a fuss about. He thinks I think it actually happened to me. He thinks I think I am the only one who empathises properly and that I therefore believe that I own the Holocaust in some way, which gives me the right to lord it over everyone else.'

'Absurd.'

'And to think I was going to take him a picnic.'

'Actually, if you remember, you weren't.'

Winkler reflected.

'True,' he said. 'Just as well. Man's a cunt.'

'Pritchard's a cunt.'

'That he is. Spawn's a cunt.'

'They're all cunts,' said Glaub, including the whole office in a wide sweeping gesture of his arm.

'Cunts, the lot of them. I'm off.'

'Probably best.'

'Fancy a drink before I go?'

'No. I've really got to get some work done.'

'Cunt,' said Winkler, picking up the ugly black briefcase with its neatly stitched handle and gold clasp and shimmering monogram, and heading off round the corner, down the corridor, towards the bright, dusty afternoon.

13

Winkler's Brief
Moment of Heroism

It didn't start heroically. Far from it. It started with Winkler, disgusted by the greasy faces of his fellow passengers as he surged home from work with his gay briefcase, full of misery, taking solace in the advertisements over the ventilator shafts in his carriage. Specifically the girls. He watched the white swim-suited, almost-nipple-showing blonde girls with caramel skin and graffitied eyes. And he began to plan a relaxing afternoon wank in his warm, empty flat.

Rising on the escalator, accompanied by recurring and changing images in small poster-boxes of half-dressed women who wanted him to buy things, Winkler felt that luxurious uncoiling that can persuade an unhappy man, briefly, that all is well. There were girls in summer dresses crouching on the covers of bad novels; sticky red lips clamped around chocolates; women with dancers' legs straddling chairs in sheer tights and begging Winkler to come to the show.

Winkler wondered whether he dared buy a porn mag at the corner shop at the end of his road (it would rather depend on which member of the family was manning the till) and plunged his not-holding-brief-case hand into his trouser pocket. Just for a tickle.

A black woman whose nipples had hardened in her pink bikini explained that you could call such countries as Nigeria and Ghana for as little as 1p (though Winkler had not even a penny's worth of things to say to anyone in Ghana). A youngish mother with her little girl and husband strolled on a hot sunny day through Disneyworld, marvelling at the gothic majesty of the magic castle – her pale green pleated skirt clung to her thigh and showed the shape down to where the golden, sun-tanned leg emerged.

Winkler tugged and watched the grey maw of the escalator-eating floor approach, wondering if he dared just bring it off now and have done with it. It would be messy in his pocket on this day of death: he had not ejaculated in days and had tumesced and detumesced and retumesced hourly, it seemed, the last forty-odd hours, pumping his bollocks to boiling point.

But a radio DJ in a white singlet and baseball cap opening her mouth to tell Winkler to tune in weekday mornings between six and nine had tits too good for radio, clambering up the inside of that little white top, screaming for egress . . . Oh, God –

'Oop, sorry.'

A man with a large holdall barged Winkler as he climbed past up the left-hand side of the sliding stair and apologised. Winkler ripped his hand from his pocket and said, in a half-squeak, 'No worries.' And settled the hand on the moving banister. And saw that there were only seconds left, saw the multi-toothed jaw of the station floor gobbling the last steps, one, two, three, four, five, six, seven, eight, nine, ten, eleven, Winkler hopped off thinking something like, 'Oh, well. It's probably for the best,' took a brief lungful of air on the pavement which, if not absolutely fresh, was at least free-range, and ploughed into the underpass, where, tapping her way nervously towards him, he saw a blind girl.

She was a Goth. She must have been struck sightless in about 1983 and didn't know any better. Those bloodless posers of post-punk still populated the world that was splashed on the screens of her blind little head. She got up in the morning, felt her way along the walls to the wardrobe and put all that shit on – little black pixie boots with the spunk-washed black jeans tucked in, black tour t-shirt and leather jacket with tassels – because she thought it made her look what, normal? Cool? Cute? Sighted?

The sun warmed Winkler's face and back and his subterranean tunnel-dwelling reptile's blood. He felt it, standing at the entrance to the subway as she came tapping, knock-kneed, dead-arsed, spastically almost, towards him with pale, possibly painted skin, big hair, black hair, backcombed, dyed black possibly, hard to tell in the lightless warren. Do blind people dye their hair? Probably not. Surely they are above, or below, or just a long, long way away from such vain gestures.

With her sunglasses, big, round, ancient in style, she was not immediately obviously eyeless. Except for the stick, light as a dreamer's imaginary baton, which she wafted ahead of her, into her future, searching for surprises, measuring an irregular beat to console herself in her unlighted loneliness.

Her clothes, all wrong for the mood of the day, set as it always is not by temperature, scent, or sound but by light. Only the blind, with the sky blue and high, and the grey concrete piling the light up in drifts, will drag on the black weeds of winter mourning because they sense a certain chill.

Then again, weirdos like her, sightless or sighted, dress like that in deference to the darkness of night, and regardless of the day, with their black kit faded to rusty green and brown, worn with resisting the light of countless mornings and afternoons. Ten-year-old tour dates flaking from t-shirts and thin chains faintly suggestive of bondage – surely a blind woman will not submit to be chained. Isn't that taking submission too far, trusting too much, isn't the four-sensed fuck kinky enough as it is?

Winkler watched her as they walked towards each other, she hugging the wall in the wide tunnel, over the grated drain, piss-puddles and wall stains, he keeping to the middle line.

Winkler stared, the better to form judgements, and then thought he shouldn't stare at fucked people. It was rude. And then thought, 'Fuck it, she's blind and can't see me staring.' And then he thought that maybe she could sense him staring. They're good at that.

And into his stare, just behind the girl, walking up quickly, came a scrawny man wearing a necklace and a baseball jacket.

'A baseball jacket,' thought Winkler. 'Haven't seen one of those in a while.'

Winkler offered the man a half-smile intended to say, 'Okay, you've busted me staring at batgirl, but so were you, so who's going to tell?'

And at that very moment the scrawny man passed the blind girl, turned round towards her, where she was tappety-tapping her way along with her stick, and punched her hard right in the middle of her face:

Blam!

The girl went down with a silent whump. A UN rice-bag famine relief sack slump. A bullet-in-the-back-of-the-head from close range while blindfolded and expecting life to continue knee-buckle and slowmo sink.

A woman with a child spread her eyes wide in astonishment and pulled the child to her as the child pulled from an orange bag with his wet hand another pickled onion flavour Monster Munch with its vinegary tang all on the front of the tongue and the ammoniac vapour all in the nose, sweet and sour and collapsing from corn into air with a mash in the mouth.

The scrawny man looked down briefly at the pole-axed blind girl, a middleweight boxer, hands dropped with no need to guard, staring down, sweat-wet, at his clubbed opponent, grunting something through the mouthguard, and then ran. Past Winkler and out of the tunnel.

Winkler dropped the briefcase of Sherwood Glaub and turned and ran after the scrawny man, shouting, 'Oi! Oi! Oi!'

Out of the tunnel and into the sunlight, round the corner into the crowds who had not seen what the scrawny man had done. And didn't know why he was being chased.

Up the stairs to the main road, Winkler shouting, 'Oi, you fucking wanker! You won't get away! You fucking bastard!' And getting closer.

Winkler was still quick. He used to be much quicker, chasing a ball driven hard to the cover boundary, bouncing and spinning through the half-shaven green-brown outfield, the steel-blue and steel-hard sky blazing all around him, diving into the dandelions, daisies, grass clippings, butter-cups and bees out down by the old tarmac tennis courts bristling with weeds, while the bowler and wicket keeper shouted and square leg, mid-wicket, slips and mid-on squatted, chewed fingernails, watched the clock, looked for girls (weren't any) or sprawled out on their backs (not allowed) to take the sun in their faces and the weight off their feet. Often he saved not just one but two, because the batsmen slowed in their run-gobbling sprint to a trot, believing it would go for four.

Pennant-Cecil shouted once, 'Run, run Winkler, you waddling dumpling, run!' and Winkler had run, dived, caught the ball and whipped it in hard over the stumps, nearly running the man out, without a word of praise from the captain, not a hint of an acknowledgement that, what-ever he looked like when he ran, he was faster than anyone else in the team.

And now he was nearly up with the scrawny man. What was he going to do? Kill him? Winkler didn't know how to kill someone. He would jump when he was nearly up with the scrawny man, jump onto his back and maybe he'd be lucky and the man's neck would break as they fell.

But what if the scrawny man had a knife? Or a gun?

'Stop him! Oi, stop!' Winkler shouted, but people hardly glanced as the two men galloped by. They ran past two long bus queues at two bus stops quite close together. Why don't they stop him, thought Winkler.

And with all this thinking, Winkler was slowing down. The gap was reopening. They were on the big hill now and scrawny man was less hindered by gravity than Winkler – who was by no means dumplingy, but was by no means scrawny either.

Slowing, but still trying, Winkler contemplated murder. I saw him, I'll catch him, I'll fucking kill him. What sort of a man punches a blind girl like that? Without robbing her or anything. Maybe it was just a domestic though. You shouldn't get involved in other people's domestic arguments, no matter what. Until he hits her, of course. Which he just had. And who would do that? Nobody. Shit. Maybe he hadn't.

Winkler stopped. The scrawny man ran on, glanced back once, and shot down an alley behind a housing estate.

What if Winkler had imagined it? No, the man had run. It must have happened. Where was Winkler's briefcase? Back where the girl was. Shit. What if she wasn't blind at all and it was just a con set up by her and the scrawny man, and when he goes back she's gone with the case. It might have had money in it, or anything.

Shit, shit, shit. Winkler ran back down the hill. What a fucking fool. Nobody punches a blind girl. Nobody. It's the perfect con. Even in this soulless, shapeless, senseless new world without community or human kinship a man with a briefcase would still drop it to chase a man who had punched a blind girl. Winkler anchored on a lamp post to swing round the corner from the hill down into the station forecourt and there she was.

At the entrance to the subway tunnel. Kneeling. Slumped. Her head in her hands. And shaking, Winkler noticed, when he got closer.

Nobody had come to help her. But then not many would have seen it happen. It would have been easy to assume this was just another drunk Goth having an episode in the subway: collapsed, perhaps, after squatting for a piss.

The case was there, too. Where he had dropped it.

He said, 'It's okay, it's okay. He's gone. I chased him away. I tried to catch him but I couldn't. Sorry. I'm really sorry. I'm not going to hurt you. I won't even touch you unless you tell me to. Don't get up. Don't get up yet. You've had a shock. Just stay there for the moment. I sound like this because I've been running, to try and catch him, but I couldn't. Because I'm not really in shape for that sort of thing. I'm going to stay here and if you need me to help you get up, or get you anything just say. Here, look, your phone was on the floor. Here.'

She put her hand out and Winkler put the phone in her hand, allowing her to feel in her cold little palm the warmth of his finger and thumb tips. She was shaking, and she could feel that he was shaking too, from what he had seen. He found himself in her head, looking around and seeing nothing. She could have, in her darkness, no idea of what had happened. Had she walked into a wall? A tiny door or overhanging cross-beam or road sign? Had she been stabbed? Or shot? Was she not in the subway at all but in the street and had been hit by a car? Or a bicycle? Had something fallen on her?

Jesus Christ. You walk around helpless as a baby, depending on the sighted world to make way for you, to help you, give up a seat on a bus or a train for you, not rip you off, laugh at you, mug you, at the very fucking least not to whack you just for the hell of it, just for the fun of it, just because doing harm to somebody else anonymously and for no reason felt good, felt powerful, doing it maybe not despite the fact that you were blind, but because of it. Because of it.

'Come on, love. Try and get up,' said Winkler, who never called anyone 'love' but wanted to sound safe and normal. A man of the people, salt of the earth, backbone of the world. 'You're sitting in a puddle there.'

'Am I?' she said. 'That's good. I thought I'd peed myself.'

She was American. Not only was she blind, she was American. She was blind and foreign and this was the welcome we managed for her. On a lovely day like this. With the air all warm and the grass smells, and the girls in skirts with bare legs and the birds singing. No, you could not hear birds here. But they were singing today, somewhere.

'No, you haven't peed yourself,' said Winkler. 'Shall I help you up?'

'I was joking about the pee,' she said.

Joking. She was joking.

'Oh, right. Shall I help you up?'

'Just give me a second.' She looked up. The sunglasses were in her hands. Her eyes were very pale and not looking anywhere. Her face was naturally pasty, not painted after all. She had some spots around her chin. Her forehead looked sweaty.

'How do I look?' she asked.

'You look fine, considering,' said Winkler. Considering what? That you're blind? That you're not especially attractive? Or that you have just been punched in the face?

'Not bleeding?'

'No, no blood. You just look a bit shaken.'

'How can you tell?'

'Well, I mean. I assume you must be shaken. And in fact there is a bit of blood, just a drop at your left nostril.'

'That's different,' she said, wiping both nostrils with the cuff of her leather jacket, which was not the ideal fabric, and only wiped a slash of blood across her cheek. 'Yeah, I'm shaken, I guess. But at least I'm not bleeding. Last time my shades cut the bridge of my nose. There was lots of blood.'

'Last time? This can't have happened before?'

'Yeah. A few months ago.'

'Was it your boyfriend?'

The girl laughed. 'No, not my boyfriend.'

'So who was it?'

'How would I know? Didn't you see him?'

'Um, yup. Er. He had a baseball jacket and, ah, a necklace and he had bad skin and he looked maybe Irish or Scottish. Have you always been blind?'

'Yes.'

'Right. So you don't know what I mean when I say he looked Scottish?'

'Not really.'

'No. Well I just mean that he looked sort of –' what did he mean? Winkler meant that the man had looked hungry, weak, drunk, ignorant, wilful, violent, sad, resentful and dirty.

'He looked small and Celtic. Dark but pale.'

'Very interesting.'

'You know what a baseball jacket is?'

'Yeah, I know what a baseball jacket is. But don't kill yourself describing if it was red or blue.'

'So how do you know . . .'

'Can we talk about that later? Right now, I'd kinda like to get up.'

'Of course. Shall we go to the police?'

'Where's the police station?'

'No idea. I can ask someone, though.'

Twice Winkler walked towards sober citizens and twice they backed off and hurried away, even though he was saying as he approached, 'Excuse me, do you know where the nearest police station is?'

With her face covered in tears and her cheek striped with a line of browning blood, and Winkler all out of breath and wheezing, and his shirt – remember – all smeared with chocolate from the morning, they must have looked, thought Winkler, like a pair of tube station drunks, full of strong cider, who had had a fight, and now the male drunk was making a big pissed gesture that went something like, 'You think I assaulted you, eh, do you, bitch? Well call the fucking police, go on, call them, call the

FUCKING POLICE! Call them. Or, God help me, I'll sort you out properly. Come on, if you think I'm going to kill you then call the FUCKING
POLICE! Oh, you don't want to. Okay, I'll call them. Better than that
we'll fucking go and see them. We'll let them decide which one of us is
FUCKING MAD! Oi mate, mate, scuse, where's the police station?'

That is how it must have looked, thought Winkler, to the hurriers-by,
when he asked them, all sweaty and chocolate-smeared and out of breath.
And so he gave up.

'Well, look,' he said. 'I only live two minutes away. We can go back to
my place and call them. And you can get cleaned up and have a cup of
tea.'

The girl said nothing.

'Look, I promise I'm not a baddie. Although I probably shouldn't suggest
going back to my flat with me because, really, in principle, you shouldn't
come. And it's wrong of me to suggest it and put you in the position of
having to decide whether I'm a mad axe-wielding rapist psychopath or
not. So don't if you don't want to. But I do just want to help. And I feel
bad because I didn't manage to catch the fucker who hit you. I feel so
guilty. I feel responsible for all the people who can see and just . . .'

'It's okay,' she said. 'I'll come. It's kind. Thank you.'

'Oh. Good. Fine. Great. Shall I hold your hand?'

'If you walk next to me and stay in contact, that will be fine.'

'Right then.'

She was from Kentucky, it turned out. Jenny-Marie. She was here
studying or travelling or something, with or attached to some sort of
organisation Winkler was expected to have heard of. Winkler took little
in, between noticing the speed of his heart and wondering whether he
was dreaming. Surprised, undermined, flabbergasted that these last hot
forty hours that had dragged so slowly by, so empty of events but so full
of something else, had come to this nightmarish hour of horrible assault
under the ground.

Feeling very small and also very enormous, Winkler walked in hope
that nobody would think – as he walked slowly along with the blind girl,
chatting quietly and touching gently – that she was his girlfriend. He
thought it often enough walking in public with Mary, who was filthy but
at least had eyes. If he should be linked sexually to this poor, stunted thing
– even only briefly, in the imagination of a stranger – well . . . Winkler
shuddered.

'Ooh. You okay?' she said, feeling him ripple. 'That was a hell of a
shiver.'

'Yeah, fine, I do that whenever I see dog shit,' said Winkler.

'At least you see it,' she said.

Winkler shuddered again. This time at the horror of dog shit, the horror of blindness, the horror of a blind girl sliding in unseen hound crap.

Winkler's street, which had surprised him that very morning with its sudden loveliness, was without features. There was no room for scenery with the foreground so full of battered blind girl.

'Careful on the path,' said Winkler, holding open the gate, feeling the dry moss and pushing her through. 'The paving is a bit uneven.'

'Okay,' she said.

Safely at the door, Winkler double unlocked it and handed her into the hall.

'Whoaaaa!' she said.

'What?' said Winkler, panicked.

'That goddamned smell. That stinks.'

The smell. And her a blind girl with the heightened senses, like a blood-hound or a rhino or a bat. He had not himself noticed it immediately, which was rare. Now she would panic. She'd identify the human-flesh-cooking smell immediately and assume that he had lured her back to his dungeon to kill her and eat her. She'd run, but she wouldn't know where to run to. She'd follow the light, like a moth. She'd zigzag through the front garden screaming, 'Help! Help! Murder! Help!' tearing herself to pieces in the thick old rosebushes with their Stanley knife thorns of great age and hardness, and then slam into the wall and fall back, bleeding, then climb the wall and run into the street and then, who knows, a car:

Blam!

But she did not bolt.

'It's gross,' she said. 'Like, grody to the total max. I hope it's not your dinner.'

Winkler laughed and said that it wasn't.

'Rabbit, man. Frozen rabbit. Nobody eats that shit back home but the black people. The dirt poor, jobless, have-to-travel-on-the-buses black people.'

'Eh?'

'Well it is. In America white people don't have to eat rodent.'

'That smell is rabbit?'

'Well, I assume so. Less what I'm smelling is someone you killed and buried under the floor.'

'I never knew what it was. I don't live in this whole house. We always thought it was, well, we had no idea what it was.'

Winkler skipped up the stairs to the landing, three or four stairs at a time, then remembered Jenny-Marie and came down again.

'There's a few stairs,' he said, heaving her onto the first one. At the landing he said, 'Can you wait for a second?'

He went to the kitchen door. He saw it running with sweat. He put his head round the door and saw that the kitchen was empty. He pushed it open wider. He went to the big, cheap, thin-walled, plastic handled aluminium-coloured saucepan on which the lid rattled violently, battered at its half-cocked edge by escaping steam. 'And no wonder it wants to escape,' thought Winkler, 'with the smell in there.'

He took a dishtowel (good thinking under time pressure: the chef could appear at any time, hearing the intruder, fearing the theft of his simmering rodent flesh) and raised the lid. Meat pieces jostled furiously in the thin brown water, nosing out of the surface scum occasionally as the soup raged.

A plastic spoon, standing by, enabled Winkler to raise pieces to his eye. Leg and thigh and breast pieces – as much like chicken as anything else. Which did not, of course, rule out rabbit.

Researching further, he poked down the stained white lid of the red swing-bin and gagged at a thicker, more murderous distillation of the smell. Polythene pieces, crumpled and pulled, were slicked with the stickiness of blood. They were not labelled. This was no supermarket meat but some povvo butcher's must-go-today sale dog meat, bought and boiled.

The rabbit theory was plausible. Before he left the kitchen he lifted the lid on the coffin freezer to make sure there were no human body parts in there. There were not.

In the flat he sat her down in the sofa facing the television.

'Is there a chair in the sun?' she said.

'Yes. Would you rather?'

'It's better when I'm somewhere new. I know where I am then. At least, I have an idea which way I'm pointing. And if you've got a hard chair, like, a sit-up chair, that would be better too. It's not so important, though. I don't want to be demanding. You're very kind. It's just that in a hard chair I don't feel so much like –'

'No, of course.' Winkler didn't want to hear what she wanted not to feel like, and pulled her up and put her on a wooden chair, it was the old-fashioned kind with a pole bent into an arc to form a hooped back inside which six canes ran into the seat either side of a 'fancily' carved piece of wood. And she said,

'Thank you.'

'Do you want a tea or a coffee, or a beer or, or a glass of wine maybe?'

'A glass of water would be just fine.'

Winkler ran a tap for the blind girl. When it was cold on his finger he filled a glass that had come free with petrol years ago (when he had the car) and was scratched almost to cloudiness. And the water was cloudy, too. And so he emptied it and filled it again and it was less cloudy. He was going to give it two more slooshes, like always, and wait for the cloudiness to settle, but then he looked through the door at her sitting in the hard chair with her pasty face turned to the window, like a sick little sunflower (and just as blind) saw her black, black sunglasses showing nothing behind at all, and her round little shoulders hunched forward, and her feet in the boots planted square on the floor, her head occasionally moving, twitching like a cat's, when one of the old floorboards squeaked or a window banged in the back. And he thought, 'How silly,' and took the water in and handed it to her, and again she said,

'Thank you.'

'You don't want a glass of wine, or whisky or something? It might help you relax. You're probably in shock.'

'I don't really like being drunk. But you're very kind.'

A car with (maybe) a busted flywheel (though Winkler knew nothing of cars) screeched up the road and slowed outside Winkler's house. They both looked at the window. More cars than you would expect with this problem came up his road. Unless it was always the same one. You can't hear how fast they're going because the screech problem does not relate to speed. It can sound like a racing car ripping the tar off a hot corner at Imola and you run to the window and it's reversing into a small space between a skip and a rusty Bedford van with no wing mirrors. The car idled down to a quiet, conventional chunter. Young men shouted at each other, oafishly.

'Can you hear what they're saying?' said Winkler.

'No,' she said. 'Can you?'

'No.'

The doors of the car slammed twice. The car screeched away. Winkler would have liked the silence to be full of crickets, but it wasn't.

'I'll call the police then.'

'Okay.'

'Shall I call 999?'

'Why not?'

'That's the emergency number. Like 911.' She knew that. 'But I'm not sure if this is an emergency.'

'Not for you maybe. But it feels kinda pressing from where I'm sitting.'
Winkler dialled the number. Explained. Gave his address.

The girl on the phone had a soft Canadian accent. Winkler said that the girl wasn't bleeding, no. And that she did not appear to be in any immediate danger (what was he, a fucking doctor?) and that the culprit had long since fled, but that he had chased and chased and very nearly caught him (hang on, maybe there was a medal in all this somewhere). He wanted to know where the telephonist worked. Was it nearby? He liked her voice. Why was a Canadian on the other end of his phone, doing this job? Was she specially trained? Was she better looking than this other native of the North American continent that he had here in his living room? He imagined her looking like the only other Canadian he had ever met. Donna.

It was a school outing. In the youth hostel was a group of Canadian schoolgirls. Winkler – fourteen, fifteen – had barely met a girl. Term time at boarding school with only boys, holidays at home with his grandfather in the flat. Winkler, whenever he did chance upon a girl, clammed up, flinched, sweated, wept.

But there on the moors, or wherever it was, after the potholing, abseiling, canoeing and climbing, after the running, jumping and smelling, Winkler talked to a girl – was it Donna? – as the sun went down and the kids on the cooking rota cooked, and the sky purpled and his arse grew damp, pressing on the damp heather.

She had blonde hair. Dyed from dark brown perfectly and without rootsplash. She had braces on her teeth. Shorts. White trainers with pink ankle-socks with two pink pompoms on each sock. A Brown University sweatshirt, grey, from her sister. They sat on the heather together. Winkler thinking, 'Here I am, talking to a girl' – and then terror of kissing raced in.

And then the bell sounded for the meal and Winkler said, 'We'd better go in,' even though he knew that the spell would break in the din of the food hall and never be recaptured, knowing that, even then – good God – in the purple evening.

And she had said, 'Let's not. Let's stay here. Or walk down to the river. I'm not hungry, are you?'

And Winkler, lying, had said, 'Yes.' Because it wasn't a question of hunger. Dinner was compulsory. You had to be there or – or, what? What did he fear? A pair of ragged teachers in tanktops and sandals scuttling after him across the heather to – what? What punishment was in their power to hurt him? Why did he go back to dinner? How did those teachers make of Winkler a boy who ran from the opportunity for first love because of his fear of missing dinner? And a man who ran from it ever afterwards, for similar reasons? How had they dared to ruin his young life? Spoil the one thing he had dreamed of to make him normal, to let him catch up with the breathtaking romantic pace of the world?

He looked, then, at her pink knees and wanted to touch them. Her pink smooth knees bent back as she sat with her heels and calves at her side, appearing jointless. Her blue eyes.

'Sorry,' he said, and got up and ran into the hostel, the big Victorian hostel with many windows, across the patched green lawn, the badminton court, the cracked terrace.

Minutes later she, too, came into the dining room where Winkler was sitting with his group – a group whose faces he could not remember now – and looked briefly at him, blinking once, and passed his table, and as she passed Winkler saw two damp circles, one on each buttock, on the khaki shorts where she had sat on the grass.

'Urghh! Winkler fancies that. She's a bloody pig, Winkler. What's your problem, spasmo? Never seen a girl before?'

In the morning the girls were not at breakfast. They had eaten early, Winkler discovered, and moved on in their big air-conditioned tour bus. Standing in the door of the hostel, looking out at the gravel forecourt in the still quite early morning, where the grit showed the deep tyre marks made by the bus in leaving, Winkler felt the violet cool of the previous evening rush back on him, and rush past and disappear for ever. If only he had had the courage to go to Nicky Raymond's birthday party three years before, he had thought even then, he might have kissed her, Donna, in the purple field. And all this would have been worth remembering.

Winkler came back into the living room, where Jenny-Marie was clutching her glass of cloudy water in her black lap.

'So where's home?' he said.

'Not far. I live with a girlfriend – the Perkin Warbeck estate.'

'Grim.'

'Is it?'

'Yes. Oh. Yeah it is. 1960s block. Real Stalinist stuff.'

'I'm not so up on architecture.'

'No, I spose not. Doesn't it smell bad though?'

'Everywhere smells bad.'

'Is your friend a boy?'

'I said she was a girlfriend.'

'Oh yes.'

'In fact, on the way here I told you her name was Emma.'

'So you did.'

'My boyfriend's back home. In college.'

'Is he —'

Blind? That's what Winkler wanted to know. He wanted to know about sex. Surely a sighted man wouldn't have a blind girlfriend. Mind you. Then he could fuck whoever he wanted, right in front of her even, and she'd never know. Did her boyfriend ever, assuming that he could see, creep up and stick his cock in her mouth when she's sitting reading and doesn't know he's there. Reading Braille, of course. Head up, mouth lolling idly: Wham! Winkler would, if it were him.

And if he were blind then how would he get aroused without the visual element? Not that the visual element is much in her case. Best if he is blind, probably. But then how does he know if he's about to come in her face or on her tits or in her ear or something? Does it sting if he spaffs her right in the eye? Or does being blind mean it's no big deal?

'— contactable on the phone?'

'Yeah but it's, like, about six in the morning in Kentucky. And what could he do?'

'Mmmm,' said Winkler, who had an erection again and felt bad about it. But he could not help the blood rushing to his dick and thickening it out, so that he had to hold his hand against it and push to relieve it a bit, shut his eyes, squeeze a bit. One eye half-open just to make sure that she wasn't — no, blind as a bat. Best say something though, been a few seconds,

'What did you think had happened?'

'I guess I knew,' she said. 'Not right the first second but . . .'

Winkler could even whip it out right here and she would never know. As long as he wasn't turned on *just because* she was there and could not see. As long as he was just going to finish his wank now the way he was planning to anyway. And just not bothering to go to the bog to do it — as he would if she were any other girl — because there was no point, since she was naturally protected from the profanity of it as it was.

'Mmm, mm . . .' he said, easing his cock out of his trousers as Jenny-Marie explained how she had at first thought it was a robbery, at least after the first few seconds when there had been no room for thought at all . . .

Winkler stroked his cock now, standing in the doorway. So relieved to feel skin on it after the frustration of the interrupted trouser-fumbling on the escalator. He gobbed on his hand to allow for nice swift sliding, but she seemed to pause at the quiet hawk and spit, and so he paused, and then she carried on talking about her initial terror and how it had happened before, not that long ago, as Winkler moved to the middle of the room sliding his hand on his cock as he moved. She paused. Or maybe even stopped. She took a sip from the glass of cloudy water.

He gasped at a particular rush of pleasure and then heard the loud squelch of his hand catching a spit bubble on the ridge of his bell-end and he realised how loud it sounded when she was not talking – like when he wanked in bed next to Mary and never knew why he tried to be so quiet, because if she was asleep she wouldn't hear and if she was awake there was no way of hiding it, and anyway he didn't give a shit what the fat bog-trotting slag thought about anything else, so why this? And so he said,

'Doesn't something like that just make you lose all your faith in community?'

'I never had much,' she said, and began talking about that, as Winkler passed his palm back and forth over the tip of his now hard-as-could-be cock.

He moved closer to her, tried not to breathe, wondered if he could come on her face and say he had tripped with a glass of warm milk.

No.

Fuck, but he could fuck her.

She could never identify him. He could fuck her and then take her out and leave her on the street and that would be that.

What would that mean about him? That would be rape. Christ. And worse. Imagine what it would mean to her. That after such a terrible random act in the subway the next man who happened by – and there were 3 billion men on earth it might have been – was one who, having stopped to help her, was prepared to rape her. What would that mean about humanity? What were the real odds on that? What would other men do? Were not all other men worse than Winkler in every way? If he could get so close as to think it then surely all the others could go that far, and then further. Millions of those might go so far as actually to do it. How many were likely to be moral men, like Winkler, driven to action always by the observance of a strict ethical code? How many men could be lured from the right and proper path by the thought of a nice warm cunt?

'Are you okay?' said Jenny-Marie.

'Fine,' said Winkler. And standing only two long paces from her he thought of Donna and her knees and the wet circles on her khaki shorts and came suddenly in a thick spurt, pulling his cock round from where it was pointing, straight between her eyes, to spray its main violent ropey gob – with outriders and lassoes of onlookers dragged in its wake – onto the grey dusty screen of the television rented from Granada rentals on the high street, and a chasing load that did not make it that far, which fell into the gritty brown carpet, and a third emission that spilled onto his fist, and a fourth that he dragged from his tubes with neat pinches into his palm.

'Absolutely fine,' he repeated quietly. 'The coppers should be here by now. It's a bit odd. I'll just get a . . . do you want something to eat?'

She was saying 'no' as Winkler skipped to the sink, flicked the sperm he had caught into the stainless steel box and ran the hot tap over his hand to loosen and drive off what was stuck there. He stood on tiptoe to splash water on his cock, and shuddered as he saw the steel rim of the sink-top not quite flush with the formica unit, and thought of an accidental topple that would see the tip, the very tip of his dick, sliced neatly across the hole by the old metal edge.

He dried himself on a tea towel that lay on the draining board (a towel with pictures of vegetables on it with their Latin names) and hung it back on its hook by the cooker.

He came back into the living room, wondering whether she might have guessed what he'd done. And decided that that depended on how frequently men did that in front of her. And then realised that by his own assumption of moral averages that must be very frequently, when the doorbell rang.

'Cool. That'll be them,' he said, and went out and down through the defrosted rabbit-smelling (rabbit-smelling!) house, opened the door and brought the policemen up, two large men in black who filled the hall and corridor and stairs with beefy weight and the rustle of synthetic fibres, and apologised for the smell, which he said was one of the downstairs lodgers defrosting rabbit, offered them tea, which they didn't take, and gave a description that wasn't much use, and listened while they spoke to Jenny-Marie and suddenly saw the now completely liquefied streak of semen on the 32-inch Panasonic screen in the corner and hoped they had not seen it (though he could not think of a crime with which they could charge him – short of masturbating in his own home in the presence of an adult he had saved from attack, who had not been aware of the act) and showed them, all three, to the door, after he had first established that Jenny-Marie did not think she needed him to go along with them all to her home.

Jenny-Marie said, 'You've been very kind,' and squeezed his hand, which he was glad he had washed. And he watched them go down the path and he called out to her to mind the uneven paving stones. And she turned and waved eyelessly at the house. And they all got into the badly parked white car with orange and yellow stripes and drove away.

And Winkler went back upstairs and wiped the television screen with a damp J-cloth and dried it with the hand-towel from the loo. And he realised that he did not have a number for her, to call and see if she was alright. But thought maybe in a couple of days he'd call the police and see what had come of it, and ask if they could give him her number, or pass his on to her. Knowing, of course, that he would never phone.

And so he sat on the hard chair in which Jenny-Marie had felt, at last, at least relatively safe, bathed in the sunbeam through the dirty window.

And he looked at the sky, which was still very blue, with a swallow crossing it very fast and quite near, and he cried and cried and cried because he had seen a random man punch a blind girl in the face, in the underpass, on his way home from work.

And the next morning, without any fuss, Winkler pushed a fat woman under a train.

LAST PART

14

Winkler Starts a New Life

Winkler danced and Winkler sang. Winkler lived life to the full.

He lived now not in the big bad house of smells and wetness up North but in the newly fashionable West of the city with Albuquerque.

Alba who?

Of course, you don't know. Mary is long gone now. The house, too. The office and Millfield Spawn, Sherwood Glaub, Pritchard and Leo Sneel. Winkler's been sleeping with a beautiful dancer, long-legged, wet-lipped, horse-eyed and smokily spoken, who lives like he does in the six-bed end-of-terrace early Victorian house of Rupert Theofrax Helmesley-DeWilde – bright and white and full of light – next door to Lady Annabel Mosketh's celebrity millinery on a street once full of hashheads and crack whores, speed freaks and demons, buyers and sellers, merchants and murderers, runners and Rastas, minicab-mongering African scumsters, burger and kebab pushers stinking of saturates, car mechanics, council flats, gun markets, pimps and poor people; now flower-smelling, feminine, scented with freshly ground coffee and suede, sun-spackled streets and flittering leaves where it all used to be rainy and grey.

Here boys and girls just up from the country, down from the University, out from the old and into the new, have made the formerly benighted quarter their own: artists and lovers, writers and dreamers, singers and – are you convinced? Is anyone?

Money and fun and nobody knows where it comes from and nobody knows where it goes, players and snoozers, winners and losers, livers, in short, of life to the full, with different rules from the rest of us, us Winklers, or rather, us examples of what Winkler once was, once, before he pushed the fat bitch − splat! − and set himself free.

Rupert Theofrax Helmesley-DeWilde. That's Ru, the friend of Will's of whom we thought Winkler did not approve. What was it he said? 'A cocksucker with silly hair and a voice like a racecourse announcer choking on a golf ball'? Witty fellow, Winkler. The old Winkler. And bitter, too, railing at Ru's 'fucking tinted spectacles and his sandals and his fucking million quid house and his fucking DJ-ing. Shit, he doesn't have the first fucking idea . . .'

But after Winkler pushed the lardy lass under the steaming choo-choo down under the ground right at the end of the old life, he knew he could not go back to the flat. Because then it would have been meaningless. An entirely gratuitous act. Any more than he could go back to the job. And, not being big on friends, he could think of no one to call on but Ru. He had his number because just to fill his phone with numbers he had rummaged in Will's address book and even in Mary's and even Meriel's address books and even, even Sherwood Glaub's (big-cocked batty-boy requires likeminded for rectal trauma and possibly something more . . .) to plug the gaps.

'Hi, is that Ru?'

'Yo. Flipside speaking.'

'Um, is Ru there?'

''Tis I, dread, whappen?'

'Oh, right. It's Winkler here, Will's flatmate?'

'Oh, yeah. Cool, man. Flipside's, like, my DJ name. Or, like, part of it. But most of my homies call me dat, pun de real world. Innit.'

'Um, this might sound odd. But I've had a bit of a bust-up with my girlfriend and just for the moment I don't have anywhere to go. I wouldn't ask, but you've always seemed pretty, er,' Winkler cringed, '*chilled* about things, and I wondered if you might have a spare room I could kip in for a few days.'

'Yeah, man. For real.'

'Really?'

'Hombre, if da bitch give ya grief, you takes your leaf. Yaaarmsenn?'

'Great. So if I come round now . . .'

'I'll sort you out, nuff said. Respec'.'

'That's great. Thanks. Thanks so much. That's brilliant.'

'Word up.'

And Rupert Theofrax Helmesley-DeWilde was gone. DeWilde One, Winkler later discovered, never said goodbye on the telephone. It might be bugged. Best keep dem Babylon guessing.

Round Winkler went with nothing at all but the trousers he stood in. And at the door was Ru, standing in even less. Just a pink sarong round his waist – through which his finely-bred genitals were nicely visible in the morning sun that fell on the porch – and his natty red dreads, frizzy and split, dangling to nipple length. A tattoo of a mermaid on his forearm and, no, wait, not a tattoo, a faded henna design, bespeaking recent sub-continental holidaying.

'Eye-ree,' he said.

That was six days ago. Since then Winkler has moved into a white-washed room on the third floor with dark unpolished floorboards, a cast-iron bed, and a large classroom cupboard full of old books – Asterix, Tintin, Jennings, William, Famous Five, Arthur Ransome, Abbot's 'O' level Physics, yards of RJ Unstead – most of which he has stacked on the floor, either side of the large black iron fireplace, to make room for the clothes he has bought round and about, as he pottered the streets, wondering what to do next, sitting at small iron tables drinking coffee, reading second-hand books he bought in shops which charged more than the books cost new – for the cachet of that 'well-thumbed look' – and staring at the girls, all blonde, hard-bodied, large-breasted, tightly dressed, on the phone, inside shades, big-teethed, leather-booted and looking as easy to fuck, he thought, as a hole in a bathsponge.

And on the third day he met Albuquerque. Walking up the stairs from the shower to the room next to Winkler's as he was coming out of his to go and drink coffee and read second-hand books: tall, gym-muscled, freckly shoulders, hair dyed blonde and the roots showing dark at the scalp where it was all tied up in a white towel, green eyes, tanned skin – standard Australian surf chick sexploitation cartoon – nice wide hips, good hard hip bones showing through, holding the stomach taut, smooth legs, hairless, quite a hairy muff though and deep oval breasts with strangely tight nipples. A silver ring through her slightly outy navel, but, thank God, no tattoo.

Winkler said nothing.

'Oh, hi,' she said. 'I'm Albuquerque.'

'Me too,' said Winkler. 'I mean, I'm Winkler.'

'That all?' she asked, holding out her hand to shake Winkler's. She *was* Australian.

'Er, some people call me Wink.'

'Good people or bad people?'

'Just some,' he said.

'I didn't think anyone was in,' she said.

'Clearly,' said Winkler.

'I used my towel for my hair,' she said.

'So you did,' said Winkler.

'Sorry about that.'

'Jesus, don't apologise to me,' said Winkler.

'I guess not,' she said, and passed Winkler – showing her brown back and every vertebra of the long straight spine from which her shoulder blades sprung like two banana leaves – and turned the door handle of her room.

'You're Ru's girlfriend, are you?' asked Winkler.

'Nope,' she said, as she closed the door. 'I'm nobody's girlfriend.'

Winkler stood on the little landing, leaning on the banister for support he did not really need. He thought about breathing deeply, but thought she might hear, then stepped off the landing on to the stairs and thought,

'Wow. Never seen one of those before, without its clothes on. I hope I see her around the place again soon.'

And then he thought.

'Jesus, what am I? A couple of days ago I killed a woman just for being fat. I'm surely not afraid to ask some hippy tart out for lunch just because she's got big hooters and a hard arse.'

And he stepped back onto the landing and rapped three times on the door with his knuckles. A hairdryer – or at least some fan driven electrical appliance – stopped blowing.

'What are you doing for lunch?' Winkler asked.

'Eating it with you, I guess,' she said. And the hairdryer started again.

Winkler looked up at the ceiling, which was showing a little damp, closed his eyes, and mouthed, 'Oh yes!' to himself.

'I'll be downstairs,' he shouted. He wondered if she'd heard, and whether he should knock to tell her. But he decided that that would not be the best thing at all.

In the afternoon they walked the streets arm-in-arm. They trawled the shops on the sunny side of the street, stopped to drink in every pub they passed and enjoyed the boys staring at Alba. At least Winkler enjoyed it. The only people who had ever stared at Mary were retired sausage-makers with a nostalgic eye for well-meated pork animals. They sat on the roof of Ru's flat and smoked joints and played games of backgammon. Which Albuquerque always won.

'You don't play chess?' Winkler asked, momentarily sad for those evenings with Will. The scent of victory was what he missed, rather than the camaraderie or location or lostness of time.

'No, man. Chess is so lame. Backgammon's way more cool. I learned to play in Ibiza with Ru and the guys.'

And Ru and the guys were mostly at home. Fine people, really, if Winkler did not think too hard about it. They sat around smoking dope, watching films, playing music, sometimes cooked meals. Sometimes people in suits appeared, as if they'd come from work. Most of them smiled a lot, wore good clothes. He wasn't sure exactly which of them lived here – certainly the guy Chambers who ran a website for drug paraphernalia which seemed to be nearly as lucrative as his trust fund, and definitely Pilko (his name was a subversive boarding school corruption of 'pillock') who was 'in wine' – but the rest of them seemed just to appear late in the afternoon, and still be around in the morning, when they shuffled off grumpily home.

The afternoon after he had lunch with Albuquerque they had come back in the house to find Ru and a couple of his friends playing video games. Ru looked up as they came in and said, 'Yo, geez, sup?'

A rich bloke with no job looking up from his telly in the middle of a weekday afternoon to see Winkler and a comically perfect *überfrau* walking into his house, and not finding it even faintly surprising.

One day, soon, Winkler would learn to be blasé. Blasé was one of the things he had definitely never been.

'Just got a load of kufte in,' said Ru. 'You wanna cheeky line before bed?'

Bed? It was only four in the afternoon. What sort of timetable were these people – oh, God. No. Let it not be so. Let it not be that Ru had just said something in front of the girl and these unknown men that suggested that she and Winkler were about to go upstairs and, no, please let him not have meant that. But nobody sniggered and Alba said, 'Yeah, course. Let me rack up.'

Which was just as well. Because Winkler would otherwise have had a slight comprehension stall there, too. Kufte? Clearly it was cocaine. In this part of town any word in conversation that you did not immediately recognise was a synonym for cocaine. He avoided it, in fact, this nasty drug, because he had always found that his life was too awful to deal with the downers. He never even got a brief zing of liveliness before he got depressed. The very feeling of the harsh alkali streaming up his nose and walloping into the thin membrane that prevented it from coating his actual brain – the moment when even the most frequent user still got at least a momentary buzz – just reminded him that in eight or ten minutes he would start to feel miserable, and in no time he'd be flicking urgently through his mental rolodex for the most awful details in his life, to turn them over and over in his mind until they swelled to the gravity of a terminal cancer diagnosis so that he could crawl into a corner to lie awake sweating and staring and weeping.

But now, hey, with the externals so damn rosy maybe there was less to worry about.

Alba filed out very long curving lines of coke on an album cover ('Vinyl only man – no CDs allowed in this house,' Ru said when Winkler moved in. But as Winkler did not even have fresh pants for the morning, let alone a music library, it had hardly sunk in). She chopped out seven or eight of them, quite messily, held up her long dyed blonde hair with her left hand so that the roots showed nice and dark and, holding a rolled up bill in her other hand, snooched the biggest one up at a blow.

Most impressive. Winkler would have held one nostril closed to ensure suction in the other, as he was taught many years ago. Winkler went down. Went up again, breathed out. Handed the note to Ru, who said, 'No man, I ain't having that filthy capitalist shit in my nose. Observe . . .' and from behind his ear came a little silver trumpet, two or three inches long.

'It's my bugle bugle, man,' and he stuck it in his nose so that the bulbous end jammed in and held itself there, held back his big red dirty mane in both hands and went down, shooting down one of the lines and back up one of the others, one of the ones that Winkler noticed Alba had chopped out beyond the literal numerical requirements of the group. He didn't think anything particularly scathing about Ru's bugle bugle, which was odd. And just then he got a bit of cokey gob-melt in the back of his throat, flinched an involuntary lemon-suck wince and thought,

Yeeeeoowww!!!

This was different from what he remembered.

More please.

Later on they went to play football in the park, picking up more friends outside a pub on the way. They played for a couple of hours, at a slow pace. Winkler was about the only one who didn't play in sunglasses. Or wear 1970s-style trainers with jeans and a beige Adidas tracksuit top with the old fashioned cuffs and waistband. Or run like a girl. Or complain that he forgot it wasn't rugger whenever he handballed. He played well. Scored a couple of times, and nobody shouted 'soloist!' when he dribbled round four men (with that scuttling run of his) and nutmegged the keeper. Ru said, 'You're bloody good, for a little feller. You should play in our league games on Sundays.'

Puffed from his effort, Winkler glanced across to see if Albuquerque had seen. He shaded his eyes against the low sun that was falling into the trees in the distance and saw her lying on the ground, propped on her elbows, talking to a girl with brown hair cut into an elfin bob, who was sitting cross-legged, rolling a joint. Or wanking. It was hard to tell at this distance, with the sun in his eyes. Alba turned towards him and smiled.

The game rushed on around him with shouts and grassiness. He was reminded of school. In a nice way.

In the pub afterwards, or rather, in some sort of bar-restaurant-club type place of the kind that they had in this part of town instead of pubs, the players sat on a terrace drinking beers brought to them on a tray by an expensive-looking Italian girl whose name they all knew, and discussed plans for the evening.

Ru listed a number of parties that were happening later on and suggested a meal out beforehand.

'About ten o'clock. You up for it, Wink?'

'Yeah, cool. Why not?'

'Alba?'

'No, sorry guys. Can't. I've got a date with some mates.'

Winkler's world fell apart. But then one of the footballers tapped his hand, raised his eyebrows and slipped a wrap of coke into his palm. So he went to the loo, reeled out a three inch line, a good quarter of a gramme, honked it down, and his world fell together again. He skipped back to the table gurgling with delight and grinned as he felt the eye-winking chemical trickle in the back of his throat.

Winkler, desperate to talk, asked the one called Baz if he would be coming for supper.

'No, man,' said Ru, interrupting. 'Baz is always fucked on Friday nights. Jewish Sabbath. He's back home eating chicken with the aged Ps all night.'

Winkler, panicked, swivelled to look at Baz.

'Tis true, bro. Tis true,' he said. 'The whole fucking works as well. Not just challa, chicken soup and a couple of amens, who loves ya, Boobah, I'm off. Since my pater died I'm in the boss seat. Sit there in me ancient clobber hunched over the Torah, davening like a nodding bloody dashboard dog till bloody midnight.'

'Least Baz gets out after,' said Jason. 'Does a couple of pills and then Bob's yer auntie's live-in-lover. I have to stay in all night on *shabbos*. If my folks caught me slipping out they'd kill me. It's almost enough to make me get my own place.'

'You're Jewish as well?' said Winkler.

'No. Quaker. We just like to eat chopped liver and go to church on Saturdays coz it's quieter.'

The coke-filled, exhausted, beer-swilling footballers laughed. Winkler thought, 'What sort of dreamworld have I landed in?' and said aloud,

'I haven't done Friday night since I was about six. And that was only a couple of times. Can't even read Hebrew.'

'Shame, man,' said Ru. 'Roots is roots. Blood. Naaamsehhhn?'

'Well, you're welcome round mine any time if you want to sit in for old time's sake. Casual-stylee,' said Baz.

'Sometime, maybe,' said Winkler, baffled.

Winkler had supper with Ru and some of the gang. 'Some of the gang.' Well, they said it. Why shouldn't he? He was elated. He had identified himself as a Jew, proactively, for the first time in his life, in an environment he had always feared would be the most difficult of all. There was nothing left for them to discover. Nothing for him to hide. He had no secrets. Well, nothing important.

At supper nobody ate much, but they drank hugely. And skipped out for drugs every twenty minutes. People came and went. Women, particularly. Most of whom seemed to be interested in Winkler.

They are a pretty closed bunch, he thought. A lot of them, but finite. They've probably all slept with each other at least once. Not much fresh blood. This is going to be alright.

After midnight they went to a party at someone's flat. A vast apartment not far from Ru's house, where the music was louder than Winkler could stand and people drank red cocktails and snorted coke off the tops of fridges, off banister turns, televisions, stereos, bookshelves, coffee tables.

All Winkler's conversations went:

'Winkler, yeah. Just Winkler. So what do you do?'

'Nothing much, man. What about you?'

'Me? Same. Nothing much.'

Up to a point, and just for the moment, Winkler was in his element.

Walking into a small, bright room where people sat on a bed, snorting coke off a large jigsaw puzzle box, Winkler saw Will.

'Wink, man, what the hell are you doing here?'

'Came with Ru.'

'Where the blazes have you been? Mary's been going mental.'

'I've been staying at Ru's is all. I had a bit of a crisis, thought it best to get away for a bit. I did email her.'

'Oh. He emailed her. I mean, *très* thoughtful, old man.'

'Don't be silly, Will. You know she doesn't give a fuck about me one way or the other. She wouldn't care if I'd been lying dead in a ditch all this time.'

'Harsh but fair, harsh but fair. I'll tell her you're feeling much better, and will get in touch soon.'

'Tell her what you like.'

Around three o'clock Winkler went to find Ru and told him he was going home to crash. Yes. Crash. He said that. Ru said that sounded like a bona fide theory and said he'd join him.

Back in the flat, Ru made tea. Skinned up. Flicked on the television. Winkler said he was going to bed.

'You planning to sleep?' Ru asked.

'I thought I might,' said Wink.

Ru laughed and got up. He went to a drawer, pulled out a brown jar and handed Winkler two white pills. 'One of these should sort you out. Keep the other one by the bed just in case.'

'What –'

'Couple of temazzies, dude. 10 mills apiece. You'll have no troubles with Lady Shuteye, man.'

And Winkler did not have troubles. He woke the following afternoon with Albuquerque ruffling his hair and saying, 'You must have had quite a night.'

Downstairs, John Coltrane was tuning his saxophone, pastel-striped mugs of tea were steaming all over the living room, the vapour rising in plumes that looked smokey in the low sunlight, and a man in sunglasses, whom Ru introduced as '"Mr Clean" our friendly neighbourhood bugle-meister', was counting twenty pound notes. Ru and some of his friends were counting bags of grass, saucerfuls of pills and little folded lottery ticket parcels of coke.

Winkler sat down in a beaten-up leather armchair and nursed a cup of tea in his lap. Albuquerque perched on the arm and said, 'We'll go out and buy you a razor.'

The doorbell rang. Mr Clean sat up hard like a meercat and Ru went to the door to peer through the spyhole.

'C'est cool, Raoul,' he said. 'It's Baz.'

The Jew walked in. Winkler felt warm and comfy.

'Chance of a cuppa?' said Baz. 'Oh, and I see something perkier may be in order.'

'Cheeky bifters all round?' said Ru, showing the buglemeister to the door and shaking his hand.

Fat lines snaked across the tinted-glass top of the coffee tables. Briefly.

'Pill, anyone?' said Ru.

'Ah, leave it out Ru,' said Albuquerque, dabbing at her slightly powdered nose with the back of her wrist, looking at it and licking it. 'It's only four o'clock.'

Ru laughed and swallowed one down with a mugful. 'Tea and whizkits,' he said. 'A drink's too wet without one.'

They all went out again. This time Alba was there too. At the first party, which was in a packed club under a motorway, they had a little kiss. And each of them swallowed an E. At the next party they went to the loo together, Winkler and Albuquerque, and had a fat line of coke and another pill. And as Winkler was bending over the cistern to snort his line, Alba stroked her hand up the inside of his thigh all the way to his balls, which made him blow mid-snort and lose some of the coke.

He was about to suggest they chop out another quicky before reentering the fray but she grabbed him, opened the door and said, 'Let's dance'.

Winkler froze.

'I —' he said. And stopped. Her face was glistening from the heat of the house and the mugginess of the room, her freckly shoulders were covered in that dyed, oh that dyed blonde hair he'd dreamed of for twenty years, her eyes were big and her smile was huge and her tits in that little brown top . . . And now, finally, for the first time since that fucking twelfth birthday party of Nicky Raymond's, Winkler was faced with a situation in which he really, really, could not say no. Well, he could. But the consequences were not worth thinking about.

And anyway, he thought, what validity would my refusal have? What would it mean? Nobody here, least of all poor, poor delicious Albuquerque, has any idea that I do not dance, so they have no inkling of the compromise it would connote if I did. And how much is it about whether or not I can do it — I'm as full of fucking pills and coke and booze as the rest of them, all human difference has been eradicated. No judgement or evaluation is asked or given. What is there to do or not do? That I will grind on her naked body tonight is a given thing. She merely wants us to touch each other standing up in front of lots of people first. Look at her, there, look at her. What could I possibly achieve by refusing?

And so as Albuquerque began to pulse and throb and shake her head and close her eyes (I mean, Jesus, she can't even see me), Winkler moved in on her, taking her sides and stroking them up and down, moving his own arms and hips and knees and feet to get in new positions around her, snaking over her like a reptile on a tree, and knowing that there could be nothing less embarrassing in the world than to be stroking the hot, wet, sticky body of a girl like Albuquerque.

So, yes, Winkler danced.

And walking home to Ru's with her, stopping every ten yards to kiss and lick and whisper (she loved the way he danced, so sexy, she said – God, the barely-dancing he did that was all he was able to do was better than the dancing that other men did, a fine time to find out now, with the dancing years so much nearer their end than their beginning), walking there she sang 'Under the Boardwalk' – don't blame her, thought Winkler, she's Australian – and she insisted that he did the bass line, insisted, or she was going home and his dick was going nowhere warm and snug tonight (she's an Aussie, he thought), and so he mooed 'under the boardwalk' as she wailed 'out of the sun' and 'people walking above' and 'we'll be making love' and Winkler didn't worry if people looked – and those that were out at that time on a Sunday morning certainly did look – because, like with the dancing, there could be nothing on earth less embarrassing than having a girl who looked like Albuquerque pawing your trousers and singing about fucking.

So, yes, Winkler danced and Winkler sang.

What Winkler did not do was fuck.

'Jesus,' he said. 'It must be the drugs.'

'And the booze,' she said.

'But mostly the drugs.'

'And the excitement of going to bed with a girl as great as me.'

'Well, I don't –' It was good to have her say it for him, and make it sound okay. Fucked as he was, and full of drugs, he could probably have managed to screw sorry old fuckbucket Mary. No pressure. You can always grind out a wank. No matter what. But Albuquerque . . .

'And Ru says you had a couple of temazzies last night. Two of those things is heaps. You've got enough shit in you to knock over a donkey so I'd hardly expect Uncle Wiggly to be up and dancing.'

Uncle Wiggly?

She bent down once more and took it in her mouth, tugging at the sorry bulb with her teeth and flicking the opening with her tongue. But Winkler, made miserable as the drugs fell away, knew that, as had happened over the past couple of hours, even if her fantastic chewing could get him half-hard, the general fuck-up mentality was set in now, and the urgency with which he would make up his mind that now was the moment to get it out and stick it in would undo all her good work. And even if he had got it partly in, as had happened when they first got home, it would lose firmness so quickly that he could not risk anything but the meagrest oscillation or it would slip out again and that would be that.

'Maybe in the morning, if we get a bit of sleep . . .' he began.

'Ah, ah. No sleep. You just relax.' And she rested her hand on his belly, which felt good, and went back to her chewing.

And some hours later, it seemed, when the dawn was a memory, and it was already too hot for the birds still to be singing, and the dustmen would have been clattering in the road and the traffic honking and the radios blaring and the smell of cigarettes wafting in off the street, if it had not been Sunday, he felt a tingling in his chest and down his arms and in his fingers – a fucking heart attack, now – like something was going to happen. Something, at least.

He felt a warmth in his arse. A warm wetness like he was about to shit himself, but then he felt that the warm, wet slippery thing was going into his arse, not coming out. She licked and probed and the tingling went into his toes, and she slipped a finger and then two fingers into his arse and he could feel he was as hard as he could ever have been, the way he had wanted her to see him so that she would know that he could be and he tried to move her now, for the fuck he had been dreaming of, but he found his hands tied fast, very fast, to the iron bedhead. Tied almost painfully tight. Yes, really painful. And she said,

'Ah, ah, not now, mate, not after all my hard work.'

And she bit him hard on the chest so that he shouted with pain, and again so that he grimaced, and again on the shoulder, sinking her teeth in. She pulled his dick up to the perpendicular and buried it in her mouth, at the same time slipping something else into his arse, hard, and bigger than fingers – Winkler suddenly thought 'Christ, she's a fucking man,' but she was sucking him so it couldn't be her dick – something she must have prepared earlier because he didn't have anything this shape in his bedroom, and then the tingling became almost painful and Winkler was about to cry out,

'Oh, Jesus, Fucking, Christ, Jesus . . .'

But she thrust a pillow in his face and held it down, leapt around to sit on the pillow, sit on his face on the pillow and he couldn't shout. And he couldn't breathe, he couldn't breathe at all.

And Albuquerque shouted, 'Hold still now, y'bastard.'

And he came hard in her mouth and his dick jumped around and rattled on her teeth and he blacked out and she took his dick out of her mouth and lifted herself from his face and whipped the pillow away and he gasped and glugged at the air, and he came again so hard that his dick wrenched out of her hand and a shot of it hit him straight in the eye and stung like nothing he'd ever had in there, and he yelled with the pain, but the yell could have been anything, and as she grabbed at his dick, which was leaping around like a shower dropped in an empty bath, she scratched his back deeply with the nails of both hands and he shot three more times, in thick stripes on her chest. Like Zorro.

And he fell back on the bed, saying, 'Fuck, fuck, fuck . . .'

'Christ, it had been a few days hadn't it?' she said.

And Winkler didn't reply because Winkler couldn't reply, he could only gasp and breathe and breathe and feel his heart in his chest banging and banging as if it were made of tin with the drugs and the sucking and the sucking and the arse thing, whatever the thing now gone from his arse had been, and the suffocating and the sleeplessness and the sweat poured from him almost noisily, almost with a rushing sound.

And minutes later, remembering what she had said, he replied, 'I can't wank in a strange house.' And thought, truth, now. On top of the dancing and the singing. And then he looked at her and said, 'Jesus, you're covered. Sorry.'

'Don't apologise. That was crazy. That was fucking crazy. I want more of that. But I've gotta go. It's nine o'clock. I've gotta work. I've got an audition at eleven. You stay there. Just like that. And we'll carry on where we left off next time.'

She untied his hands, kissing him on the forehead as she did so, picked up her clothes from the floor and walked out, naked and sprayed, onto the bright landing.

15

The Beginnings of a Police Investigation

Winkler did not wake until much later. It must have been much later because when the doorbell rang nobody answered it. And when it rang again still nobody answered it. Winkler put on his pants and poked his head out of the door.

'Ru?' he said. 'Someone at the door.'

But Ru's room was empty, and nobody else, for once, seemed to be in the house. There was an intercom for the doorbell on the wall next to Ru's enormous bed in a bedroom that took up the entire second floor. Winkler pushed the button and said,

'Hello?'

'Good afternoon,' said a voice that did not sound like one of Ru's usual callers. 'I'm sorry to trouble you on a Sunday afternoon, sir. But would you mind opening the door. It's the police.'

'The police?'

'That's right sir, DCI Porfiry and Sergeant . . .'

'Right. Well there's nobody here.'

'Apart from yourself, of course.'

'Yes. But I'm asleep. Rupert will be back later. Bye.'

Winkler let the intercom button go, and thought to himself what a close run thing that had been. He caught sight of himself in Ru's full-length mirror.

'Wow,' he said aloud. 'I don't feel *that* bad.' He straightened his hair and felt his beard. He didn't feel terrible at all. He didn't get hangovers, and anyway he'd sweated out the worst of it in bed with Albuquerque hours ago. And as she had kept having to go and get more water to keep her mouth from drying out he had drunk plenty, too. So there was just fluffiness from the drugs. And some mild post-narcotic depression, but

Winkler had woken up depressed every morning of his life so far, so he didn't know it was that.

The buzzer went again.

Who could it be?

'Sir, if you wouldn't mind letting us in, it'll only take –'

'Oh, it's you again.'

'I really do need to talk to you, sir. I can come back with a warrant if you'd rather but –'

'There's no need for that,' Winkler said into the wall, kneeling there in his pants on Ru's bed, holding the red 'talk' button down. 'I've never seen a search warrant. You can just wave a parking ticket or something and I'll believe you've got one.'

This quietened them down. The buzzer didn't buzz again and Winkler got as far as the door to the stairs. Then the buzzer buzzed again.

Who on earth could it be this time?

'Sir, I don't know whether you find this –'

'Not you again? Jesus. Okay, okay. I'll put some pants on and come and open up. No, wait, I appear to have pants on already. I'll be right down.'

Winkler clunked down the bare wooden stairs to the living room and crossed the floor to the front door, noting as he went how messy everything seemed in the late afternoon sunlight. The house-dwellers and visitors had all, he assumed, fled to the country or some swanky local restaurant for Sunday lunch with their 'aged Ps' and hadn't even bothered to tidy the place. These bloody Hoorays. Never lifted a fucking finger. Expected everyone to tidy up after them. 'Just leave it to the Jew, lads, he's not even paying rent, reckons he's onto a nice little thing, reckon he's . . .'

Wait, no, that was not how these people were. That was not how it was here. Winkler smiled. He was so happy. But still the place was a mess, he noticed, as he raised his hand to the latch to open the front door: newspapers everywhere, trainers, CD covers, ashtrays and their contents in no sort of symbiosis, pizza boxes – yuk, with all that money they've got they'll still eat that greasy shit – fag packets, books dragged out in the heat of a cokeflush to read out the best description of a grouse-shoot in the history of the whole wide world ever, mugs and milk cartons, video, DVD and Playstation boxes, hats, rizlas, empty snap-top plastic packets, scrunched lottery tickets, dented soft-drink cans with compass holes punctured in little burnt nests in the dimple of thumb-dents, roaches, Ru's stupid nose trumpet, burnt spoons, meths swabs, scraps of blackened aluminium foil, varying lengths of plastic drinking straw, pieces of a smashed bathroom mirror (ha!), dust of cocaine splashed everywhere and pills all over the place, whole, halved, crunched and powdered, including those evil little blue ones (Winkler knew little of drugs) which the bloke Chambers had insisted on pounding in a pestle and mortar and scooping into all the joints.

Of course, fuck it. The police were here because of the drugs.

Mr Clean, my arse. A twat in sunglasses walking around looking like that, selling thousands of pounds worth of drugs to the kind of twerps that lived round here was never going to last long. It was a drugs bust. That was why it was top brass. DCIs, sergeants. The works. The big cheeses wouldn't show up to advise on the neighbourhood watch scheme or to tell them to watch out for a team of catburglars currently at large in the community (though Winkler knew little of police work). He'd open that door and fifty of the fuckers would burst in wearing the night helmets with infra-red sights, carrying little chunky automatic rifles screaming, 'Nobody move, this is a raid.' The first one in would drop Winkler like a pheasant. A rookie, unused to the pressures, fresh off the shooting range, 'Motherfucker at three o'clock!'

Blam! Blam!

Winkler goes down murmuring: 'Mother, oh, mummy, why did you let me go? Oh, oh, Mary, I, I . . .' and expires.

When the place is given the all-clear — no motherfuckers hiding in the cupboards — DCI Porfiry comes in, looks around, crosses to the kitchen, stepping over Winkler's body without a glance as he does so, and says, 'Anyone dead?'

'No sir, just this Jew.'

'Okay bag him and book him. The fucking kikes, sheesh,' and he tips his hat back on his head and plants his hands on his sides and shakes his head. 'You'd think they'd stop short of peddling drugs to children to satisfy their lust for gold.'

'These people have no respect for human life, sir. It says so in the Bible.'

'You're right there, sergeant. Luke 22, verse 3. First they kill the Son of God, now they want our children. Makes you sick. Don't bother with the bag on second thoughts, sergeant. String the yid up from the lamp post outside and let him be a lesson. Now, check the attic. They're always hiding in attics, these people. Then torch the place and let's get out of here.'

Winkler went to the window, very slowly, to see how many vans were parked up. To assess his foe. But there was no sign of life in the street apart from the blinking hazard lights on a double-parked green Ford

Sierra. Ghia. The model with leather trim and heated seats (Winkler knew little of cars, but he had looked at a Sierra a couple of years previously when he thought he was about to be promoted to a job that came with wheels).

Winkler looked round towards the front door and his eyes met those of a tired looking middle-aged man in short-sleeved shirt and tie with a jacket over his shoulder, peering in at him. He jumped. The man indicated his watch and jabbed at it urgently a couple of times. Behind him a younger man was standing back down the steps (or 'stoop' as Ru called it – he liked to have stoop parties there, sipping a gin and juice, checking the bitches, rapping with his homies), looking up at the house for signs of life.

'Just coming!' shouted Winkler dumbly at the double-glazing. 'I couldn't find a shirt!' and he pointed to his naked nipples with the index fingers of both hands. 'Two minutes, I'll be two minutes!' and he held up a victory sign of fingers for Porfiry to muse over, then spun round into the living room.

Into the kitchen, bin bag, and into the bin bag everything including the trainers and the DVDs and the cans and the ashtrays – clunk, bang, smash, rustle, fuck, fuck, fuck.

Winkler stood back. Not bad. He went for a cloth for the table and then thought, 'Aah, fuck it,' picked up a gym membership card from the mantelpiece and scraped it in random swooshes across the table until he had a nice grey-white tumulus of cocaine, dust, fluff, ash, tobacco, hash, ketamine, speed, grass and seeds, mashed pills and dandruff and then pulled Ru's bugle bugle from his back pocket where he had put it seconds before and snarfed the whole lot up in one go.

'A job well done,' he said. And then sniffed hard to try and get down a clotted chunk of MDMA powder the size of a Monopoly house that had, not surprisingly, lodged in his sinuses. Or maybe it *was* a Monopoly house. Had they played Monopoly at any time over the weekend? Probably. If it was a Monopoly house he was fucked. But then if it was a gramme chunk of MDMA he was fucked as well. He chucked the bugle bugle in the bag, swung it twice, holding corners, knotted it and knotted it and knotted it again and went out to the kitchen and into the yard (it was a garden, but Ru called it the 'yaaaard', and had allowed it to collapse into a state of relatively convincing yarditude) and heaved it into one of the big wheely bins by the side gate, dusted off his hands (actually dusted off his hands: paff, paff, paff) and then came back inside, locked the door and put the kettle on. Then he sat down at the kitchen table and pulled a

double-folded *Daily Telegraph* towards him and the pen that was lying on
it, to see if he could do any of the missing crossword clues. Ru always
had the *Telegraph* crossword half-filled in the house. It was the only broadsheet crossword he could come even close to completing.

'Border poet's hirsute growth . . .' Winkler read aloud. Border poet.
What has borders? Everywhere. Wales. It had to be Dylan Thomas. But
it was a nine letter word. Bob Dylan. That had nine letters. And Bob
Dylan had a beard. Some of the time. And it counted as one word because
it was a name. Winkler wrote it in: 'B-O-B-D-Y-L-A-N-'

'Fuck.' It was only eight letters. Wait. Winkler wrote an S in the last
space, and put an apostrophe before it. 'Bobdylan's'. Which border poet's
hirsute growth? Bobdylan's. Fuck. He wasn't Welsh. But America had
borders too. It had to be that.

Excellent work. And in Winkler's slightly fucked state, too. Most impressive. He went to the cupboard to get a mug for his tea.

The doorbell rang.

Who could that be?

Fuck, the police.

Winkler ran to the door and rattled it until it opened. He had never
quite got the hang of it. There was a thing to turn and a thing to lift
and then you had to pull the door and, anyway, there the door was:
open.

'We meet at last,' said the middle-aged man, presumably Porfiry.

'Had trouble with the door,' said Winkler, becoming aware just then,
of the fact that the Monopoly house had moved further back into his
head. Which meant that it must have melted a bit to be able to shift.
Winkler snorted with horse-like power, and it seemed to shoot an inch
and then stuck again. 'Must be MDMA after all,' he said aloud.

'I beg your pardon?' said Porfiry.

'I said that I was just making tea for us all.' And just then the hissing
of the kettle became audible away in the kitchen.

'Very thoughtful,' said Porfiry. 'Weren't you going to put a t-shirt
on?'

'No, a shirt,' said Winkler.

Porfiry looked down at Winkler's chest. Porfiry stared hard at Winkler's
chest and nodded towards it. Winkler looked down. It was bare.

'Right,' he said. 'But I couldn't find one. What with putting the kettle
on and everything I just didn't have time. I didn't want to keep you
waiting too long.'

'Very thoughtful, once again. If we might . . . ?'

'Oh, of course, come in, come in. Sit down if you want. I'll just go and grab a t-shirt.'

Winkler tossed his newspaper down on the newly-cleaned table, ran up the stairs, into his room, grabbed a t-shirt from the floor by his bed and shuffled it on over his head as he bounced downstairs again.

'There, all done,' he said.

The two policemen stared at him.

'Uh, sir,' began the younger one. But Porfiry hushed him with two closed fingers swiftly raised to shoulder height.

'Really, have a seat,' said Winkler.

'I will, thank you,' said Porfiry.

As Porfiry and Winkler hunted for clean space to sit in amongst the rubble that was still there after the hurried clean, the younger man looked around him. He walked to the bookshelves and glanced at the spines of some of the books, his hands behind his back, his head tilting sideways to read. He picked up a sock from the mantelpiece.

'It's a bit of a mess in here, isn't it, sir?' he said, addressing Winkler. But Porfiry interrupted:

'Don't be impertinent, Tolkien. Mr Winkler has just spent the last ten minutes cleaning up for us.'

Winkler started.

'Um. You said Winkler?'

'Yes. That's you, isn't it?'

'Yes it is. But I, ah, how did you know?'

'Why, Mr Winkler. It's you we've come all this way to see.'

'All what way?'

'From – oh, of course. We haven't introduced ourselves. How rude. I'm sorry. I'm Detective Inspector Porfiry and this is Tolkien.'

'Sergeant Tolkien, sir.'

'Yes, yes. Sergeant Tolkien. He's very keen on that. He waited a long time for promotion. Passed over by many much younger but abler men over the years, and now he can't seem to do without it for even a moment. It's Sergeant Tolkien this, and Sergeant Tolkien that.'

'Right, and you've come all the way from . . . ?'

'From Northstead CID to ask you a couple of . . .'

Northstead! Northstead was Winkler's local station. What on earth were they doing here? Unless. Unless it was about the – fuck, he snorted and the lump of MDMA shot into his throat. He swallowed it. It burned.

They were here about the fat woman on the train, in front of the train, that is, under the train. Smashed by the train, mashed by it and flattened.

Winkler's murder. The murder. Nearly a week ago now, and given not a thought since.

That bright morning. Of course bright, all the mornings were bright. It was just a morning last July. No particular morning.

That bad night of Holocaust dreams. Gas chamber dreams. Inside the chamber and out. And of Malcolm Pritchard finding it all so boring. And Sherwood Glaub, and his grandfather. Will and Mary. All bored. The Werther report always there, hanging, and Millfield Spawn. The rattling train, Winkler clinging to the chocolate machine – wondering: what if he pushed? The conspiracy theories of Leo Sneel. And the gnus milling silently, sniffing the air. Miss Maxwell dragging him by the ear for breaking his vow of silence. The blind girl helpless in her hard chair in the sunbeam. His grandfather helpless in his stairlift chair, endlessly unvisited, picnicless. The endless repetition. Day after day and train after train and always the same, and the Holocaust stories always the same, but seemed so much fresher to Winkler than this every day up above the streets and houses and into the steaming human swarm around the deathless puddle under the bridge. His clumsy equation of the tunnels of the train with the tunnels of the what? The sewers of the city and the streets of the ghetto? The little fat women everywhere all in black. The snakes and the spiders threatening danger. The shivers and the shouting, the old Jew with the blackheads and the apple – wondering: what if he pushed? – and the screaming boy robbed of chocolate, the scrawny man chased up the street, the ball chased to the boundary, Ginger Bill, the little pile of shoes on the bed, the milkmaid severed at the head, and the sperm sprayed silently on the television's screen.

Down into the Underground in the early morning and the platform's already rammed. Down to the business end, the rocketing hammer and anvil, cylinder and piston, death-dealing steelthump at its most merciless and in among the jostling jostlers knowing where the doors will fall and elbowing, shuffling, kneading the doughy populace for position, the woman in the grey suit with black, blocky rubber-soled half-smart work and rape-escaping footwear, white t-shirt and cheap-necklaced piggy-face (like Mary, the broad bean then in his life) flat-permed wattle-necked slack-kneed gigantic pointless ugly ill carrying a too-big handbag, great sack of shit and supplies and reading a folded magazine designed for a woman like her full of help that won't and advice that can't, chewing a banana (diet number 23, and that only this year: eat anything yellow during daylight and then as much fish as you like after midnight) not noticing the space opening in front of her right in the space where the doors won't fall and the herd knows it. Winkler as the rumble rumbles moving through the herd, pressing through the weak points where shoulders touch shoulders, and the rumble rumbles louder, more and more metallic, tinnier and higher, Winkler at a tripping trot there at the last minute as the heads down in newspaper pages look up and the pages are folded away for the press onto the train, one or two stepping involuntarily back from the line, Winkler at the last minute with his hand out, rushing for the gap before the train and if she moves now, now at the last minute, over goes Winkler like he always feared, into the onrushing slam of red and grey but she is big enough to stop him, hand out into her back, her back and side and no movement from her at first as his hands sink in and she all yielding and fleshy, rumbly, like a waterbed, the rest of her wobbling around as Winkler sinks in deeper, but more conviction in his lean as her head starts to turn and a stagger and a stagger and all eyes firmly on the approaching train, and, oof, there she goes. There she goes. Thaaar she blows, the great whale, the magazine flies, the bag is clutched, oddly, pointlessly, oh, it's all timed so nicely for an aerial collision and it's touch and go which will go, it may be curtains for the train, but no

Blam!

Screaming, obviously. Not hers. Too late for that. She is multicoloured mist and smoke. Winkler's scream is first out of the hole.

Well, shit, he was nearest. This is going to fuck him for life. Him and the driver. Though the driver will get counselling.

Oh, they're all screaming now. Like they've never seen death before. Jesus. One life extinguished – without pain or anguish, remember – and they're all going nuts. It's not as if there's a shortage of people. Six billion more where that came from. That's right: a thousand times as many people left alive after the fat slag splatted as died in the boring old Holocaust. And still they scream. Like to see how they'd have made out in the ghetto.

Winkler screaming loudest of all though, still. And then suddenly an alarm wailing over the tannoy and instructions. Stay put? Get the fuck out? Who knows. Winkler runs. Of course. Backs away into the crowd, stepping on toes, but after surging forward by Christ they're backing off now, too. The train has stopped not quite at the end of the platform. And Winkler, by the time he gets to an exit from the platform, notices it's quiet. A bit of crying. But quiet.

Instructions calmly slide out of the speakers but whatever they say Winkler is off up the escalator with great speed, up the left-hand side, never stands still anyway – and hates the ones who do – left or right – it's a moving staircase so that people can travel long distances up and down between the light and dark with more efficiency and speed, not so they can stand still and be dragged down and up, fattening up nicely and burning not a joule (He said joule, not Jew). If the man who invented the escalator had wanted that he would have invented the lift.

Seven or eight quickskipping men in pale blue have passed him on the downside (on the downside, the bitch is dead: on the upside, Winkler is not) in case there is something they can do. Winkler could shout, 'Relax, there's nothing for you there, I caught her just right. All you need is a mop, and a bag for jewellery,' but that would be incriminating. Wouldn't it?

Proper cops pass him at ground level, with that funny little run of theirs, and a couple of policewomen too in those horrible shoes and black tights on their trunky little legs.

Winkler feels for his ticket, can't find it. Before and behind him urgency and irritation as people hear the station announcer announcing that the station will close and alternative routes will have to be found, and all because of Winkler. They don't know that though. His peers, they are. The jury of his peers. They'd send him down for years and years. Just for making them late. Fuck, where is it? If I can't get out I'm fucked. Not as fucked as the fat fucker I just fucked down in the bowels of the town under the screaming heat and the traffic roar –

Ah! Got it.

And now out in the street. Bright, of course. And with the feeling of her doughy fatness in his hand and arm, and her scent, and sweaty from the run upstairs. Breaking a step to run, and then remembering. No need to run. Nobody chasing. Just Winkler in the sunshine, at last, with a job that needed doing done. The smell of diesel and tar quite spicy in the sunshine. Grass seed he could smell, and bread, the smell of breakfast. No need to go to work. His time suddenly his own to do with as he pleases.

And it was a beautiful day.

'You alright, sir?' said Sergeant Tolkien, peering into Winkler's face.

'Hmm? Oh. Yes, fine. Fine.'

'You look awfully sweaty, sir.'

'Um, yes. I am rather sweaty, aren't I?' Winkler clutched up the bottom hem of his t-shirt and mopped water from his face. It was the drugs of the last few days, or more likely the MDMA he had just swallowed, that was doing it. The moisture on the t-shirt smelt terrible. 'I had a rather heavy night,' he said.

'Clearly,' said Porfiry. 'Tolkien, get Mr Winkler a glass of something cold. I dare say there's a beer in the fridge. And make us all a cuppa with that water he so kindly boiled for us while we were standing outside.'

'Look, how do you know my name?'

'We went to your home address this morning and they said we might find you here.'

'My home?'

'In Black Park Hill. Number 32.'

'Who said I would be here?'

'A girl.'

'Irish?'

'Possibly, I didn't pay much attention.'

'Beefy girl, face like a broad bean?'

'I suppose. I thought she was rather pretty, myself.'

'Bitch.'

'Look, Mr Winkler. I don't want to keep you any longer than I have to. I'm here because a woman's been killed.'

'Killed?' said Winkler. Because that is what you have to say in such situations. But he was wondering how on earth they had got to him already. And hadn't everyone just assumed it was an accident? Or suicide? Must be the fucking CCTV cameras. Bastard fucking cameras. Well that was it then. All up. Six days of life as he had always hoped it would be, fine fucking, friendship and fun, and now prison. For ever. Well. No. Couldn't be that bad. First of all there was the insanity plea. Nobody in their right mind would do a thing like that. Not a nice well-adjusted person like Winkler. And he could just claim it was an accident. He tripped and grabbed her for support, she shrunk back, and – he felt terrible, of course, and was trying to deal with it as well as he could, which was why he had not come forward until now. He was planning to. On Monday. Why did he run? He didn't run. He walked. Because the tannoy said to leave the platform (didn't it? He thought so). Oh, he was caught on camera running. Well, that was because he couldn't risk being late for work and had to be first on the bus. What, how did they know his work arrival time wasn't very important? Glaub. That snake-in-the-grass! Winkler would kill him. It wouldn't be his first murder. But it would be his first murder with a motive.

'Markings on the body do not indicate a struggle and –'

'Markings? Good God. That must have been messy work.'

'Not particularly. And there was no sign of a break-in, so we have to assume that she knew her killer quite well.'

'Who?'

'Jenny-Marie Rollins – the blind girl I've been talking about.'

'Eh?'

'Mr Winkler,' Porfiry almost barked. 'You are not the first man ever to have a hangover. Though, God knows, it looks like you've consumed some stuff in the last few hours that compassion would prevent me putting out to poison the foxes. I have come here to talk to you about Jenny-Marie Rollins, a poor bloody helpless foreigner in this country, a poor blind girl who was murdered at her home last night by an intruder. Raped and murdered, Mr Winkler. So do please pay attention to me. I have been made aware that you were known to the dead girl, and I want to know if she said anything in your meetings that might help us identify the attacker.'

'Oh, thank God,' Winkler wheezed.

'What?' said Porfiry.

'Nothing.'

'Did you say "Thank God"? Mr Winkler, what is wrong with you? An innocent girl has been murdered. And you were among the last people to see her alive. It is nothing to be glad about. It is something to take very seriously. Very seriously ind– for crying out loud will you stop making so much bloody noise Tolkien!'

'Sorry, sir. I was just –'

'You were just what, Tolkien? Looking for clues?'

Since returning from the kitchen, where he had stood for a while wondering what he had gone in there for and then given up, Sergeant Tolkien had been strolling round the walls of the flat, his hands behind his back, peering at things, picking things up, turning them over, replacing them, or dropping them, or banging them on each other, mirrors, pictures, books, lighters, carved ebony fertility icons from Burkina Faso, a fur-covered polystyrene Womble about the size of a fat man's thumb whose name was Orinoco, glasses, mugs, pipes, a number of commemorative snowstorms, a flashing amber warning light stolen from roadworks, a sound-sensitive ornamental electric dildo whose illuminated tip wiggled to music from the stereo and ejaculated (if you filled it with a suitable fluid) at key changes; and he was now holding a half-crushed Tizer can which he had picked up from the floor under the television. A charred depression in it was scored with dozens of little holes as if with a pair of compasses and Tolkien had been blowing into the pouring hole and sliding his fingers around the little burnt punctures.

'It appears to be some sort of primitive musical instrument, sir.'

'It's a makeshift crack-pipe, Tolkien, for the Lord's sake, were you born in a barn? Leave the gentleman's personal effects alone and try and pay attention to the matter in hand. Perhaps there is something you'd like to ask Mr Winkler.'

'Am I a suspect, or something?' Winkler asked.

'Well, as a matter of fact —' Sergeant Tolkien began.

'Nobody is a suspect yet,' Porfiry interrupted with a raised voice. 'Except clearly this man who assaulted the late Miss Roland in the subway pass on the afternoon —'

'Rollins, sir.'

'Tolkien?'

'The girl's name was Rollins, sir. Not Roland.'

Porfiry sighed. 'Very good, Tolkien.'

'Sergeant Tolkien, sir.'

'Very good, Sergeant Tolkien,' and Porfiry rolled his eyes conspiratorially at Winkler, who was in no mood to conspire. 'Perhaps, Sergeant Tolkien, you would like to continue the conversation with Mr Winkler while I smoke a cigarette. I shan't ask your permission, Mr Winkler, since I imagine that if I harvested the fruit of every tobacco, cannabis and coca plantation south of Mexico and set fire to it here on the carpet I could hardly be accused of compromising the wholesome atmosphere.'

'No, go ahead,' said Winkler. Porfiry hadn't laughed. So Winkler didn't either.

Sergeant Tolkien took a notebook from his pocket and flicked through it until he found what he was looking for.

'We have it on good authority from our colleagues on the beat,' he began, importantly, 'that you witnessed an attack on the deceased last Thursday afternoon in the subway underpass beneath the R1 dual carriageway at Northstead south junction by a, and I quote, "Scrawny looking man in a baseball jacket, possibly Scottish". Is that true?'

'I saw it, yes. I chased the man for about a mile and then I —'

'Mr Winkler is a hero, Tolkien,' Porfiry bellowed, exhaling cigarette smoke at the ceiling as he lay back on the sofa with his head sunk deep into some of the exotic beaded cushions which Rupert Theofrax Helmesley-DeWilde had brought back from Goa with a view to selling on the internet, but hadn't quite got around to yet. 'He chased the assailant out of the subway, up the hill, quite a hill, that, and only lost him when he ducked into the Perkin Warbeck estate and became suddenly invisible. Though there are no witnesses to this extraordinary pursuit and no bravery medals have been applied for.'

'What? I didn't ask for any medals.'

'Which is what I said.'

'I was worn out and worried she might nick my bags.'

'The blind woman?'

'I didn't know she was blind at the time.'

'Despite the fact that she walked with a stick.'

'It might have been a trick.'

'A trick?'

'To steal my briefcase.'

'And what was in your briefcase?'

'Papers.'

'Valuable papers?'

'No. A photocopied mid-term report on a German fuel company called Werther.'

'Why would a mugger want that?'

'He might have thought it was valuable.'

'Was it an expensive looking briefcase?'

'Quite.'

'May I see it?'

'No. It's not mine.'

'Whose is it?'

'It belongs to a work colleague of mine called Sherwood Glaub. He leant it to me so I could go home early that day and take my work home with me. But I left it at home, the home you've just come from. And I don't have it here.'

'Why did you want to go home early?'

'What?'

'Why did you arrange to leave unusually early that particular day?'

'I was going to go and see my grandfather.'

'And did you?'

'No.'

'Why not?'

'Because –' Winkler stopped. 'Listen,' he said. 'Do you really want my whole life story?'

'Is it exciting, relevant, sexy, unusual, pacy, exotic and well-plotted?'

'No.'

'Then spare me. Nobody's accusing you of anything. Just tell us again exactly what happened, like you told the officers who came to your house.'

So Winkler did.

'And did she say anything about who she thought it might have been?'

'No.'

'Are you sure?'

'The police asked her in front of me, and she said not.'

'But it's rather more important now, isn't it Mr Winkler? Seeing as she's dead.'

Winkler thought for a minute. What if when they went round to the flat today they found traces of the sperm? Like in the carpet or something, and matched it to his DNA. Did they have his DNA profile? But what would that prove? That at some time during his occupation of that flat he had had a wank in front of the television. Embarrassing, but not criminal. Devastating for Meriel, of course, who would realise that his bollock-scratching story had been a red herring. Anyway, surely he cleaned away the sperm when the cops had gone. Didn't he? He couldn't remember. Surely he had.

'Poor Jenny,' Winkler said suddenly. 'Poor little Jenny. God. It's just awful. She was so sweet. And scared. And even then I was appalled by the thought of her vulnerability and wondered who on earth would do something like that. And I never dreamed . . . hang on. She did say she had a couple of funny phone calls. I remember now. I was asking her if she had any idea who it might have been and she said that she'd had a couple of scary phone calls recently.'

'She said nothing to the attending officers in her statement.'

'Maybe she didn't think it was relevant. I was saying, just to make conversation, that it was a dangerous city and you never felt safe, and how we'd had a crank caller at the flat. And she said she'd had one. A bloke who just hung up. Didn't breathe or talk or anything. Just rang, and then hung up. And she was saying how terrible this was because an invasion of her aural space like that, it's much worse than for us because it is all she has left for orientation. She inhabits an almost entirely aural world and so . . .'

'You seem unusually interested in it.'

'No. I just remember what she said.'

'Well, Mr Winkler, I won't keep you any longer. You clearly have a lot on your plate today. This little visit has turned out to be quite worthwhile. But we have got another individual in the frame. Albeit an unknown, a variable, an "X" that requires a value ascribing to it.'

'Inspector Porfiry nearly got a maths degree,' Tolkien interjected.

'Shut up, Tolkien,' said Porfiry.

'Nearly?' said Winkler.

'As good as,' said Porfiry.

'It was the drinking wasn't it, sir?'

'Shut up, Tolkien.'

'He blew it the night before his last exam. They found him under a hedge out by the ring road with two empty bottles of Johnny Walker and an inflatable –'

'Tolkien!'

'But he never touches the stuff now, Mr Winkler. Not a drop. He says –'

'Right, Tolkien, that's it. We're off. And you've had it. I never wanted another partner after poor old Ransome died. I don't mind telling you now that I took you on purely as a favour to old Dodgson. But that is positively the last time you're coming out with me on a murder inq. Mr Winkler, I am sorry for the idiocy of my colleague, PC Tolkien –'

'Sergeant Tolk–'

'Not any more, Tolkien. Not any more. Mr Winkler, if you would be so good as to attend the station tomorrow morning at 11 o'clock,' said Porfiry, rising to his feet and looking in the mirror as he gathered himself to leave (smoothing his hair as he spoke to the reflection of his face that stared at him from beneath the word 'Revolushun' in flaming red, yellow and green letters painted on the glass), 'I would like to have a statement regarding this mystery caller, and anything else you can remember. I am delighted we found you. And I wish you a very good day.'

'What, up at Northstead?' said Winkler. 'It's a bit of a schlep. Can't I do it round here?'

'No you can't do it round here,' sang Porfiry. 'I am sure the police stations are very delightful in these parts, with lots of pretty girls and I dare say their own cappuccino bars attached where you can get a nice little sun-dried tomato smoothie while you give your story. But the down-side is that they do not have *me* there, listening to you and deciding what is true and what is not. So if it's no trouble . . .'

'No trouble at all, Mr Porfiry.'

'Good, good. You can take the tube, can't you? It's only forty minutes.'

'Dangerous place the tube, though, sir,' said Tolkien. 'Only the other day there was that woman who –'

'Come on Tolkien, no time for your bloody trainspotting stories,' said Porfiry, glancing down, as he turned, at the folded *Daily Telegraph* on the coffee table. He frowned, then picked it up and looked at it for a few seconds.

'Sideburns,' he said.

'What's that?' said Winkler.

'Border poet's hirsute growth. It's not "Bobdylan's". That's two words and it has an illegal apostrophe. And it has no logic at all. The answer is "sideburns". Border is "side", Burns is the poet. It is merely serendipitous that he is a poet from north of the border. The hirsute growth in question is, or are, sideburns, made when the two words are elided.'

'That's remarkable, sir,' said Tolkien, holding the front door open for Porfiry.

'On the contrary, my dear Tolkien,' said Porfiry, walking through onto the porch. 'It's a piece of piss. Good day, Mr Winkler. Until tomorrow, then.'

'Bye,' said Winkler, closing the door, and muffling slightly the sound of Sergeant Tolkien saying,

'But the speed you did it sir. It was amazing. It really is a shame about that degree. If only you'd −'

And Winkler was alone again.

Walking back to the kitchen to make tea he caught his reflection in the mirror that moments ago had held the grizzled visage of Inspector Porfiry. He noticed the writing on the t-shirt he had grabbed from the floor of his room. Dull as his mind was, he had to read each back-to-front letter aloud to himself to develop a picture of their collective meaning, squinting as they diminished to squeeze onto five lines:

'L-i-k-e m-y t-i-t-s, d-o y-o-u? T-h-e-n s-t-o-p s-t-a-r-i-n-g a-t t-h-e-m a-n-d b-u-y m-e a d-r-i-n-k.'

And he laughed. After all, it was really quite a funny t-shirt.

On the other side of the door, Porfiry and Tolkien were enjoying the last of the sun and taking the steps down to the pavement slowly.

'Did you see all those drugs, sir?' said the junior man. 'Shouldn't we send somebody round about that?'

'Oh, don't worry about that stuff, Tolkien,' said the hoary old detective. 'These university boys with their bloody family money, it's all they do. I dare say his daddy's best pals with the chief commissioner. He's probably sitting with him now over a large whisky and soda at the club and they're swapping stories about their tearaway sons. We can't touch him for that. A few pills, a few grammes of cocaine, he wouldn't even get community service, though he could do with it. And there's no point scaring him away. We're going to nail him for something much bigger, aren't we Tolkien, my old pal?

'Are we sir? You don't mean . . .'

'The murder of Miss Rawlinson, I do indeed.'

'Rollins it is, sir. You don't really think he's capable of it, do you?'

'You saw the way he was. Pretending to be relaxed. Pretending to be surprised. He's a desperate young fellow. Confused. Alienated. Riddled with drugs. Friendless. Unhinged. Rootless. Spoilt. Chased the assailant away, my arse. There was no assailant, Tolkien. It's all in his imagination. He whacked her himself that afternoon and then bottled out of the rape – the nihilistic act that would crystallise for him in his mind the desperate philosophical circumstances in which he found himself. And then he went back to copulate with her dead body last night. Hoping it would look like a sex game gone wrong.'

'But sir, a posh graduate's existential estrangement from his fellow man is one thing. This poor blind girl was brutally tortured. She was tied to the bedstead so tight the cords cut into her hands, sir. She was tortured. Sodomized with a blunt instrument. There were bite marks, deep bite marks and scratches. And the asphyxiation with the pillow was so brutal that her neck broke.'

'I know that, Tolkien.'

'But it's not just that he did all that, sir. It's that he ejaculated only after she was dead. In her mouth, sir, and all over her dead body.'

'I know that, Tolkien. Don't get hysterical.'

'But, sir. He just doesn't seem the, well, you know, the type.'

'There is no such thing as types, Tolkien. When you've been in this game as long as I have – which of course you won't be – you'll understand that.'

'But you've let him go, sir. If what you say is true, he'll run.'

'He won't run, Tolkien. Running is the action of a scared peasant, a victimised prole. Our Mr Winkler believes himself to be rather more than that. Cowards run, Tolkien. And Mr Winkler believes he is a Romantic hero.'

'A Romantic hero, sir?'

'A Romantic hero, Tolkien.'

16

The Truth About Albuquerque

'Is this a stroke of luck, or not?' Winkler wondered, wishing he had not snorted all that crap off the table, because he needed to think clearly and not be any more depressed than was absolutely necessary.

Winkler was off the hook on one crime – hardly a crime, the spiritually expedient culling of a single faceless, well, practically faceless, and certainly faceless now, fat and useless prole. Useless. Ugly. Fat. Less than Winkler. Less than Mary. Less than Sherwood Glaub. Less than Porfiry. Less even than Sergeant Tolkien. (Tolkien. What sort of a name was that for a policeman?) Yes an unproveable, unpunishable incident, for which he was not ashamed of being responsible. He could hold his head up high about that one. He really would. He simply would not accept that a single individual death in a world overpopulated with invalid souls was something for which one needed to weep. The killing had set him free. Just like Wallenstein had said it would. Winkler, thanks to the trainsplat of fat, was free of the fear of death that had held him back for so long. Free of the fear of exposure. Free of Winkler.

But this crime of which Porfiry suspected him – clearly, he suspected him – was something different.

Why?

The blind girl was young. The blind girl was not fat. The blind girl was blind. Winkler's eugenic code allowed for the disregard of human lives that were unproductive, ugly, brutish and too voracious of the resources – air, food, space, beauty – of which we humans have only a finite supply. Fat people consume far more, for no greater return. They are the massy horde grazing dumbly and moving on as the feeding grounds shrink and shrink. But like elephants on a wildlife reserve, they could not be allowed to multiply indefinitely and kill all the trees. But Winkler was not out to exterminate the vulnerable. It was not about killing disabled people. It was not about racial or genetic purity. He had very deliberately pushed a white woman under the train lest his act be misinterpreted (by himself above all) as a race killing. People cannot help certain things and thus cannot have their cultural value judged by them. Fat people can help it. Fat people can be judged.

The killing of the blind girl was an ugly act. A vile and cruel and cowardly act. An act from which its perpetrator derived pleasure. A rape. Nice smooth white arse, cool skin, soft brown hair. Winkler had derived no pleasure from the murder he had committed. It had been a matter of urgent necessity, not of pleasure-seeking.

Poor Jenny-Marie was a person.

Poor, poor girl. Poor girl. And to think: if she had died under a train – as blind people must fear doing more than the rest of us – or under a lorry or car, how much more painless for her, being blind, than for the rest of us, by comparison with the alternatives. A rape and murder is total invasion of her remaining senses: touch, sound, scent, taste. I dare say, Winkler dared say, that a woman who is being raped closes her eyes anyway. Even Jenny's little advantage is taken away from her in the moment of death. Hit by a hurtling passenger vehicle, she has that tiny edge on the rest of us: she does not see it coming.

How much more heinous to commit the crime of which Winkler was suspected, than that of which he was guilty.

And how much more punishable in the eyes of the law.

What an irony.

What a fuck up.

Winkler phoned the old house. Mary answered.

'Hello?'

'Hi, Mary. It's me. Have the police been round?'

There was a pause. Quite a long one.

'Christ. Wink. It's you.'

'S'what I said. The plod. Have they been round the house?'

'Where the hell are you?'

'I'm round Ru's. You know that. You told those coppers. Ah, there you go. Superfluous phone call. They have been round. What did they do?'

'Thank God you're alright.'

'Course I'm alright. What about those coppers, did they go in my room?'

'Wink, for God's sake. I haven't seen you for days. What's happening? You can't just start on about the police. Yes, some old inspector came round with his idiot friend and asked all sorts of questions about you but they wouldn't say what it was about. I was worried sick. I thought –'

'What questions?'

'Wink. Stop it. I'm your girlfriend. Don't I deserve an explanation?'

'No.'

Silence. Winkler put the receiver down on the table and went into the kitchen, found a packet of cigarettes. Lit one. Came back into the living room. Looked at himself smoking in the mirror. Listened to his name being shouted into the cushion by the telephone. Read the word 'Revolushun'. Laughed. Said, 'stupid t-shirt,' and tore it off with one hand, failing to rip the neck-hole until it was stretched almost to his waist and hurting his neck with the force of it. Picked up the phone again.

'Look, calm down, Mary. Calm down. Don't get hysterical.'

Was this the first time he had ever told someone not to get hysterical?

'I will not calm down, I came home from work one evening and you weren't there. Fine. You're free to come and go as you please. We've always said that. And so am I. And I do. But you don't. That's the first time in three-and-a-half years that you've –'

'Christ is it that long?'

'Yes it is. What do you mean? What do you mean, "Is it that fucking long?"'

'I didn't say "that fucking long". I just said "that long". I was surprised. It doesn't seem so long.'

'Darling, listen. I just want you to come home. I miss you.'

Darling? Did she call him that? Is that what she called him? What did he call her? Honeypetal? Scrumblebum? Fluffimooch? And she missed him.

'Do you?'

'Of course I do, baby. The bed's so empty and . . .'

Baby?

'. . . saying is that if you're going to suddenly disappear for this long then at least phone so that I know you're okay. Let me at least know that. Or . . . or just let me know where you are. I thought you'd had an accident. And then when those policemen came I . . . I . . . I . . .'

It sounded like she was crying.

'Incidentally, how did you know where I was?'

'Will saw you at that party on Friday night, don't you remember?'

'Oh yeah. I was fucked though.'

'He said.'

'Did he now?'

That snake-in-the-grass. I wonder if he said about Amplitude. Ampleness. What was her name? Ampleforth? Alpaca? Alabama wasn't it? Yes. No. Anyway, if he had then . . . no, wait, she wasn't there on Friday night, that was just the boys. The boys – how excellent: a boy's night out. Then again. No bad thing. Have Will see him with a bird like that. Good if he did tell Mary, even. Shake her up a bit. What was her bloody name, though?

'Wink?'

'Alba! Albuquerque!'

'What?'

'That's her name. Albuquerque.'

'Whose name? Nobody's called Albuquerque.'

'This girl is. The girl I –'

Came all over after she'd tied me up, scratched me, spanked me, sodomized me with some enormous dildo and suffocated me. No. Even the new Winkler couldn't say that, out loud, on the phone to his girl-friend.

'The girl I had to turf out of her room so I could stay.'

'Very gallant.'

'Mm. Look all I want to know is –'

Winkler heard voices on the stoop. Singing.

'. . . is: did they do anything funny with the telly. Swab it for evidence or anything, or whatever they do?'

'Eh?'

'Or the carpet near the television?'

If they found his sperm there they'd know he'd wanked in her face. And a man capable of that was capable of – anything. Except, no, like he said before, it would just mean he had had a wank there sometime in the last few years.

There was the rattle of a key in the lock.

'Wink I just don't understand. What did the police –'

'Did they go in my room?'

'Yes.'

'Whaaaaaat? You let them?'

'Yes.'

'They have to have a warrant.'

'What do you mean, a warrant? You were practically a missing person. I wanted them to find you.'

'Oh you stupid, stupid cow. Did they take anything?'

'I don't . . . I can't imagine that they . . .'

She was crying.

'DID THEY TAKE ANYTHING?'

The door opened and Ru and four of the lads staggered in singing 'You're not singing anymore! You're not sing-ing any more!'

'I don't think so.'

'Well they're not allowed to, you see. So it doesn't matter. They have to have my permission to get a DNA sample. If they took it from my hairbrush or something without my permission it's inadmissible.'

'What sample? You haven't got a hairbrush. Wink, please. What's going on? What's wrong with you? Come home, please. I want to be with you when you're going through something like this. I love you. I'm your girl-friend. I can −'

'Okay. If that's the problem here then the answer's simple. You're chucked.'

'What?'

'You're chucked. You're not my girlfriend. Fuck off. Sorry, gotta go. Bye!'

And Winkler hung up.

The five boys had stopped singing and were standing looking at Winkler.

'Bitches,' said Winkler.

'For real,' said Ru.

The five of them were wearing football shirts. They'd been round Baz the Jew's house watching football. They'd won.

'Ya haffi tell dem bitch: a man gyaat fi do wat a man gyaat fi do. Ya naaaaaam sehn?' said Rupert Theofrax Helmesley-DeWilde, flopping down on the sofa, patting the top pockets that his burger-chain-sponsored synthetic football shirt did not have, and said, 'Who's got the chang?'

Baz the Jew said; 'Tis I, me bredren, who have the fine white residue of da fountain of yout.'

'Who had all the chang? Who had all the chang? You fat bastard, you fat bastard, you had all the chang!' sang two or three of them, pointing in synchrony at Baz, while Ru said,

'Plenty maaar fish in de sea, sehhhn?'

'Absolutely,' said Winkler. Who was feeling a little chastened by his reflections on the blind girl's death, the likelihood of his conviction and cruel punishment and the end of his relationship with Mary. He was sliding down off the coffee table snort and heavy night's abuse into a reality that was suddenly less perfect than it had seemed only hours before.

'Clear the way for Alba and all that.'

The bredren fell silent. Stared at Winkler. The one called Chambers glanced up from his position hunkered over the coffee table with a note in one nostril and a finger holding down the other. Baz scratched his head. Ru pursed his lips and gave him an Arnold-out-of-Different-Strokes stare.

Then Ru laughed. Clapped Winkler on the back. Said,

'Don't kill yourself over that one, man. We've all been there. Alba's not for hire.'

'Eh? She said she wasn't your girlfriend.'

'She's not.'

The boys laughed.

'She said she was nobody's girlfriend.'

The boys laughed louder. Ru said,

'She isn't. She's engaged, man. Got a fiancé in Melbourne. And she's tight as a drum, bro. Doesn't so much as put her knickers in the same washing machine as mine. While back she broke all our hearts, me say laaaang time sin'. But we gave up trying. She's cool, geez. I see her more like a sister, now. And if I see a guy so much as look at her I . . .'

Ru made a soft fist and his Georgian signet ring glinted not very menacingly on his little finger.

'But last night I −'

Winkler paused. Hadn't they seen him with her last night? No, they left the party quietly and got home alone. But at the party. No, she grabbed his balls in the loo. That was their first contact. And the dancing? That was pretty − but then maybe to people who dance all the time, for whom dancing is no big deal, that is just what dancing looks like. Shit. Interesting.

'You what?' said Ru.

'I, ah, oh, nothing. Damn, that's a shame. I just thought she looked cute in that little brown number at Marky's party. Thought I might be in with a shout of some jiggy-jiggy. But I guess she's just a tactile girl. If she's taken, she's taken. Plenty more bitches in the pound.'

'For real,' said Ru.

'Dat a true,' said Baz.

'Big up respec fi ya mates' bitches an ting,' said Chambers.

'Get your sneezing gear round some of that,' said Ru, pushing a newly striped album cover towards Winkler across the coffee table.

Winkler did as he was told. Rapped knuckles with each of the guys in turn. Said,

'Where is she, out of interest?'

'Back in Oz. Flew out this avo.'

'What? She said she was going to an audition.'

'Yup. And then straight on to the airport. The job, if she gets it, starts Tuesday fortnight, so she's gone for some sort of special occasion.'

'The annual Roo shoot,' said Chambers.

'The Mingashagga charity Beerathon sponsored by Castlemaine,' said Baz. 'Most Australians wouldn't even try to spell XXXX . . .'

'Incest week at Fuckyasista Creek,' said the other one. A bloke with a beard and sunglasses wearing a tracksuit.

'Now there's a week to love Albuquerque like a brother, man,' said Baz.

And Ru said, 'Raaaaaz claaaat. Boooomber style!' And they clanged knuckles again. Like the skinny Muslims of Winkler's forgotten mornings.

Okay. Good. Fine. This was no time to be settling down again. Chuck Mary. Come all over Alba. And move on.

Dread.

Ras-Ta-Far-iiiiiiii.

17

Containing Twenty-Five Little Chapters in Which an Awful Lot Happens

'You up for the cricket, then, man?' said Ru, as he and Winkler sat out the last minutes of Sunday together on his great ancestral (or possibly not ancestral) leather sofa in front of the television, watching a cable news channel with the sound off, drinking cocoa, wearing dressing gowns, smoking long chillums of pukka charras, listening to Mingus.

'The cricket?'

'My Pa's game. You said you would on Friday. You said you'd show us a bit of the left arm tweaker magic. Lord Morcester's XI versus the village. Oh, come on. It's a wicked day. Big lunch for the whole village on the croquet lawn. Local holiday. Ox on a spit. Maypole. Morris dancing. Local wenches. The lot. We get really bugled up afterwards, probably take out some of the old man's Le Mans classics and tear up the tennis courts a bit. Then it's three hours each either side of tea. Whack a few sixes into the lake and laugh at the yokels. Then the plebs are sent packing with a clap on the back from Dad and a bottle of something cheap and fizzy and supper is toffs only in the house. Hookers in from town later if we fancy. Bit of a laugh. Say you will.'

'It's just that I'm supposed to be seeing the police tomorrow.'

'Oh, man. Fuck da police. Fu- fu- fuck da police. Fuck da police.'

'They think I raped and killed a blind girl last night.'

'Whoah. Not mellow. By no means mellaow. Did you?'

'Shit, no. I was upstairs with . . . With my sweet dreams. Crashed in the bedroom.'

''F you say so.'

'Well, of course I fucking was.'

'I can't give you no alibi, brother. I wasn't here.'

'Don't worry. It's cool. I'll postpone the police thing.'

'Cool. Cricket it is.' Ru got up and began to dance in the mirror, smoking his chillum at the ceiling, under the letters that spelt 'Revolushun' and singing, 'I don't like cricket. Uh-uh. I love it . . .'

'Funny thing is,' said Winkler, unheard. 'I pushed a fat woman under a train eight days ago and nobody seems to give a shit.'

'Me nah like reggaeeeee . . .' replied Rupert Theofrax Helmesley-DeWilde. 'Me loooove ittttt – ah . . .'

Winkler picked up the phone. Rummaged the phone book for Northstead station. Dialled the number.

'Oh, hi. Hello. Is Inspector Porfiry there?'

'No. It's gone midnight. Is this an emergency?'

'Not as such. Only, I'm supposed to come and see him tomorrow morning at eleven.'

'Then you better had.'

'Yes. Except, I can't. My grandfather is ill. Very, very ill. In fact, he's dead.'

'I'm sorry.'

'Not your fault. Only I have to deal with certain things. Arrange a burial as soon as possible. He's Jewish, you see. I'm Jewish. We're all Jewish. We have to bury him by nightfall on the second day. So I just can't make it. Can you tell him for me? Can you say I'll be there at eleven o'clock on Wednesday, prompt?'

'I can leave him a note.'

'Do that. That'd be great. Excellent. Thank you so much. Bye.'

And so that was that done.

'Sorted,' he said to Ru. 'I'm all yours tomorrow.'

'Great,' said Ru. 'We better kip down then. Early start tomorrow. Up at nine and away by ten to make the old place by lunch. It'll be such a laugh. And we should give the locals a real thrashing this year. We've got a very respectable side for once. A couple of county fellows and also my old school captain, a roaring middle order bat and a very dear old pal of mine. I can't wait for you to meet. He's just your sort of bloke.'

'Really?' said Winkler.

'Really. He's called Rupert, too. We Rus like to stick together. You'll love him to pieces.'

•

The drive out to Morcestershire in Ru's 1958 Lotus 7 was hairy. Winkler in the passenger seat rolled joints while Ru, with his school cricket cap perched on top of his dreadlocks and a pair of skiing goggles on his face, replaced endlessly the CDs in his too-loud hi-fi, always with another hiphop tune which Winkler had to check out, this bit, this rhyme coming up now, if he was to understand where Ru was coming from. What he was dealing with.

Winkler was particularly uncomfortable in a long traffic jam that snaked for miles through the poor black neighbourhoods in the far western reaches of the city. Ru's hear-me-now volume drew the attention it was supposed to. And in amongst his head-bopping he threw what appeared to be nods to the young black men who glanced at the car.

Maybe they were nods, maybe they weren't. Certainly the men did not nod back. Maybe they were admiring the music. Maybe, as anyone would, they were admiring the car. But the look in their eyes did not seem to Winkler much like admiration.

It was possible that Ru was not aware that he was white.

And white he most certainly was. As white as anyone Winkler had ever known. Whiter than Winkler by a considerable distance.

•

When Winkler came downstairs that morning the front door was wide open and sunlight was pouring into the hall, glinting off the bicycles parked against the radiator, flashing the light into the living room in sparkles that bounced off the mirror that said 'Revolushun' and clattering among the copper and steel saucepans that hung from a ceiling rack in the kitchen. A plane was passing low over the street, very slowly. For a long time. Winkler went out to investigate the noise.

At the foot of the stoop, the Lotus – by no means an aeroplane, but gun-metal grey, striped down the middle of the bonnet with a pair of white lines and stamped with a number 53, upholstery red, exhaust vast, double and glistening with polished chrome, quietened down to a growl as Ru looked up from where he had his head in its jaws and a spanner in one of its teeth. Ru turned the spanner a little more, still looking at Winkler, and the growl simmered down to a gentle purr.

'That sound right to you?'

Winkler, who knew little of motor engines, shrugged.

'She was ticking over a bit hastily. Used nearly a tank of gas getting her here from the lock-up. It seemed like a Lotus sort of a day, don't you think?'

Winkler, who knew little of days and the classic automobiles to which each was specifically suited, nodded and said: 'She's very lovely.'

'Dad drove this at Le Mans in '64,' said Ru, climbing the steps to the front door, wiping his hands as he came on an oily chamois leather, turning and looking down at the quietened lion. 'Got bumped off the road by a pair of Gerries in an illegally modified Porsche, spun fourteen times and broke pretty much in two. Killed his co-driver. Which was a bore because old Cloughie, Clim my dad called him, was the head gamekeeper on the estate. And after he croaked the shooting went rather to pot. Still, got the car back in shape finally, which was something. You ready to rumble?'

'More or less. Cup of coffee. Get dressed. Have to stop and get some kit on the way.'

'Oh don't worry about kit, I've got a few pairs of whites, plenty of shirts, bound to be a pair of boots in the house that fits you. We'll get you a coffee on the way. Go on, put some clothes on and we'll get going.'

'Do I need anything smart?'

Ru looked at him.

'Not really,' he said. 'A jacket for lunch and tea would be nice and supper is black tie, of course. But otherwise Pa's pretty casual.'

'Oh, right.'

Ru laughed. 'For fuck's sake, Wink, what do you think the dress code is?' He threw his hands wide, presenting himself: surf shorts, singlet with a Japanese rising sun on it, a broken pair of Dunlop Amber Flash.

'For evening I add a chichi cricket sweater to the ensemble,' said Ru, 'and bob's-yer-auntie's-quickie-with-the-milkman: the well-dressed Englishman at rest.'

When Winkler came down again, dressed and with a change of under-wear, a toothbrush and a book to read on the boundary packed in a supermarket plastic bag, Ru had put the cap on his head and the sweater round his shoulders. At his feet was a vast cricket coffin of the type Winkler had never owned because he was a bowler, and bowlers did not need kit. (Because he was a bowler, and small, he was not allowed to bat higher than number eleven. So there was not even the faintest suggestion that he needed his own pads, or bat or even box. He just borrowed what he needed if he found himself, due to some collective failure of the other ten, required to walk to the wicket and do what he could with the heavy wooden object with which he was not allowed to practise. And if Winkler was walking out to bat then it meant that all was lost, anyway.)

'Take a sweater for the ride,' said Ru, offering the coffin with a flick of his palm. 'It'll be chillier than you think with the lid off and nothing keeps the British weather out of a Lotus like a good triple-knit Shetland cricket sweater.'

Winkler bent to the coffin to rummage for a sweater. The base smell was the leather of the case and of the dozen or so balls that rattled around at

the bottom, a couple of them all but new, match balls barely tickled in a
disastrous second innings collapse, but most were ancient and pinked, swollen
from nights out under hedges in a rainy September, but were still carried
for sentimental reasons and for knocking in new bats. There were three
bats: a twenty-year-old child-size Gray-Nicholls four-scoop for knocking
about in the road if the groundsman hadn't arrived yet to open the gates,
and a pair of newer bats, one heavier than the other (the weightier one
for squaring up to quick bowlers on a hard wicket and driving them back
over their heads, the lighter one for protracted innings against spin, not too
tiring, and facilitating the cutting and sweeping, nipping and nurdling that
such bowling, particularly on a slow wicket, demands). The bats gave a smell
of wood and linseed oil, and the handles a rubbery tang. Disturbing the
sweaters, Winkler released the gentle scent of expired mothballs and the faint
memory of old chests of drawers lined with blue and white checked lining
paper. One pair of pads was old and made of nubuck with leather straps
and metal buckles and gave off that smell. Another pair of pads weighed
nothing and had wide straps of Velcro but no smell at all. Boots smelled of
whiting from a squeezy applicator with a foam brush nozzle, and the mud
stuck between the spikes was earthy and dusty and dry. The short-cut grass
that was swirled up and fossilised in the mud, and the grass in the bottom
of the case which was old and dry but still green, as well as brown, smelled,
deceptively, of outfields newly cut. Coins rattled and dropped, pencils clinked,
there was a foxed old scorebook, a curled tube of Deep Heat for muscle
strains, smelling lightly still of eucalyptus, sweatbands, ankle and thigh straps,
bandages, scissors, tape, a squash racket, a bent library hardback of the Arden
Pericles, a girl's shoe, a bicycle pump, stud tighteners, a pair of Green Flash,
pellets of purple foil of Dairy Milk or Fruit and Nut, a strapless digital watch,
miscellaneous keys, two feather shuttlecocks, cue chalk and caps of many
colours smelling of must and curtains. Mysteries. It smelled of last summer,
and of summer twenty years ago, and of summer before the War and of the
long, long summer at Hambledon, where giants played.

Winkler had not been so absorbed by a smell since the smell of . . .
the house. Two smells from opposite sides of the universe. Winkler
laughed.

'What?' said Ru.

'Nothing,' said Winkler, straightening up with his chosen sweater in his
left hand and clapping his right onto Ru's shoulder. 'Really, it's nothing.
The smell of the coffin brought back memories is all. I haven't played in
a long time.'

'I should throw most of that junk out,' said Ru. 'But I never get round to it. And then when I'm about to it always seems like a shame. I see you've gone for the I-Zing. Excellent choice.'

Winkler looked at the red, black and gold neck-stripe of the sweater. The colours of I Zingari, the oldest wandering club in the world. The first cricket colours, the red, black and gold indicating 'the ascent from darkness through fire into light' and named in 1845 after the Italian for gypsies. Winkler put it on. He found it scratchy.

'Come on old stick,' said Ru. 'Help me get this bastard strapped on the boot and we're all done.'

'Right,' he said, leaping over the door and into the car a few minutes later as Winkler opened the passenger door and climbed in, finding the seat awkwardly low and the sill inconveniently wide. Ru turned the engine over and gunned it loudly in neutral, 'We've got 95 miles to drive, we've got a full tank of gas, a half-pack of Camel, it's night and we're wearing shades . . .'

Winkler turned and looked at him.

'It's from *The Blues Brothers*,' said Ru.

'Oh, I see,' said Winkler.

'Obviously some of the details are wrong. But here's some riz, the last of that charras and some Silk Cut. You can skin us a fat one for the road. You can manage can you, in the car, with the roof down? I'll drive easy till you're done.'

Rupert Theofrax Helmesley-DeWilde pulled the skiing goggles out of the glovebox in front of Winkler and said, 'You can roach that if you want,' indicating the original 1958 owner's manual that was lying there in a sealed plastic pouch. 'I'm sure Dad wouldn't mind.'

He pulled the goggles onto his head, gunned the engine again, settled them down over his eyes, threw back his head and laughed like Vincent Price. Then he turned to Winkler and shouted,

'Poop! Poop!' And roared off down the road, covering Winkler with the insides of the cigarette he had just opened and the thumbful of charras he had crumbled into his palm. He turned sideways and said,

'Toad. From *Wind in the Willows*.'

'Yes,' said Winkler. 'I got that one.'

•

A couple of hours later, Winkler, for the first time in a long time, saw fields. Real fields. Not sickly imagined vistas of what may or may not have once lain beneath his tarmac world. Green fields netted by hedgerows, containing flint houses with grey slate or thatched roofs, rivers, sheep, leaves. Containing also this horrible road and these horrible cars, but then that would always be the case with fields that one saw from a car.

As they approached Ru's village the hedges at the side of the road towered higher either side of the car as the Lotus roared through the tunnel of green, through explosions of light and shade that burst and flew depending on the trees above and the angle of the sun, until they rounded a corner and Blam!

The landscape opened before them and fell away through fields that were small and each of a different green, shades of green that ran all the way to purple, stitched together with hedgerows where small birds swooped and sang. We're here, we've made it. Winkler's Never Never Land.

Down below, the road turned and swooped to the house and the car followed it down, skirting vast oaks, swerving round to go out of sight of the house and then come in again as Winkler's eyes rushed across high grass and deer to low-cut grass, a brown wicket and stumps casting no shadow at the dead of noon, a pavilion and scoreboard and the house again. Big, grey, mid-18th century, nothing special. Pluck one out and stick it in: Brideshead, of the book or the Castle Howard television series proxy, Blenheim if you like, or Longleat, though much too grand. Althorpe, maybe. Without the memorial island. You don't even need to imagine those. Take Winkler's landscape, do the crucial edits, whack in a great big house.

'Fucking hell,' said Winkler.

'Welcome to the 'hood,' said Ru.

•

'Dad, this is my friend Winkler.'

'Mr Winkler,' said Lord Morcester, gruffly. Shaking Winkler's hand very hard as they stood on a path through the rose garden, which was the way they were walking back to the house after dumping the kit in the pavilion.

'Mr, er, Lord, ah, your, um. Hello,' said Winkler. 'What a wonderful place.'

Lord Morcester stared at Winkler and blew through his nose.

'You half expect to see Isaak Walton sitting under that tree with his wooden rod, thumbing through the Bible,' said Winkler.

'Where?' said Lord Morcester, turning round and looking at the tree, which hung over a bend on a stream that ran round the back of the kitchen garden and out through an arch in the medieval brick wall that surrounded the immediate grounds, and where flies skittered in a shady patch and trout watched them greedily from below. 'On my land? Can't see him. Isaac who did you say, man?'

Winkler froze.

'What's he blathering about Rupert?'

'Nothing, Dad, he was making conversation,' said Ru, putting his arm round the old man and leading him towards the house. 'Let's go and say hello to Mummy.'

•

Left outside the house, Winkler had no idea where to go or what to do. He wanted to go inside and look around, but it was a private home. He couldn't just go in.

Outside the pavilion a few of the cricketers who had recently arrived were tossing a ball at each other and strolling out to inspect the square. Winkler walked towards them.

'You them or us?' shouted a tall man in a blazer.

'Us, I reckon,' called Winkler. 'Unless you're the village blacksmith or the postman or something.'

The man laughed and hurled the ball high in the air in Winkler's direction. Winkler lost it in the sun, saw it again going behind him slightly, stepped back two paces, raised his left hand high above his head to sight the ball and allowed it to fall past his upstretched arm into his right hand, which was cupped at his waist.

The man in the blazer clapped. Winkler lifted the ball to his nostrils and sniffed at it, looking out across the pitch as he did so, to the little churchyard on the other side where generations of Morcesters or Helmesleys, or whatever they were, were presumably buried.

Then he tossed the ball back underarm, but too hard and it flew over the chap in the blazer, bounced once and struck the knee of a short fat man with white slacks, brown brogues, a yellow chambray shirt with a Ralph Lauren logo and a bald head, who was talking to a skinny woman wearing an Alice band and restraining an excited Labrador on a lead.

'Steady on,' said the fellow. 'I wasn't looking.'

'Sorry about that,' said Winkler. 'I haven't played in a long time.'

'And anyway, you should have been looking, Ru. It's a cricket pitch,' said Blazer to the little bald man. And then to Winkler, who was now within handshake distance, 'Either way, good to meet you. Field in the deep with a pair of hands like that and you won't need to worry about the dodgy underarm. Ledgard, Adrian Ledgard.'

'Winkler. My friends call me Wink.'

The little bald man was upon them now, 'Only kidding about the knee,' he said. 'Barely felt it. Just an excuse when it won't straighten up later.

Didn't catch your name. I'm another Rupert, I'm afraid. Rupert Pennant-Cecil for my sins.'

•

In the kitchen of the house, Ru was smoking a cigarette and flicking the ash into the fireplace while his mother inspected the lunch and his father sent a scrofulous midget down into the cellar to bring up a case of that awful champagne the local MP had sent him at Christmas and two cases of the Bulgarian merlot they'd bought too much of for the mulled wine last November 5th.

'I do wish you wouldn't do that Ru,' said his mother.

'What, smoke or flick my ash in the fireplace?'

'Both.'

•

'Bloody hell! Of course. Of course I remember. Sorry, it didn't click just then. Jesus, Mary and all the Hey diddle diddles. How the devil are you? Still sending down those little left-arm tweakers?' And Rupert Pennant-Cecil made the door-opening gesture with his left hand raised to head height that is familiar across the planet to men who bowled spin quite well at school and are forever afterwards being asked if they can still do it. Which they never can.

'Hardly,' said Winkler. 'But I'll do my best.'

'Best little spinner at the Prep,' said Rupert Pennant-Cecil to the one called Ledgard. 'Didn't turn it much but it was all in the flight. Got hatfuls of wickets. Did you carry on to any sort of level, old bean?'

'Not really,' said Winkler, who was stunned by the fact that Pennant-Cecil had not only failed to grow since the day he last saw him, but had lost most of his hair and become so . . . nice. 'I played for a while at my next school but then things got on top of me a bit and I lost interest. You were playing England schoolboys weren't you, Rupert? Surely you went on to greatness?'

'First off, it was England *private* schoolboys. I always played that one a little higher than it was worth. But, yes, I played some club cricket at Eton as well as captaining the Colts. And I played some County juniors, too.'

'And then?'

'Then my old man died and –'

'Oh, I'm sorry.'

'Don't be. He was a bastard and bloody old. Seventy-eight when he died. I was sixteen and mother was left on her own and I felt that I couldn't spend all my weekends playing, it was bad enough being away at school, so I gave up and used to spend my weekends with her.'

'I don't remember your father from the Fathers' Match,' said Winkler suddenly.

'Which Fathers' Match? Oh, of course, *your* father's match. What a match, eh? No, my old man never played, he was too old. But he took it upon himself to be the non-playing captain. God, that was embarrassing. He was determined to do what he could to beat my team even though he couldn't play. Came out for the toss with me and then sent a local bloody professional in instead of himself. Told the school he paid the damn fees and he could do what he liked.'

'I'd forgotten that,' said Winkler, who was reeling.

'And the thing was,' said Pennant-Cecil, turning now to Ledgard, who looked bored, and was, 'the thing was that although in my other Fathers' matches the fathers always won easily, this time they very nearly lost. Because Winkler's uncle got them all pissed on the field.' Pennant-Cecil paused to laugh heartily at the memory.

'Do you remember, Wink? God, I was so jealous. That huge red-headed chap with the beard. Your uncle. Just so not like all the other dads. This beefy bloody Jewish feller looking like Ernest Borgnine in *The Wild Bunch*, swats a few sixes and then goes off to get hammered. Anyway, Adrian, it was hilarious. Because we had to get about a hundred and fifty to win and –'

'A hundred and forty-three,' Winkler interrupted.

'Yes, a hundred and forty-three. I say, well remembered. And we would never have got close, as usual, until Wink's old man, his uncle, starts passing round the hip flask. The dads lapped it up. Rule breaking like when they were little kids. They got ratted. Couldn't bowl or field a damn thing. Even the pro my Dad had paid for was blotto. And it really looked like we might win for the first time in, well, yonks and I was batting at the end, with you I think, Wink –'

'Yes, with me.'

'And I mean if old Wink was batting it meant things were running pretty close. No disrespect, old stoat. Anyway, Ledgard, I slashed at a half-volley outside off-stump, didn't move my bloody feet, thought I was David bloody Gower, nicked the bastard and it went like a rocket to second slip. I remember thinking we had it, then. They were all so pissed none of them could have caught a ball travelling like that, and suddenly there was Winkler's bloody Uncle Bill. Swallowed it like a python. And they carried him off on shoulders singing his name. I was inconsolable, I don't mind saying. After seven years of sporting achievement at that horrid little school my last act on the cricket ground was to fail because of a blinding catch by a drunk old chap who'd never played cricket in his life. Fair play, it was a blinding catch. But I never quite got over it. I probably wasn't very gracious at the time, Wink.'

'Not at all,' said Winkler. 'You were as charming as ever.'

'Was I?'

Winkler raised his eyebrows. And the pair of them laughed loudly and for a long time. Then Pennant-Cecil clapped his arm round Winkler's shoulder (which had been happening a lot recently) and said, 'How is your Uncle, by the way? Bloody excellent man, he was. They still talk about him, some of the boys.'

'To be honest,' said Winkler, 'I really don't know. I haven't seen him in years. I should look him up.'

'Absolutely you should. There's not much family these days. And a chap like that is priceless. I thought uncles like him were only in children's books. When you speak to him do send my regards.'

'I'll do that,' said Winkler.

'Right then,' said Rupert Pennant-Cecil. 'Let's get inside. I'm ravenous. It must be lunchtime about six times over. You don't get a belly like this standing around chatting. I say we stock up on pies and a couple of bottles and go and scoff them down by the river and catch up on old times. That old dragon Morcester, whom you've no doubt met, will have dragged out the very boggest standard of plonk from that wonderful cellar of his. But I reckon he'll be changing about now and if I time it right I should be able to slip down there and pull out something decent.'

•

'He's not a drug-dealer, he's my flatmate,' said Rupert Theofrax Helmesley-DeWilde.

'Another one? Oh tosh, boy. Tommy Rot. How many bally flatmates can you have? Bloody lugubrious little face he's got. Mischief. You can see it a mile away. You promised you were off that stuff,' said Lord Morcester.

'I am,' said Ru. 'And he isn't a drug dealer. He's a bloody good man. He's a mate of a mate and I'm putting him up for a few weeks because he's fallen out with his girlfriend.'

'Boyfriend more like, the way he's dressed.'

'I told him it didn't matter what he wore. He hasn't got much stuff.'

'Sold it all to buy drugs I dare say.'

'That would be if he were a drug addict, not a dealer. What I meant is he hasn't got much stuff round mine. And he's dressed fine.'

'Bloody plimsolls. Bloody little collarless shirt thing. Looks like bloody nightwear. Your other friends at least know how to dress.'

'Winkler isn't like my other friends.'

'And don't tell me he's not a drug dealer. What would he be hanging around you for if he wasn't?'

'Dad. Don't.'

'Well, it's true. Have you got a job yet?'

'Stop it.'

'Still spending the capital? Anything left in it?'

'Why are you doing this?'

'And I see you've brought the car out. I dare say that will have impressed Mr Vinkler.'

'It's Winkler.'

'Oh, is it? I do beg your pardon. Vinkler, Winkler, I know all about his sort. Bring him to Morcester Hall for the cricket, for Christ's sake. What are the damn locals going to think?'

'There isn't anything to think. He's as good a man as I am.'

'Well I won't argue with that.'

'Or as you are, Father.'

'You dare,' roared Morcester, 'in my own home?'

'Fuck it, Dad. This isn't the Middle Ages.'

'More's the pity.'

'Winkler is fine. It'll be fine. Stop being silly. Let's go and have lunch.'

'Feed him at my bloody table,' muttered Lord Morcester. 'My own damn home. Home of the Morcesters. Fine, is he? Eh, what? Fine? We'll see about that.'

●

At Northstead police station Inspector Augustus 'Gus' Porfiry was losing his patience.

'Where is this blasted man to mend the window, Tolkien?'

'No idea, sir. I can call and find out if you like.'

'Excellent idea, Tolkien. Sorry, Sergeant Tolkien. Initiative. Lateral thinking. That's what the force is looking for in a detective. You do want to be a detective, don't you, Sergeant Tolkien?'

'Absolutely, sir. Yes.'

'Well, if the window is opened in the next ten minutes, I'll put in a good word for you with the chief.'

'Very good of you, sir.'

Inspector Porfiry stood up and went to the window. And tried to pull it open again. Reddened in the face. Cursed. Gave up. Observed the dark wet patch under the arms of his light blue shirt. Said, 'This bloody heat is killing me, Tolkien. I'm not asking for bloody air conditioning. Oh, no. Not in an English police station. But a bloody window would be nice. That's not unreasonable, is it?'

'No, sir. It isn't.'

'No. It isn't. A window that a man could open isn't too much to ask, is it?'

'No, sir.'

'If I have to take off any more clothes I'll be stark bollock naked. And I can't interview a murder suspect stark bollock naked, can I, Tolkien?'

'No, sir. You can't.'

'Except we do not have a murder suspect to interview, do we, Sergeant Tolkien?'

'No, sir. We don't. He should have been here an hour ago.'

'I know that, Sergeant Tolkien. But my day is not going very well, so far. If both of them do not turn up in the next fifteen minutes, then both of them are going to be very sorry.'

'Maybe Mr Winkler called and left a message with the duty desk last night, sir, and she forgot to pass it on. You know what these YTS people are like. Maybe something urgent came up. There's probably a perfectly good explanation, sir.'

'Oh there better had be, Tolkien. There really better had be. Because if there is not. If either the window man or our Mr Winkler is sunning himself somewhere with a cool beer on this lovely day while I am sitting here in this godforsaken city, sweating like a Bernard Matthews Christmas Special in a small domestic oven recently turned up to brown, then people are going to die, Tolkien. Do I make myself clear?'

'Diamond, sir.'

'Crystal, Tolkien. The traditional response of the indignant underling, asked by his immediate superior if he has understood his instructions clearly, is, "Crystal." Now, when you've called the oddjob man I want you to call the house at Black Park Hill and see if anybody there knows where Mr Winkler is. And try the mobile number you got for that friend of his, that Will.'

'Crystal, sir.'

'I didn't ask you if it was clear, Tolkien. I just — oh, look just get me bloody Winkler, now!'

•

At 32 Black Park Hill the windows were working perfectly well. They were all open, the flatmates were sipping some delicious homemade traditional lemonade just that morning brewed up by Meriel, and any passing pigeon peering in would have seen Meriel herself sitting at the hard chair by the table, the one in which a now dead blind girl had recently sat, nursing in her lap the head of Winkler's ex-girlfriend, Mary. Still attached to the rest of her, of course.

'Oh, Mare, Mare,' Meriel was saying. 'We'll find him. I'm sure he's alright. He's just having a bad patch at work, I'm sure that's what it is. He loves you, I know he does. And he'll come to find you just as soon as he finds himself again.'

Mary looked up at Meriel, her face was wet and red and swollen with crying and her little Irish eyes were like a colon rolled over onto its side, which is to say: little and black and piggy. She tried to speak, gasped, burst out crying again and collapsed once more into the lap in which Winkler, not so many days ago, had dreamed of burying his own face.

The phone rang. Mary looked up. Looked at Meriel. Stood. Ran across the room. Picked up the phone,

Said 'Hello? Wink?'

Then said 'Oh.'

Then said: 'No I haven't got a fucking clue where the bastard is. So just fuck off and leave me alone, okay.'

Hung up. And burst into tears again.

•

On the other side of town. Out of town, in fact. Over the rolling hills and meadows south of the city, south even of the Emerald City, in a large grey prison building, in a cell about the same size as the away changing room at Morcester Hall, a very large inmate, about sixty-five years old, with grey hair on his head and a long beard which was still red at its extremities but almost white near to the face, was holding a wiry, tattooed and much younger man in a headlock under his arm, and occasionally twisting the younger man's neck hard and making him writhe and grunt.

'Take it back, son,' he was saying. 'All you have to do is take it back.'

The younger man was slapping at thin air and going purple. He was not even breathing, let alone taking anything back. The big man wrenched him again.

'Will you take it back?'

The younger man managed a nod. The headlock was loosened. He clutched at his throat. The bearded man said,

'Come on Sal, I haven't got all day.'

The younger man gasped, 'I take it back, Bill. I take it back.'

'Say it then, Sal. What am I not?'

'You are not a grey bearded old cunt.'

'What am I?'

'I don't know. Just an old man with a fucking bastard of a headlock.'

'I am a *red*-bearded old cunt, is what I am.'

'Eh?'

'I may well be a cunt, son. This is a prison, we are all cunts. If we were not we would not be here. And I am old, my boy, because I squandered my youth frittering about with little fuckwits like you. But my beard is red, you sorry little *schmendrick*. Look, look,' and he tugged at the still orangey extremities of his great two foot bush of chin hair. 'The beard is red. I am a red-bearded old cunt. Or at a push, ginger. I am no longer sensitive about that.'

The young man with the tattoos looked at the old man as if he suspected him of real insanity.

'What am I?' said the old man.

'You're a red-bearded old cunt, Bill,' said the younger.

'Good. Well done. Don't forget it. The only reason I didn't break your scrawny little goy neck is because you remind me of a nephew of mine who I haven't seen in a long, long time. A funny kid. Completely nuts. Never happy, never had any friends. I never figured him out. I played a game of cricket with him once. And then I fell out with his granddad and never saw him again.'

Ginger Bill stared into the distance for a minute. Then pulled himself together, turned to the scrawny little man and said, 'Right, you can go now.'

The younger man looked at him the same way as before.

'Are you still here?' said Ginger Bill.

'We're locked in, Bill.'

'So we are, Sal. Well, just fuck off over there and get on with something then. Read a book. Improve yourself.'

•

At the offices of a right-leaning daily broadsheet newspaper situated on the twelfth floor of the biggest of the Emerald City's seven towers, on a desk staffed by five men in their twenties wearing suits of linen, light tweed or seersucker, and all wearing brogues, a mobile phone rang out the tune of the Eton Boating Song. Four of the men reached for their breast pockets. One answered his phone. It was Will, the former flatmate of our hero. Winkler is still our hero, isn't he?

•

'Cricket, on a Monday?' roared Porfiry.

'Apparently so, sir. It's an annual event. The locals all get a day's paid holiday. It's a local bylaw or something, since the 1700s they said. Mr Winkler appears to be a friend of Lord Morcester's son, sir.'

'The 1700s, Tolkien, is the brief spell of time between 1700 and 1709. Cricket was almost certainly not being played in Morcestershire at that time, or anywhere else. Though there is every possibility that *this* game was being played, God blast it, in 1763, for example, or 1791, which are dates in the 1760s and 1790s respectively. The collective term for all of these dates, however, is the eighteenth century, a little confusing, I know, seeing as the number eighteen is not the cardinal with which each of the dates therein designated begins, but it is, nonetheless, correct. The 1700s is not correct. Though it is a creeping idiocy that is in danger of becoming ubiquitous.'

'1704 I think was the date he said, sir.'

•

Winkler moved across instinctively to the offside as Barney Clapp, the village mechanic, speared another yorker at his leg stump, dropped his bat quietly across his ankles and attempted to clip the ball down to third man. He missed, the ball whacked painfully into his heel and Rupert Pennant-Cecil, batting at the other end, cried, 'Waiting, waiting, yes, there's one there, run it, Wink, old boy, run it!'

The bowler cried, 'Owwwwwozzzeeeee?'

The umpire, an old fellow wearing medals on the breast of his long white coat, shook his head and said, 'That is not out!'

Winkler turned and shouted, 'Yup, one more, go go go!'

Cyril Magwitch, the village's elderly and myopic optician, deceived by the sun, trod on the ball and turned his ankle.

Rupert Pennant-Cecil cried, 'One for the throw!'

The old man stood up, squealing with pain, and underarmed the ball back to Fat Albert Sneep, the butcher, who was keeping wicket.

The crowd – there were possibly seventy of them including staff, wives and the photographer from the *Morcester Globe and Advertiser* (incorporating the *Morcet Herald*) – rose and applauded.

Winkler, puffed, met Rupert Pennant-Cecil in the middle of the wicket.

'What are they clapping for?' said Winkler.

'That's your fifty, you daft bugger. Bloody good knock. It's considered meet on such occasions to acknowledge them.'

'But I didn't hit it, it's a leg-bye. I should say so.'

'Don't embarrass the ump, if you didn't hit it he'd have to give you out LBW. Just raise yer bat. You don't get fifty every day, I'll wager.'

'Never got one before,' said Winkler with a grin and raised his bat to the corners of the ground. 'You never used to let me have a go, remember?'

Winkler had gone in at six because Ru had persuaded his father that his bowling might have suffered in the twenty year lay-off and it would be nice to give him a chance to get involved in the game. He had asked his father to put Winkler in at five but Lord Morcester had said,

'One of them? In the top half of the Morcester XI's batting order? Never!'

So six it was. And Winkler had repaid Ru's faith with the first fifty he had ever scored. The bowling was terrible, though. All but four of his runs had come on the leg side and now he had moved to the first batting milestone of his life with three erroneously credited runs, had only really made 47, and had failed properly to acknowledge the crowd. The moment so long awaited was a little tarnished. He was run out two overs later while backing up, after an unscrupulous appeal from Gerry the Gyppo, the local vagabond, who was bowling roundarm daisycutters from the other end, for 52. Which was really only 49.

Lord Morcester declared at 278 for four and said to Rupert, as they went in for tea, 'In C.B. Fry's day a gentleman didn't even run if the ball went to leg.'

●

Angelena Kafka, the sultry and mysterious Czech pathologist who was working at Northstead CID on a placement from an exchange programme the city had initiated as part of a wider British attempt, sixty years after the event, to make up for doing nothing to defend Czechoslovakia from Nazi occupation in 1938, and on whom Inspector Porfiry had had his eye for some months, burst breathlessly into his office, where he sat with Tolkien, waiting for Winkler and hogging the measly wheeze of the only electric fan in the building.

'I heff done vot you esked me, Herr Inschpektor,' she said. 'Ze DNA results from ze blind girl's clotheses.'

'Thank you, my dear, very kind,' said Porfiry, wondering how he could turn this brief conversation into an agreement on a dinner date and then giving up on it, in the heat. 'It would have taken weeks if I'd gone through the normal channels.'

'It iz my pleezure,' said Dr Kafka.

Porfiry mopped his brow with his already soaking wet handkerchief and then wiped the back of his neck. He glanced at the piece of paper she had put on his desk, and compared it with another that had been sitting there all morning. He looked back at the new piece of paper and back at the old. And at the new and at the old.

'Get the Sierra, Tolkien,' he said. 'And rustle up a couple of officers in a squad car to follow us. We're going for a little drive in the country.'

'Are we sir? Where's that then?'

'Morcestershire,' said Porfiry. 'It's such a splendid day, I feel like watching some cricket.'

●

At Northstead General Hospital Doctor P.A. Paphides stood at the foot of a bed and looked at the clipboard hanging on it. 'Nurse, would you call Mr, er, Christ, this is illegible, can't anyone round here get the hang of the Roman alphabet? Mr W – Woojamaflip, let's call him, would you mind calling Mr Woojamaflip's nearest and dearest and telling them that there's nothing else we can do for him now. There's no point keeping him here, he's unlikely to make it through another operation – it would be a waste of everyone's time and money, frankly – and without it he'll be dead by Thursday. He might as well go home . . . And if you're not doing anything later, do you fancy a curry?'

●

Winkler decided not to ruin his day by bowling. For the first time in his life he had contributed significantly with the bat, so he decided to enjoy the onset of a warm evening rather than panic about whether, after all these years, he would be able even to land the ball on the square. So when Lord Morcester muttered to him, as they crossed between overs, 'Vinkler, next over that end,' he said, 'Ah, Lord Morcester, I was going to say. If it's all the same to you I'd rather not bowl at all today. I haven't in fifteen years and I'd hate to let you down.'

'You're the only spinner in the side, Vinkler. Next over that end.'

'But –'

'Don't answer me back, boy. They only need another 60 for their last four wickets, the pitch is dry and the ball was turning for their bowlers. You've had some fun with the bat at the expense of some others who drove a considerable distance in their own cars and might well have scored a lot faster than you did and given us a few more runs to play with. Rupert said you could bowl. Now bowl.'

'What was that about?' Ru asked his father, trotting over to hunker down next to him at second slip.

'Bloody drug dealer of yours doesn't want to bowl.'

'He's probably just nervous. He doesn't want to let you down. He hasn't played in a long time.'

'What did you bring him for, then?'

'For a nice day out. It's not a test match, Dad. Don't be so tough on him, you'll make it harder for him to bowl.'

'Bloody wimp. They all are. His lot. No damn bottle when it comes to it. That's why – damn it!'

The ball shot through Lord Morcester's legs and Ru turned to run after it. The over ended and Morcester walked up the other end to set a field for Winkler.

'Can I have a deep square leg, please?' he said. 'I haven't bowled in years and it could go anywhere. I need some protection out there.'

'No you can't have a deep square leg,' said Lord Morcester. 'We need wickets. A left-arm spinner doesn't need a deep square leg, damn it. If they hit it there it's because you're not bowling properly.' And he stormed down the wicket to retake his position at slip.

'Bloody wimp, your exotic friend,' he said to his son as he passed him. 'Protection! Damn his eyes.'

'Best of luck, Wink,' said Rupert Pennant-Cecil. 'Not that you'll need it. They won't know what's hit 'em.'

'No,' said Winkler.

He trotted in for his first ball, turned his arm over and watched the ball soar over the batsman's head, who ducked at the last minute, over the wicket-keeper, who was not expecting it, and down towards the boundary. Lord Morcester with his dodgy knees had to chase after it.

'Loosener,' said Rupert Pennant-Cecil. 'You'll have the rhythm soon.'

But Winkler did not have it soon.

His next two balls both bounced twice and were spanked for four to the square-leg boundary.

'He's doing it deliberately,' said Lord Morcester.

'No he isn't,' said Ru.

'I thought you said he could bowl,' said Lord Morcester.

'I thought he could,' said Ru.

'At the end of the over Ru said to him, 'We'll give you a couple more. I'm sure it'll get better.'

'No, really,' said Winkler. 'I think I've done my shoulder. I'd really rather not.'

'Bloody hypochondriac,' said Lord Morcester. 'You'll bowl another bloody over.'

'But, Dad, you didn't want him to bowl at all,' said Ru, grasping that Winkler was not injured but seeing his discomfort and trying to help.

'Changed my mind,' said Lord Morcester.

•

Millfield Spawn perched his vast arse on Winkler's desk. Opened the top drawer and rummaged in it. Found nothing interesting. Closed the drawer. Said to Sherwood Glaub,

'Do you mind bagging up Winkler's stuff, Sher? It'll only take a minute.'

'But he's only been gone a week.'

'I know, I know. It's not my decision. You know what the Bosses are like. One minute you're –'

'Actually, I don't know what they're like.'

'So you don't. Well, anyway, there's a new fellow starting next month and in the meantime we can use the desk for a temp.'

'After all the years that Winkler's been here? All the times he's saved your arse . . .'

'There's no room for sentimentality in business.'

'Because he misses one week of work?'

'A week is a long time in business.'

'He's having a bit of a crisis.'

'Not for the first time, Sherwood. Eventually we all have to grow up and learn about responsibility.'

'He used to be your friend, Millfield.'

'Used to be, Sherwood.'

'I can't believe I'm hearing this. What about loyalty? What happens if I start having a breakdown of confidence myself? What happens when I have to take time out to stand back and look at my life?'

'You won't, Sherwood.'

'I –'

'Do you know what we were paying Winkler, Sherwood?'

'No.'

Millfield Spawn told him.

'No? Shit. Why? No? That's more than twice what I get. He does, did, the same job. Why, Millfield? He was never here. I've been here nine years, at my desk every day at eight. I eat lunch at my desk. I'm never home before ten at night. I've sacrificed my personal life almost completely. And he just swanned in and out when he chose. Never took any responsibility for anything. He was drunk half the time. He never even dressed properly. He spent the time he was here harassing the secretaries and being snooty about everyone, and bitter. And he was being paid how much? Fucking hell. What does he think we are? I can't believe it. And that Werther report, he was going to trick you into thinking he'd done it by the end of week but I'll bet . . .'

'He didn't do it at all, Sher.'

'No? But he – Christ. I feel such a fool. And he's probably outside somewhere in the sunshine having the time of his life. While we –'

Millfield Spawn, with his wide arse slightly numb from perching on the edge of Winkler's desk, smiled.

Sherwood Glaub got up and yanked the big black plastic bin liner from inside the bin and, as Millfield Spawn walked away, round the corner, past the gnus up to his new little office on the same floor as the bosses, began pulling out the drawers from Winkler's desk and tipping their contents into it.

From the direction in which Spawn had disappeared, Leo Sneel, sensing upheaval, loped into view. Approaching Sherwood Glaub, he glanced to his left and glanced to his right and then to his left again. Then he leant towards Sherwood Glaub's left ear and, hiding his lips from the rest of the office with the back of his right hand he said,

'So, Sherwood. It begins.'

•

Winkler's two overs had cost twenty-nine runs and the game was finely poised, with a couple of the village team's wickets having fallen, when Winkler, who was staring over the fields towards the churchyard beyond the boundary and wishing, not for the first time, that he had never been spotted in the playground by the geography teacher, saw a green Ford Sierra Ghia crawl in through the gates and around the boundary, where afternoon shadows were sliding out towards the square, to the spot where other cars were parked in a row next to the pavilion, followed by a marked police vehicle.

•

'Wonder what they're after?' said Ru.

'Come for your bloody drug dealer I hope,' said Lord Morcester.

'Maybe they just want to check the gun cupboard,' said Ru.

'Six of them?' said Rupert Pennant-Cecil. 'You must have a hell of a lot of guns.'

•

'Should we wait until the match is over, sir?' said Sergeant Tolkien.

'I certainly don't think there is any need to rush out there and arrest him now,' said Inspector Porfiry. 'There's no need to embarrass Mr Winkler more than is necessary. Let's go and get a pint in the pavilion and see how things pan out.'

•

Winkler was watching Inspector Porfiry indicate to Sergeant Tolkien that his glass was now empty, when he heard his name shouted by Rupert Pennant-Cecil. And by Rupert Theofrax Helmesley-DeWilde and by Adrian Ledgard and, most frighteningly of all, by Lord Morcester, who cried, 'Mistaaahh Vinklerrrrr!' And he looked up, and saw only the sun, and then, coming out of it, the little black speck of ball. He put up his left hand to sight it, saw it going behind him, far, far behind him, started jogging back, caught his heel on the slightly exposed socket of a water-sprinkler, tripped, fell, landed on his back, and heard the dull thud a second later of the ball hitting grass a yard behind his head.

'Oh no!' cried Lord Morcester. 'Damnation. What was he doing? That bloody . . . bloody . . . Jew!'

•

'There now,' said Porfiry. 'It's over. I told you it wouldn't be long. Let's cuff him boys. Oh, shit. What's he doing, now? Bugger, come on lads. I think he's about to do a runner.'

•

But Winkler wasn't about to do anything of the sort. He was standing over Lord Morcester and preparing to hit him again.

'Come on,' said Winkler. 'Get up you old cunt. Get up and say it again.'

Lord Morcester sat on the grass, touching his nose on his sleeve and looking at the small drops of blood soaking into the wool.

'Come on,' shouted Winkler. 'You're not hurt. Fucking get up. You fucking old hypochondriac.'

'He's broken my damn nose. The insolent little –'

'What, you old cunt? Say it! Say it!'

'I will say what I like on my own bloody land, you bloody little Hebrew Jew.'

Winkler's kick only missed the old man's right ear because he was falling to the ground under a diving tackle from Sergeant Tolkien, who wrestled him onto his front and knelt on the small of his back.

'Sharp work,' said Rupert Pennant-Cecil, with a grin, to Adrian Ledgard, who, like everyone else, was looking on motionlessly. 'I think Wink would have killed him.'

'That would have been amusing,' said Ledgard. 'Bloody spoilsports.'

'Yes, rotters,' said Pennant-Cecil. 'There's never one around when you want one and then six –'

'Officer, arrest that man!' cried Lord Morcester, recovered now, and on his feet.

'Obviously, sir,' said Porfiry. 'That is why we are here.'

'Bloody drug dealer,' said Lord Morcester. 'That's it, Rupert. You get off my land this instant. And your bloody friends, too. The lot of you. Bloody Jew drug-dealers and pimps the lot of you.'

'Dad –'

'No, Ru, leave it. I'm off,' said Rupert Pennant-Cecil. 'I don't really fancy supper.'

'Me neither,' said Adrian Ledgard.

One by one, the players sloped away.

Rupert Pennant-Cecil, on the way to his car, went to say goodbye to Winkler, penetrating the ring of policemen as Sergeant Tolkien was saying,

'. . . Winkler, you are under arrest for the rape and murder of Jenny-Marie Rollins. Anything you –'

'Bye, Wink,' he said, interrupting. 'Well done. Bloody well done today. Shame about the bowling but you can't have everything, eh? Bloody good day otherwise.'

'Terrific,' said Winkler.

'And don't forget,' said Rupert Pennant-Cecil, slinging his cricket bag over his chubby shoulder and heading off towards his big black company Lexus, 'send my regards to your Uncle Bill.'

'As I was saying,' said Sergeant Tolkien. 'I am placing you under arrest for the rape and murder of Miss Jenny-Marie Rollins. Anything you say . . .'

'Will be totally ignored by the great tattooed beasts who will thrash the living daylights out of you day and night, Mr Winkler, when they get wind of what you did to that poor little blind girl,' said Inspector Porfiry. 'By God, I hope you enjoyed your cricket match. Because you are not going to be playing again for a very, very long time. Cricket or anything else.'

'Indeed not,' said Sergeant Tolkien. 'I am placing you under arrest for the rape and m–'

'Will you shut up!' cried Inspector Porfiry.

18

De Profundis, Bill

South of the City. On the bank of a wide, desolate, polluted, filthy, life-less river, stands a town. One of the true fuckholes of the whole country. In the town there is a fortress. In the fortress, a prison. In the prison, already confined for three days, is unbailed convict number 20710, known to us, and to everyone else, as Winkler.

To an impartial observer (and aren't we all?) he appears to have been unlucky. This is where they send you when you have been charged with murder, until such time as a jury of your peers (and they're talking culturally rather than morally) can be rustled up to take a look at you, not like the look of what it sees, and send you back for ever. But Winkler has not been charged with murder yet. Really, he should be being held at cosy little Northstead, pottering about a large clean cell created with middle-class drink-drivers in mind, eating reasonably well, kipping down on a clean mattress, joshing with coppers who have known him for years.

But Winkler has refused to provide a DNA sample to the police these last few days. Without it they do not have much in the way of evidence and are reluctant to charge him. They are not supposed to have held him this long without charge but he has not demanded to be released. Not by any means.

Where would he go? He couldn't go back to Mary. He couldn't bear to go back to Ru's place, after the embarrassment of the cricket match (the embarrassing bowling, the embarrassing missed catch, the embar-rassing racial abuse, the embarrassing arrest for rape and murder), and anyway it wouldn't be fair on the lads, all those police around all the time,

getting in the way of their drug abuse. And he couldn't go to his grandfather's place. Not to him, of all people.

So he kept nice and quiet. And here he seemed to be, in the blackest
keep of the darkest fortress, in the deepest, dampest, grizzliest dungeon
in all the length and breadth of merry England.

But he had no complaints. Food. A place to crap. Walls. A roof. It was
how men lived before things got all fucked up. Winkler had no complaints.

He did give them an alibi. Alba. In Australia. Likely story. But they
hadn't been able to get her. They were trying. Oh yes. But there was
nothing from the mobile phone. And Australia is still a long way away,
whatever you think. A long way away, and big. But she would surely show
up in time.

And so Winkler waited. Waited for them to find Alba. Waited for something to happen. Waited as he had always waited.

And, anyway, maybe he did kill the girl.

'It's not impossible. Christ. Can it really not be impossible? Technically,
it isn't impossible, I suppose.'

Winkler paced up and down his cell. One, two, three, four, five, six,
turn. One, two, three, four, five, six, turn.

'Suppose I was so fucked up by all those stupid drugs that I don't properly remember what happened that night?'

One, two, three, four, five, six. One, two, three, four . . .

'Suppose I never went to bed with Alba at all? Ru says she's never
shown any interest in anyone else. Maybe I dreamed it. Maybe I was so
confused after pushing that woman in front of the train, so whacked off
kilter by the noise of her fat body splitting when the train like a great
metal mallet whacked her wide arse inside out – can that have been what
it was? – that I . . .'

Five, six. One, two, three, four . . .

'No, no time to worry about that now. That was unfortunate for the
fat woman. There will be time for remorse. I'll have to be remorseful. I
was planning to be remorseful, all along. That was part of it. How remorseful
would I be? This was part of the truth of things that would become clear
to me when the kill was complete. But I can't worry about that now.
Not until later. That'll only confuse me.'

Five, six . . .

'So I left the party with Alba after we did that line of coke in the bog.
She never stroked my balls. Obviously. I imagined that. I left the party
with her because I was obviously too fucked to stand up and – Damn!
I didn't dance after all. Fuck it. I knew it was a dream. Shit. What a shame.'

One, two, three, four, five . . .

'She took me out in the street because she was being nice, and she hailed a cab. And in we got. And I passed out on the back seat. Must have done. Head back, lolling, snoring. Maybe muttering directions. But maybe we didn't go home together at all. Maybe she looked at me lolling there and thought – being Australian – "Sod this for a laugh, I'm going back to the party." And then she got out of the cab and said, "Take this guy home," and slammed the door. That's what happens in my life. That's what girls do. They don't come back to my room and stick their tongues up my arse. God, what was I thinking?'

Six. One, two, three . . .

'As the door slams the driver says, "Where's home 'guv?" And I grumble and snore myself awake and say, "What?" and he says, "Where d'you live, mate?" And I say, "32 Black Park Hill," obviously, and pass out again. He drives me back to my old home and I get out of the cab. I guess I pay. I guess he says, "You alright, guv?" and I say that I am.'

Four, five . . .

'I try the key in the door but can't get it in. Not surprising as it is the key to Ru's house. I think about ringing the door bell. But it is very late to wake everybody. I stand there on the broken old path staring up at the horrible house all peaky and gothic against the stars and I remember old Wallenstein the scary man, and the Nazis, and I freak out and run away. I rummage in my pocket and find a piece of paper. It's the piece of paper with the blind girl's address on. I go round there. I ring on the doorbell. She answers on the intercom. I say it's Winkler. She says what do I want and I tell her I'm locked out and I want to call a friend to see if I can go and stay with him. She reckons it's safe to let me in because I rescued her and because – oh, oh, the poor girl . . .'

Six. One, two, three, four, five, six . . .

'She lets me in and we go upstairs. She makes me a cup of tea with her finger in the mug to know when it's nearly full, which is a bit gross but fuck it, she's blind. I take the tea and our hands touch. And I put the tea down and pissed as I am, I am so fucked and full of drugs that all I want is to fuck somebody, I try to kiss her but she doesn't want to. But I remember how I wanked in front of her, spaffed all over the television, and how powerless she is, and I grab her and –'

One . . .

'Can this be how it was?'

One, two, three, four, five, six. One, two, three, four, five, six. One, two, three, four, five, six. One, two, three, four, five, six.

'Can it? That I grabbed her and dragged her into the bedroom, or onto the sofa and thought I was with Alba and that it was what she wanted, and all the time it was the little blind girl and she didn't want it at all. Tore off her clothes. And . . .'

One . . .

'What did Porfiry say? "It was a sex game that went wrong, wasn't it, Winkler? I'm not saying you went round there with the express intention of killing her. But you went round, the two of you got to kissing and cuddling –" he was revolted, I could see he was revolted, "– and you tied her up because she wanted to be tied up, and then when she said it was too tight you gave her a couple of slaps, because she liked it rough, didn't she, she liked to be knocked around a bit . . ."'

Two . . .

'Tied her up? Was it me that was not tied, but did the tying? Was I not spankee but spanker? Was it my tongue? Her arse? Did I grab at something? A rolling pin? A broom? Was it not my arse full of blunt object, but hers? (How did my anus feel in the morning? How should it have felt? What does it feel like to have been done up the arse with a rolling pin sixteen hours ago when you are so full of narcotics that you are incapable of registering pain?) Was it not I who was bitten and scratched but she?'

Winkler pulled off his shirt and found the bruises and strafings of bites and scratches.

'But was that her, the blind girl, defending herself? Or Alba playing? The teeth marks are faded now, but you can see the bruises. These are the bites of a wide mouth, like Alba's. Not a small one like Jenny-Marie's. Why haven't they tested them against her teeth? That's all they need to do. They don't need DNA.'

Winkler looked at the marks again.

'Are they big though? Or have the bruises just spread? Was it not I that was suffocated to the point of orgasm and then released, but her? Was it I pressing on, leaning on, sitting on the cushion on the poor girl's face until there was a little snap, and I pulled off the pillow, and it was too late. For both of us. As she expired and I exploded all over her little dead body?'

Three, four, five, six. Winkler leaned his face on the cold wall of white-painted brick, feeling the bubbles in the mortar through the paint and his hot cheek.

'Can that be how it was?'

Can it be?

Can it?

'The Gestapo went after the blind, believing their condition hereditary. Which it sometimes is and sometimes is not. The Einsatzgruppen went round with mobile gassing lorries. Not Zyklon at this stage but just plain old carbon monoxide, that which we breathe everyday on the streets of the city, only more of it. Only sixty at a time, and pretty damn slow. Diverted diesel exhaust is all. Clunk, click. Give them twenty minutes. Then open with the doors, phew what a pong, dig, dig, dig, heave ho, you lot. Right. Fill, fill, fill. Pat, pat, pat. Lovely job. And off we go. That's where they got the idea. Right from about 1933, or close enough, the mentally ill, the halt and the blind and the deaf. And later, when they were all gone, they had a system ready for the Jews.'

Was Winkler a Nazi?

One, two, three, four . . .

Clang! The metal window in Winkler's cell door slid open. A pair of eyes stared in.

'Oi, you. Stand up.'

Winkler stood.

The eyes retreated. Another pair of eyes appeared, peering.

'Wink?'

Winkler nodded.

'Bloody hell. It *is* you.'

The door shut. Winkler heard muttering, then the door opened and the guard was standing there showing in a heftily-built man of about sixty who, but for his long white beard, just ever-so-faintly tinged with orange at the extremities, would have been the spitting image of Ernest Borgnine, just before he died.

'Watch this one, Bill. He's a nutcase. Hasn't stopped talking to himself since he got here. All day all night. And he repeats his police interviews over and over verbatim. And not deadpan or anything. Dramatic like. And he'll do the police in different voices.'

The guard retreated and locked the door.

'Wink? It's me.'

Winkler stared at Ginger Bill with his head on one side, like a dog. Barely understanding.

'Uncle Bill?'

'Yes, Winky. It's your Uncle Bill.'

'I'm not allowed visitors, Uncle Bill.'

'I'm not a visitor, Winky.'

'What?'

'I'm on the inside. I'm just pals with some of the warders, and when I heard there was a Winkler in here on remand, I arranged to come and see if it was you.'

'Oh. Yes, I'm afraid it is me. It's funny. Someone was asking after you only the other day, and I thought how long it had been. How long have you been here?'

'Seven years.'

'Seven years? What did you do?'

'Less than you, from the sound of things.'

'Oh, Bill. You don't think I'm a rapist, do you?'

'Of course not, Wink,' said Bill, gently. 'Of course not.'

And Winkler started to cry and Bill put his arms round him. And they stood like that for a long time.

'Me? Oh it's a long story, Wink. No, it's not. Armed robbery. Accessory to murder. Guilty as charged, convicted and punished. Not much I can say. Very stupid. My fault.'

'I never heard. I never knew.'

'Well, they keep this sort of thing from the kids, I suppose.'

'Tell me, then.'

So Ginger Bill told him.

'It was Maurice Mogelbaum's idea. You remember Thin Maurice? I've always had money worries, as you know. And I've done a bit of time before now for knocking people about. Maurice comes to me with a plan to knock over a jeweller's shop. I say what is he thinking of? I am an honest citizen for nearly a dozen years at a stretch and by no means intend to compromise my liberty for a few grand. And furthermore, I say, I am very nearly three score years of age. I do not wish my life to be measured as threescore years and as long as I can survive in chokey at this ripe old age, which will not be very many, if I am any judge, and possibly less.

'But then he says to me like this, "Bill," he says. "It is not a few grand that you will profit in this enterprise, but thirty grand. Will you give yourself a break for once? Or do you choose to be a *schlemiel* all your life?"

'By and by he persuades me that it is money for lighting my own wind. He has a couple of pros lined up for the hard work. All I have to do is act as lookout and protection. They will be packing sawn-offs, which they are instructed not to use at any time. Although they are loaded. I say okay, okay, thirty grand is thirty grand, but I do not carry a piece, no matter what. And this is agreed.

'Winky, my boy, I cannot list on all my fingers and toes the things that go wrong. The other two are small-timers who have never done anything like this even remotely. And in the car on the way I realise this and try to impose some authority on them. But this offends their professional sensitivities. So communication breaks down more than somewhat.

'Furthermore, it appears when we arrive that Thin Maurice's plans of the place are forty years out of date. And probably then some. Still, the ding-bats Maurice has hired fall to loading their little bags with the cheap crap this sparklemeister is passing off to his customers as the real McCoy, although I am frankly suspicious for my thirty grand when I see that the place is no longer called "Sheldon's Sapphires" but "Ginsberg's Cut-Price Trinkets and Small Stones".

'Suddenly, the alarm goes off. The guys look up and from nowhere a security guard shows up and goes for his gun, I whack him and put him in a headlock but while I'm holding him the other guard, who isn't armed – there weren't meant to be any guards at all – goes for me with his baton.

'Reg Tripp, one of the other guys, looks up from where he is frantically loading some sparkly rubbish into a black bag – even with the armed guard in a headlock, I can see from across the room that it is nothing but zircon and nine-carat bangles, and no doubt at prices I could find the same stuff for half if you let me tell you where – and blasts him stone dead, the silly fucker.

'Naturally, we leg it for the car, which is being driven by Maurice's cousin Les. We get away quick and for a few minutes as we race through the streets it looks like I am going to end up with nothing more than a sore conscience for a few years about the dead guy, and already I am figuring how to spend the seven or eight quid which I reckon is my cut of the paste necklaces and rheumatism bracelets with which Reg's bag is laden down, when we turn a corner at speed and collide head-on with a dustcart.

'It seems the black and white street map on which Maurice has drawn out our route with a pink highlighter pen is no less than fifty years out of date. I am not surprised if it indicates the many shops and houses positioned desirably along the length of London Bridge, the dozen or so bear pits within easy reach at Southwark and the especially good wolf-hunting to be had in the forest at Soho. Alas, it does not register the invention of the one-way street, one of which we have just turned down at the very moment that the dustcart is making legal use of it in the opposite direction.

'Cousin Les is killed instantly. Reg Tripp, too, when his head is smashed in by his friend, who is sitting behind him without a seat belt. The friend dies slowly next to me, and I never find out his name. For myself, I am relatively unscathed, thanks to my habit of wearing a seatbelt at all times, even on short trips and especially in the back, which is more dangerous than people think. I am trapped, however, in the wreckage of car and dustcart and my dignity is further compromised by my being covered not only in the blood of my deceased companions but also in thousands of tiny little glass beads of different colours, the two swag bags I am holding having exploded on impact, which cause me to glisten and twinkle like a Christmas tree, providing much merriment to one and all when I am finally surrounded by armed police and firemen with cutting equipment.'

'And so here you are.'

'And so here I am. And here I will ever afterwards be, is my guess. But you we can save. Surely. So long as you did not, which I am sure of, rape and murder this poor blind girl. Do you want to tell me what happened?'

'Hmmm,' said Ginger Bill. 'You can't blame them for arresting you. You were probably the last person to see her, more or less. And you can see how your story about the mugging in the subway, without witnesses, could look suspicious with hindsight, given the murder. But it's all circum-stantial. Assuming that this girl of yours shows up in Oz, you should end up fine. If she gets hit by a car, of course, you're finished.'

'Unless I dreamt it.'

'Oh, you didn't dream it, for God's sake. The killer will be a mad para-noid schizophrenic out on care-in-the-community. It always is. Some Armenian probably. Some asylum-seeking fascist Croat here to wash wind-screens with an oily rag and rape and murder our women. He'll confess in the end. They always do. But until he does it's almost impossible for the Old Bill to do anything. They like to make an arrest. They whack up a few yellow signs in the road and wait for a confession. But they can't go after the gyppoes every time there's a rape and murder. The Home Office PR team would do their nut. So they wait for the gyppo to confess. And they always do. Weird Slavic guilt thing. Raskolnikov complex.'

'I hope you're right.'

'Of course I'm right. So there are similarities between your screwing of the Australian girl and the rape of the blind girl. So what? Dirty violent sex is only rape with consent. And anyway it was you who was on the receiving end.'

'I think.'

'And you didn't give consent to your Albuquerque girl, did you?'

'No. What are you trying to say?'

'I don't know.'

'She didn't rape me, Bill.'

'A pole up your arse, though, son? Isn't that a bit extreme?'

'Mmm, well, you know . . .'

'Look, they've got a lot of good reasons to hold you. But none of them is water-tight. Why don't you do the DNA test?'

'I don't know. I held her all the way home, stuff like that. She could have had a few hairs on her or something. Then they'd charge me and I'd be fucked.'

'A couple of hairs on clothes wouldn't be enough to convict you. It's no secret you met her. No secret you touched her. It's the sperm they'll want to match up.'

The sperm. Christ. Winkler's sperm had been sprayed all over the place when she was sitting just feet away. What if . . . ? Oh Christ.

'Listen, Wink. The best thing we can do is find out what the coppers have, what they know, what they're going on. I've got a few friends up at Northstead, I can get in touch with them easy. I'll have a word and see if that helps us. You get some sleep. You look like you need it.'

'I'll try.'

'Cheers then,' Bill hugged Winkler hard. And then banged on the door with a fist so big and red and powerful that it made the three inches of iron sound like a child's tambourine.

'Bill,' said Winkler. 'I didn't kill the blind girl.'

'I know,' said Ginger Bill.

'But I did push a fat woman under a train. Last week. Thursday.'

'Sure you did,' said Ginger Bill.

The door opened, Bill left, and then it closed heavily. Not sounding at all like a tambourine.

'Visitor,' said the guard, towards the end of the following morning.

'Wotcher,' said Ginger Bill. 'I brought you some fags.'

'I don't smoke,' said Winkler. And then he remembered that he did, now. And so he said, 'No, wait. I do.'

'You're sure? Decide in your own time.' said Ginger Bill.

'No, I smoke,' and Winkler took the cigarettes.

'I spoke to an old mucker at Northstead. He knew all about you. It's a big deal for them. He wouldn't say much on the phone. But he's coming down. Arnold Finkel. Maybe you're related. Winkler, Finkel, in German they'd sound about the same.'

'Maybe.'

The two men sat in silence for a minute. Then Ginger Bill said, 'Oh,' and handed Winkler three packets of Rothmans. Winkler said, 'Thanks,' and put them on his bed in a little stack. They sat quietly for a while. Winkler took one of the packets, unwrapped it and plucked out a cigarette, he offered the packet to Ginger Bill, who shook his head. Winkler patted his chest with each hand and said, 'You got a light?' Ginger Bill said, 'No.' Winkler rolled the cigarette in his teeth and rolled the rectangle of gold foil from the packet between his finger and thumb and flicked it across the room. It hit the opposite wall almost instantly with a loud noise and bounced onto the floor. And even rolling briefly on the brick floor it sounded noisy.

'Quiet in here,' said Winkler.

Ginger Bill nodded.

'I pace a lot,' said Winkler.

'You'll stop,' said Ginger Bill.

'Oh, yes, I was going to say. Rupert Pennant-Cecil sent his regards.'

'Who?'

'My school cricket captain. From the Fathers' Match?'

'Good Lord, yes.' Ginger Bill looked at the ceiling and sighed. 'What a long time ago that was. My word, you hated that boy. And he seemed such a polite little fellow.'

'Mm, well he's alright now. I bumped into him the other day and he sent his regards.'

'That's nice. What a day that was. Me pretending to be your father. Driving that old Rover of your grandpa's. And then getting in trouble for feeding you hamburgers.'

'Thanks for the hamburger. And thanks for coming. That was a great day for me.'

'And for me. It was like having a family.'

'Pennant-Cecil remembered you as a real hero. Like W.G. Grace.'

Ginger Bill laughed. 'That's two of us, then.'

'You had a row with Grandpa afterwards.'

'Only about the hamburger.'

'No, it was about me.'

'We disagreed on some things.'

'You didn't like me being at that school.'

'It wasn't for people like you, Wink. I could see how unhappy you were.'

'It wasn't up to Grandpa. It was my father's money that sent me. And Grandpa couldn't really have me living there with him.'

'Why not? There was nothing to get in the way of. Apart from his occasional afternoon bridge games. And the Wednesday night poker. It was a sad house. It would have been better with you there. Woyzeck was the saddest man I ever met. And he might have been happy with you there.'

'But my father –'

'Your father had nothing to do with it. He was thousands of miles away. You know how it was.'

'Not really.'

'You knew he was in Israel?'

'No. I knew he was somewhere a long way away. I thought maybe Manchester.'

'No. Worse even than Manchester. Hebron.'

'Wow.'

'It was his penance. His atonement. You don't know about all that?'

'What's to know? I know my dad had a wife and three beautiful Jewish kids. He fucked his secretary. She had me. Dad bought her off. Gave me to Grandpa. They all fucked off to Manchester or Hebron or wherever. And he sent money for me to go and get fucked up the arse in a boarding school until it made an Englishman of me.'

'Not his secretary. The girl he first loved. His school sweetheart.'

'Oh?'

'He was in love with a girl from school, Delia Lockheart. They dated for a year or two. I was only a kid then. It was tolerated. And then your Dad, Solomon – Solly he was known as – went home one day and says he's getting married to her.'

'Solly?'

'What?'

'I didn't know they called him Solly.'

'Yeah, Solly. Or Sol. And anyway, your grandfather did his nut. No way was your old man marrying a *shikse*. You know what a *shikse* is?'

'Yeah. A slag.'

'A gentile woman.'

'Whatever.'

'So he says, "To heck with you," and runs away. Literally. Sandwiches and money in a cloth on a stick. He's maybe eighteen, but we were slower to grow up then. He runs round to Delia's to tell her that his family have forbade him from marrying her but they're going to elope to Gretna Green. He rings the doorbell of her house, she only lives round the corner. Up in Eastgate, off the dual carriageway, those little mock-Tudor semis

with the garage in the side and space for a car in the front garden, behind
the big municipal cemetery – you either know them or you don't – and
who comes to the door but her old man. He's a big yok in a string vest,
or maybe not in a string vest, he was a car salesman, I think. Anyway he
opens the door and he's holding a shotgun.'

'A shotgun.'

'Yeah. God knows where he got it. The goyim always had guns in the
old days. He points it straight at your dad and tells him to get off his land
and get out of his country or he shoots him. He gives him ten seconds.
In the background is Delia Lockheart weeping and screaming and being
held back by her mother. It seems she has told her parents of her plans
to marry Solly Winkler, the boy who rides the bicycle for the Jewish fishmonger on the high street. Even before he finds out that such a marriage
is already vetoed by your grandfather old Lockheart is tearing around the
neighbourhood talking about what will and will not happen over his dead
body. Although of course it is not his body that is most likely to end up
dead, as your papa clearly identifies before doing the decent thing and
scarpering. You want a light for that?'

'Mm? Oh, I suppose,' said Winkler. Who had been fingering the cigarette all the time Ginger Bill was talking. Putting it behind his ear. Sucking
it. Dropping it.

'Hey, Dermot,' shouted Ginger Bill, banging on the little window cover
in the cell door, which opened. 'You got a light?'

'Sure, Bill,' said the guard, passing a disposable lighter through the grill.
'You alright in there? Want a cup of tea or anything?'

'Tea, Wink?'

Winkler shook his head.

'No, that's all Dermot, ta.'

Bill sat down again and tossed Winkler the lighter.

'He goes straight home again, your dad. Unpacks his handkerchief. Puts
away his stick. Eats his sandwiches. Hates his parents for evermore. And
gets on with his life. Years pass. He falls in love with the boss's daughter.
He is a lawyer, so there is no danger that his boss's daughter is not a Jew.
Dolly Spiro. Ugly girl, great body, very rich. Dolly and Solly. It's all lovely.

'They marry. They get a big house with a conservatory and a Rover
– it's the same Rover your grandpa had, the one I came in to the cricket,
only back when it's new it is quite something as a car. They have a kid,
Rachel. But after the kid your mum – no, not your mum, sorry, this Dolly
woman – she goes nuts. Although I suspect she is always nuts in the first
place. She turns out to be a mad frummer, it's Jewish this and Jewish that,

she shaves her hair off and gets this hilarious wig so that she looks like a, I don't know what, a kind of Anglo-Saxon serf, except Jewish. And she makes everything mad kosher and then comes the '67 war and suddenly it's Israel this and Israel that, she's sending all the family money to Israel for the army and the charities. And then she declares she wants to go and live there.

'"And I will do what? And Rachel will do what?" asks your father. They will go with her of course. But this he will not have so he puts down his foot. And he does not often do this, and she is surprised and so they stay in England and for a while things are quiet. Very quiet. She sleeps alone now in another room and your father cannot come to her unless it is for procreation, and even then it is through a hole in a sheet which is a great shame because his wife, as I said, has a face like a pig but the body of an angel and if the sheet is to be anywhere it should be on only her head so that he can think he is with Raquel Welch, which presumably he does anyway, seeing as he cannot see her when he is diddling her. And then anyway to cut a long story short –'

'Too late,' said Winkler.

'Sorry. Was I too much on the screwing? Sorry. I was just remembering what a fine pair of knockers she had. Anyway. By and by your old man is losing interest in his marriage, his wife is always on about Israel and how there is great real estate to be had in all the new territories and she is sleeping in another room and he doesn't get to screw her at all which is a damn shame with her body, and anyway the body after three children is not what it was, when walking down the street one day who should he bump into?'

'Eh? Oh. Er, I don't know. My mum?'

'Exactly. Delia Lockheart. She is unmarried still and unhappy, but she has kept in shape and she is wearing this tight little –'

'How do you know what she was wearing, Bill?'

'Good point, I have no idea what she was wearing. Or even if she'd kept in shape or not. I was just sort of imagining these nice firm little hooters with –'

'Well, that's fine, but it's not really relevant to why I went to boarding school is it?'

'No, it isn't. Sorry. I've been inside too long. Really, I'm sorry. Forget your mother's nice firm hooters. The point is, your old man took one look at them and biff boff, they're off. Carrying on royally. Little flat. True love finally blossoming. She goes down on him in a way that his wife would never –'

'Bill!'

'Oh yeah, sorry. Anyway, one day she calls him up and says she's pregnant. He's gutted.'

'Thanks.'

'Well, if I cut the sex out that's all there is really – married man knocks up childhood sweetheart on the side, she has baby, he fesses up to his wife. She does her nut, leaves him, he starts new life with fresh doris. But these are different times. The wife does not leave him. He does not leave the wife. Unmarried mother kills herself.'

'Yeah, I knew that bit.'

'Maybe she didn't mean it. She was depressed, she was on pills. She'd been dead more than twenty-four hours when they broke the door down. You could have died.'

'Big tragedy.'

'Your dad obviously wanted to take you in. But his wife wouldn't have it. The moment she recovered from the news that you had been born she said that if the family was to stay together then they would have to move to Israel. And when your mother was dead even more so. But you will not go with. Oh, no. Not over her dead body.'

'Lot of dead bodies, it seems.'

'These were times of great conviction. Anyway, so you went to your grandfather. There was a nanny for the first six years, which your father paid for. And then boarding school.'

'And then what?'

'And then you know.'

'I mean with my father.'

'Your grandfather never spoke to him again. The school bills were sent directly to him. Your grandpa accepted no money for your upkeep. He was so disgusted with your father that he swore never to mention his name again.'

'Because he had an illegitimate child? Or because he had an illegitimate child with a *shikse*? Or because he abandoned the child? Or because he went to Israel?'

'I don't know. He was just generally disgusted. He was like that, your grandfather. A hard man. Always making vows, cutting people out, forbidding things to be spoken of. He never liked the wife anyway, and the more Jewish she got the less he liked her. And the more he regretted forbidding your parents to marry. And then she took away his son and his grandchildren and . . .'

'Yes, I remember he didn't like Dolly. It's one of the small things I do know. I was talking to him about the Holocaust the other day and suddenly he went mental about her, well, he went mental generally, as soon as I brought the subject up, but particularly about how she came from a survivor family and always whinged about . . .'

'You talked to Woyzeck about the Holocaust?'

'Not exactly. I was just saying that I'd been talking to this survivor and . . .'

'Just like that? Out of the blue, you brought up the Holocaust? Does this happen often?'

'No. In fact I don't think it was ever mentioned in the flat when I was living there, except sort of tangentially very occasionally. And so –'

'And you don't know why not?'

'No. He didn't seem very interested in it. I suppose he thought it didn't involve him so it wasn't his problem.'

'No, no, no. Quite the opposite. That's what I meant about him forbidding things to be spoken of. But, look Wink. That's another long story and you've heard enough from me for one day.'

'No I haven't.'

'No, well I've got to be going anyway. Talk to your grandfather. If he wants to talk about it he'll talk about it.'

'I'm not sure that we're talking about anything just at the moment.'

'Don't let that happen, Wink. Don't. It happened with your dad. It happened with me. Make it hard for him. Talk to him. Don't let him cut you out.'

'Well, I'll see. I'll try. But don't forget, we Englishmen aren't good at talking about sensitive stuff.'

Bill laughed.

'Yes, but they didn't really make an Englishman of you, did they?'

'Didn't they?'

'Oh come on. You're a Jew who plays cricket. That's not the same thing at all.'

'My mother wasn't Jewish, was she? Isn't that the deal? So then I'm not. I'm not anything, then.'

'You're a Jew. The Gestapo come to the door, you've got one Jewish grandparent, your mother's mother, your father's father, you're a Jew – blam! Who's to say what a Jew is and what he's not? The Gestapo's definition is as good as any.'

'I don't read Hebrew. I wasn't barmitzvah'd. I don't know what the Talmud is.'

'Details. We are what ever they say we are. If we weren't, then why would they say we were? What we think we are is meaningless. To them you're a Jew. So be a Jew. What does it matter? It's easier once you've made a decision. You think your Christian friends read Latin? You think they know what Michaelmas is? It isn't about knowledge. It's about belonging. I've really got to go.'

And Ginger Bill banged once more on the iron door.

'Do we Jews believe in Heaven and Hell, Bill?'

'No. No virgins, no loaves and fishes, no blind faith. No Heaven and Hell.'

'Where do Jews go when they die?'

'In the ground.'

'That's it?'

'The Book of Life. Our names are inscribed in the Book of Life.'

'Even if we murdered someone?'

'But you didn't.'

'Even if we pushed a fat woman under a train?'

'Probably. But as you didn't I suppose we'll never know. See you tomorrow.'

And out went Ginger Bill, worried for his nephew, but not too worried. The first few days are always the hardest.

'We'd never know anyway,' said Winkler, when the door had clanged, and the bolt had slid, and he was alone again in his cell.

19

The Truth About
Arnold Finkel

On the fifth night Winkler slept. Or the afternoon. He wasn't sure which. It felt like the small hours of the morning when the little metal window slid open and the voice of his guard (his guard!) cried,

'Visitor!'

Bill, again?

In walked Sergeant Tolkien of Northstead CID.

'Sergeant Tolkien!'

'Morning Mr Winkler. Sorry to get you up so early.'

'Don't worry, I dare say I'll find time to get a siesta later on. What time is it?'

'Five o'clock when I left home, must be five-thirty I suppose.'

'Has something happened?'

'No, no. I wanted to see you before work. They don't know I'm here.'

'Oh?'

'Your uncle gave me a ring yesterday. I had no idea you were related to the Goodmans.'

'*You're* Arnold Finkel?'

'Was, yes. I guess Bill didn't know I'd changed it. It's a bit of a sensitive subject at home.'

'You're a Jew?'

'Shhh, not so loud. The goon outside will hear,' whispered Sergeant Tolkien. And in a whisper he went on, 'Yes of course I'm a Jew. If you're related to Bill we're practically cousins. My sister Esther married Barry Hilfgott, the son of Heinz Hilfgott, the German convert who disappeared, you remember it was said, with another man. Well, Barry is a third cousin of Yoshi Neumann – from Neumann's Leather and Fancy Goods up by exit twelve off the East Circular, you surely know it, lovely gloves they do for driving, with proper bone buttons on the side, and if it's just one you want, for golf, they'll make you a price on a single, very reasonable – and it was Yoshi's daughter Bella who married Red Sid, God rest his soul, Bill's older brother. So, in a way, as I said, we're practically family.'

'I didn't know Bill had a brother,' said Winkler. 'But then it's turning out I don't know very much at all – why Tolkien?'

'Spur of the moment. When I applied for the force I decided it was better not to be a Jew. They're very simple people, policemen. So I changed it by deed poll and when I went to fill in the forms I didn't have a name in mind. And I was obsessed with television police at the time. Morse in particular. I wrote Semaphore down on the form but it looked awful, Arnold Semaphore. So then I thought of Sergeant Lewis. C.S. Lewis. Famous Oxford-based intellectual crazyman Christian authors of children's fantasy books with too many pages . . . Tolkien!'

'Arnold Tolkien?'

'A.R.R. Tolkien, I wrote. And they said I had to put what the initials stood for and I said, "Really?" and they said, "Yes." And I said, "Oh". And so I wrote Arnold Ridley, because he was the old chap in *Dad's Army* and he definitely wasn't Jewish. And the only other "R" I could think of was Ruben, which wouldn't do at all. So I wrote Ridley again.'

'Arnold Ridley Ridley Tolkien?'

'At your service.'

'Does Porfiry know?'

'That old Cossack? God, no. It's people like him that make me glad my name is Arnold Ridley Ridley Tolkien. No, I play the big dozy copper with him and he's totally convinced. You don't think I overdo it?'

'I meant, does he know you're here?'

'Oh. No. I came down because Bill said you wanted to know the score. Porfiry would kill me.'

'Is there anything worth knowing?'

'I'm afraid so. You're in here because we got a DNA match for you at the girl's flat.'

'But you haven't taken a sample from me.'

'Yes we have. When we went round to your flat the other day Porfiry took a clump from your hairbrush.'

'I don't have a hairbrush.'

'But you occasionally use your girlfriend's, no?'

'So maybe it was her that did it.'

'Mr Winkler . . .'

'Well. Isn't that illegal?'

'Course it is. That's why we haven't charged you. It's just the easiest way to save ourselves legwork. We do the DNA test so we know if it's worth going through the rigmarole of interviews and evidence gathering and waiting for a confession, or beating one out of you. But we can't tell you we even did this, or our whole case is buggered and you might end up slipping off on a technicality due to illegally gathered evidence. We can't really hold you even, because we can't tell anyone we did it.'

'So why are you telling me?'

'Family's family.'

'Oh.'

'That and the international Jewish conspiracy.'

'Eh, I'm not, er. Oh.'

'Joke.'

'Mm. But I helped her home, I could easily have —'

'You could easily have left hairs on her clothes, yes.'

'Exactly.'

'Except that the samples at the scene were taken from semen,' said Tolkien, quietly.

'Oh. Well I'm screwed then, aren't I?'

'Did you do it?'

'No.'

'Good. Then this'll be good news to you: yours was not the only semen we found. There was a lot more of somebody else's. Porfiry thinks it's your accomplice.'

'Great.'

'So he'll be down here later to find out who your accomplice was. And he'll probably get violent now.'

'Goody.'

'So what we want to do is prove that the other sperm belongs to the true attacker and that yours is there for some other reason, totally unrelated to the attack.'

'We?'

'I'd like nothing better than to stiff that old Tartar. He pisses on my parade day in, day out and he's a crap detective and unless I can get one on him soon he's going to have me back on the beat. You heard the way he talks to me.'

'That just sounded like office banter. And anyway he only does it because you pretend to be a fool.'

'Well if he knew I was a Jew it would be ten times worse, "Ooh hark at the Rabbi over here", "Lend us a tenner will you, Finkel, I'll pay you back, with interest of course", "Get us a bacon sarnie will you, Finkel? Ooh, sorry, didn't mean to offend" . . .'

'Yes, yes, I know how it goes.'

'And he's delighted you turn out to be a Jew.'

'Do I?'

'That business in Morcestershire. He thought you were some well-connected public school boy who was going to know all the right people. Now he's delighted. Last thing he said to me last night, in fact, was, "Right, Tolkien, early to bed early to rise and nail the perfidious Yid."'

'Lovely.'

'He's persuaded Lord Morcester to press assault charges. But I doubt it'll get anywhere.'

'Particularly if I'm doing life. All they can do is slap three months on the end of it, to be served when I'm dead.'

'Exactly,' said Tolkien. 'So the thing to do is to prove that your sperm got sprayed all over the crime scene for some reason other than that you raped and murdered her.'

'Okay.'

'So?'

'So what?'

'Did you have intercourse with her?'

'No.'

'Are you sure?'

'Of course I'm sure.'

'Okay, it just seemed the most likely answer, that's all. Save her from mugger. Take her back to yours. Ooh thankyouthankyoukindsir. Smoochy smoochy, sucky sucky, wham bam, we have something to go on.'

'Well I didn't.'

'Shame.'

'Not really. She wasn't so much my type.'

'I mean because it doesn't give you a let out.'

'Oh.'

'So?'

'So what?'

'Oh do come on, Mr Winkler, I'm trying to help. How the hell did your sperm get all over the dead girl? Did you cum in a bucket for months for a practical joke that involved perching it on top of a door so that it fell on your flatmate, but came home unexpectedly early because of the episode with the blind girl, forgot that you'd set up the trick, and then blam! Imagine your surprise when a bucket of your own cum fell on her as you were showing her into the telly room?'

'No.'

'Did you offer her a glass of milk and then beat off into it because she'd need a protein boost after the shock, but then she swallowed it, realised what she'd done, thanks to her heightened senses of taste and smell, and puked it all over herself?'

'No.'

'But I'm getting warmer, aren't I?'

Winkler said nothing and stared at his feet.

'Just tell me what happened,' said Tolkien.

So Winkler told him.

'On the television?'

'Mm. You didn't notice?'

'No. I suppose if I'm ever seconded to the anti-masturbation squad I'll know what to look for.'

'Can we not joke about it. I was in a very fucked-up way at the time.'

'Hence this big drug spree of yours out west?'

'Exactly.'

'Well you can live like that if you want. But those people aren't happy either. It's just another kind of pain. Better to face your problems and look into yourself for the answers.'

'You'd make a great Rabbi.'

'No I wouldn't. My dad said I wouldn't. I did think about it.'

'So, look. I've told you. And I'd like you first of all to swear never to tell anyone. And then to tell me how it helps, because, like I said, I came on the television screen and on the carpet, not on the girl.'

'And there was a lot of it, you say?'

'Well, yes. I'd been sort of aroused for hours, on and off, and you know how it builds up . . .'

'And where is the television?'

'It's in the corner opposite the door, by the window where the girl was sitting.'

'It's between the door and the window?'

'Yes.'

'And you're pointing at the girl, standing between her and the door, blocking that line, and you swivel to ejaculate away from her towards the television?'

'Yes, do we really need to go over this again?'

'And you come really big, like a three day whopper, which is always quite a shock on the body, so you probably stagger back a step or two as you're grunting and rolling your eyes back at the ceiling . . .'

'Steady on.'

'My guess is that not all that much hits the television, it just looks a lot because of the way it glistens and immediately slides down the screen leaving a trail. Most of this not inconsiderable gloop hits the deck, directly in a line between where the girl is sitting and the door. So then, in my opinion, it's like this: when the girl gets up to go she walks through your sperm, wading through the froth like the Israelites crossing the −'

'Except that she's not an Israelite.'

'Oh yes she is.'

'No? Oh, Christ. I had no idea'

'And that makes it worse?'

'Um, well, in a way, yes.'

'Anyway she gets your gack all over her shoes and then she goes home and treads it all over her floor at home and, being blind, there's every chance she treads on items of clothing that are lying about and even gets it on her hands when she's taking the shoes off. Then along comes the rapist and, well, does what he does, and so when we get to the fine combing of the place, we find two sets of sperm.'

'So can I go?'

'No. We still have to prove that's how it happened. Proof is the thing. We have one piece of inadmissible evidence against you and some circumstantial stuff and a detective who doesn't like Jews. If we can refute that single bit of evidence you're laughing. No need to do the test or take a hiding from Porfiry.'

'But we can't prove it.'

'Of course we can. If it happened like that then we only have to go over the squad car that picked her up and if we find so much as a trace of your gizz on the carpet then your story holds up. It was on her shoes before she even got home.'

'So that will mean telling people that I banged one out in front of her in my flat.'

'Well, only Porfiry and a couple of others. If it had come to court you'd have had to choose between going down for murder or admitting on public record that you're the kind of sick loser who wanks in front of blind people for laughs.'

'Well, I suppose I'm over the moon, then. I should thank you.'

'Forget it for the minute. Let's see what we find in the car. Who knows, if we're lucky we'll probably find your spaff all over the attending officers' boots as well.'

Well. If Winkler did not kill the blind girl (and I am sure we are all very relieved about that) then perhaps he didn't kill the fat woman either.

What do you mean, 'We saw him'?

We did not.

We knew it was always likely. We knew everything seemed to be tending that way. We know he thinks he did. And we know that the whole episode rushed through his mind when he was full of recreational drugs and sitting opposite two ludicrously sketched policemen. But we can't be sure. Just as we can't be sure that he did not kill the blind girl. Although it's getting less likely all the time. Unless you reckon the other sperm belongs to her lover and was there when Winkler arrived. No, I know she told Winkler she didn't have a lover. But do the blind never lie? Would you know if they did? You couldn't tell just from looking them in the eye.

'Maybe I didn't kill the fat woman either,' thought Winkler, relatively elated, lying on his hard little bed, wondering why he had not been reminded of the Gestapo by all the interrogation of the last few days. 'Maybe I tripped.'

There you go. Maybe he tripped. Just because he was planning to kill her, it doesn't mean he did. No murder mystery in the world would ever grip an audience if there were not characters other than the murderer who had motive, means and opportunity. Innocents with an unrealised motivation to murder are what makes murder mysteries go round. So don't hold it against Winkler that he wanted to push a fat woman under a train. Fat women fall under trains all the time. You can't blame it all on Winkler.

'Maybe I was hustling for position on the platform, no longer scared of the train because I had reached such a low point that I didn't care if I died, tripped on the brightly polished brogue of a heavily built stock-broker and instinctively put my arms out to stop myself falling.'

There. It's not impossible. It's just unlucky for the fat woman that she was the one between Winkler and the train.

'It's just unlucky that the fat woman was between me and the train. Well, unlucky for her. I fell on her, my hands sunk in her fleshy back, I

grappled and grabbed to try and stop her falling in front of the train, to
hold the two of us there on the platform as the executioner's hammer
crashed past, but couldn't get a grip on her, vast and wobbly as she was,
and so over she went. Doomed by her own obesity.'

It's possible.

'It is possible.'

The possibility that Winkler had not ever killed anybody at all, ever,
in his whole life, just like everybody else, troubled him deeply. Was he
glad that he might be innocent of all blood, or desperate that it meant
he was back where he started?

Worrying about it kept Winkler awake all morning.

At around lunch time, or at least the time when they gave Winkler his
lunch, whatever time that was, Sergeant Tolkien returned.

He stood in front of the door, which the guard had not locked after
him, grinning wordlessly. He looked as Jewish as Winkler had ever seen
him look. But still he would not have guessed.

'Well?' said Winkler.

'Spunk all over the motor. On the carpet, on both sides of the back
seat from where she got in on the kerb side and then slid across to the
other side to be in the sunlight, and on the transmission casing in between,
on the gas pedal and on the mat on the passenger side. It's a wonder the
car isn't pregnant.'

'And is it mine?'

'Yes, of course it's yours. Some of the flatfoots are a bit slack, but they
don't yank themselves off in the motor with an assault victim in the back.'

'We'll know if the car has a Jewish baby, I suppose.'

'Although it won't be Jewish because its mother is a gentile. All cars
are gentile. Except perhaps Daimlers.'

'It'll have one Jewish grandparent. That's all. Good enough for the Nazis
to take it away and put a bullet through its neck in a forest.'

'You're very strange,' said Tolkien.

'So the case against me weakens?'

'It falls apart. You're free to go.'

'Really? Just because I impregnated a police car?'

'And your alibi came through.'

Winkler danced and Winkler sang.

'No?'

'You sound surprised by that.'

'I'm surprised by everything.'

'Yes, she confirmed every detail. The police in Canberra took it all down. The parties, the timing and the night she spent in your bed. She got up to go at nine and you were still asleep, she said. So that's really all there is to it.'

'I really danced,' Winkler whispered to himself.

'And you actually got tied up by an Australian girl and fucked with a carrot,' said Ginger Bill, appearing next to Tolkien through the open door. 'Alright Arn?' he added, clapping his shoulder.

'Fucked with a what?' said Tolkien.

'My guess is a carrot,' said Ginger Bill. 'Although I'll grant that a parsnip is also possible. Myself, I'd rather it turned out I was a rapist.'

'I'd best be off,' said Tolkien. 'There is this business of Lord Morcester's assault charge. But I'll let you know about that. Don't leave town.'

'I rarely do,' said Winkler. Tolkien shuffled off.

'Bye, then,' said Ginger Bill, hugging Winkler with his great bear's grip and burying him in his beard.

'Thanks for everything, Bill. Really. Everything,' said Winkler as they left the cell and the guard came over to open doors, one for Bill and a different one for Winkler.

'It's nothing,' said Bill. 'Family is family.'

'I guess.'

'There is one thing you could do for me, though.'

'Anything, Bill. Anything,' said Winkler.

'Go see your grandpa.'

20

The Truth About Winkler

Winkler rang the doorbell a third time.

He walked back from the house and looked up. The bedroom window was open. His grandfather never left it open when he went out. Not even a crack. You never knew how thin a burglar might be. He read a newspaper story once, years ago, it might have been in the *Sketch*, no he tells a lie, it was the *Manchester Guardian*, where a house-breaker actually trained a snake to –

'Hello? Hello? Who's that?' crackled the white box screwed into the wall by the door at perfect mouth height for a man or woman no taller than four foot six.

Winkler ran to the door and said, stooping, to the intercom, 'It's me.'

'Me?'

'Your grandson.'

'I have a grandson?'

Poor old chap. His marbles really were going, tumbling through his fingers and plinking into darkness down drains and rabbit holes.

'It's me, Winky, your grands–'

'I had a grandson once,' said the frail old voice. 'But he died.'

'No Grandpa it's –'

'He was on his way to see me a little over a week ago, with a picnic lunch he had been promising to bring for me. But he was tragically hit by a bus whilst crossing the road. He saw it coming, I'm told, but he was so laden down with goodies – such as a bigger than average sacher-torte from Wilkomirsky's and a roast chicken and salami and hummus and potato salad – that he could not leap out of the way. I feel in part guilty, myself. But what could I do? He was such a loving boy, like a son to me, that I could never stop him visiting me with gifts. But in the end, life goes on.'

'Yes, Grandpa. Very —'

'Fzzzzzt!'

The lock whirred and the door popped open.

'I'm upstairs!'

Winkler climbed into the stairlift and threw the lever. Very, very slowly it began to hoist him up the stairs.

One.

How crap to be old and fucked.

Two.

What if the machine broke down and then there was a fire?

Three.

Why doesn't the old man go and live in a bungalow?

Four.

Really, it was pretty bad that Winkler hadn't been to see him since April.

Five.

Can it really have been April? The old man did have a tendency to magnify his persecutions.

Six.

'What are you doing sonny?'

'I'm coming!'

Seven.

'It's not a toy. Dear oh lore. I'd have thought at your age —'

Eight.

'I'm nearly there. Only fifteen steps to go.'

Nine.

Winkler was bored. He hopped off and the seat picked up speed, beating him to the top of the stairs.

'Smart arse,' he said to it when he arrived at the landing.

'You took your shoes off, I hope,' said his grandfather from the bedroom.

'Of course,' said Winkler.

He put down the white box he was carrying and yanked off his trainers. He put both shoes on the seat of the stairlift and hit the blue button in the wall. The seat set off again, hurtling downwards at nearly a stair a second.

'What are you doing?'

'Sending the stairlift down again,' said Winkler, picking the box up.

And plucking the toes of his socks out and curling the ends under his toe-knuckles to conceal the holes.

'Why?'

'Somebody might come in and need it.'

'Who's to come?' said his grandfather as Winkler stepped into the room.

A little yellow man in a brown silk dressing gown was lying in a big pink and green bed, three-quarters propped on a pile of pillows. A hard-back book was open, face down, on his lap. An ashtray beside him on the bed was fullish and steamed gently in a plume that swayed in and out of the beam of sunlight entering through a crack in the curtains. Two mugs sat next to a teasmaid on the bedside table. The room smelt, apart from cigarette smoke, of fart and aftershave.

'Still in bed?'

'I'm going out on my pogo-stick later.'

'But it's the best part of the day,' said Winkler, because his grandfather said that to him every morning for years. After clattering round the flat for hours, singing in the shower, hoovering outside his room, banging the Hoover against the door, and finally, unable to contain himself any longer, barging in and throwing open the curtains with a cry of, 'Best part of the day!' All because he was old and couldn't sleep and Winkler was young and couldn't do anything else.

'I brought you a *sachertorte*,' said Winkler, putting the box down on the bed and kissing his grandfather on his cheek. Feeling the chicken-soft skin over the cheekbone above the bristles. Smelling the cold creaky smell of his flesh.

'Ha, seven inches,' said the old man, opening the box and looking in. 'I said so. No freezer box then?'

'No.'

'I'm glad you came, son,' he said, putting the chocolate cake down on the bed and his hand on Winkler's hand. Winkler sat by him on the bed, making the ashtray tip to an angle that came close to tipping out its contents onto the pink and green quilt. 'Where have you been? I called to talk after last time because I made a fuss. But they said you weren't there, at work. And they didn't know where you were. And the same at home. I had a feeling they weren't telling me something. When you're my age you get used to people not telling you something. Usually it's because someone is dead. But you're not, I see.'

Winkler laughed.

'Oh, Grandpa, I'm so sorry,' he said. 'I was staying with a friend for a while. And then . . .'

'And then?'
'Then I was in prison.'

At the word 'prison' Woyzeck had winced, tutted his palate noisily and drawn his lips into a tight cat's arse of condemnation, wrinkled his nose and narrowed his eyes and sighed, 'Ooooh', just as he used to do if Winkler confessed that he had got a parking ticket, or if he swore in conversation, or clanked a plate against another in the kitchen while Woyzeck was trying to hear the radio.

There were no levels to the old man's disappointment. He was either disappointed in Winkler or he wasn't. And he was. To bring the disruption of 'prison' into the calm, foetid air of the bedroom – with its deafening 'Clang!' – was as bad as to be guilty of the rape and murder about which he would have no choice but to talk.

The way the old man saw it, there was no smoke without fire. No, no, no, he wasn't saying . . . Dear Lord, why didn't Winkler get a grip on himself? Rape, that such a word should be said in his house, of course not, his own flesh and blood could never, but he was Winkler's grandfather and he had brought him up and if he couldn't say what he thought about it then who could? And this was a case of Winkler embarrassing himself by getting messed up with the law because he simply –

The old man had always said that if Winkler didn't get married, get a proper job then this sort of thing – there was no need to shout, was this how he behaved with the police? No wonder they locked him away. If a man is not respectable then he is not respectable and so when such a terrible thing happens nearby then the eye of suspicion can fall on him. Had he not instilled in Winkler some morals? Some of the common decencies? It's like the time with the car, the Vauxhall, such a nice little car, but oh no he had to – dragging? He wasn't dragging anything – and with the store detective in the big book shop, if he hadn't been dressed like such a tramp . . . Even that he lives in such an area, where such a thing can happen must be looked at, must it not? That a grandson of his should live in such an area –

Of course he understood that Winkler was totally exonerated that he . . . no he wasn't behaving as if his grandson had been let out on some sort of legal technicality, he was only observing that he was, how old, now, thirty-four, thirty-five? Okay, twenty-nine, so it's the same, he was twenty-nine and by now such things, no of course he knew the age of his own grandson, he was an old man, numbers to him looked all the same lately, he felt he must tell him that in all his eighty-four years never did he have so much as a parking ticket. Never had a policeman rung his doorbell. No, he only meant that they must have had a reason to suspect him. What did he mean, he didn't know? He didn't ask? He is put in a prison cell all this time and he doesn't ask why they suspect him? How does he know he is off the hook now? After a certain time they have to let him go, don't they? Because they have no evidence to charge. But if they find some then maybe he'll be charged again. Why must Winkler take that tone with him? He was clearly aware that if he hadn't done it then there would be no evidence. But what if . . . he didn't know, but it was possible. Why had they let him go then? Why was he no longer a suspect? What sort of a mistake? Well, he had plenty of time. Time he was not short of. If it took all day, it took all day. Of course he would understand. What was his old grandfather, stupid? So, then if Winkler wanted to be like that he could be like that but his grandpa would find out tomorrow from Bill easily enough. So.

What did the Irish girl think about it, anyway? They aren't so forgiving, these Catholics. For her family that Winkler should be held in a cell for . . . how long? Eight days? Eight days! He hadn't said it was eight days, that was a sentence in itself. Eight days they don't hold you without charge, it wasn't realistic, Winkler's story. So. Eight days he is held for sex crimes and murder, what do they say, the parents of the Irish girl? Mary. Yes, Mary. Mary, Susan, Kathy what does it matter? If they had met, if Winkler had not been too ashamed then maybe names would be . . . gone, was she? Well that did not surprise him. Oh, it was Winkler who left? And before this all happened? Why leave? Who was he going to find now, at his age, at thirty-four, to marry and . . . twenty-nine, then . . . who would want to settle with such a feckless . . . already? What was this now, a new one so quick after the Irish? What was this, a little Indian girl? A Black? What was he saying, she was an Austrian? Did Winkler have any idea about Austrians? Did he know Hitler was an Austrian? Austrians are Germans only more so. Oh. Australian then. It's an Australian girl Winkler was canoodling with now. Irish, Australian, what was wrong with him? Why was it always foreigners? Like these men who take a bride from a catalogue, from Thailand – what was wrong with him that he couldn't make something with an Englishwoman? Of course he was English. What nonsense. What else did he think he was, a Dutchman? A Jew? Not this again. This Holocaust nonsense. This mad old man under the stairs with his stories. Winkler was not a Jew. He could read no Hebrew. He was not barmitzvah'd. Did he believe in God suddenly? He could be sentimental all he liked. To be a Jew was not just to whinge whinge whinge about the past, this was why so many Jews made so much trouble for themselves, it is not just to cry over the past and make a big song in front of the goyim and blame everybody, and weep over stetls and cheders and synagogues and Warsaw and some idea of this lovely Europe before the War where everybody was so happy and the Jews had all such a lovely time and the ancient communities and Salonika and all this nonsense, it was always, always terrible to be a Jew, always, Hitler was nothing, a beginner, for thousands of years it was the same. How long did Winkler think the Germans were in Germany? How long? 1,400 years is how long. And the Jews? Longer. 1,700, 1,800 years. The Jews from the East were there in Germany before the Germans came, in the forests, in the fields and even then was it good? Ha! The Romans, the Romans made it a misery. Now suddenly it is sixty years ago the Holocaust and so maybe Winkler thought it was funny to be a Jew, but he knew nothing, nothing. It made him sick to think of. Why now did it come, this Jewish rubbish? After the schooling and the cricket and the girls and the drinking and the university and the football and the beer and cigarettes and the idleness: such an English, English child and now he wants to be a great Jew with a beard, what, now, a rabbi, perhaps? A cantor in the shul humming there and bowing, or tied up with his tefillin and muttering in a corner, and then one day petrol in the letter box and then his cricket bats and his tennis sweaters and his English novels and his Shakespeare and his American comics and his tweed jackets will make a nice fire for the hoodlums. Why? Why did he want this? Winkler was no Jew. His mother was a, was a, she was a –

So quickly it had changed, Winkler's mood. His feelings about his grandfather had shifted from the moment of the hand-on-hand contact and the sympathy for his decrepitude, and admiration for his humour, and disgust with himself for his neglectful ways, to the same old anger with him for being the way he was, in a way which made it impossible to believe he had felt so differently so recently.

So when the old man talked about morals, and the instilling of decencies, Winkler carried on protesting but was not thinking about his words, just letting them roll out, protestingly. What he was thinking was that the old man had instilled in him nothing but table manners.

'Table manners was all it was. All you were good for. The sum total of what you had to pass on in terms of right and wrong. Your Ten

Commandments bellowed to Moses across the table on the mountain. Your Polonius moment – neither a gobbler nor a slurper be – your Damon Runyon leaving home moment, when his father told him that one day a man would show him a brand new deck of cards on which the seal was not yet broken and bet him that he could make the jack of spades jump up out of the pack and squirt cider in his ear, that same speech that ended up in the mouth of Sky Masterson's father in a flashback in *The Idyll of Miss Sarah Brown* and then in *Guys and Dolls* in the mouth of Marlon Brando.

'Well, I got my earful of cider, because all I had had to keep it dry was table manners, and they weren't enough. Elbows off the table. Don't talk with your mouth full. Don't eat with your mouth open. Finish what's on your plate. Eat what's put in front of you. Don't play with your food. Don't reach, ask. Don't ask, wait to be offered. Chew before you swallow. Don't leave the table without asking. Don't interrupt when I'm eating. No combination mouthfuls. You don't drink soup, you eat it. Side of the spoon, side of the spoon. Nice people don't have ketchup. Don't mix cereals in the bowls. Eat the fat, it's good for you. Put your knife and fork together when you've finished. Don't bang your knife on the plate. No orange squash with soup, it doesn't go. Don't eat with your fingers. Cut with the knife, don't tear.

'But what about, Don't wank in front of blind girls. Don't punch four-teenth earls in the eye on their own land even if they call you "bloody Jew". Don't think intolerant thoughts about Muslim women or Asian boys. Don't sit and do nothing when your boarding-school chums pile shoes on your bed. Don't lie about your father. Don't lie about your reli-gion. Don't lie about your race. Don't chuck your job in because an old Jew killed some German kids in the War. Don't treat your girlfriend like a bag of shit. Don't push fat women in front of trains. Where was all the useful stuff, you old cunt? Where was the advice that might have helped?'

And, anyway, look at him now, the old man. All the time they were talking he was eating the sachertorte, spooning spherical mouthfuls from the glistening cake and pushing them into his yellow-sticky mouth and chewing with the terrible slurp and drool of a camel eating treacle. The noise of Woyzeck eating was the noise of Winkler's death. Eating cake it was all smack smack smack and the sight of it going round all brown and shining in his mouth turning over and diminishing in size as it rolled from right to left and right to left and right to left. Eating nuts it was all crunch crunch crunch and the separate seeds all mulching down noisily to a goo until the crunch crunch crunch became a smack smack smack like the cake of the sticky brown nut butter becoming part of his grandfather, and the sighs and breathy winds of him taking oxygen and shedding carbon dioxide as he ate, the mouth always open to let him breathe and eat. A man's got to breathe. A man's got to eat. And the white spit-strands that stretch in the mouth-corners as the lips separate go gradually brown as the chocolate joins in the fun. And of course he talked. Talked as he chewed and as the cake mulched in his maw. Each chocolatey ball yielding to saliva and enzyme as he voiced his criticisms of Winkler's life around the mouthful and over it and under it, and as he spoke and as he ate carving off another chocolate ball and holding it there in front of the yellow lips as he spoke and then – is he going to stop talking to put it in? Is he going to finish this point first? Surely. The spoon poised. The mouth open. Yes. No. Yes. In it goes – no room for Winkler to interrupt, the old man's still talking and he's taken on enough chocolate cake to keep him going for quite a while.

Winkler looked at him, yellow, bent, half-propped under the green and pink quilt next to the half-tipped ashtray of curled cigarette canoes. When he ate chocolates from a box he did not put them in his mouth, he stuck out his long, yellow, fur-topped tobacco-stinking tongue and placed a chocolate on the end of it and then drew the tongue into his mouth (like a frog with winged game) and chewed it with a great bulge in his cheek, sometimes keeping his mouth closed to keep the sound down so he could hear the television but making a terrible smack as the sticky lips separated eventually to take on air.

If Winkler could stop him doing it, maybe he would visit more often. Visit sometimes. Not just the noise and horribleness of it. The hypocrisy. The constant reminder of the table lessons given over all those years that were good for nothing and meant nothing. Lessons that were doled out purely for the pleasure of correction. If he could only tell him, and stop him. But now? Was this any time to bring it up, fresh out of chokey and the old man about to croak?

When it came to shouting, Winkler shouted loudest because he could. When he said, 'You didn't want me to be happy, you wanted me to be quiet,' he said it so loud that his throat roared red with soreness and across the street men reached for the remote control to mute the sound and hear what was going on outside.

When he said, 'It wasn't my fucking fault they left me with you,' he was gasping for air and drowning in snot and the 'you' at the end of the sentence was unintelligible, an endless, tapering avalanche of vowels.

When he said, 'Why do you think I never come and see you? You think I deserved to be locked up on suspicion of murder and in the same head you can't understand why I don't come?' he was not really making words at all and half way through 'understand' he gave up and cried, 'Aaaaarghhh,' or something like it, and swept round for something to smash. There was nothing breakable but a mirror on the wall above the bed, a full length mirror free-standing in a corner, the teasmaid and the old man, and they would all have been too messy to clear up afterwards so he screamed and punched with his left hand the pine door front of the old man's wardrobe containing laughably wrong-sized suits which had not shrunk as he shrank, and crunched through it nicely and withdrew and punched again and again until lots of the suits were visible, mostly in the dry-cleaner's polythene they had worn home after their last clean, years and years ago, when Winkler was still at university probably, even school. And by the time he made his last punch and felt the pain of his broken knuckles all soft and blue under the skin and noticed light smears of dark blood on the wood he had said, 'You never loved me,' a number of times, very loudly indeed, and also, 'I did love you once and I stopped a long time ago,' but that only once. But all very loud, with swearing, and punching and snorting.

And when he told his grandfather that he knew nothing, nothing about what Winkler was like and even as he criticised and criticised he had no idea of how bad his grandson really was, he was still loud, but tearfully loud rather than screamingly loud. And when he told him that his grandson, his own grandson, yes, his own flesh and blood, was so much more than disrespectful, lazy, foul-mouthed and whatever else the old man thought he was, he was getting quieter, but was still louder than just talking. When he said that he was hate-filled, resentful, bitter, sick with unhappiness, gleefully revolted by every, *every* other human on the planet and that he was also murderous, really truly murderously bad and had proved it by pushing a fucking fat woman under a train and appeared to have got away with it, he said it only as loud as a teenage boy tells his parents to fuck off when they tell him he can't stay out after midnight.

And when he told Woyzeck not even to bother saying that he was hysterical and that he had let his imagination run wild and what nonsense was this with the train, because it was true, he had done it because it was time to do it and it was partly the fault of the old man under the stairs and partly his own fault and partly everyone's fault and quite consider-ably his grandfather's fault, when he said that he was only loud because he was crying and fighting to vomit the words out over the wet and the heaviness of his breathing.

And when he fell on the carpet holding his destroyed left hand in his cool (it felt cool) right hand, sobbing and gasping for air with seal-like honks that almost embarrassed him through the pain, he felt relieved, finally, that he had made enough of a demonstration now of how he felt, and must surely have got his point across.

Winkler rolled over onto his back on the carpet and up against the frame of the divan and the dirty pink valance that hung pointlessly over it, and stared up at the grey-white ceiling, textured with the fan-like trails a trowel leaves in plaster by way of ornamentation in council-owned properties built before the 1970s. A step up from wood-chip, or maybe a step down.

He breathed in and out a few more times but the incoming air was hard to get down and sounded more like crying than breathing, and now that he had stopped crying he didn't want to be making the sound anymore so he tried not to breathe except through his nose.

And then he felt something cold on his forehead. His grandfather's hand. Not a familiar feeling. And he heard a voice saying, 'My boy, my boy.'

At first, Winkler kept one foot on the floor like a pre-war Hollywood lover (in Hollywood a woman had to keep one foot on the ground to signify 'not fucking', thought Winkler, while at the same time, the same time, a German woman caught fucking a Jewish man was paraded through town with a placard saying, 'I have committed race defilement' round her neck, while the man, well, there's no point worrying about the man) but eventually he drew it up onto the bed also, because now was not a time when his grandfather would make a fuss about 'feet on the furniture'. And anyway he wasn't wearing shoes, so that made it okay.

The polyester sheets, which were so easy to wash because they dried so quick and didn't need ironing, warmed quickly where his face and clothes touched them, the noise of his clothes moving on them was not pleasant, if your ear was to the mattress, but Winkler did not move much. Movement would have changed everything.

His head rested in the old man's armpit and half up on his chest, and he smelt, up close, like a supermarket shelf-stacker. His head moved up and down fractionally as the old man breathed, each weak rib easily felt by his hot ear. The feeble heart beating regularly, it sounded like. The lungs not making any heavier work of respiration than he would have expected. Sounding a little more lively when they sucked cigarette smoke than oxygen, but that was illusory, surely.

Surrounded by smoke and the chewing and swallowing of sachertorte, and the warmth of the room, and fart and shelf-stacker and old sheets and mattress and a skein of light sweat on his face and salt stripes dry on his cheeks, Winkler lay close – like a feeding baby.

The old man, half-propped, thin as nothing, smoking, yellow-chested, big eyed in his shrunken face, told it like this,

'Siri came from Budapest. I met her in a coffee house in Leeds where she was working in 1944. I was out of conscription because of a medical certificate I had from my cousin Albert. You know about that. She had long legs. And her hair tied up for work showed her neck like a swan. A strong, creamy swan. She carried things, trays, urns, crates of milk, like they weighed nothing. But she wasn't big. I remember how she looked from behind when she was working the coffee-grinder – it was a manual one, you saw them a lot then – in the brown woollen skirt she always wore which smelt of naptha (of course, so did the jacket smell of it, but I liked to think I knew the smell of the skirt separately). She looked strong but not wide and her calves had muscles, from dancing in high shoes she said, in Vienna and Bratislava, everywhere – she ran with a fast set in the old country.

'She served me every day. I always went at the same time, after work in the shop, although obviously I went home first to wash so I wouldn't smell. Not because it mattered then to smell of fish. But because fish felt to me like a poor smell. It was a saying people back then had for a person who talked big and wore flashy clothes but who you suspected had it all on the lim, "He smells of fish," we would say. But it wasn't the same as "He smells fishy," it was specific. Anyway, it was said in Yiddish, "*Riech nach fisch . . .*" or something, I didn't speak it properly, only to pepper a sentence for fun. Your great-grandfather, he hardly spoke anything else. The smell of fish on a man meant that even if he claimed to be a "businessman" or "in property" really he was a fish porter, or fishmonger's boy and only had dreams of something better, or sometimes that he was recently a fish man and would be back schlepping herrings soon as the market turned. But anyway, when I saw Siri the first time I decided at least to wash now whenever I came in.

'For a long time I tried to get her talking. And this took a very long time. For a few weeks I could get maybe a smile here or there, and I would leave bigger and bigger tips, but it never made any difference. Because of business I could always get eggs and fish and butter, even cigarettes and alcohol, and I thought to make such offers, but then I thought I didn't want to appear flashy, or appear to bribe her. Always she looked at me with her big brown eyes and my heart stopped. I knew the first time she looked at me that she was Jewish. And of course it was a kosher shop so she couldn't have been anything else. But she never smiled. She never spoke to me. Even to say thank you. Beautiful and grumpy she was. At first I thought beautiful and sad, but then I decided beautiful and grumpy.

'I asked another girl, Leila, what her grumpiness was about. "Why does she never smile or speak to me?" I said. "She never speaks to anyone, Woyzeck," Leila said, because she knew me, all the girls there knew me, I had a good camel overcoat and shiny shoes and they knew sometimes I would leave a big tip. "She is from Hungary," said Leila. "Her English is not so good and she prefers to say nothing."

'And so I stopped trying to talk to her. But I went there every day anyway just to look at her. One day I took Maurice with me, thin Maurice, he was thin even then, not as thin as now, but he was young so it was more of a thing, I took him just to show her to him, because it was all I could do now and I had given up hope of anything else. "She's lovely," said Maurice, when Siri had brought him his lemon tea and put it in front of him with a noise on the table so that a little spilled from the glass into the saucer. "And what a window-box," Maurice said, "Oy, such fruit on a young tree, but also what a moody? Dear oh lore," he said. "What would it cost her to smile?" And when she came back with sugar he said to her, "Cheer up, darling, it might never happen." And she banged the sugar bowl down on the table and everyone in the place looked round, the other waitress, too, Leila, and all the old women with their cakes, and Siri stared at him and then she said, very calmly, with a strong accent I had never heard before,

'"It hess aul-reddy heppenned."

'And then she turned to me and said, "Your friend is a fool, Mr Vinkler. You may valk me to my home, vhen you choose." And she walked straight out of the place and stood outside the front door, with her arms wrapped round herself from the cold, and stamped her feet a couple of times. Maybe to be warm and maybe to show anger. When I had finished laughing I stood up and looked around, everyone was still staring, and I looked across at Leila and she nodded towards the door and I put down some coins and started to go, when Leila called, "Mr Winkler!" and held

out Siri's coat. A fur coat, no less. So I took it from her and thanked her
very much and went out into the street. I put the coat over her shoulders. And your grandmother said, "Senk you. I do not liff far. You do not
heff to valk me." I told her I wanted to and she said, "I know you do."
And so we walked.

'Do you want a cigarette, son?' the old man asked Winkler.

'Yeah, okay,' said Winkler.

'Good, this packet's empty. There should be more in the drawer over
there.'

Winkler got up and went to the dressing table and rummaged through
his grandfather's underwear.

'At the bottom. At the back,' said his grandfather.

Winkler wondered why the old man bothered to bury them, and noted
with displeasure a pair of yellow Y-fronts with a darkish track in the gusset,
many times washed but many times soiled, a defeat now accepted by the
fabric.

He lit a cigarette for his grandfather and looked at the tip and lit it
again and then handed it to him, and the old man sucked it weakly and
made a faint glow at the end. Winkler put one in his own mouth and
then took it out, and put it back in the packet, and put the packet on
the table on his side of the bed – 'his side', this was like Morecambe and
Wise – and reassumed his position while his grandfather smoked.

Eventually the old man started talking again. 'It turned out Siri was
married,' he said. 'Her husband was still there, in Hungary, some town or
other. A big shot businessman. He had shops. A newspaper. A fleet of cars.
Even, I think, an aeroplane. Though I can't remember when she said it
about the plane, before when she was boasting, or after when she was
twisting the knife. I wondered if she had made that up. An Eastern Jew
with an aeroplane in the 1940s? Anyway, she was married to this man on
account of her family. Her father also was a businessman, but a failed one.
He knew this man, Furtwangler, the husband, from previous deal-makings,
and this was how he came to meet Siri, and to fall for her. And her father
was very insistent that she should marry him for the good of the family,
you understand, son, for his money. He was older than her by twenty
years but already at this time Siri was thirty-one herself and her father
said that if not Furtwangler then who?

'She did not love Furtwangler. She told me a thousand times. And each
time she told me it made it a little better.

'And so she married him, and it all went well for the family. And she
moved into his house. A great mansion in the countryside with a dozen

servants and seven automobiles including a Rolls Royce. Like Hatfield House, she said. Although that did not seem very likely. The immigrants at that time were terrified to be thought poor and desperate, and they had also a terrible pride, so there was always some house waiting for them back in the old country that was like Hatfield or Hampton Court.

'Until early 1944 it was thought the Jews in Hungary would be safe. But later, when eventually the husband's friends persuaded him it was time to leave, that the Nazi occupation would come any day and it would not be safe to be a Jew, he first of all sent her to England. He was a rich man. It was still possible to cross Europe with real money, Schindler-type money, and to leave through Sweden. She wanted him to go with her, begged and screamed for him to go with her – this she told me even though it was not good evidence for the story about how she did not love him – but he would not go until he had made his businesses safe, or what he thought was safe, and sent enough money on ahead, which was nearly impossible at that time. And he told her that she had to go and he would follow soon after.

'So she travelled across Europe on her own. Left her mother and father without tears because they after all had put her into this marriage, and her sister, Shula, and all of her friends – although she never mentioned any friends so maybe she had none – and all the life she had in that town that is no longer there any more in the way that it was before, so help me I forget its name completely. Left all the things she owned and people she had met, and knew to nod at, and the places she had been, perhaps for ever she thought, and definitely for ever as it turned out, all that gone as if it never had happened, and she was not a child who can just kick over the traces and start again, but a woman, the same age as you, more or less, imagine that, if it was you who –'

Winkler, of course, imagined. Or tried to imagine. A few weeks ago the idea would have fascinated him, leaving Glaub, Spawn, the office, the puddle, the Werther report, Leo Sneel, the Asian boys, the Gnus, the dog shit, the smell, Mary, Will, Meriel, Grandpa, the always imminent death under a train, his books, school, cricket kit, parks and pavements and bus stops and shops, fields and gardens, dreams and visions, shapes and sizes . . . but now, as things stood, he had said goodbye to all those things already, or most of them. Yes. It was all quite easy to imagine. What lucky fellows those refugees were. What a blinding excuse and dazzling opportunity to flee.

'. . . and into the bus or lorry or whatever it was came a young Gestapo officer. He engaged her in conversation and told her all about his family and how he hoped one day to become a famous footballer and flirted with her – and she always talked about him, about how polite and handsome he was, as if politeness and being handsome were exonerating features in a Gestapo officer, as if they all were polite and handsome and that was why it was such a shame they were murderers, as if you could say what you like about Hitler but there was no denying that the Gestapo were polite and handsome – and when they came to whereever it was they were going, he helped her down with her bags and kissed her hand and wished her a pleasant trip and good luck for the future and said maybe they would bump into each other after the War.

'It was very important to your grandmother, this story of the Gestapo officer who was in love with her. She was, as I said, in her thirties by then and always had to have some younger man flirting with her. If she had been misty-eyed when she told her story, it would have been one thing, but it was always with a dirty smile, as if she wanted me to know that they had found a quiet corner of the bus and . . . well, you know how it is. This is what I later thought maybe had happened. But whether she taunted me just to hurt me, or because it was true, I don't know. I was very jealous – this was finally the great love of my life and she came with her past locked away from me, and only chose to let out little pieces as it suited her. I could not see in, and so I could not know what had made her how she was, and what she had done and seen.

'A lover is always a mystery, and unravelling the mystery is what falling in love is. But Siri I could not unravel, she was tightly wound and then knotted and then she bit off all the loose ends. Other men, other loves, whether they were there or not, or meant more or less than I did, or than Furtwangler, I didn't know. And this disappearance of her past made her present seem the more fragile. Was this how she was in love? I had nothing to compare. Had she been like this with others? Would she again? All this perhaps made me behave to her in a way that made her feel suffocated and to make me back away she had perhaps to talk like that about the German, and other men, but . . .'

Winkler pulled his grandfather onto his chest and held him while he heaved for breath and shook, and wetted Winkler's shirt, dark blue linen, short-sleeved, with his cold old tears.

Laughing and sniffing, then, Grandpa Winkler said, 'Of course I was jealous because I saw how easy she did it with me. It is always six of one and half-a-dozen of the other with such girls. So good to have them part their thighs for you, but then you can't help wondering . . . Well, anyway, after I walked her home I began to do so every night, and she told me all about her husband and how she did not love him, but she must wait for him to come from Hungary before she divorces. And for just as long as it was decent she put off even a kiss, and then she cooked dinner for me one evening when her landlady was not there, and I stayed with her for the night, and after that, well, we were in love, I thought.

'The husband didn't come, and then the Germans occupied Hungary. And the deportations began immediately, as we later heard. And she heard nothing and heard nothing. And soon she was pregnant with a son. Your father. We pretended that we had married on the quiet, for the child not to be a bastard, but we didn't because she still thought he'd show up, this Furtwangler. And then when he never came and never came, long after the war, we carried on pretending, because she never accepted that she was a widow. All there was for evidence was the liquidation of Hungarian Jewry. Total. But no death certificate. So she never would go through with it.'

'You never married?'

'Never.'

'Shit.'

'It's not such a big deal. Everybody thought we were married. I felt God would see that I had the done the right thing. Apart from fornicating, of course. And I paid my price in the end.'

'Because she killed herself?'

'Oh, they all killed themselves. No, I paid and paid and paid for loving a girl whose sugar daddy never came back from the war. Who knows but at the moment of our first love-making he was marching through a forest somewhere with a shovel over his shoulder to dig his own hole to . . .'

'Grandpa, you —'

'Yes, but that's what she said, Sonny. She wouldn't leave it alone. Lying there together in bed in my room over the fish shop, late, late in the war, with your father there in a box on the floor, and us lying there smoking after more lovemaking while he cried from the noise, she would start to wonder where he was now, this Furtwangler. She imagined him always in the gas chamber, clawing at the doors until his nails bled, and wept because his nails were always so beautiful, because he had them manicured every week by a woman who visited the house. . . such a terrible shame for someone so sensitive as him to go through that, she thought. And imagined him hiding in an attic somewhere, living on God knew what, the shame and indignity for such an important man. And all his

money could not help him, this astonished her, and was as close as she got
to seeing the worthlessness of it. But still for her his wealth made the suffering
and the death more tragic, in a way that I could never understand.

'And then if I went quiet while she talked she would roll over and tell
me she never loved him, as if this made us suddenly close again But it
was always there, the Holocaust. The death camps, the marches, the shootings, always wondering where did he die, and how, and where was he
now, and her parents, of course, but less so, and all the things she might
have had if he had only left when she left. Such clothes she had before
the War and such jewels and furniture and cars and overcoats of every fur
you can imagine – and now, look, she was here over this fish shop in this
stinking city in this stinking country of savages – and there, of course,
she never saw the irony that it was the greed of Furtwangler that made
him stay on in Hungary and in the end killed him. I went so mad with
it that I began after the War trying to persuade her that he was not dead
but only used the Holocaust as a smokescreen for fleeing his debts, that
he took another identity and fled to America. I don't remember if I
believed this, or whether I made it up to force her to get over it or just
to hurt her. But it didn't stop. Even after we moved to a bigger flat, still
she filled it with her dead. And it only got worse after her sister came.'

'Her sister?'

'Shula. She appeared in 1947. What a sight. Like a ghost at the front
door. The front door was also the front door of the pub. We lived over a
pub. And it was a Thursday evening when she arrived, unannounced, like
a skeleton in her grey slip dress and her little bean shaped round-toed
grey lace-up shoes with ankles like pipe cleaners. Like a tiny stick-woman
that a child would draw, with a big round head. Not more than four foot
ten, maybe five stone, eyes deep like thumb holes in a bowling ball. Hair
white. Asking at the bar in German for Herr Vinkler.

'Siri never told me they had been corresponding, or that she had invited
her. She said it didn't seem ever a good time to bring up the subject.
After Auschwitz Shula had tried to go home, but in Hungary almost none
survived so there was nothing to go back to. So then Palestine, where
Siri's letters found her, and now here. Like a mouse in a dress. Silent and
shivering always. With a disgusting big purple scar inside her left forearm
where she had carved out her tattooed-number with a pen-knife after
they laughed at her in Budapest and told her it was no longer a place
for Jews.

'She and Siri would sit talking to each other in Hungarian and ignore
the boy completely. She hated her son, and so did her sister. Or perhaps

only cared nothing for him at all. The flat always had to be boiling hot like a sauna, otherwise the sister complained of the cold, and then she would suddenly demand fresh air and make me open all the windows, which would make her cold. This was the late 1940s, there was not much money around, and she came to be a real extravagance. She would eat practically nothing. She was fearsomely kosher – unlike Siri who didn't care what she put in her mouth – and complained and complained and complained until she was brought such and such a delicacy and then complained that it was too big a portion, or ate only a mouthful. And if she ate more she often vomited it back right there at the table. And if I said anything, anything, then Siri flew at me with how can I say such a thing after all her sister has been through. She had returned from the bowels of hell, where Siri's poor dear husband had died, and every second that was given to us to be with her was a blessing. If she wanted to be warm, was that so terrible? If she wanted a little chicken? A little choco-late? Was it such an effort? Was I not prepared to sacrifice . . . On and on like this it went, with the ghost of Furtwangler's money always there too, which might have made Shula (and, of course, Siri) so comfortable. So what was I to do? Leave them? I could not imagine it. What would they have done? These two young but now suddenly old Hungarian women over an English pub? They would have . . . well, I couldn't imagine. And the boy. Your father. He would have . . . he would have . . .'

'You could have taken him with you,' said Winkler.

'I couldn't take the boy,' said his grandfather.

'But if she wasn't fit to –'

'I couldn't take the boy,' said his grandfather again. 'And by the winter of '48, she was dead, the sister. She wouldn't see a doctor. She was briefly very sick but it wasn't such a big change from normal. And then one morning she was stiff as a board and I had a friend I knew in the under-taker three doors down come and box her up. Some rabbi's assistant said a few words. It was just me and Siri and the boy. The ground was frozen hard but they had knocked up some clods for us to push into the grave. Well just for me to push, it isn't for women. I pushed in the shovel and heaved a clod over the edge, it was huge and rock hard and hit the coffin like a hammer, as if it would crack it. Siri looked at me and said, "You bastard". And we went home separately.

'She insisted it was the cold flat that killed Shula, and blamed me. 1948 was cold in England, but not as cold as the places she survived. And the heating was on permanently. I thought it was blood-poisoning from her knifework to remove the tattoo. Or maybe tuberculosis weakened her lungs in the camps and it was just bronchitis that did for her. Still, it seemed a blessed release.'

'For who?' said Winkler.

The old man turned and looked at him. 'For Shula, son, who do you think?'

'After that we didn't speak much. I loved her so much, it was terrible. She talked only about the old days and Furtwangler, and his cars. She started to believe, after all, that he was in America, and wrote to all sorts of Jewish organisations there, and in Israel. She even went to Israel to look for him. Four months she was gone, without a word, until I thought she wasn't coming back at all, and it would just be me and the boy. But then one day she walked in the room when I was washing up some pots and pans and the boy cried out "Mama!" and she took him in her arms, and we never spoke about it. In the summer of 1953, a few days after the coronation of Queen Elizabeth, she took pills. And when I came home from work, there was the boy brushing her hair, and her lying on the bed, stiff like her sister, with her eyes open. My big Hungarian love with the great behind who I met in the coffee shop.'

Winkler pulled his grandfather onto his chest again and held him. He didn't know if he was crying and didn't look. He thought probably not.

'Why couldn't you leave with the boy?' he said eventually.

'Just couldn't,' replied his grandfather.

'When was he born?'

'October 13, 1944'.

'And you met Siri when?'

'In the spring of 1944.'

'When in the spring?'

The old man peeled himself off Winkler and sat up. Then he got out of bed in his striped dressing gown and put his yellow feet into his tartan slippers and padded over the carpet to the electric button that opened the curtains and buzzed himself enough space to open the window.

'It's stuffy in here,' he said. 'It reminds me of the flat when Shula was having one of her cold spells.' He went to the dressing table and picked up an aerosol with a pink lid which he sprayed into the air until Winkler got the whiff of pub toilets in his nostrils. Then he lit a cigarette and stood by the window, looking out at the street through a gap he had opened in the nets with his non-smoking hand. 'There's a lovely big space right outside you could have parked in,' he said, 'if only you still had that car.'

'So the end of this is that you're not really my grandfather?' said Winkler.

'She was already pregnant when you met. The boy was Furtwangler's. She slept with you because she thought he might never come, and wanted you to think it was yours, just in case. And you pretended to be married to her so she wouldn't feel ashamed.'

'Of course I am your grandfather,' said the old man. Still staring out at the street. And then turned back into the room and with his wet eyes looked at Winkler. 'Of course I am.'

'When did you know?'

'Always.'

'When did she tell you?'

'She never told me. But I knew. There wasn't time for it to have been mine. It was possible, I thought. Just. But she did not pretend even that it was early. He was a big boy. So big I thought maybe the Gestapo officer . . .'

'Christ. Don't say that.'

'Look at yourself, Winky,' said his grandfather, spinning the dressing table mirror round on its stand. 'You're not a Kraut.'

Winkler sat up and walked to the dressing table and looked in the mirror. He was red and moist and warm from lying there and being sad and being moved and being smothered in smoke.

'Does my father know?'

'Of course he does. It's why it was so easy for him to leave. He remembers his mother. And when I told him about Furtwangler he started remembering a childhood where I was a monster who hounded his poor refugee mother to her death. He made a performance about not having a father. He probably thought his real father was out in Israel somewhere, too. And so when the scandal with you being born came out, he was off. Two birds with one stone, he probably thought.'

'And yet he asked you to take me?'

'She would not have you, the wife, so what was I to do? It was that or an orphanage.'

'A Jewish orphanage?'

'I dare say.'

A Jewish orphanage. Fun and games after lights out, Talmudic study by day. Winkler would have known Hebrew, understood his people, had a close and trusting relationship with his little penis. Been trained to something worthwhile, a dentist or solicitor or, who knows, rabbi. Spoken a little Yiddish. Met a Jewish girl. Lots of Jewish girls. Had sex early in the fraught, parentless chaos of the big house full of young Jews. Married her. Been by now a father of four or five. With a beard. Outside of the

mainstream – as he was anyway – but with another self-sufficient community to be part of, which did not always threaten to uncover the horrible
truth of his race. Although of course he would never have played cricket.
Never known the joy of concealing an arm ball after four dot balls that
looped and bit the dusty track and turned away past off stump so that
the batsman, tall and blond and descended from sixteen generations of
English soil, let the fifth one go, only to find it skid off the top, not break,
and brush past his pad into the tinkling wicket . . .

The old man, seeing Winkler's silence, mistaking it for emotion, reached
to touch him. Surprised him.

'So you took me. Even after he rejected you like that?'

'It was not for him I took you. But for you. In your little carry cot,
a few months old, a fat little piglet like your father, twenty-five years
before. I could not let you go to a home. And I had nothing else planned
for the next thirty years.'

'And you took me.' Winkler didn't want to cry. Because it would look
like self-pity. And it might set the old man off. And the pair of them sniv-
elling there would be a revolting thing.

'I took you.'

'I wasn't even a pretend non-biological son I was . . .'

'A pretend non-biological grandson. We are not much related you and
I, Winky. I'm sorry.'

'But Grandpa,' Winkler decided it didn't matter if he cried. The old
man would be pleased. 'But Grandpa.'

'Son?'

'I wasn't your son's son. I wasn't your grandson.'

'No, Winky. I'm sorry.'

'You didn't have to take me. All those years. You didn't have to do it
for me, or for him. It's just a man and a woman from Hungary who had
a son. And then the son had a son by mistake with another suicidal woman.
And again you . . .'

'Wink, I'm sorry. I'm sorry,' said Winkler's grandfather.

'No, Grandpa,' said Winkler. 'Don't be sorry. Don't be. I love you. I'm
so glad. I love you. All that time you had me. And fed me and bought
me birthday presents. My Geoff Boycott book. And we tried to find me
a dad and in the end Ginger . . . oh. I suppose he's not my uncle then.'

'That depends on what you think an uncle is.'

'And what you think a grandfather is.'

'Yes, son.'

'Or a father.'

There was quiet in the gaily painted hot little bedroom. The old man let the curtain drop and stubbed his cigarette in a small porcelain ashtray with a faded rose motif in the middle. Winkler put his arms round him and felt his weak little body. And the old man clasped him, and Winkler felt his strength too. Winkler told him over and over that he loved him. And the old man said many times that he loved Winkler. And Winkler said, 'I won't talk about bloody Wallenstein any more, or the War or the boring bloody Holocaust. I'm sorry.'

And the old man leaned back out of the hug and looked at Winkler with his red eyes and said, 'You talk about whatever you like, son.'

Then the old man was tired and got back into bed. And Winkler opened the window wider to get some proper air in there. Then he sat down next to the old man and put his hand on his shoulder – the old man was lying on his side, facing away towards the window – and said,

'Things will be different now.' And he fell half-asleep leaning back against the chrysanthemums embroidered on the bed head. And half-waking he said, 'I'm moving. I'm going to get a proper flat, with plenty of room. We'll live together. We'll do all sorts of things. We'll read to each other. And go to the cinema in the afternoons. We'll go to the zoo. We'll go to museums. The War museum. We'll go shopping and go out for dinner. Maybe we'll go to Europe, on a trip. Drive around and see what we see. We'll go to Israel. We'll go to the countryside. We'll watch cricket. We'll go and see Ginger Bill in the nick. I'm going to look after you, now. It's my turn. I'm going to look after you until . . . until . . . Grandpa?'

The old man lay silently, lit across the cheek and one big ear by beige, curtain-filtered light. Winkler rubbed his shoulder but he didn't move. Winkler touched his head. It was cool. Winkler panicked and rolled over to listen to his chest and heard nothing. His grandfather was dead. Or perhaps only sleeping.

Winkler went to the dressing table and picked up the mirror, brought it to the old man's side of the bed, squatted so that they were eye-to-eye, held the mirror at his face, like you always wonder if you ever will. Nothing appeared steaming on the surface. How much should there be? He pushed it closer to the pale mouth and a puff of condensation mottled the glass. And shrunk away. And then another one.

Winkler replaced the mirror and went to the door. He turned and looked at his grandfather for a while and said, 'Bye, Grandpa.'

And the old man said, 'Bye, son,' without looking up.

Winkler did not use the stairlift on his way out.

21

The Truth About Wallenstein

Everything seemed so simple now. The streets were wide and cambered
lazily to barely parked pavements, unlike the car-jammed narrow teeming
streets of Winkler's less suburban neighbourhood. Trees and hedges sighed
in the breeze and gently whirring sprinklers murmured the obvious way
forward:

Call Millfield Spawn fairly soon and take him out for dinner. Explain
the whole thing in terms of the great personal journey he had recently
taken, which had opened his eyes briefly to the horror of life and precip-
itated his disappearance and wrongful arrest for rape and murder. Explain
that now everything was resolved. Everything. The legal and the spiritual,
the physical and the familial, the social and the sexual. He was, now, positively looking forward to a day of sustained and thunderous brilliance on
Werther 2000. He could really use an office of his own, at some time in
the near future, so as to avoid the distractions which sometimes, he knew,
made his deadline observance unreliable. But he was ready, now, to come
back. If they'd have him, of course, he would add with a wink, or some
gesture that approximated to a wink.

As if they wouldn't. What, like they've already cleared his desk or something? This is Winkler we're talking about.

And then Mary. It was time to settle down. He was thirty next month.
Makes a chap think. Not everyone gets to marry Albuquerque. And
Albuquerque is not right for everyone, anyway. And will not make every
man happy. Any more than Siri. His grandfather would have been better
off with a girl like Mary. And Mary was quite good enough for Winkler.
And he would be good enough for her. The three of them would live
together, and have some proper little Winklers, at last, who were born to
parents that . . .

Except that, strictly speaking, they would be Furtwanglers. Just as he, too, was a Furtwangler. What a name. At school, what, Fatwanker? Furtive Wanker? And to his friends and relations? Furty? And so next month, then, Furty turns firty?

No, he was Winkler, like always. And Mary would be, too. And all the little Winklers they would have and bring up to be proper little . . . well, whatever they turned out to be. And bring them up all nice with Grandpa in a little house in one of those wide streets with very few cars and quietly murmuring sprinklers.

He would return to the house – which smelt only of rabbit now – and wait for Mary to get home. And tell her all about it.

Winkler travelled home by bus, for a change, instead of taking the Underground, and it stopped – whaddya know? – right outside Northstead Police Station. Sergeant Tolkien was on the steps with a younger officer, drinking from a can of diet cola and taking the sun on his upturned face with closed eyes as he drank, while the junior man smoked a cigarette.

Letting the can down and opening his eyes he saw Winkler.

'Mr Winkler, what a stroke of luck,' he said.

'Hello,' said Winkler.

They shook hands. The smoker regarded Winkler suspiciously. But he was a young policeman and regarded everything suspiciously.

'I was just this minute about to call you,' said Tolkien. 'As soon as I'd had five minutes of sun. I wanted the five minutes. Television says the heat is nearly over. I could have sworn I felt a breeze earlier this – there, did you feel it?'

Winkler felt nothing.

'It's funny. One makes such a fuss about the heat wave and then when it looks like coming to an end you know you're going to miss it. I kept meaning to take a few days off and take the missus out to the country somewhere. Have a picnic by a lake or something.'

'Maybe it isn't over,' said Winkler. And just then he felt the breeze on his ankles and on his neck.

'We'll see, I suppose,' said Tolkien.

'Why were you going to call me?' asked Winkler, noticing the stare of the younger policeman just in time to stop himself saying, 'Where have you found my sperm now?'

'Just to say you can stop worrying about the assault charge. I don't know if you were worrying or not. But anyway, I've had two Ruperts on the phone who say they're prepared to swear in court that Morcester started it. One of them claims to be his son. Porfiry put this to the old boy and he told him he didn't want to pursue it. Porfiry was beside himself.'

'Maybe he'll bring me back in for the murder now. It's not impossible that I spermed in the flat and also killed her, you know.'

'No, we've got our man. Asylum seeker. Schizo. The full profile. We matched up the DNA the same time as we got yours in the panda car – and got an automatic reading for this Albanian scumbag. Pot luck, though. They take DNA for all asylum cases and whack it in the computer records. Porfiry didn't tell him that, though. He beat a confession out of him just for fun. But it got you out of his system. And the Albanian will recover. Well, probably.'

'Poor chap,' said Winkler.

'I suppose,' said Tolkien. 'Still, life goes on.'

'Yes it does,' said Winkler.

'I've got to crack on, I'm afraid.'

'Yes, me too. See you soon.'

'I'm sure you hope not.'

'No, I mean. You know, around. Now that you're here, and we turn out to be . . .' Again, the inquisitively staring junior officer stopped him finishing his sentence. He was going to say 'family'. Instead he said, 'I'll drop in some time and maybe we'll go for a sandwich.'

'I'd like that,' said Tolkien. And Winkler nodded and raised a hand to wave, and then carried on up the hill towards the bridge.

As he went, the younger policeman said,

'Wasn't that the bloke from the posters?'

'What posters?' said Tolkien.

'The ones we had up about the woman pushed under the train. The geezer in the photo looked like that bloke you were just talking to.'

'It was a suicide, Rowling.'

'Yes, I know we think that now. But those CCTV pictures were very suspicious, sir. I know things weren't clear but we did think at the time that . . .'

'I know what we thought at the time, Rowling. But the family are satisfied that it's suicide. It's simple enough. The poor woman got pregnant late in life after years of fertility treatment, miscarried quadruplets, got depressed, got fat, got more depressed, the husband fucked off with a younger woman, and along came a train like the hammer of God and out she jumped. Blam!'

'But, sir, there was no note. And on the video it looks like —'

'Hammer of God, Rowling.'

'But, sir —'

'Of God, Rowling! That stone age machine on the platform takes a still every four seconds. Some guy might have stumbled, we couldn't tell if it was before or after she fell. He might have been trying to save her. The stockbroker with the brightly polished brogues couldn't tell us anything and he was right on the spot. It's why we took the posters down again. We didn't need him. Families do not offer you a suicide verdict so easily, Rowling. The Hammer of God, man. It is merciful and without mercy.'

'Yes, sir.'

'Yes, sir, is right, Rowling,' said Tolkien with a shiver, looking up at the sky, where clouds were not yet lowering, and drawing his jacket more snugly about his chest and belly, though a shaft of evening light fell full upon him between the roofs opposite and played behind him on the station window and flashed brightly in the glass above his head. 'She took her own life because she was cast down in misery, Rowling. And may God forgive her for it.'

He scrunched the cola can in his hand as he said this, and looked up the road to where Winkler was approaching the bridge.

'Forgiveness is everything, you see, Rowling,' he said, pulling open the heavy station door and letting it fall behind him on its big iron spring with a creak that muffled a very quiet, very distant rumble of thunder.

Up the old hill walked Winkler with a slight limp, he realised. A limp? Just tiredness making his feet drag. Winkler was so tired. He would soon be up the hill, past the gardens and the close-parked cars and children visible in sunny back gardens through dark houses; soon into the house, not noticing the smell now that it was nothing but rabbits returning from the ice, and up the stairs holding the banister, the smooth curling banister, for support (mmmmm, he could sleep leaning on the banister), and glance only briefly at Madame Moranges' door, and Wallenstein's door and the door next to it containing the old woman, up to the landing and the tasselled table and lamps and the heavy telephone, clunking the bolts of the door to his own little apartment, and up those stairs, to the first turn, and there heave the window door open and step out onto the tarmac, still in the sun, and the green and white striped deckchair that must still be there, and slip off his shoes and peel off his socks and stand feeling the gritty roof with his toes and looking out at the city in the last of the sun – and perhaps the last of the sun for a while if Tolkien was right about the weather forecast. And flop down, then, into the deckchair and wait for Mary to come home. Explain. Explain properly. About the past few days. And the past few years. And the past fifty years. And his plans for the next fifty. And then out later, with Will and Meriel, maybe, to celebrate. An evening walk in the park, come on, it's nearly the end of the summer and we haven't been once yet. We can stop for a drink or two when it gets dark and then go for a curry. Come on, like old times. To celebrate. That Winkler is back at last.

But at the brow of the hill Winkler saw black cars outside the house. And men in black suits milling about, and a few people from the street standing in the road, too, having a little look, and one or two from the house, there, Madame Moranges, and there, good Lord, the old woman from the room next to Wallenstein. Winkler had never seen her in daylight. She was wearing black. From the open front door of the house emerged a small, pale coffin, borne by more men in suits. Too small to contain Will. Or even Meriel. Mary, possibly. Which would have made Winkler break into a trot. And he didn't, so it couldn't have been.

So, what? Obviously it's Wallenstein. It's too late to introduce anyone new and care that he's dead. Except maybe the rabbit-eater. Poisoned by refrozen defrosted rabbit parts inadequately stewed. But what would that prove? Or somebody beaten by Mulligan's hoodlums? Who cares about Mulligan? We've already forgotten about Mulligan. He didn't turn out to have much to do with anything.

No, it's Wallenstein. No surprises. Well, maybe one. One little one. Or maybe you won't be surprised.

Winkler approached the two women he knew by sight and said, sombrely, 'Is it Mr Wallenstein?'

Madame Moranges blew her nose and nodded.

'Poor fellow,' said Winkler. 'It was so cold in that flat. It's as if Mulligan had killed him with his bare hands.'

'*Comment?*' said Madame Moranges.

'Cutting off his electricity at the mains.'

The older woman laughed. 'Who told you that?'

'He did.'

The old woman laughed again.

'Is nonsense,' said Madame Moranges. 'Ze man was just too mean to pay 'is bills. He never 'ad heating in zere in fifty years. Zees was long before Monsieur Moolligern came. Ze 'usband of Sylvie wouldn't put 'is hand in 'is pocket for . . .'

'Whose husband?' Said Winkler.

'Sylvie's 'usband,' said Moranges, nodding sideways at the old woman and whispering, 'Estranged. They had not spoken since nineteen seventy sree.'

'Of course we had spoken,' said the old woman sharply. 'You don't live in the room next to someone for thirty years and not speak.'

'She is upset,' said Moranges.

'I am not upset,' said the old woman. 'Well, of course I am upset. He was my husband.'

'I'm so sorry,' said Winkler. 'I didn't know he was married.'

'Why should you?'

'We were quite friendly.'

'Really? How unusual. He didn't go in for friends much.'

'Well, "friendly" is probably pushing it,' said Winkler as the suited men, on a silent count of three, swung the coffin down to hip level and launched it into the back of one of the cars with an air of self-importance that was almost intolerable, to Winkler. 'I sat with him one afternoon last month and we talked.'

'About what? You must be quite a talker. I never got more than a few sentences from him even when we lived together.'

'No, actually, it was him who did all the talking. Mainly about the ghetto. But also about the resistance in the forest. The groups he fought with. The friends and family he lost and the world that was destroyed in Poland. And his vow to avenge the death of Jews by . . .'

Mrs Wallenstein – well, that's who she was – put her hand to her mouth, gasped. Looked on the point of tears. Madame Moranges had turned away to harangue the men in suits for their lack of decorum.

'The old fool,' said Mrs Wallenstein. 'Fifty years it's been. I'm surprised he still remembered the old lies.'

Winkler's fragile new world wobbled on its axis.

'He ended up, did he, trapped between Soviet and Allied forces, was picked up by the Palestine Brigade and came eventually to Britain?'

'Yes.'

'Tell me. Do you remember the names of his family?'

'Not the parents. Er, his sister was Yitke, wasn't she?'

The old woman mouthed the word 'Yitke' and nodded.

'There was Issy Dalman from . . .'

'Solec,' she interrupted. 'They called him skinny Issy but it was funny because in the ghetto everyone was . . . oh.' She put her hand to her mouth.

When she spoke again she said, 'Was there a businessman, Dosseker? And Viktor and Abba and Grosstein and boys with heads trodden into the gutter at the wall of the ghetto and a boy Solly and his sister Rushke . . . I haven't heard those names in sixty years.'

'I didn't know she was called Rushke.'

'She wasn't. She wasn't. She wasn't called anything. She was from a book. If she had a name I doubt it was Rushke. I made her up for him, like all the others. But he never needed them in the end.'

'Sylvie, Sylvie, we go now!' cried Madame Moranges.

'I don't understand,' said Winkler, who didn't.

'Come, I'll tell you in the car.'

'What car?'

'Come. We didn't need two cars anyway. It was only for dignity. It's only Dennis and Amelie and me. It would be useful to have another mourner for the old bastard.'

Winkler looked over and saw Mulligan, in a tight-fitting suit, with his hair brushed into a parting, and his big red face strangled by his collar. He was helping the French woman into one of the cars. And when he looked up and saw Winkler he smiled embarrassedly and raised a hand in greeting.

'Come,' said the old woman again. 'We'll ride behind with Pavel.'

'But –'

'Come.'

And so Winkler got into the silent, carpet-smelling hearse with the old woman and the body of her husband and a man who asked if it was okay to remove his cap for the drive. And they drove northwards out of the city to put an old man Winkler had met only twice in the ground. And, while they drove, the old woman told Winkler the truth about Wallenstein.

Another story for Winkler to listen to. One last story.

The driver raised the divide and cut himself off. Possibly turned on the radio. Winkler and Mrs Wallenstein sat next to each other in the slow-moving car as it maundered northwards, through acres of Asians, similar to those near Winkler's office, but less colourful. Through miles and miles of suburb, little mock-Tudor houses along the long dual carriageways, round roundabouts and over flyovers, through traffic that thinned and thickened, past vast town halls and gigantic schools and tiny old churches, and occasional small brick buildings with uneven lines, old centres of forgotten villages and townlets. A great public school rose over the brow of a hill, which was once, Winkler imagined, a great hill outside the city which townspeople could see from afar and dream of escaping to from the smell and the rats and the plague, and then it was the centre of a rural spa, and then the school was built, a great country school, raising men to go out and run our Empire, and they did, but slowly the Empire collapsed anyway, despite the men and despite the school, and the men came back, and slowly the suburbs crept out to gobble the school (as the shadows in late summer creep out to gobble the wicket) and the suburbs filled with the people of Asia whom the men educated at the school on the hill had been sent out to rule. Following them back to Britain in search of the so much better world they clearly came from. And they came and came until the school was surrounded. And the only white men were inside the fortress on the hill, and the natives surrounded them. History, if nothing else, has a sense of humour.

It seemed that when Sylvie first met Pavel – which is to say, Wallenstein – it was in a town in Italy whose name she chooses not to remember. It was in a factory gutted by bombs which had been turned over to UNRRA, the United Nations Relief and Rehabilitation Administration, for the sorting and processing of refugees from all over Europe.

The town was heaving with confusion and panicked souls. As well as UNRRA there were centres of the Joint Distribution Council (JDC) and the Red Cross, functionaries of various Jewish agencies as well as Supreme Headquarters, Allied Expeditionary Force (SHAEF), and all around it temporary Displaced Persons (DP) camps. The streets heaved with refugees in the clothes of peasants, in the stripes of the camps and in uniforms of the Red Army, the SS, the Polish army, all stolen or borrowed or bought, so that you had no idea who anybody was. And among them, one had to assume, some real soldiers. But mostly British or American, or Jews from the Palestinian Brigade of the British Army looking for displaced soldiers to join the battles that would follow as the War moved to the Land of Israel – and looking also for those fighters of the ghettoes and forests, those war-hardened Jews who would be invaluable in the new killing that must be undertaken now.

In the open spaces all over town were tents and half-made shacks full of DPs of all ages. Except not so many old. And not so many young. And none very old. And none very young. And not so many women. And also people just lying out on the ground in rows in the sun.

Everyone there had run from something, lost everything, possessed nothing. Their choices were gone. All they were was what they appeared to be at a glance: in a cold snap a camp survivor strips a Red Army coat from a broken soldier and suddenly he is a Communist, and the Americans are suspicious of him. So he strips to his stripes again and the Americans pity him, but the Russians suspect him, and the Poles fear and hate him. So he swaps clothes with a peasant and everyone ignores him.

Everywhere there were organisations to help: charities, armies, medical corps, repatriation committees – and everybody should have someone to turn to, and most do. Not all, but most.

In the narrow streets, people roaming in search of something. Sylvie thought they were seeking content for their lives. In the morning they got up without knowing what for. The day passes and night comes and so on . . . the present is superfluous and its only job is to bridge between the life that once was and what is yet to come. The sense of the provisional is felt at every turn. There is no stability, neither material nor spiritual. Yesterday they were in hell and tomorrow they will be in an earthly paradise and betwixt and between only emptiness and idleness.

The people are crazed with loss and sadness and heat and hunger (some are hungrier than they have ever been and others not as hungry as they have been recently) and what is worst of all is there is no choice at all for each individual – except to choose who he is.

The Old World was destroyed already. They all knew this much. Even before the bombs of August and the separations and inventions at Yalta. The Old World was over and the identities of the Old World were gone forever. And a man did not have to be what he was before, in the Old World (this was clearest to those from the East, and especially to the Jews among them – but to all of them it was clear enough).

And here in the market place, in the town whose name she chooses not to remember, where there was nothing on sale, the only thing you could buy was an identity. Here, for the first and last time in the world – Sylvie did not want to sound too portentous, maybe only the first time in Europe – here for the first and last time men and women could choose who they wanted to be.

Sylvie was involved in the registration of DPs. She manned a table where they took names and birth dates and birth places and wrote down trades and languages spoken and asked to see papers and made no fuss, for the first time in years, when none were produced. The camp survivors had none, of course, nor the resisters who could not risk identification during the War, nor the POWs who had them confiscated, nor the collaborators

whose names would appear in SS registers, some of the homeless peasants had them, but not all, or even most.

And to the front of her queue came Pavel.

'Wallenstein,' he said. 'Jude, oys Majdanek, Treblinka, Auschwitz-
Birkenau.'

She wrote this down and then looked up at him. He was in camp
stripes, ill-fitting, faded, worn. But he was all there. It was hard to explain
but –

The car slowed suddenly as a road worker manning a contra-flow spun
a stop-go lollipop to red and Sylvie grasped Winkler's knee to stop herself
sliding forwards on to the floor.

. . . But he was all there. There was fear and loss and hunger, but behind
that, behind the eyes, plenty of life. Yes, he hunched his shoulders and
rolled his eyes, but she had the impression that he was trying to appear
sicker than he truly was. His back was straight and his head did not hang
low. His limbs moved freely at the joints.

This was not how it was with those who came there from Auschwitz,
even the Hungarians that went late into the camps and were there only
weeks or a very few months before the liberation, even these were like
ghosts. And not least because only those sick to the edge of death were
left behind when the marches left. And here was this man saying he was
from Majdanek, Treblinka, Auschwitz. The Grand Tour. And he was not
a ghost but a man.

She asked Wallenstein in Yiddish what his name was. She didn't know
much Yiddish but they had been given a few phrases to use with those
who spoke nothing else – although as it turned out very few of the survivors
were speakers of Yiddish only. The ones who made it here made it, in part,
because they spoke German, Russian, Polish. This was just to test him.

She said it again.

He shrugged.

Sylvie later learned that he had thought she was speaking German and
that she suspected him of being SS and was trying to trick him into
revealing this. He was just a Pole and did not know the one language
from the other.

She leant across to the girl next to her, a Pole and a Jewess, but kept
her eyes firmly on Pavel's (which is to say, Wallenstein's) eyes. And she
saw how blank they were. And how terrified. And she saw in them that
he was wondering if he should make a break for it. She said what she
thought to the Polish girl and the Polish girl looked at him and smirked
and said,

'*Redest kein Yiddish, bist kein Yid!*'

Which is to say, 'If you don't speak Yiddish then you ain't no Yid!' And then she laughed. And her laugh terrified Pavel.

Sylvie took pity. She didn't know why. She scribbled the address of the place she was staying on the back page of her book of registrations and tore it out and pushed it into his hand as the Polish girl shouted louder, and without laughter, '*Redest kein Yiddish, bist kein Yid!*' And then in Polish, 'You haven't a damn clue what I'm saying, have you?'

Pavel looked pleadingly at Sylvie then shrunk back into the crowd and pushed his way quickly out of the room into the hot sun as the girl rose to her feet to shout for the military police to stop him. But Sylvie grabbed her arm and said,

'He's just a Pole. He thinks we think he's SS.'

'Just a Pole?' said the other girl. 'There is no such thing as just a Pole!'

But she sat down again just the same because you'd never catch him in that place and there were so many people there to deal with, all heaving and surging against the row of trestle tables, shouting and cursing in a thousand languages (literally, Babbling) and waving pieces of paper and calling everyone else a cheat and a liar. And half of them getting to the front were angry that the women had no food for them and could not believe that they had spent all day in the wrong queue. A queue with no food. If not food, then what was to queue for?

The next day he showed up at Sylvie's building. There was a knock at her door and the landlady said there was a man to see her who spoke no Italian.

He was in clothes now. Only the filthy overalls of a farm worker, but clothes. Not the striped uniform. He was holding his hat. Sylvie told the landlady it was okay for her to go, this was her friend.

When they were alone Pavel handed her a piece of paper on which was a note in English written for him by someone he had found whose grasp of both Polish and English was only basic, even to Sylvie who then spoke only stumbling English herself, 'I am Poland. But not bad Poland. Resistance. Partisan. I fight in forest three years. Mix band, Russian, Germany, Jews even. I have homeless. No family. All dead. But they not believe. There are from my own band who hate me. They announce me for Nazi believer. If they see me they do again. We will here for probably months. Every day the Jews leave. Tell them I am Jew. Tell them I am Jew, please. I am good Poland. Not bad Poland. I am good spirit. Pavel Pilnik.'

But she told him, 'They are going to Palestine, the Jews. Palestine. You can't go there.'

He only looked at her.

'Palestine!' she said louder, almost shouting. 'Israel! They're going to Israel. You cannot go to Israel!' And she shook and shook her head. But all he understood was 'Israel'. And so he nodded frantically saying,

'Israel. Ja. Israel. Israel. Israel,' and pointing to himself.

And she shook her head still more and said, 'They will not be fooled Signor Pilnik. Not for a second. You cannot go to Israel.'

But he kept nodding and saying 'Israel' over and over and then began making gestures of hanging himself and shooting himself with his fingers and cutting his throat and shaking his head wildly. And then he fell to his knees weeping and clung to her knees and cried.

And she wept, too, to see him. And thought of her husband. Her Vicenzo, who was also dead. She thought of him in his uniform before he left, laughing and posing for a photograph in the village. She had nothing either. Nobody there had anything. And they spent all day not crying. And she had not cried because she had nobody in front of whom to cry. But now she had this weeping Pole in his stolen clothes (Winkler thought briefly, only briefly, of Ginger Bill) who was terrified of something that he thought he could escape by pretending to be a Jew. And so she cried too.

And after a while Pavel Pilnik looked up and saw that Sylvie was crying – she was something of a beauty then, very much admired – and he took her to the bed and made her sit. And sat next to her. And pulled her hair back behind her ears. It was black then and long and when it was back it showed off her shoulders and her neck. And he handed her a dirty rag to blow her nose. But she didn't want to make a blowing noise in front of . . . of . . .

The old woman turned round in her seat to look at the coffin. Blond wood, plasticky fittings, a mostly green wreath sitting on the lid.

She didn't want to make a blowing noise in front of him. And so she shook her head and pushed the rag back at him. And he pushed it back at her. And she laughed and shook her head. And so he put it away in the belly pocket of the overalls. And kissed her forehead. And kissed her eyelids. And kissed her cheeks, which were wet with cold tears on hot skin and salty. And kissed her lips. And she did not pull away her lips. And she thought she was only kissing him because she could not speak to him and so felt awkward. And she was afraid somebody would come. But nobody came. Not for hours. Not before morning. And even then, not.

All that night she did not sleep, though Pavel slept beside her and snored, she said, like a baby. And as she lay there she thought to herself, 'What would I do if I were him?'

He had something to escape. But she did not know what. She thought, at that time, that he feared he would be taken for a Polish collaborator, a Nazi, a kapo, some sort of war criminal . . .

And then, what? Hanged? Possibly. Imprisoned? Tried? They wouldn't bother with such small fry. Most likely they would hand him over to the Red Army. If the Red Army do not believe he is a partisan but a collaborator then pof! A bullet in the neck and a hole in the ground. And anyway the partisans were rife with anti-Communists so anyway then pof! And a hole in the ground. And if they believe he is a Jew, the Russians, then probably not much better.

He had to go west, he knew that, clearly. And he could not pretend to be other than a Pole, since Polish was all he knew. So he must pretend to be a Jew. Not a thing that comes naturally to a Pole. So where were the Jews, if not dead? If you were a Pole then you knew it was Auschwitz. That was all. Polish Jews were either dead or saved from the camps.

But he did not look as if he had been in the camps, as Sylvie had explained. So what if he claimed to have been a Jewish fighter in the ghetto? A Jew in the forests, working alone or in a small band that is now all dead. She was only thinking. Imagining what he might say if he wanted to get away. She had met such Jews. They were not so thin as those from the camps. Not so broken. Not ghosts. They were prouder. Undefeated. And with nothing to return to they looked defiantly to the Land of Israel to continue their war there. Pavel would pass more easily for this kind of Jew.

So Sylvie made this story for him. That he had been interned in the Warsaw Ghetto, fought his way out before the Uprising (because by then the numbers were small, almost all died and those that did not knew well who was there), fought in the forests, through Poland and as the Russian front moved he came down through Germany south and west to Italy. From her registration lists she created names, putting first and second names and birthplaces randomly together, to give him a past and to give him comrades in arms. These she wrote down for him to memorise. From what she had heard from the soldiers and partisans she made stories for him to tell, composed of truths and half-truths and lies in equal measure – a soup of Jewish war experience – and all of it hung closely at least to where he claimed he had truly been and the places he knew. And this way his story would be easier to tell. And it would be harder to disbelieve, being a Jew's story. He spoke no Yiddish or Hebrew, it was true.

But many of those truly assimilated in Warsaw did not. And what was to disbelieve? A Pole would rather be anything than a Jew. Rather be dead. And even more important, at that time, after the thousands of visas for Palestine became available to surviving Jews – She'erith Hapleitah they called themselves – then the Palestine Brigade were giving first priority to any fighter who would go. And the Allies and Americans after the first few months stopped dividing and testing the Jews, because of the uproar that that was behaving no better than the Nazis. So with this story it would be easy.

Sylvie's friend Rula, from the registration depot, did not approve of the plan.

'How do you know he is what he says?' she said. 'He may be Josef Goebbels for all you know.'

'Goebbels has a club foot,' Sylvie said, laughing. 'And anyway, the Russians found his body last week. A woman just knows. You know that.'

Rula looked at Sylvie scornfully and said, 'A woman does not know. A woman just lies there and watches the plaster flake on the bedroom ceiling.'

But she agreed, in the end, to explain Sylvie's plan to Pavel. And so Sylvie told Pavel the story of his life – the story, she supposed, which he had told Winkler so recently – and Rula translated as they went. And Pavel wept for joy and gratitude. And also for himself. And also for this Yitzhak Wallenstein, this unhappy Jew he had become.

She told him to stick to generalities if questioned, so as not to tie himself in knots. But as time went on – and especially on the boat to Palestine – he embroidered his story more and more, became more and more enamoured of it, obsessed with detail, grilled others on their experiences and rehearsed his newly elaborated story with her each night.

For, yes, she went with him. On the day he got his visa he presented her with a ring bought with the exchange of a pistol he had concealed so far from the Americans – all weapons were forbidden to DPs and were worth, Sylvie said, a fortune.

She showed Winkler the ring, a thin band of silver with a setting for a large stone which was not there. The stone they had sold in Palestine to pay for transit to England.

She went with him to Palestine because she had nothing to return to in Europe either. More than Pavel Pilnik. And more still than Yitzhak Wallenstein. But still nothing.

And in Palestine there was nothing for them either. They were among Jews fighting with the British and fighting with the Arabs. Pavel did not

want to fight anymore. And Sylvie did not care one way or the other.
And so they came here.

They came from the Holy Land in early winter as brown as Indians,
she said. And there was no difficulty in persuading people that Wallenstein
was a Jew. With assisted rent they came to live here, in the house. First
in the big apartment upstairs. Winkler's apartment. Then on the middle
floor, with all the rooms, and then when the blacks came and the old
landlord, the Jew Nader, saw that each room could be let separately and
paid for at a premium by the benefit agency, to the rooms under the
stairs.

They joked that there was nowhere lower they could go unless the
next landlord put them in the cellar. Or buried them in the garden.

But this was the last joke they shared. Soon afterwards Sylvie went to
live alone in the little room that was the bedroom and he lived alone in
the room that was to have been their living and eating room.

He had stopped sleeping. And he made her nervous. For nearly twenty
years after the end of the War they talked little about it. He learnt his
story so well that it was as if he had come to believe it himself. They
lived by the story she had made, and such people as they encountered,
who were few, believed it too. But then after the capture of Eichmann
suddenly what happened to the Jews in Germany and Poland during
the War stopped being a taboo. More and more details came to be
published, more and more stories. Wallenstein devoured them frantically.
And tossed and turned at night, shouting in Polish things she could not
understand.

Members of the resistance, former SS men, camp and ghetto survivors
began to talk and write and thousands and thousands of books appeared.
And there were the Nazi hunters, hundreds of them, finding old crimi-
nals in the darkest corners of the world from the north of Europe to the
southern tips of the continents and trying them before the world for
ancient crimes unthinkable in this new world that had replaced the old.

And she gradually came to the conclusion that Wallenstein had something more to fear now, about which she did not want to know. The
complicity of the Poles in the slaughter of their Jews became clear. Indeed
it was more than complicity. The Germans, some said, only lit the touch-
paper of what was truly a Polish Holocaust. The very notion of an innocent Pole – just as her friend Rula had insisted – was becoming untenable
by the early 1970s.

Wallenstein read and read, and grew unbearable. Polish and English
newspapers. The English press from Israel. Court transcripts. Book after book

after book. Fine-tuning his story and testing it again and again. He never left the house. The doorbell, on occasion, made him jump.

His decision to stop leaving the house except by night, and then only if absolutely necessary – which is when Sylvie decided to move next door – came after the high profile trial in 1973 of a German accused of having personally slaughtered nearly a hundred young Jews, a work detail of boys between twelve and sixteen that had been forgotten in the rush to begin the marches, in a gas chamber at an abandoned satellite camp only a couple of miles from the front at the end of the war. Two witnesses brought late by the defence swore it was the work of a Polish officer left to guard the boys when the Germans fled. The Pole himself had panicked, killed them and run himself. It was not believed, of course, and the German was convicted and hanged.

Her husband stopped going out after that, declaring it was no longer the time or place to be a Pole. Even with his watertight story. And she, not only because she had begun to have intimations of the truth about Wallenstein's past, but because it is no fun living with a man who will not leave the house by daylight, moved out.

The following year, mad with the fear of discovery, he had the 'procedure', which was almost unknown at his age and was performed outside of formal medical care because he would not risk exposing himself – literally – as a gentile. It did not go well. There were subsequent operations that did not make things better. But as she had left his bed by then she never knew how it affected his 'duties as a man'.

And so. They were nearly at the cemetery.

Winkler climbed out of the car in silence and went to help Wallenstein's wife out of her door. But the chauffeur beat him to it. At the car park was the entrance to a Jewish chapel and the beginning of Jewish tombstones that stretched for what seemed like miles to the edges of wide, warlike fields.

Winkler was glad of the sombreness of the place, and the silence. The unwelcomeness of spoken words. He could not have been somewhere where speaking was required. He could not have been where there was anyone he knew. While big men rolled the old man in his box out of the car and took it to a trestle, Madame Moranges nattered and smoked and Mulligan fiddled with his tie and Winkler touched Mrs Wallenstein's elbow and wandered towards the graves, where he read name after laughably foreign name surrounded by the illegible ugly-beautiful script of the

ancient Jews, identifying the bones of little old people mulched in the
English mud. And when too many of them offered also the names of
relatives killed between 1942 and 1945 whose wherabouts and exact date
of death was unknown but who were here commemorated on the stone
of their beloved husband, wife, son, daughter, father, mother, cousin and
sometimes, most awfully, friend, Winkler returned to the body of the old
man and its three mismatched mourners.

The short procession to the grave began. Wallenstein turned, in this
last, honest hour, away from the Jewish chapel to the higher, grassier
ground closer to the road, where the low, level acres of non-denominational burial space stretched far and wide.

As they paused to cross the road, a car full of boys chose not to give
way but to slow and wind its windows down and shout 'Yiddoes!' mistak-
enly, taking them for what they were not. Winkler smiled. A last little
triumph of deception for Yitzhak Wallenstein.

He was put in the ground without words. The hole was deep. Winkler
did not know what name would be put on the stone when the earth had
settled. A spot of rain fell on his face. And when he looked up he saw
the sky grey with clouds.

'Good for the farmers,' said Mulligan, edging past him cautiously at
the grave's edge and hurrying towards the cars, fearful that the first drop
would not be the last.

'Will you come back for a cup of tea?' said Sylvie Wallenstein. 'Madame
Moranges has made cakes.'

'No, thank you. Thank you, Mrs Wallenstein. I won't. I'll hang around
up here for a bit and go for a walk. I've never been to a cemetery before.'

'Suit yourself. But it looks like rain.'

'I'll be alright,' said Winkler, unsuitably dressed, as much for rain as for
funerals.

'He hadn't told his story in thirty years,' she said. 'It must have got very
elaborate with time. I imagine he wanted to tell it one last time, to
whoever would listen. Pavel knew he was near the end. I'm glad you
were there to hear it.'

'But the photographs,' said Winkler. 'The photographs of Issy and his
brother and of the men on the airfield and the dog. And what about the
stamps he bought for his dead father? He gave me the stamps.'

'Issy and his brother were pictures submitted for ID cards by refugees
who never returned to collect them,' said the old woman. 'There were
plenty of these, who died waiting. The men with Pavel on the airfield are
probably friends in the Polish army, if it is truly Pavel you saw. The dog

was I don't know what. Maybe he thought there should be a dog. And the stamps were a present from a Polish boy I allowed to help me with errands at the depot. Pavel took them for a prop.'

Winkler took the stamps from his pocket and held them out without speaking.

'I don't want them,' she said. 'I don't want anything to remember him by. You keep them. Sell them. I dare say they're worth something by now.'

She held out her hand and Winkler squeezed it briefly. Then she and Mulligan and Madame Moranges left in one of the cars.

Winkler stood by the hole in the ground that contained the body of Pavel Pilnik and Yitzhak Wallenstein. The rain fell hard on the dry edges of the deep hole. Winkler took the envelopes out of their plastic pouch and tore off the four stamped corners which, after sixty years, was a very noiseless tear. He dropped them, fluttering, over the grave. Two fell in, one flush on the coffin top, one down the gap at its side. Another stuck on the wall of the grave, facing in. And another blew over and away and settled softly in what would soon be a puddle.

A puddle, thought Winkler. The puddle will like this rain. Tomorrow it will be deep again, and wide and wet.

A few yards away a long dark procession was making its way out of the Jewish chapel between the thousands of squat little grey stones, behind a small coffin on a cart, draped in black. From his vantage point in his own godless field Winkler saw a pile of earth by an open grave. Two shovels stood rooted in it. And he knew that the column of Jews in dark clothes, when they had negotiated the low, easy maze of their dead, would queue to cover the coffin with clods and say prayers he could not understand.

And he watched them. With the rain on his face, lashing horizontally, whipped by the wind over the Jewish graves and over the not Jewish. And the prayers were muffled by the traffic roar of the dual carriageway close by and the noise of the rain falling on Wallenstein's coffin, and everywhere else.

And when he had watched the strange, foreign-looking Jews file out of their field and away and pause to wash their hands in the icy water of a tiny stone basin at the cemetery gate, he took a last look at the field of stones – for it was not often that Winkler saw fields – and then he turned towards the road himself, into the rain, so that it washed through him, through his eyes and nose and mouth and through his clothes.

At the roadside was a red telephone box, glowing from the inside with yellow light, like a lamp. Inside, it was dry. But water was beginning to puddle on its concrete floor. Winkler picked up the receiver and felt the cold black plastic on his ear. The rain drummed hard on the little glass windows of the phone box.

Winkler felt condensation muster in the tiny dimples of the keys, where his finger pads settled on them. He wondered who to call. He wanted to phone somebody and, when they asked, to tell them his name.